# ENMA
## THE IMMORTAL

Fumi Nakamura

translated by Neil Nadelman

VERTICAL.

Published by Vertical, Inc., New York

ISBN 978-1-932234-90-9

Manufactured in the United States of America

First Print Edition

Vertical, Inc.
451 Park Avenue South, 7th Floor
New York, NY 10016
www.vertical-inc.com

# Table of Contents

# Prologue

*A.D. 1859 (Ansei 6)*
*Hagi, Domain of Choushuu, Yamaguchi Prefecture*

"Sister, I'm going to change the world."

She pushed through the grove of trees and came out to a clearing, the vastness of the sea spreading out before her eyes. Maybe that was what made her recall the parting words of her younger brother. Sawa smiled wanly. He'd always been childish, but saying something that arrogant had taken it to a whole new level.

Their entire nation had been dozing for a terribly long time, surrounded by ocean and darkness. But then the black ships had come from far across the sea from a place called America, and with them came myriad expectations, an eagerness to finally wrench open the night in which they'd been living. An eagerness from within the nation as well as from without. But, she thought, even if the names of the people in charge change, my life won't. It was meaningless for the common people. What could a mere woman hope to do? What could she hope to accomplish?

Sawa was desperate. She'd lost the slimmest glimpse of hope. All she cared about was taking care of her younger brother, but she wondered if she could do that when she hadn't even managed to get herself married yet.

The sea breeze was cold. She rubbed her chapped hands together for warmth, her frail body shivering beneath the crude short-sleeved *kosode* kimono she wore. After she'd gazed at the sea for a while, she trudged onward. The calls of the food vendors echoed into the clear autumn skies. Children shouted with joy as they dashed through the streets. Even in these troubled times, the town possessed a certain energy to it.

She heard other, more valiant, voices coming from the young samurai gathered by their schools and training halls. They proudly boasted about how they were going to change the world. Well, that explained where her brother had gotten his crazy ideas. She followed along the white plaster walls and came to the river. The setting sun sparkled dazzlingly on the water, and the surrounding trees swayed in the wind, the first hints of autumn color on their leaves. It gave the town an air of elegance which Sawa liked very much.

She continued along the riverbank and proceeded towards the mountains, leaving the town behind. The twilight deepened and her surroundings grew more desolate, the wind rustling the tall pampas grass into undulating waves. In their shadow she spied the black arc of a stone bridge. A lone young man stood idly in the middle of it.

*Well, now…*

He was a youth possessed of an elegant profile, his long hair knotted in the back and his slender body wrapped in a fine reddish-brown *kosode.* He had an almost unearthly quality, and it was impossible to tell what sort of business he was in. But it wasn't his appearance which caught Sawa's interest. It was his eyes, eyes darkened with anguish, eyes which seemed to cry out for a quick death.

"You aren't thinking of…" she stammered. "Don't be hasty! You mustn't kill yourself!"

At the sound of her voice, he turned and looked at Sawa. A faint smile came to his lips.

"Don't worry. I'm not going to die."

Was he not intending to die, or did he simply lack the courage to do it, she wondered. Either way, she could sense that he was a very unhappy person.

"You look more like someone ready to die," he said.

Sawa's eyes widened. She'd never met this man before, and yet for some reason, she couldn't bring herself to deny what he'd just said. Her weak heart reeled under the gaze of this man who had just given her an invitation to paradise.

"Perhaps I am…" she answered.

"You poor thing," he said, nodding his head, the smile never leaving his lips.

Sawa stood there, petrified, gazing into his eyes. She knew she was in danger, and yet she could do nothing to defend herself. The man held out a reddened maple leaf.

"Shall I kill you then?" he said.

## Chapter 1

# The Eternal Beast

*A.D. 1866-1867 (Keiou 2-3)*

### —1—

The long autumn rains were hard to deal with. They might have given the streets of Kyoto an elegant air, but when they dragged on this long, it just got irritating.

Besides the rain, there was the cough he had to endure. Clicking his tongue in annoyance, Baikou went outside, coughing as he did. Tipping the bucket he carried, he dashed the water he'd wiped from his body onto the ground. Muddy water spattered onto the hem of his kimono, but he barely noticed.

Bungo Bridge looked frozen in the rain. The sun was not yet down, but a gloom like diluted ink hung in the air. Not a soul was in sight. There was only the sound of the pouring rain, with nothing to dispel the feeling that everyone in the city had died.

It was amidst this that he heard shouts in the distance, drawing Baikou's gaze. Running footsteps were splashing closer and closer. A figure passed by the alley of the row house across the way, soon followed by three more men running after him. They seemed to be gaining.

He couldn't tell who the fleeing man was, but his pursuers were definitely the Shinsengumi, the special police corps of the Tokugawa shogunate which ruled Japan. Even in the gloom, their gaudy *haori* coats made them unmistakable. Baikou couldn't fathom how anyone could be proud to wear such a ridiculous get-up.

"Bullshit," he grunted. What would it matter who got to play the new king of the mountain?

Baikou went back into the house, leaned down on his rolled-up bedding and flipped open a sketchbook with an air of boredom. It was filled with Sanskrit designs, Kurikara dragon figures, dragons and tigers, cherry blossoms and ivy vines. Whatever you asked him to tattoo on you, Baikou Houshou would deliver a work of art. Sickness now prevented him from completing the really great projects that he had put his strength into, but he'd never lost his passion for the art of tattooing. He used to have customers come all the way from Echigo and Satsuma. Those who traveled so far were seeking the name of Houshou more than they were the fame of Baikou himself. They all had varying expectations, but he had never disappointed any of them. Despite that, he'd only done two tattoos so far this year. The battle between pro- and anti-shogunate forces had been extremely violent. With the battle at Hamaguri Gate and the sword battle at the Ikedaya Mercantile, Kyoto now was too violent a place to be worrying about getting tattoos.

Perhaps spending money and time having your flesh carved into was too extreme a pastime. It was better suited for a more boring world.

A plum blossom bloomed on the palm of Baikou's right hand. While still a young man, his master had tattooed it onto him when he had sworn to dedicate his life to his craft and inherit the Houshou name. It had required three days of cutting and had hurt so much that he couldn't sleep. He'd intended at first to do it on his own, but such dedication was too much for someone as weak as he.

He didn't have much time left.

He probably wasn't going to make it through the winter. That was clear to him now. Pressing his hand to his tightening chest, he swallowed hot water steeped in the last bit of the medicine he took for his chronic illness.

Fifteen years earlier, Baikou had moved from Edo to Kyoto. He hadn't planned to make the move permanent. He'd been invited by an extraordinary request from a man who'd retired early with too much free time and money on his hands. His commission was for a huge skull to be tattooed across his back. Sadly, he'd died before it could be completed. He'd wanted to return home, but then the illness he'd had since birth had worsened. He didn't have the strength to make the return trip to Edo.

He was seventy years old now. Fine, he thought. That's a good run. He'd lived a good life as a master tattooist. But even as he thought that, he was also conscious of a black regret deep within his heart which trapped him.

He had no family, nor anything else to give him joy. His entire life was ruled by the desire to tattoo, never fading, just growing more intense. The demon that dwelt within his old body would never be satisfied. Its avarice knew no bounds, and it continued to devour the soul of its host without mercy.

Only now did he realize that the flower blooming on his fist was a curse. Clenching his right hand, he lay down.

He looked over to a cat curled up in the corner of the room. The cat with its disdainful stare had just showed up one day and, before he'd even noticed, had moved in. Baikou called it Kuro, and its fur was as black as the name implied. The cat was cold and apathetic to most people, yet for some reason it had taken a liking to Baikou. As for Baikou, he liked animals about as much as he liked people, which was not very much at all. Still, he tolerated the furry freeloader because it reminded him of a cat which his old master used to have as a pet.

Kuro slept, his eyes thin slits, seeming to enjoy the sound of the rain drumming on the roof. All the cat ever did was sleep, as though not knowing what to do with all the time on his hands. Lulled by this notion, Baikou closed his eyes.

A sound woke him from his sleep, like someone knocking at the door. He got up slowly. The room was pitch black, but he knew his home without needing to see it. It wasn't too much trouble. Wrapping the sleeved quilt tighter around his shoulders, he fumbled to light a candle and then stepped onto the dirt floor in front of the door.

"Somebody out there?" he asked in a loud whisper. There was no answer.

Baikou unbarred the door and opened it. Nobody was there. The rain had stopped, and all he saw was the full moon which illuminated the night sky.

He shivered. The night was dreadfully cold. He was about to go back inside when he spied what looked like a person's face out of the corner of his eye. Holding the candle higher, he saw a samurai slumped on the ground behind the hedge, beneath the eves of the house. He was breathing, just barely, but his body was soaked and he looked frozen. The back of his kimono was split open in a thin line, and blood was oozing from the wound.

It was probably the man he'd seen fleeing earlier.

Well, this was going to be a pain in the ass, he thought. If the Shinsengumi were after him, that meant the samurai was one of the dogs working for the rebel lords in Satsuma or Choushuu. Either way, this wasn't somebody he wanted to have anything to do with. Still, if he just left him there, the man would surely die.

Baikou squatted down next to him and reached out his hand to brush the long hair away from the man's cheek. He looked to be about twenty years old, his pale skin as smooth as Portuguese glass and cold as ice.

"Hey," Baikou said, shaking the man's shoulder. "Wake up."

The samurai responded with a groan.

"Am I…going to die…" he asked.

"Probably," replied Baikou coldly.

"I want to live…" the man said. "I don't want to die…"

The words came, full of pathos and mixed with the blood he was vomiting up as he spoke. Hearing them, Baikou wasn't even conscious of the smile that had come to his lips.

"Someone said it," Baikou whispered.

He was wild with glee. Whatever shred of reason he had left was swallowed up instantly by the urge to work his craft.

"Someone just said that they didn't want to die!"

* * * * *

For generations, the Ichinose family had been country samurai in Choushuu province. They were samurai in name only, having won the right to have surnames and wear swords in the Edo period. The fact was that they were little better than peasant farmers.

The youngest child, Amane, had been born to his father by his second wife when he was past forty. Because of that, both of his parents had died by the time he was ten years old. To his older brother who was more than twenty years his senior, his little step-brother was nothing but a burden.

The only one who had shown him any kindness was his next-oldest sibling, his sister Sawa. She was smarter than any of his other brothers and sisters.

"If I could just live by teaching children," she'd say, "I wouldn't care about anything else." It was a dream which could never come true, though. The times she lived in demanded that a woman could never hope to be anything more than a wife and mother. It didn't matter what other desires she might have.

No matter how hesitant she was about marriage out of her concern for her little brother, by the time she was past twenty the matter had become unavoidable. She obeyed her older brother and agreed to be married the next month. She was to be the second wife of a man seventeen years her senior. Her husband-to-be had fathered a child with his late wife, and while there were rumors that she had been bullied to death by her mother-in-law, it wasn't definite. Still, he didn't think this was a fitting betrothal for his sister.

Sawa often told her little brother, "Life is too precious to be misspent. Never be in a hurry to waste it." Having been treated like trash all his life, Amane had little concern for his own well-being and wondered what his sister had meant. He'd been greatly concerned over her fate, but in the end, Sawa didn't seem to have as much attachment to life after all.

His sister was dead.

It had happened on a clear autumn day, when she'd gone into town to deliver some sewing. Her corpse was cold when they'd discovered it the next morning. Her heart had been ripped out of her chest. There were no signs of a struggle, and her face had borne a calm expression in death. The news of some maniac who was after young women threw the town into a frenzy, but it was just as quickly forgotten when no other victims appeared.

After losing his sister, Amane grew even more isolated.

Choushuu was one of the main provinces pushing for the overthrow of the Tokugawa shogunate which ruled Japan. Many feudal retainers, their eyes on a new age, fell in the rebellion. It was inevitable that Amane, who felt that he belonged nowhere, would end up living his life drawn to places which stank of blood. In the summer of his sixteenth year, he finally joined the rebellion. While he had no real political leanings, Amane felt that, if the world was changing, he wanted to be in on it, too. First, he bought himself a sword, then he became an escort for an official direct inspector for the shogunate, wrapping himself in the illusion of patriotism…

After the inspector had committed suicide by ritual disembowelment, Amane became an assassin. Being unafraid of death and impervious to pain, he felt it was a good fit for him.

He hadn't been able to sleep the night he first killed someone. His opponent's sword tip had grazed him just below the right eye, splitting open about an inch and a half of skin, but that hadn't bothered him. It was the feeling of when his sword hit the man's bone… That feeling lingered in his hand. It hadn't been exciting, just… cold. What was it the man had muttered at the moment of death? Probably a woman's name. He felt like he'd murdered another person as well.

"What we do is mete out heaven's punishment. Don't shrink from it," someone had told him.

He'd felt like vomiting.

He'd never had the will to kill someone. He began to feel he should run away to somewhere. That he *had* to run away.

...Burning.

He felt pain in the palm of his hand. Was the hand which had murdered a man burning up? Well, it couldn't be helped, could it?

* * * * *

The first thing he saw was dingy wood grain. A spider crawled along it.

A ceiling... Amane let out a short sigh and then covered his eyes with one hand. The realization that he was still alive filled him with an indescribable feeling. It was neither joy nor despair, although, if pushed, he might describe it as vague disappointment. He remembered being slashed with a sword. Pain running through his back, he'd stumbled into the river and had thought he was done for.

He felt sluggish, as though he'd been sweating terribly. There was a burning sensation in the hand which covered his eyes. It was only when he raised it a bit that some sort of character on it caught his eye.

Sanskrit?

It seemed to dance across the palm of his right hand, clear despite the filth on it. He thought that was strange, but Amane soon lost interest.

He slowly got up and looked around. The house was small and old, and he was lying on a thin futon. A man was standing in the direction from which he could smell miso. The man's back was turned, but Amane could see that he was old and feeble.

"Where am I?" Amane asked. Startled, Baikou turned to face him.

"You alive?"

"I think so," Amane replied. "Assuming this isn't hell," he thought to himself.

A grin coming to his toothless face, Baikou quickly tottered over to him. Cradling Amane's cheeks in his hands, he drew his face close.

"Oh yes, alive. Definitely alive. Impressive!" His wrinkled, worn-out old face beamed with delight.

"Did you save me?" Amane asked.

"Hell yes, I saved you. You wouldn't be here talking to me, otherwise!"

Amane felt like saying he shouldn't have bothered, but just couldn't bring himself to ruin the old man's obvious joy.

"I see," he said instead. "I'm in your debt."

"Not at all," Baikou replied. "Thanks to you, I could create a fine souvenir for my death."

Amane didn't know what he was talking about, but didn't care enough to inquire any further.

"Do you think you can gulp down a little miso with green onion? You've been asleep for two days straight, so I'm guessing you're pretty hungry."

So, it'd been two days since it had happened. As if on cue, he suddenly felt intense hunger.

"Thanks," Amane said.

"No problem," Baikou replied. "You wanna live, you gotta eat," he said as he cheerfully fixed their meals and then brought them back to the dirt floor.

What a kind old man, Amane thought without a hint of suspicion. He didn't know that Baikou seldom smiled. If anybody who knew him were to see Baikou in a good mood like this, they'd probably find it creepy.

"You live alone?" Amane asked.

"Yeah," the old man answered. "No family. Just that cat, and he moved in here without asking me first."

Amane saw the cat asleep in the corner. As though sensing his gaze, the cat opened its eyes and stared back. It seemed to be laughing at him, but that had to be Amane's imagination. And as much as the cat seemed to be laughing, Amane sensed an air of scorn from it, too.

"I'd better get out of here," Amane said.

He'd leave Kyoto at nightfall. He didn't see much problem with him dying like a dog on the roadside at the hands of his pursuers. It was only fitting for a young, half-baked loser like himself.

"Like I already told you, I live alone and have no relatives. It doesn't matter to me if I get mixed up in your troubles," the old man replied.

"But..."

"Don't worry about it. Besides, the Shinsengumi probably think you're dead now."

Startled, Amane looked up. This man knew that much about him?

"I saw those guys in the fancy Dandara-patterned *haori* coats chasing somebody. I assume that was you."

"If you know that much, then you should throw me out of here at once."

If they thought the old man was a comrade of his, he'd be killed for sure.

"Don't wanna. I won't get to see you healthy and running around again, otherwise."

"Are you this kind to everyone?"

Baikou roared with laughter, as though he'd said something hilarious.

"Nah, I'm just happy to see you're still alive, that's all."

The words of a saint, delivered with the leer of a wild animal.

"Get some rest before we eat."

Picking up a pot and a small charcoal brazier, Baikou went outside. Soon the pleasant smell of miso came wafting in. Amane lay down and closed his eyes, not caring what this overly kind man's expectations of him were.

In the end, despite how heavily his eyelids drooped, Amane couldn't sleep. After their meal, even as the night grew late, sleep simply would not come to him. His back would ache every time he turned over, but not unbearably so. He was in strangely good health considering he'd been on the verge of death not long ago. The meal had been delicious, too. He had some questions about how he'd recovered so well in only two days, but thinking very deeply about anything was hard.

"You hurt much?" Baikou suddenly asked from where he slept beside him.

"No, not especially," Amane replied.

"Really? Good. Then wrap up in your futon and get to sleep. It's cold tonight."

He could hear a draft howling like a beast. It seemed cold enough to chill the very marrow in his bones.

"I can't sleep."

"Probably slept too much." The man's raspy voice echoed in the little house.

"I wish I could have slept forever," Amane sighed, a slight grumble in his tone. It wasn't the sort of thing one should say to a man you owed your life to.

"What are you saying? You came knocking on my door in the middle of the night and then asked me to save you."

That wasn't how he remembered it.

"That can't be. After they slashed me, I fell in the river."

"What, you think a weak old man like me could just hoist you out of the river? You wanted to live so badly that you crawled out and came here."

In the darkness, Amane smiled bitterly. What an embarrassing story. In the moment when he had been slashed and fallen into the river, thinking he was about to die, he'd felt rather relieved. And then, despite that, his terror of dying had made him crawl out and go looking for help. It was ridiculous.

"People don't want to die. They want to live so badly that they'll do anything. They'll kill in pursuit of it, even commit heresy. Heaven above, what's happening to Kyoto now?"

It hurt Amane to hear this, since it was exactly the sort of things he'd done.

The draft was quickly blocked up and soon Amane heard snores coming from the side where the old man slept. Unable to sleep, all he could do was spend the night trying out the various names he could now call himself. Burden… Fool… Traitor… On and on and on.

He thought about leaving Kyoto in the morning and heading for Edo. He had no intention of going back to being an assassin, mainly because he'd been wrong about his suitability for being a professional killer. Maybe he had the skill for it, but for a guy whose first thought when faced with killing someone was to hide in bed, it might not be the best career choice.

The wooden shutter across from him shook in the freezing darkness.

Amane's father was already old by the time he'd grown out of babyhood, which was why people often mistook him for the elderly man's grandson. His father was still healthy, though, and taught Amane swordsmanship. He probably thought that a second son, unable to inherit his house and land, would need to be taught a skill with which to earn a living. The nation of Japan had just begun opening back up to the outside world at the time, and the possibility of war was in the air. He'd foreseen this and, out of love for his youngest son, gave him a skill he thought might be useful in the coming years.

The hair Amane wore bunched at the back of his head was the only remaining evidence of his samurai heritage. Although it really wasn't a true topknot, he still decided that it was time to cut it off and end that part of his life once and for all. He grasped it at the nape of his neck and then roughly cut it down at the root with a short sword. His forelock hung over his eyes, but having cut his hair didn't make him feel any better.

"So, how's it feel to have short hair now?" Baikou called out, standing on the dirt floor in front of the doorway as he cleaned himself.

"It feels good to be free of old bonds," Amane answered. "Wow," he added. "Those are some amazing tattoos you've got there." He spoke with genuine admiration as he saw Baikou's half-naked body. The old man's arms and shoulders crawled with vivid Kurikara designs, while the goddess Benzaiten smiled bewitchingly across his back.

"Oh, this?" the old man snorted. "Terrible! Look at Benten's face back there. Expression's totally dead."

"I think it's excellent." Amane couldn't really judge how good or bad a tattoo was, but he could recognize an epic work when he saw one.

"I practiced on myself when I was still learning the craft," the old man explained. "That's why there are so many different figures."

"You're a tattoo artist?"

Amane still couldn't quite figure out if this man was honest or a member of the yakuza, so he didn't think the question was unexpected.

"That I am," the old man replied. Baikou put his arms through the sleeves of his kimono, then put the bucket with its dirty water out onto the dirt floor. He turned to face Amane, coughing as he did.

"Heaven's gift to the art of tattoo: the great Baikou Houshou, at your service."

Amane was completely clueless as to whether that name was supposed to mean anything to him or not, but it was only then that he realized that he hadn't asked the old man his name.

"I'd rather not tell you mine," he said. He'd decided that it would be safer for both of them that way.

"Really," Baikou replied. "Then why don't I call you Enma?"

"Why would you do that?"

"Because Great King Enma is in the palm of your hand, that's why."

Baikou went outside and dumped his bucket of water into a plank-covered ditch. As he did, Amane took a hard look at the Sanskrit figure on his right palm.

"This thing?" he muttered. "It's not a bruise and it won't wash off. What is it?" After seeing the gates of hell itself, he hadn't thought the new mark on his skin was very important and hadn't paid any attention to it.

"What's it look like," the old man answered. "It's a tattoo. The Sanskrit character for Great King Enma, the lord and judge of the dead." Refilling his bucket with fresh water, he staggered back inside. Upon hearing it was a tattoo, Amane began rubbing it with his fingers, utterly dumbfounded.

"But, how...? I don't remember ever getting this."

"Well, you had one foot in the grave at the time, so I'm not surprised you don't remember."

Was this man saying...? Amane's eyes widened, not believing what he was hearing.

"Come on, strip down," the old man said. "I'll get you cleaned up now."

Without waiting for Amane's say-so, the old man had his kimono open and pulled down to his waist in a twinkling. He admired the younger man's skin, so pale it seemed to glow faintly blue, and squinted his eyes at the brilliance of it.

"You tattooed me?"

"Yeah."

"While I was dying?"

"Yup."

The blood started to rise into his face. How dare he! He was lying there dying, and this crazy old fart had tattooed him?!

"Why would you do that?!" he sputtered.

"Because I wanted to," the old man replied, washing Amane's slender arms.

"I haven't been getting any customers these days, and my hands were just itching to tattoo somebody."

Amane's mouth just hung open, no words able to come out. The thought that this man had saved him only for that reason turned all of his thoughts of gratitude into annoyance.

"You are a piece of work, old man!"

"You're the one who said he didn't want to die, so I saved you! I don't remember you complaining about it!"

"What?! You saved me by tattooing me?!"

Baikou tilted his head up and smiled slyly.

"The fact that you're alive right now is proof of that."

That smile, so full of devilishness and self-confidence... Amane faltered before it.

"Look at this," Baikou said, spreading his right hand out to show the younger man.

"A plum blossom..."

"The design doesn't matter. This is called an *oni-gome*. You tattoo it on the palm of the dominant hand. It's a kind of magic charm."

Upon hearing it referred to as a charm, Amane stared at his palm again.

"Just as I once swore to live my life as a tattoo artist called Baikou Houshou, your wish to not die invited an *oni* into your body."

"An oni... A demon?!"

"Exactly. You have now become almost impossible to kill. The oni possessing you won't allow it."

Amane gulped, his throat tightening.

"That's impossible," he said.

"Then what about the wound on your back? It's practically healed already."

He probed the sword wound on his back with his finger. There was still a scar, but it was quite well healed over now.

"Pretty soon, all traces of it will be gone."

Amane felt the scar beneath his right eye.

"What about this scar on my face?"

"That one was there long before the oni-gome was performed. Old wounds don't get healed."

That difference was proof that something strange was happening in Amane's body.

"It hasn't even been three days, and it's already healed that much with only a little shochu liquor for disinfection and exposure to the air." There was a hint of pride in his voice as Baikou wiped Amane's back vigorously with a towel. It didn't even ache now.

"You are the work I'll leave behind. More than that, you're my masterpiece. You've got great skin, the very best. I wanted so badly to tattoo your entire body. With a body like that, you gotta polish it up as much as you can!"

Amane couldn't even hear the man's shiver-inducing laugh. Of course he'd have a scar on his back. What was he doing, taking this old man's nonsense so seriously? The wet towel glided along his skin like a sticky tongue. As it wiped his body clean, Amane looked down in a daze at the mark of the lord of hell who now inhabited his body.

## —2—

Amane left the house while Baikou was taking a nap, leaving a short note thanking him for his kindness. He really didn't believe what the old man had told him about the oni-gome charm, figuring that he was just a little crazy. Squeezing his right hand into a fist, Amane quickened his pace.

It was dangerous for him to be wandering around in broad daylight like this, but if he kept away from the Shinsengumi's station, he should be able to avoid them. Being a deserter from his domain's authorities, he didn't want to run into anyone from Choushuu, either. There was a civil war going on, and he'd managed to end up on the run from both sides.

Crossing through the alleyways running along the private residencies, he headed for Sanjou Bridge. There was no doubt that it was already snowing in the mountains, so he'd have no choice but to make his escape along the Toukai road. He figured the journey to Edo would take him half a month. He didn't have enough money on hand to make the trip, but he might be able to manage if he pawned the tortoiseshell comb he kept as a memento of his mother.

The winters in Kyoto were cold, with ashen skies hanging heavily over sunken earth.

He could see Kiyomizu temple off in the distance. He'd been in Kyoto not even a year, and never expected he'd be running away with his tail between his legs. Back home, his brother had succeeded to ownership of their land and was living there with his children who weren't that much younger than he was. He really had no place he could return to.

Arriving at Sanjou Bridge, Amane stopped. Two retainers from Choushuu that he was acquainted with were standing atop it. Their backs to him, they seemed to be waiting for something, giving no impression that they planned to move any time soon. Amane reluctantly turned back a bit from the bridge to buy a pair of sandals.

Well, it was the least he could do to prepare for a long journey.

Just as he was walking under the sign curtain in the front of the shop, he ran into an exiting customer. It was a young, fit samurai.

"Bastard!"

The samurai's expression changed upon seeing Amane, his eyes now flashing with rage. Amane backed away.

"So, traitor," he said. "You're still alive."

Quicker than the man could draw his sword, Amane turned. Faster than he could bring it down, Amane ran. He lost a sandal, but kept threading his way through the crowd as he fled. The young samurai's hatred was such that he'd likely chase him to the ends of the earth.

To have gone so far, only to run into him…! Amane ran until he finally lost his enraged pursuer. At last, he fell to his knees, panting, under Bungo Bridge. It looked like he'd run back almost to Baikou's house. The sky was starting to grow red in the west. Amane lay on the withered grass, looking at his palm.

He'd truly come face to face with Great King Enma himself, with his violent glare which said that he'd never, ever forgive him.

Why had he run? If killing me would make him feel better, Amane thought, then I should have let him kill me.

Because he had indeed betrayed that man—Seinosuke Okazaki.

* * * * *

Bitter memories welled up inside of him.

"I'm the third-born son of my family," the man had said. "What's your story?"

Okazaki had been chatting amiably with him when he'd enlisted in the Shinsengumi.

"I'm from Inaba," Amane had replied. Since he couldn't say that he was from Choushuu, he instead claimed to be a country samurai from Tottori domain. Young, his face still not yet known by the enemy, Amane had been ordered to secretly infiltrate their organization and spy on them. It had been just before February.

The Shinsengumi were originally a squad of ronin—masterless samurai—known as the Miburou. Through the repeated enforcement of their strict code of conduct, they had become a military power that was recognized by the shogunate itself. Amane had been ordered to investigate what their movements were from inside of the organization, but as a junior officer, he'd had no opportunity to get close to their commander, Isami Kondou. As a result, he'd been unable to get any really useful information.

"The Tokugawa have kept the peace in this land for the last 260 years," Okazaki had proudly boasted. "Did you know that no other country can claim to have been at peace for all that time? The shogunate will repay us handsomely for protecting it from these disloyal conspirators."

Amane had been a low-level member of the movement to overthrow the shogunate to that point, and had always just assumed that justice was on their side. However, entering the Shinsengumi and directly hearing their ideas, he thought that they had a valid point, too. It all may have simply been a case of differing points of view.

For better or worse, while Okazaki was a man of fiery passions, he did look after Amane well. Having been recruited as a regimental soldier along with Amane, he took care of him in many ways. From the start, Amane had seemed like a slightly undependable and aimless youth. Maybe it was Okazaki's nature of not leaving things alone which had led him to sense it.

That Amane was a spy for Choushuu.

Okazaki was as angry as a man could have possibly been. There were no words which could ever ease the resentment and scorn he felt. Amane knew that much about him. The pro-shogunate forces had infiltrated their own fair share of spies into the anti-shogunate forces. Both sides were equally guilty, and Amane could have argued that he had no reason to feel guilty about it, but he just couldn't bring himself to debate the point with Okazaki.

* * * * *

The sun set, and as the darkness deepened, Amane grew cold. He shivered in the chill that seemed to penetrate down to his bones. If he stayed there, he would freeze to death.

His right palm throbbed.

He heard a shriek from somewhere, the urgent voice of a woman. Freezing, exhausted, and so sleepy he was nearly ready to fall over, Amane got up, one hand pressed to his head. He hurried towards a large nearby medicinal seed wholesale store. Kyoto wasn't safe these days. Hardly a night passed without someone being robbed and murdered.

It was as he'd guessed: the store's shutters were broken and a woman in her nightclothes ran from inside.

"Robbers," she said. "Help me!"

She clung to Amane, terror on her face.

"Hide," he ordered her. Then, drawing his sword, he plunged inside.

He just couldn't get to sleep. Thinking about the young man who'd disappeared, Baikou tossed and turned.

To tattoo immortality... That may have been his dream.

He'd corrupted the skins of nearly a thousand. He'd tattooed over a hundred oni-gome. But he'd never tattooed an immortality charm.

He didn't have much longer to live, and Baikou wanted to leave a great work behind that he could be proud of. He'd fought the temptation to tattoo immortality into someone, and then came a man literally to his doorstep who had begged him to not let him die. How could he have refused?

Oni-gome had three taboos attached to it.

First, you could not do it to commit suicide. Second, you couldn't use it for murder. Third, you couldn't use it for eternal youth and eternal life. It was true that Baikou had gotten requests over the years to give people strong will so that they could commit suicide or be able to kill without hesitation. However, he was not supposed to tattoo a charm that directly affected matters of life or death.

Among these taboos, immortality was in a class by itself. All oni-gome essentially reinforced the bearer's willpower, but being immortal went well beyond that. You were basically invading the territory of the gods when you tried it.

With that on his mind, Baikou wondered where Amane had gone.

*Damned kid. Running off like that!*

His hand had created an immortal. He regretted nothing. Breaking the taboo had meant that he had exceeded his master. He had never been so happy. It was out of a selfish need for satisfaction that he had victimized a young man.

Baikou had tattooed many images of Buddha in his life. He'd even once had a foreigner ask him to tattoo a crucifix onto them, but Baikou believed in neither Buddha nor God. The only thing he believed in was the oni, because he knew that the oni lived inside of him.

The plum blossom which bloomed on his right hand... Baikou had asked his master to tattoo it onto him when he'd first begun his apprenticeship. He'd sworn to the oni-gome that he wanted to devote his life to only his craft when he inherited the name of Houshou. His master had repeatedly told him not to do it. Inviting an oni to possess you would never give you happiness. It was a curse. It was a trap. It was destruction. Baikou accepted all of it and let the oni possess him. Such was his fascination with the works of his master.

Baikou had loved a woman across whose back was tattooed a brightly colored mandala. The first time he saw it, Baikou couldn't stop trembling. He wept, he screamed.

It was the moment which decided his life. He immediately sought out the man who had done the tattoo and begged him to let him be his apprentice. That had been fifty years ago.

There'd been some commotion outside a few moments before, but things had quieted back down. Maybe the pro- and anti-government groups were attacking each other again, or maybe it was a break-in. In other words, the usual foolishness that went on.

Kuro suddenly awoke and crawled out of the futon. Probably needs to do his business, Baikou thought. He was a clever cat that way, and wouldn't raise any fuss. But Kuro simply went to the doorway and meowed loudly at it.

"Ah, he's back."

Cats were fickle creatures, but there were times they could act as guard dogs. Baikou went to the door and opened it.

"You coming in?"

Amane stood before him. "Yeah," he finally replied.

Amane's kimono was stained with blood down to his *hakama* trousers. Much of it was from someone else, but the blood from where his shoulder had been split open was clearly his.

"Got yourself cut up again, I see."

"It's already healed."

Baikou smiled. "That's what I like to hear," he said.

Amane grabbed a fistful of Baikou's nightclothes and dragged him close.

"It had barely been cut open when it started healing!"

"Yeah, well, that just shows how good I am at this, doesn't it?"

Amane exploded in anger at Baikou's complete lack of concern.

"Don't screw with me, old man!"

"I told you already. Maybe you think I was having fun with you, but I wasn't lying."

Amane lifted him with both hands.

"I'll kill you!"

"Do it," Baikou replied.

Amane looked distraught, then relaxed his grip and squatted down where he stood.

"Damn it all," he sobbed.

"What, you're not gonna kill me?"

Baikou snorted, then offered a towel to Amane.

"Clean yourself up. You're gonna get blood all over my house again."

Amane took the towel without a word and wiped the blood off of his hands, revealing the mark of Enma it had obscured.

"I chose Enma as the design because I didn't care if I'm going to be judged by him in hell," Baikou said. "Tattooing immortality into someone is forbidden. If death is the price I have to pay for doing it, then so be it. If you want to kill me, you can indulge yourself at any time."

Amane shook his head, his body trembling.

"Enough," he moaned.

He'd just killed the three burglars at the wholesaler's. He hadn't gone in there intending to kill anyone, but it was dark in the store and he couldn't tell what was going on. The battle with the thieves had gotten so bad that there was no way he could have shown any mercy.

He'd stood there a long time, dazed and drenched in blood, until the Shinsengumi had come running. Amane had then gotten out of there immediately. Okazaki probably would have been among them. While the group was generally called the Shinsengumi, it consisted of about two hundred people, all with their own points of view and ways of thinking. Quite a few had joined for the same reason Amane had become an assassin for Choushuu: not out of any particularly strong motive, but because they were just trying to find a place for themselves in the world. Among them, Okazaki was particularly diligent, and no one hated criminal activity more than he did. If he'd heard about the burglary, Okazaki would have been leading the pack. Amane was fleeing Okazaki more than he was the Shinsengumi. Those intense eyes of his scared him.

Amane had hidden himself under the bridge again and had eventually become aware of the pain in his shoulder. He must have been stabbed by an assailant and hadn't noticed. Fortunately, they hadn't cut to the bone, but the wound wasn't shallow, either. He'd leaned against the bridge for a while and endured the pain.

His body was cold, but the wound was tinged with warmth. He could feel that the bleeding had stopped. The split skin was growing increasingly sticky, being forcibly knit back together. The pain had been so great that he'd lost consciousness.

He could feel the wound healing, fast enough to have been seen with the eye. The sublime agony he'd felt must have been compensating for that. He'd only had to suffer the pain a short time before he'd healed. Baikou had spoken the truth after all.

"Have I become a monster?" Amane muttered to himself.

"Sorry about that," said Baikou as he lay on his futon, looking at Amane. Then he laid his head down. "I can extract the oni, too."

"Will I go back to dying?"

Baikou scratched his white-haired head.

"Yeah, you will. In your case, you'd probably drop dead where you stood."

"What do you mean?" Amane quietly asked.

"You should have gone to hell long ago. The death being held back in you would hit all at once. I'll do it if you want me to. It'd be a waste to erase that oni after having planted it inside of you, but that can't be helped, can it? I'm an old man and never got an apprentice, so you'd better make up your mind about this before it's too late."

So, eternal life or drop dead where he stood. Amane frowned. What a bastard the old man was.

It was true that he still didn't really care what happened to him, but when he asked himself if he wanted to die, the answer was no. Being asked out of the blue to answer a question this big just left his head spinning. He'd only become aware of his strange situation a few moments before, and it was a lot to take in.

Any man was scared of dying. It was his fear that kept him shamefully on the run like this. But how badly did he fear not dying? Amane still couldn't imagine that, and the things you couldn't predict were even worse than the fears you knew.

"Oni-gome doesn't work just through the power of the tattooist," Baikou explained. "The one being tattooed has to desire it from their own heart. Because you just wanted to live, without any hesitation, you've gained immortality. The same goes for my extracting the oni from you. Unless you accept death from the bottom of your heart, it won't work."

The old man fixed his gaze on Amane, as if saying, "Your move, now." Amane wasn't the sort of person who could die without any hesitation. He was young. Contrary to his desperate words, Baikou could see that he still had many attachments to this world, which was why he pressed him so hard for an answer.

"Dammit…" Amane was so drained that he could only summon up that short curse as an answer.

"You think I've done you wrong," Baikou said. "While I was trying to deepen the practice of my craft, I've burdened you with a difficult fate. That's why I'm leaving this up to you."

Amane didn't care. He closed his heavy eyelids.

"I'll think about it tomorrow," he mumbled.

He was so terribly tired.

* * * * *

Seinosuke Okazaki stood at the scene of the burglary, scowling in annoyance.

One of the robbers was dead from a stab to his side, but the wounds of the other two weren't fatal. According to the shopkeeper, a young man had run in by himself, fought the robbers, and then run off. From their description of the man and especially his hairstyle, Okazaki had a hunch who it was. There was also the sword wounds the robbers had sustained… As though they were inflicted by somebody waving a long sword who hadn't wanted to kill.

*Could it have been Amane?*

He hadn't told anyone that he'd run into Amane Ichinose. As far as they knew, he was dead. This latest act confused him, though. Why was he helping people when he could have been saving himself?

Okazaki still couldn't believe the man was a spy. There'd been something unreliable about him, in the way he'd sometimes dress with his clothes inside out, or spill his soup at meals. Like he was a little kid. True, he could handle a sword well, but he couldn't use it in combat. Maybe his lords in Choushuu needed to select their men better, or perhaps they'd decided he was useless and were sacrificing him as a pawn.

At any rate, there was no way he'd ever forgive him. They'd spent nights discussing their ideals, even talking about their lives and hopes. All the while, Amane must have been laughing at him inside. More than that, Okazaki couldn't forgive himself for having been taken in by him so completely.

He'd apparently been injured in the scuffle last night, and Okazaki had heard that he'd also taken a sword slash across the back a few days earlier. In that case, he couldn't have gone far. He must still be somewhere in Kyoto. With that in mind, Okazaki used city patrol duty as an excuse to continue looking for Amane. Normally, patrols were conducted in teams of two men, but as Amane had been his partner, Okazaki went out alone.

Naturally, he didn't wear his Dandara-patterned *haori* coat. That was much too easy to spot. He'd never really liked wearing it. Actually, very few of the members did.

The rules of the Shinsengumi were strict, and Okazaki could be executed for not reporting that Amane was still alive. Even so, he wanted to try and settle this himself if he could. He no longer had any blind aspirations for the Shinsengumi, because no matter how high their advertised ideals may have been, in the end it was a place for power struggles. Anybody who disagreed was purged. Those who survived were those who thought in the correct way.

How empty it all was. Okazaki glared at the grey sky above.

If Amane was in the official residence of the feudal lord of Choushuu in the city, he couldn't touch him. But from seeing him yesterday in the vicinity of Sanjou Bridge, the odds were good that he was trying to leave Kyoto. That meant he wasn't planning to go back to his people.

For now, Okazaki decided he'd investigate the vicinity of the wholesaler from last night. Coming to a neighborhood of old row houses, he saw an old man emerge from one, coughing as he did. He tottered along, looking not at all well. Just as Okazaki was thinking he might be in trouble, the old man fell.

"Are you all right?" Okazaki called out as he ran over to help.

"Thanks," the old man replied.

Okazaki caught sight of tattoos beneath the sleeve of his kimono that had been pulled back. The old man didn't look like he was yakuza. More likely he had just been a little wild when he was young. Okazaki picked up the *hakama* the old man had dropped, retying its wrapping cloth and beating the dust off of it. Something else must have been wrapped up inside, because it was surprisingly heavy.

"That must be heavy for you," he said. "Let me take it. I'll give you a hand."

"Oh, this?" the old man replied. "This is nothing for a samurai to trouble himself with. My grandson showed up with nothing but dirty laundry. If I didn't get these washed, he wouldn't be able to go out."

"That kid sounds promising."

Okazaki noticed some sort of flower design on the old man's right hand.

"Is that a tattoo also?"

"A man-eating flower."

Okazaki gazed at it.

"It's a plum blossom, isn't it?"

“That’s what my grandson calls it. He doesn’t seem to like it much.”

Maybe, from a child’s sense, even a tattoo could seem scary. That wasn’t even going into where it was located.

“This is the first time I’ve ever seen one on somebody’s palm.”

“There aren’t many people who can do one there,” the old man replied. “It hurt like hell, and still does.”

There was a note of pride in his voice. Okazaki wondered if the old man was proud of being able to withstand the pain.

“After fifty years, the color hasn’t faded. Pretty impressive, huh?”

He stroked his palm, almost lovingly, then suddenly looked up.

“Good grief! I have to get home! If you’ll excuse me.”

“Right. Take care now.”

Bowing his head several times in agreement, the old man took his leave.

Okazaki wondered if maybe the man had once been a construction worker or a fire fighter, but the thought passed just as quickly and he soon lost interest.

He wouldn’t remember the old man’s wrinkled face until the following year.

## —3—

“There you go. You’re getting good at that, aren’t you?”

Baikou nodded as he looked down at the drawing of a lotus blossom on paper.

White breath spread from his mouth each time he opened it. The brazier was lit, but it barely affected the drafts that poured through the old house. It had gotten even colder after New Year’s.

“Liar,” Amane replied. He put the brush down and blew on his hands for warmth. His hands shook from the cold, and he couldn’t draw the lines straight.

The design of the lotus he saw in the book bloomed much more grandly than this, didn’t it? He should have simply been able to copy what he saw, but it was harder than he’d expected. Could he ever work up the nerve to draw this on a person’s skin and then color it in with a needle? Amane began to lose his nerve.

“I feel an apprentice grows through encouragement.”

“Who said I’m your apprentice?”

He hadn’t set out to be the old man’s apprentice, but while he was making up his mind between immortality and instant death, winter had arrived. And so now he found himself lodging with Baikou. It had begun with him simply drawing some pictures in order to pass the time.

“Why not try doing it seriously?” the old man suggested. “Your career as an assassin is ruined now. If you find yourself a good career, you can live a long life without any worries.”

A long life… Amane shivered at the words and stopped drawing.

“How about it? Will you inherit the name of Houshou?”

“There are other people you can get to be your apprentice,” Amane said. “Why does it have to be me?"

Baikou shook his head sadly.

"I've had three already, but none of them worked out. Two of them had no talent for it, so I gave up on them quickly. The third one looked like he was going to work out, but then… He was a fool who chose the wrong path to follow. I haven't taken another pain in the ass apprentice since."

An unusually bitter expression came to his face. Probably because of whatever this "foolish pupil" had done.

"The Houshou name has lasted a long time. That was pretty irresponsible of you."

"A pupil who masters oni-gome usually just takes the Houshou name. That's how it's managed to have been passed on all these years. There really aren't many other details to sweat besides that."

Amane warmed his frozen hands over the brazier.

"In that case, you don't need me to take over the name, do you?"

"Perhaps, but if you take the Houshou name, you'll gain its prestige. It'd earn you an income. If you want to live a long life, that's not a bad thing to have."

Amane didn't like how the old man smugly assumed that he couldn't choose death. But what irritated him the most was the fact that he couldn't die without asking Baikou first. The power of life and death over him was held at Baikou's whim.

Amane had drawn pictures since he was a child, and he enjoyed it quite a bit. His sister Sawa had been skilled at drawing, and she'd taught him well, so the idea of his becoming a tattoo artist wasn't that disagreeable a notion. However, he was reluctant to simply go along with Baikou's plans for him.

"Of course, you'll need the proper skills to do that," Baikou continued.

"It'd probably take me years to learn them."

The old man's favorite phrase was "I'm not long for this earth." He may have been the sort of man who could hold off hell itself, but the truth was that his health was poor. He never seemed to stop coughing now. With each coughing fit, he'd take a potion of boiled *kikyo* root, but it was growing less and less effective.

"Oh, yeah," he replied. "So I'll just teach you the basics and the rest you can learn by trial and error. You'll have plenty of time to practice."

"I'm going out for a walk."

Having him shut up in here out of public sight was also what Baikou wanted. Amane wanted to get out under the sky and breathe fresh air.

"Then use this," the old man said, tossing him a hood. Wearing a hood over your head was normal for a man at this time of year. Amane wrapped it up to the bottom of his nose. His hairstyle now looked so different that it would be difficult to recognize him like this. He was very glad that it was wintertime.

One step outside and he immediately hugged himself tightly. Apparently the rickety old house really was staving off some of the cold.

"Come back before it gets dark!" the old man called out.

*What am I, a little kid?* Amane wondered.

Despite the blue sky, snow was falling. The road was wet and white.

Head down, Amane walked along the riverbank. A few waves lapped weakly in the dull waters. To avoid recklessly sticking his nose into any quarrels he might find, he'd left his sword in the house, but its absence from his waist made him nervous.

He hoped the snow wouldn't pile up too much. He was a little unsteady on his feet. It would snow occasionally in Choushuu, but it didn't get nearly as cold. As he stepped to avoid slipping on the snow, a girl in front of the sweet shop laughed at him.

"A sweet shop, huh…" he said to himself.

Amane pulled a purse from his pocket. There wasn't very much in it, but he could afford a bit of candy.

"Do you have any cough drops?" he asked. He wasn't buying them for Baikou's sake, he told himself. His coughing was just annoying.

"Thanks. Hope you feel better," the girl said. Amane smiled bitterly. Dressed as he was, it was no wonder she thought he was sick. He popped one candy into his mouth and then pocketed the rest.

He hadn't noticed when, but the snow had stopped falling.

Just as he was thinking he should be headed back, Amane suddenly realized how thankful he was to have a home to go back to. Now that he could not return to his family, the Shinsengumi barracks, or even the residence of the lord of Choushuu, Baikou now loomed large in his life. Maybe because he'd never felt as comfortable living anywhere else as he did with the old man.

*Come back before it gets dark…* His sister used to say that to him, too.

Dusk was falling. He could hear a bell toll. Amane wheeled around and had started back the way he'd come when he heard shouts behind him. Probably a quarrel, he thought. He quickened his pace, not wanting to get involved.

"The Miburou are being attacked!" someone shouted.

Amane stopped in his tracks. Miburou was another name for the Shinsengumi. It was a name the people of Kyoto called them with fear.

If the Shinsengumi were nearby, it was all the more reason for him to get out of there quickly. Reinforcements might be arriving soon. If they were fighting the guys from Choushuu, it would be even more dangerous for him.

But… The image of Okazaki's profile, cornered by enemies, filled his mind. What if it was Okazaki and his men who were being attacked? Thinking that, he couldn't just run away from there.

He just had to be sure that he wasn't seen. Amane ran off towards the trouble.

A group of townsfolk were watching the scene from afar. Two men in the *haori* coats of the Shinsengumi were backed up against the river, surrounded by four ronin.

It was Kuwata and Saki, two guys in his group. Amane didn't recognize their opponents. They were yelling something in Tosa dialect. Relieved that they weren't from Choushuu, Amane hid himself behind a willow tree. Looking around, he saw no sign of help coming from any other Shinsengumi.

The faces of the two Shinsengumi men were tense. Saki, who was young even compared to the other members of the force, was backing away. His hands shook as he held his sword. Kuwata, likely feeling some duty to protect the younger man, took a step forward. In this cold, they would be risking their lives to jump into the river. Melting snow had raised its waters higher than normal. There'd be no easy escape that way. Besides, to make such a shameful retreat in front of all these people would have disgraced the Shinsengumi as a whole.

The ronin were slowly closing in. Kuwata's eyes wildly swept back and forth, trying to figure out which would attack first.

Amane chewed his nails nervously, wondering what he should do.

He didn't want to see Saki die. He was barely more than a kid. Cheerful and gentle, he'd adored Amane and Okazaki like older brothers.

*Saki…!*

Had he not been unarmed, he might have leapt out to help them. As he put his hand to his breast in frustration, Amane felt a hard bulge inside.

One of the ronin stepped forward, swinging his sword down from above Kuwata's head. Kuwata only barely deflected it in time, but he was knocked off balance, falling to the ground on one hand. The momentum slipped one of his sandals from his foot.

The ronin, thrusting his sword to finish him off, suddenly stopped and rubbed his face. A cough drop had just flown smack into the middle of his forehead.

"Now!" Amane yelled, without thinking.

Still holding his sword, Kuwata leapt up and tackled the ronin. His sword plunged into the man's belly, piercing all the way through. Screams erupted around them.

"What the…?!" The remaining ronin faltered, losing their nerve. Facing each other, as if coming to a consensus, they turned and all fled at once.

As they were doing so, Amane too beat a hasty retreat from the scene. He ran intently through the deepening gloom, regretting his careless shout. He spotted a group of Shinsengumi running along the way, but they passed by without paying him any mind. They were in too much of a hurry to get to the scene of the battle to pay any attention to passers-by. Amane had spotted Okazaki among them.

It looked like he'd have to refrain from any more spontaneous strolls from now on. It was thoroughly dark by the time he got back to Baikou's home.

"Took you long enough," the old man gruffed. "Here, get over by the fire. Your face is turning blue."

He was thankful that the old man had waited for him. He may have had a cracked smile like an old toad, but it made him feel good, in a strange way. Handing him the remaining candies, Amane made his decision.

"Teach me how to tattoo."

* * * * *

Kuwata was pale as he spoke, having only barely escaped the ronin from Tosa.

"Something small, a pebble, I think. It flew into that outlaw ronin's head. That's what saved us. Someone in the crowd must have helped."

One of the townsfolk had helped the Miburou? Okazaki tilted his head, puzzled. The Shinsengumi weren't exactly liked in this town. More like feared, but of course some of those people must sympathize with them. Even so, he doubted that any of them would recklessly involve themselves like that without a good reason.

While the others cleared away the bodies of their fallen comrades, Okazaki searched by lamplight for the "pebble" thrown by Kuwata and Saki's savior. He found something that looked a bit like a pebble, but when he picked it up, he saw that it was a round hard candy, still fresh. It looked like a cough drop, and it smelled of quinces. He suddenly realized he smelled the same sweet aroma on the forehead of the dead ronin.

"Are you all right, Saki?" he asked the younger man. Saki was still pale. He was young, baby-faced. He looked so childlike that it was a wonder that he'd ever been allowed to join their ranks.

"Y-Yeah," Saki replied.

"Looks like you had somebody help you out. Did you see anything?"

Saki weakly shook his head no.

"I had my eyes closed."

This kid wasn't going to survive long in this job. Once again, Okazaki thought he should be discharged at once.

"Um..." stammered Saki.

"What is it?"

"Ichinose-san really is dead...isn't he?" Saki asked.

Okazaki drew a sharp breath.

"I heard that they never found his body."

"The river was swollen with rain that day. It probably washed his body away. Why do you ask?"

"Because I could swear I heard his voice before. It's strange, don't you think?"

Okazaki paused before asking his next question.

"And what did this voice say?"

"'Now.' I think he was telling Kuwata-san what to do."

Okazaki considered this for a bit, then smiled.

"Even his ghost wouldn't have done that," he laughed. "He was a Choushuu lapdog, after all. There's no way a guy like that would ever be on our side."

Saki nodded sadly. "Maybe I just wished it was Ichinose-san," he said.

Okazaki clapped Saki on the shoulder, telling him that paranoia was rife in their ranks now. If he started worrying about things that he shouldn't, he might be unjustly suspected of something. "Just forget about him," he said.

What had he been thinking by doing this? Okazaki clenched the paper-wrapped candy in his fist.

Amane, you idiot.

* * * * *

By the time the plum blossoms were in bloom, Amane was able to draw rough sketches on bare skin. He had to use his own leg for practice, so it tickled a bit.

"Oh, you numbskull!" Baikou roared angrily, hovering over him. "How many times do I have to tell you?! You gotta draw the lines straight!"

Baikou's instruction was strict; apparently, his claims of developing talent through praise were just a lot of hot air. After each tirade, he'd erupt into a violent coughing fit. His hacking was so painful that it was worrying Amane.

"All right, all right!" he exclaimed. "Just get some rest!"

"Oh, like I can rest when you can't do this right! Are you trying to kill me?!"

The old man's eyes sparkled as he spoke. It was obvious he was relishing having a student after so long. Even so, the winter cold had taken its toll on him, and he was visibly emaciated. If he hadn't been set on making Amane the successor to the Houshou name, he might have died already.

"Still, there is a sexiness to your drawings. That, at least, I can compliment you on."

"Sexiness?"

That might have applied if he'd been working on a portrait of a woman, but Amane was drawing a rising dragon just then.

"Sexiness is a good thing to have in a drawing, even if it's of a dragon or a fish," Baikou explained. "You'll probably get women as customers, too. My master always said that my drawings had an air of bloodlust. That's probably why I only ever got bastards as clients."

Amane thought he'd be reluctant to cut into a woman's skin to tattoo it. Even as he was studying the craft, he still couldn't quite understand why anyone would pay money to have themselves tattooed.

"Are there women who get tattoos?" he asked.

"Plenty," the old man replied. "You just don't normally see them. Prostitutes get tattoos of the names of the men they love. Of course, when they get a new man, they waste no time burning them off with a hot set of tongs!"

Baikou smiled as he said this, but there was a strangeness to how he said it that Amane couldn't quite put his finger on. All he could think was that it was sad that a woman would subject herself to pain twice for such a trifling thing. He kept this to himself, however, since he had a feeling that saying it to the old man would just lead to a lot of teasing about how he was just a stupid kid who didn't understand the workings of a woman's heart.

"You don't like tattoos?" the old man asked. Amane found that he couldn't deny the question.

"When I was a little kid," Amane replied, "I saw the body of a man who'd drowned. He had the kanji for 'dog' tattooed on his forehead. My big brother told me that meant he was a criminal. I think having that tattoo made him so miserable that he jumped into the water to die."

Amane looked at the mark of Enma on his palm.

"That tattoo was *irezumi*," Baikou replied. "What we practice is *horimono*. Don't mix the two of them up."

Apparently, *irezumi* was a tattoo given to a criminal as punishment. *Horimono* was a tattoo that you got willingly to express your creativity and flair. Horimono was art. Irezumi was just ink on skin.

"So, that means my Enma mark is an irezumi, doesn't it?"

"Oni-gome is a two-edged sword," the old man replied. "For better or for worse, it cuts both ways."

Baikou's cough suddenly worsened. Amane quickly began pounding his back. When he finally quieted down, Amane placed a candy in the plum blossom on his palm. Amane would always buy the candy for him whenever he ventured outside. He realized the risk he was running, but there was no way Baikou could buy them himself in the state he was in now. Fortunately, he hadn't run into any of the Shinsengumi when he did.

"There's something I have to tell you," the old man began.

"Never mind, just get some rest."

He lay Baikou down on the futon and drew a sleeved quilt over him.

"To draw an oni out after it's been placed inside of someone, you just need someone who knows how to practice oni-gome," Baikou said. "But you can't drive out the oni yourself."

The oni wouldn't allow it, Baikou explained, a self-mocking smile floating to his lips.

"There's that other guy who took the Houshou name for himself, isn't there? Couldn't he do it?"

"If he's alive," the old man answered. "But I told you, I cut all ties with that failure of an apprentice. I don't know where that little shit is or even if he's still alive."

Amane shook his head in despair.

"It doesn't matter what kind of guy he was. I can't look for him if I don't know what he looks like."

Baikou stopped coughing and smiled.

"He was young, really handsome. Well, handsomer than you, anyway."

Amane smirked at hearing that. He didn't fancy himself a man with particularly gentle features.

"Even if you ask someone to draw the oni from you, your immortality will make it difficult. If drawing it out means death, then the oni may not allow it. Honestly, I've never heard of anyone being able to extract an oni when it knows that it'll die in the process."

He imagined that the basic human instinct for survival combined with the oni's tenacity in not letting him die would make doing it very difficult.

"Still, there are other ways that you can die. If you're beheaded or have your heart stabbed with one thrust, you'll die before you can heal. That should be easy enough for you to arrange."

Amane smiled a bitter, exhausted smile.

"Definitely," he said. He was on the run, after all. He should have many opportunities to die like that.

"Aside from that, you can probably die from being ripped apart or strangled. No matter how hard the oni may try, people don't change. Immortality and eternal youth are imperfect things. I've even heard that an oni will leave of its own accord when it gets tired of someone. And this is my own opinion, mind you, but I think the oni may have a limited life span of its own."

"A life span?" Amane asked, frowning.

"Even an oni can't live forever. It'll die, someday. Just like we humans return to the soil, it'll melt away back into the ghostly ether it sprang from. At least, that's what I think it does. You know, in a way, immortality really is a curse. It's almost like killing somebody right away.

"When you no longer value your life, you become reckless," Baikou murmured.

"Did you know a man like that?" Amane asked.

"Long ago, when I first began my apprenticeship, there was another man who was immortal and eternally young."

The old man closed his eyes, as if he were dredging up the memories inside.

"Did you tattoo it into him?"

"It was my master who did it. He liked to gamble, and he was in over his head with debt. His bookie threatened him and gave him a choice. If he didn't have the money, he could either make him immortal or else cut off the tips of all of his own fingers. What else could he do? And to be honest, my master was sorely tempted to try and tattoo an immortality oni-gome." It was the nature of the Houshou, Baikou said, his mouth growing slack. Even though it was forbidden, all those who bore the name may have been doomed to give in to the temptation.

"And what happened to the yakuza?" Amane asked.

"He died. He lasted about a year with the oni-gome. He was a real scumbag, after all. Got to be known as Tatsuzou the Unkillable, and ran riot all over the place like he was the hottest thing around. Ended up getting executed for his crimes. Once they cut off his head, there was nothing the oni could do to save him."

Knowing for certain that a guy like him had been killed gave him some relief for now. Hearing this story lightened Amane's mood considerably.

"And even though he died in the end, he was still the 'unkillable man.' His grave was robbed, not a shred of flesh or bone left, taken by people who wanted to share in his miracle. People can be disgusting, sometimes."

Baikou fell silent, as though depressed by his own tale. Then, recalling one more point, he added: "A man who invites an oni into his own body and becomes half monster isn't receiving a blessing. He's just a hopeless fool."

"You're one to talk," Amane said, considering how he'd made another man a monster without even asking permission. As he indicated the Enma mark, Baikou smiled without a hint of regret.

"Damn right I am."

Was there a limit to how infuriating this old man could be?

Amane opened the window and savored the scent of the plum blossoms outside. Cherry blossoms, which added such color to the springtime as they blossomed, were fine in their own right, but their fragrance was sadly lacking. He preferred plum blossoms, which weren't as showy but whose scent could turn your head as you walked by.

Baikou wasn't a great lover of flowers, but as the character for plum formed one part of his name, he'd planted a plum tree in his tiny garden. It comforted the heart of the man who was now caged like a bird in the old house.

"Close that window!" Baikou said. Amane obliged him.

"Are you cold? I told you to get some sleep."

"The wind's going to blow my papers away," he replied. He'd been feeling a bit better today, and so he'd been up since early morning, working on new designs.

"Look, don't you think you should go see a doctor?" Amane asked.

"When you get old, your health goes. That's a fact of life. Going to a doctor isn't going to change that."

Well, his mouth at least was still healthy.

"Anyway, why don't you try tattooing something for real?"

"What, you mean on a person?"

"Unless you plan on using a pillow as a pin cushion forever. Don't you want to tattoo someone?"

Tattoos lasted forever, so practicing on someone wasn't something to be attempted lightly. That was the reason he'd been practicing using the pillow.

"But there's no way a total amateur like me could ever get a customer—"

"Don't be an idiot! I meant practice on your own leg. That way you'll know how much it hurts, too."

Of course. Amane still had a certain resistance to the idea of tattooing and didn't really want to scratch ink into his own skin, but this was the only way he'd ever get any experience.

"How can you ever be a tattooist if you hate tattoos?" the old man said. "Now get ready!"

"What should I tattoo?"

Setting out a needle and ink, he extended his leg. He wiped the inside of his calf with a towel.

"Why don't you start with a flower? There we go, this one. Just take it slow and do this," the old man said, pointing to a cherry blossom in his design book.

Amane carefully drew a rough sketch on his skin and then began etching the ink into his skin with the needle. It didn't hurt as much as he'd thought it would. Sweat dripped from his brow and the hand holding the needle grew damp and trembled. A bit of blood ran down his leg. He'd grown used to being stabbed and stuck, but the strain still wore at him.

"Don't be so nervous. Be quicker with your movements."

"You just told me to take it slow, didn't you?!"

Amane paused to wipe the sweat away.

"If you don't hurry, it'll disappear!"

"Tattoos don't disappear."

"Your body is a special case. Remember the wounds on your back and shoulder? You don't have any scars from them, do you?"

He didn't normally think about the sword wound, since he couldn't see it, but he knew that no scar remained there.

"Wait, that applies to tattoos, too?"

"As far as your body knows, it's just another wound to heal," the old man replied.

Amane looked down at the cherry blossom he was tattooing. There still wasn't any change that he could see.

"You must be doing it right," Baikou mused. "A bad tattoo probably wouldn't stay. That'll make it great for you to practice on, won't it?"

Oh, he had to be kidding. Amane hurried the tattooing, not wanting to see it fade. The last thing he wanted to do was directly confront evidence of the monster he had become.

"Ow!"

The needle slipped from his hand. The skin upon which he was tattooing the cherry blossom had begun to hurt intensely. It was just like the time when his shoulder had been slashed. The condensed pain wracked his body, although he couldn't tell if it was pain or a sort of itchiness. He tried to pick up the needle again, but couldn't, instead clutching his leg and doubling over in pain.

"Dammit!" the old man cried. "I told you to hurry up with the tattooing, didn't I?!"

"Shut up," Amane hissed through gritted teeth. "Dammit…!"

His painful writhing didn't last long. Finally getting up, Amane timidly looked at his leg. The wound was closed, the cherry blossom fading before his eyes.

"By tomorrow, your skin will look like it never had a wound on it. Now try it again."

Amane picked up the needle and flung it at Baikou.

"Fuck you!" he spat.

Seeing his strange healing power had left Amane shaken.

"Oh, just suck it up already! What are you, a child?!" Baikou yelled in disgust.

Shooting a piercing glare back at Baikou, Amane stalked off to a corner of the room and sat down, hugging his knees to his body. His body felt heavy, like it was covered with mud.

After several days of the same thing happening, Amane was forced to accept the reality of his situation. He also accepted the pain that came in direct proportion to the time it took for a wound to heal. The Enma which existed on his palm was judging him, he thought. Well, until somebody separated his head from the rest of him, there was nothing he could do about that.

Today, Amane was drawing the freshly severed head of a warrior. Using shading, he had given it a faint air of melancholy.

"You know, now you're just making me jealous," Baikou said. "You've gotten that good with only this much training."

If Baikou was saying that, it meant he'd done a very good tattoo. As the burning pain came, the bewitching severed head vanished from his leg. It seemed to resemble Amane in some ways.

"You may have a talent for this that's even better than mine," the old man added.

It was rare for him to offer praise like that. Baikou had done a small bodhisattva tattoo on his upper arm as an example, but the Buddha he'd made had a ghastly air to it. The one Amane had done seemed tepid in comparison. Of course, it soon vanished from his arm. He'd actually been a little sorry to see it go.

The sluggishness hit after the pain had passed. He lay down and fell asleep, where the usual dark dreams awaited him.

* * * * *

"Come on, get up! You're going to be late!"

That was how Okazaki had always awakened him. Amane was almost useless in the morning, so Okazaki would physically haul him up and throw his *kosode* and *hakama* onto him to get him dressed. One might have thought he was playing the fool in order to hold down any expectations of performance in battle, but the truth was he wasn't making any special effort to fool Okazaki. His inability to wake up and his general carelessness were entirely separate matters.

"Aside from Saki, I have no idea how you got accepted into this outfit," Okazaki had said. "What happens if somebody attacks you while you're waking up?" He tied up the cord of his *hakama* and then dragged him along to the sink. The sun wasn't even up yet, but there was a lot of work for the new recruits to do.

"Ichinose-san, you have terrible bed head today," Saki said as he washed rice at the sink, laughing his pleasant laugh. The boy wore his sword on his right, but he remained stubbornly left-handed when it came to writing and using a kitchen knife. As a result, he'd constantly be bumping elbows with anyone he was next to when they did any work lined up with each other. It was kind of funny how he'd apologize each and every time he did it.

"Never mind about that, Saki," Okazaki angrily yelled, "what are you going to do about this dog?!" He'd nearly tripped over a puppy which followed him around underfoot. Saki had taken him in the night before.

"Can't I keep him here, sir?" he asked timidly, picking the puppy up and holding it to his chest.

"Look, if the captain had taken it in, that'd be one thing. But there's no way they'd allow underlings like us to keep a dog in here!" Amane nodded in agreement.

"But, maybe if we raised him to be a good guard dog, he'd allow it then," the boy suggested. Saki was remarkably persistent when it came to matters of the heart.

"If he became a guard dog for the Miburou, he'd be the first to die if anyone attacked us. Just forget about it," Amane said. The others around them nodded. It hadn't taken long for even those who had joined casually to figure out exactly what sort of place this was.

"All right, I get it," the boy answered.

In the end, Saki took the puppy back to where he'd found it. He looked so sad and lonely, seen from behind. Okazaki and the others thought the same things that Amane did, even though he was their enemy. As they fought over and over, blood being washed away with more blood, they didn't even know what they were fighting for anymore. Maybe Saki had wanted to try and save the puppy to make up for how powerless he felt.

That had been the day.

The people Amane had been connected to had been captured, and he'd been quickly found out. Seeing the look in the eyes of his captain as he'd approached, he'd quickly figured out what had happened. He hadn't been slow to realize the murderous rage being directed at him. He had run for his life. Then the pain had run along his back…

* * * * *

He awakened.

It was dark, despite his being awake. Night must have fallen as he'd slept. There was a sleeved quilt over him, no doubt laid there by Baikou.

"Hey, old man?"

There was no answer. Could he have gone out at night like this? What if his back gave out and he fell? Amane fumbled for the lantern and lit it. He wiped cold sweat from his brow. The scar on his back may have healed completely, but that dream of how he'd gotten it had been so vivid. When he flipped up his sleeve, a faint image of a tattoo remained. A thin smile came to his lips.

"How convenient…"

Stepping down onto the landing in front of the door, he drank the water in the bucket.

Although he'd come to the red light district with his comrades, Okazaki wasn't used to seeking out female companionship there. He was naturally straitlaced, and he disdained the thought of paying for sex. After having a cup of hot sake, he'd excused himself, saying he was heading back to the barracks. He looked up at the moon, pale as fish paste.

Face powder from the girl who'd poured his drink clung to his sleeve. It didn't smell like blood and sweat. Its fragrance suggested paradise. Brushing the powder off, he walked along the streets at night. An old man carrying a paper lantern crossed in front of him.

"Let me walk you home," he offered. The streets of Kyoto at night weren't safe for an old man walking alone.

"Nah, don't worry yourself," the old man replied. He was carrying a wooden box packed with sushi. He didn't seem drunk.

"It's dangerous out here. Look, let me walk along with you while we're going the same way. Don't worry, I'm with the Shinsengumi."

The old man became visibly uncomfortable, but Okazaki was used to this reaction.

"No need to be afraid. The Miburou only bare their fangs at the lawless."

That's right, he thought. They weren't wild animals. True, they'd once been thought of as a collection of outlaws, but now their strict discipline let them maintain order and justice. They just needed to make more people understand that. Besides, he'd seen this old man somewhere before. Where was it…? Okazaki wracked his brains, trying to remember.

"Really, I'm fine," the old man insisted. "My grandson's hungry and waiting for me at home. I'll go straight back there, I promise."

Grandson… The image of a plum blossom tattoo floated up through Okazaki's mind.

"Oh!" he exclaimed. "It's been a while. You're the one who had the plum blossom tattoo on his palm, aren't you?"

The old man squinted his eye, trying to place him.

"The samurai who picked up that bundle I dropped, right?"

"So, you remember me."

Did the old man trust him a little more now? His face betrayed no emotion.

"Is your grandson well?"

"Yup. Impertinent and causing me trouble."

If his grandfather was looking after him like this, it probably meant that the kid had no parents.

"Still, he's dear to me. Can't have the young dying before the old, can we?"

It was the times they lived in. Very often, the young would die before the old. Despite the bluntness of his expression, Okazaki could sense the deep love the old man felt for his grandson.

"Sounds like he's the apple of your eye."

"More than that. He's my treasure."

"He must be a happy child."

The old man tilted his head, considering it.

"Well now… I'm not sure if he is."

It seemed strange for him to say such a modest thing.

Okazaki and the old man continued walking side by side. The night grew deeper, until the light of their lanterns could barely penetrate the darkness. Spring may have been near, but the night was bitterly cold. The old man coughed, in obvious pain.

"You got a cold? That's no good."

"It's nothing, really," the old man replied. He drew out a small paper package from his breast pocket and from it extracted a candy. He passed a piece to Okazaki while popping another piece into his mouth.

"Please, have one. My grandson buys them for me to help with my cough."

The candy smelled of quinces.

"Your…grandson, you say?"

"Yeah. Oh, we're near my house now, so I'll say goodbye. Thanks for the company."

"Sure… Take care."

Bowing his head over and over, the old man disappeared down an alley lined with residences. Okazaki thought of walking him to his house, but bid him farewell there.

Then, as the old man turned right, Okazaki followed along, watching him, making sure not to make any noise as he walked. Maybe it was just a coincidence, he thought, but he couldn't just leave without making sure. The old man had said that his house was nearby, but he walked on for a while. Every once in a while, he looked around, as though keeping on guard.

At last, the door of one small house opened.

"You awake?" the old man called out. "Look, I got us some sushi."

He couldn't see inside, but there was light from in there. Okazaki hid in the shadow of a plum tree and waited to see what would happen.

"Never mind about dinner," he heard someone say. "You know it's dangerous for you to go out at night."

"Yeah, it was pretty dangerous."

"Why, did something happen?"

"Nah, forget about it."

The voice coming from the house was definitely familiar. After a moment of hesitation, Okazaki silently departed.

Even though the door was closed, it was still a run-down house. The gaps in the boards could do nothing to stop the penetration of sunlight inside. Even so, it was nearly noon when Amane awoke. Thanks to his off-again on-again sleep schedule, his sense of day and night had gotten out of whack. Turning his head to stretch, he went outside to wash his face and nearly stepped on Kuro as the cat rubbed against his feet. He was still half-asleep. As he lowered the bucket into the well, a young girl ran over to him. She was the neighbor's girl, and had charming rosy cheeks.

"Here," she said, holding out a piece of paper she had clutched in her hand. "The man told me to give it to the grandson next door."

To the neighborhood, he was known as Baikou's grandson, but there was no way Amane could be getting a message from anyone.

Thanking the little girl, Amane opened the paper where he stood. Inside was a piece of quince candy and a short note. He pondered it for a moment, then looked up at the sky. He washed his face and went back inside, where Baikou was coughing violently.

"I need you to teach me oni-gome. Right now," Amane said.

Baikou looked up at him, frowning in surprise.

"Don't be ridiculous. You can barely tattoo. It's way too soon to teach you that."

"I want to learn everything before the day is out. I know this is unreasonable, but..."

Baikou looked up at Amane, his eyes probing him, then stood up with an air of resignation.

"Well, get ready," he sighed.

The sudden cram session lasted late into the night.

Oni-gome was like sorcery, definitely not a technique meant for man to know. While he couldn't see it, he could sense signs of something not of this world. They came wriggling out of the noise and darkness. A ghostly aura hung over the tiny room like smoke, transforming it into the spirit world. When the time came to teach him the most forbidden technique of immortality, even Baikou's practiced hand shook.

"It'd be better if you didn't know this, but I don't want your education to be incomplete," he said.

The oni peered down at them from above, enveloping both men like candlelight. Amane felt a wet sensation gently brush his cheek.

He felt a bit more of his humanity slip away...

As Amane was feeling as though he was being stepped on by a heavy darkness, he heard Baikou's cracked voice.

"I tattooed a Yasha demon on the lower back of my foolish apprentice, and he took that for his name as a tattooist. He made an oni-gome of immortality for himself. And, in doing so, he became a true monster."

"A true monster?" Amane asked.

Baikou nodded.

"It's what happens when you give yourself an oni-gome. You become a monstrous cannibal who devours others, and so he devours life. If he doesn't, the oni he carries will start to go out of control and torture him with unendurable pain. It's only fitting for a fool who goes fishing for dead flesh to eat. You must have heard stories, legends of how eating the heart of another will give you eternal life. Every country has them. The crazy bastard ended up just like that."

An immortal madman. Amane couldn't begin to comprehend what a horrible existence that would be. At the same time, he suddenly thought of his dead sister. Sawa's heart had been ripped out of her body when she'd been killed.

*Was it possible...?*

This was Kyoto, and Sawa had been killed in Hagi.

"It's no simple matter to give yourself an oni-gome, since you have to tattoo it onto your dominant hand. That's why he didn't tattoo anything complicated. On his right hand is a *mikazuki*, a crescent moon. That is his oni-gome of immortality."

Mikazuki… A thought suddenly came to him: perhaps he'd taken that name for himself, the way Amane had taken that of Enma.

"As much as I'd thought him a fool, perhaps I envied Yaksha for challenging the taboo. That's why I… Forgive me," the old man said. Hearing how wrung out his voice was, Amane lost any last feelings of blame for him. Even in the short time he'd been studying, he'd learned enough. He could understand the madness that Baikou had fallen victim to.

"If you should ever meet him, if it's at all possible… Kill him," the old man said.

It was a hell of a thing to ask of him. He wanted to tell the old man to be serious, but he didn't refuse. He simply replied, "If I get the chance."

He knew better than anyone else that he would never get that chance.

*Forgive me, old man…*

I'm going to die very soon.

## —4—

Opening the window, he saw the sky growing faintly light. Baikou had been so exhausted by the all-night oni-gome training session that he was deep asleep with barely a snore. Taking his sword, Amane silently exited the house. It was a shame that Baikou would never have his apprentice and that his posthumous work would be lost, but this, too, was fate. In the end, death was catching up with him.

The sky in the east was now tinged with red. It would be rainy today. He hoped the old man's back wouldn't bother him too much—he was a bad-tempered old fart, but when Amane was with him, his feelings changed. Amane yawned, as tired as you might expect. Sword fighting was hard work, so there was no way he was going to live through this. Seeing that he was half-asleep, there wasn't much question of that.

He could see Bungo Bridge now.

If he didn't make a real effort in this duel, he would just make Okazaki even angrier. He wasn't the sort of man who'd simply kill a man with no questions asked.

Grasping his sword, he ran to the area around the bridge. They would need to get this settled before the crowds started to gather.

"You're late," Okazaki said, brusquely. With a grim face, looking as if he were at his wit's end, he thrust out the point of his sword. Amane could see that he was resolved to do this, but he also saw a hint of hesitation in his eyes.

"I'm sorry. Let's get this over with."

Not wanting to allow Okazaki to lose his nerve, Amane continued on without stopping, launching straight into his attack. His sword blade slashed through the air just in front of Okazaki's face as he swung.

"You son of a bitch!"

Not just late, but also attacking without warning. Amane could see how angry he was now. It was the perfect means of ensuring that Okazaki would show him no mercy.

"The old man just helped me when I was hurt. He has no relation to me besides that," Amane said.

Sparks flew as blade met blade.

"I'm only after you," Okazaki replied.

"I'm grateful," Amane answered with relief.

"Don't act like you're the good guy here!" Okazaki spat back. "We weren't enough for you? You had to trick an old man, too?!"

Amane smiled bitterly as he blocked a terrific blow aimed at the crown of his head.

"Sorry about that."

"You keep saying thanks and that you're grateful. Are you a moron?!"

The sound of the two swords crossing reverberated into the morning silence. Guessing each other's moves, neither man took distance from the other, both simply thrusting their swords again and again. Okazaki was irritated at how Amane wasn't talking the way he thought would be appropriate to the setting.

"I mean, what is it with you?" Okazaki exclaimed. "Every morning, you couldn't get up by yourself. You even needed someone to get the bones out of your fish. That was all just a ruse to throw off suspicion from you, wasn't it?!"

"I could get those little bones out by myself, but you just had to do it without me even asking, didn't you!"

"Shut up!"

Okazaki's sword skimmed his breast, laying open a wound lengthwise along Amane's neck. Amane gulped. Whether it was that he felt afraid of dying, now that he was directly confronting his foe, or whether the oni inside of him was not going to allow him to die easily, Enma fought with an earnestness he had never felt before.

"You certainly get quick when you're fighting," Okazaki said. "Were you really a Choushuu assassin?"

Sounding more and more pissed off with every strike, Okazaki's sword barely skimmed the bridge of Amane's nose. Most of the young recruits didn't have any particularly strong devotion to the cause or high intentions. They joined up because they were looking for a job, or perhaps because they were attracted by the gallant atmosphere. But Okazaki was different. Maybe that was why he couldn't forgive what Amane had done.

"Still, I have to thank you for helping Saki and Kuwata before," he said as he lunged forward with murderous intent.

"You should really get Saki out of there," Amane said.

"I agree," Okazaki replied.

"You should quit the Shinsegumi, too."

"Don't mock me!"

Swinging his sword with all of his might, Okazaki cleaved Amane's shoulder apart. Flesh and bone ripping in a wave of searing pain, Amane went down, but kept his eyes on Okazaki.

"Damn, you are strong, aren't you?" he said.

"Did you hold back?" Okazaki asked, thrusting his sword at Amane's nose and grinding his teeth in anger.

"No, you're just stronger than me, that's all."

Having spent as much time as he could inside of Baikou's house, Amane had little strength, and he was already panting for breath. Having taken a severe wound, he couldn't even move a finger now.

"If you're going to finish me, either take my head or stab me through the heart. Otherwise, I won't die."

Okazaki felt a little let down by this. Having finally reached this moment, it seemed like Amane was just making fun of him. In actuality, even Amane wasn't sure if he'd really die or not. By the time he was sure, he'd already be dead.

"You're all set to die, then? Fine," Okazaki replied. He placed the tip of his sword against Amane's breast. He would be killed before he ever had a chance to heal. It was a bit of a shame the sky was grey with a heavy layer of clouds. Amane had hoped to see blue skies in the end. The same blue skies that ran all the way back to Choushuu.

And thus would end his life as an assassin. He felt rather grateful that it was Okazaki who would be finishing him off.

"I never thought this day would come," Okazaki muttered in anguish. "I really liked you."

"And I really liked you," Amane murmured in his heart. He didn't say it out loud for fear of making this even harder for Okazaki to do.

"Just hurry up and kill me," he said. While they were wasting time, the wound was already closing. They didn't have time to sit here and mourn their parting.

Okazaki drew his sword back to build up some momentum for the final stab. His manly face was twisted in anguish. Amane closed his eyes, thinking that watching the blow coming would make it hard for Okazaki.

"Stop it! Stop it, please!" an old cracked voice called out. Baikou ran towards them, one hand pressed to his heart.

"Old man, stay back!" Amane yelled.

His plan to have the early-rising codger sleep through this had come to naught. Apparently Baikou had seen through the shallow thinking of the younger man. The old man forced his way between the two younger ones and clung to Okazaki.

"Don't kill him, I beg of you!"

"It's too late," Okazaki replied. "Even if I let him go, he'd just die from that wound. All that's left is for me to finish him off."

One of Amane's arms barely hung from his body by a thin flap of skin, and the wound extended all the way to his chest. It was only natural for Okazaki to think it was fatal.

"This boy is more precious to me than my own life! He's my greatest masterpiece! I beg of you, don't finish him off!"

Amane's value was in his continuing to live on. His work would be meaningless if Amane died before he did, Baikou wanted to scream. Okazaki wouldn't understand the meaning of this, and would probably just assume the old man was begging him to spare Amane's life.

"This man is a spy, an outlaw ronin from Choushuu. I have to take his head and bring it back to headquarters."

"Then kill me first…"

Baikou collapsed, wheezing, onto the ground. His face was dark red, twisted in pain.

"Is it asthma?" he asked, bending over the old man and rubbing his back.

"Asthma…? No, just a cold I can't shake," Baikou wheezed. "Don't kill him," he sobbed. "He belongs to me… He belongs to me…"

Baikou seized hold of Okazaki's arm. Gasping painfully, his expression once again dead set that Amane would die over his dead body, he no longer looked human. Even Okazaki gasped at the sight. And then, suddenly, like water being let out of a vessel, all the strength left him. His hand fell lifelessly away.

"Old man! Old man!" Pressing his shoulder, Amane staggered to his feet as he screamed at the corpse of what had once been the man named Baikou.

"He's dead," Okazaki said. A bit of blood dripped down his arm, drawn by Baikou's fingernails digging into his flesh. The scratches were clear evidence of the old man's tenacity.

"Just go," Okazaki said. "Disappear somewhere. Even if you live, never cross paths with me again."

"What about my head?" Amane asked.

"You belong to the old man," Okazaki replied.

Okazaki picked up his sword and moved off, as though he were being dragged. As he watched him walk away, Amane let out a long sigh.

Night had given way fully to day, but the sky was still dark and gloomy. Before long, a pelting rain began to fall. Getting up, Amane closed the old man's eyes, rage-filled even in death, and then simply said one thing to the corpse.

"You old fart…"

Greatest masterpiece, huh? To the very end, the old man had simply seen him as a project to be worked on. Baikou was just trying to protect his posthumous work.

The rain wasn't letting up, so Amane dragged the corpse under the bridge. Turning at the sound of a cat's meow, he saw Kuro slowly drawing near. The cat had probably seen the entire episode from beginning to end.

Kuro licked Baikou's hand. This beast knew that his master was dead. More than that, he was mourning him.

*That's true. A debt is a debt, after all.*

After being given shelter and food, even a beast could feel a sense of obligation, more or less. Amane hugged Kuro to him, enduring the pain as he did. By the time the worst of it was over, the rain had stopped.

First of all, he'd have to find this guy Yasha. That was the only goal he had in living now.

Leaving the old man's corpse, he walked away, Kuro still in his arms. Amane walked on, headed towards the shafts of light peeking through the clouds.

Amane Ichinose was dead. All that was left of him was Enma Houshou.

## CHAPTER 2

# THE PROMISE

*A.D. 1883 (Meiji 16)*

### —1—

The year 1868 (the fourth year of Keiou) saw the end of the Tokugawa shogunate's reign, and with it came a new name for Edo: Tokyo. And while voices cried out for enlightenment to follow the restoration of imperial rule, peace did not come quickly or easily in this world. After cycles of bloody disturbances rocked the nation, the means of battle changed from force of arms to discussion. But, even then, these discussions weren't especially free.

Just as much as people had dreamed of a shining new age, there was much that they had to give up. Still, everyone found some way to live, balancing illusions with reality.

*April 1883 (Meiji 16)*

It had been sixteen years since Enma had begun his new life in Tokyo, and it was getting near time for him to move again.

The lady hairdresser next door had a keen eye, a result of her trade, and she was noticing that age left no mark on his appearance. She would stare at him each time they met, and when she'd tilted her head in contemplation the last time, he knew that it was time to go. He'd moved between Kyoto and Yokohama and lived in Nagoya, Kobe, and Tokyo.

Today, Enma was slurping down a bowl of soba noodles, considering where he should move next.

He'd just finished a big job: a tattoo of the Buddha Acala, which covered his client's shoulders, back, and buttocks. It had turned out to be a very convincing portrait, with the transition of colors he'd chosen making it almost seem to move. Naturally, he hadn't taken another commission after that.

It was risky, but he wanted to return to Yokohama. Being single and free, suddenly breaking ties and moving away without telling anyone would mean no work for a while. For a tattoo artist who couldn't operate openly, losing personal connections was a matter of life and death. But in Yokohama, he wouldn't have to worry about customers.

There were foreigners there. In their eyes, the tattoos of this country reflected great artistry. Besides, some of them would want to have angels and devils tattooed onto them, and Enma thought it'd be fun to do those again after such a long time. He'd even once had an enthusiastic merchant invite him to come to America, and that hadn't sounded like a bad idea. The world was vast and offered an abundance of destinations for him to move to. But, in the end, he didn't have the resolve to go through with it.

There was also the matter of killing the man Yasha, the task entrusted to him by Baikou. He'd heard no word of him thus far. He probably wasn't living under the name of Yasha Houshou. It was doubtful that he'd even continued to be a tattooist in the first place. Besides, he couldn't rule out the possibility that he'd gotten himself killed already. Immortality brought about by an oni was far from perfect.

It was like trying to find a single pebble in a vast dry riverbed. If he'd known this was going to be the case, he'd have asked Baikou for more information about Yasha's appearance.

*Tattoos of the Buddhist deity Yasha and a crescent moon, huh?*

It wasn't like he could just walk up to strangers and ask to see their palms, and he certainly couldn't ask them to take off their clothes so he could check to see whether or not they had a tattoo on their lower back. He had no way to look for the man.

For now, he wouldn't go looking for him. He felt sorry for Baikou, but in abandoning the name of Amane Ichinose, he'd also given up being an assassin. He'd sworn to the oni on his right palm that his hand would never kill another man again. Even if it was the man who'd killed his sister, that wouldn't change.

Killing the murderer wouldn't bring Sawa back to him.

*Anyway, I have to decide where I'm moving.*

There was no point in just thinking about Yasha.

Enma considered moving to Osaka, since he'd never lived there before. He'd been in Yokohama just ten years ago, and if he ran into anyone who knew him, there'd be no talking his way out of that. There was also a danger in moving to someplace so close to Tokyo. He'd best leave Yokohama for a later move.

Thinking back fondly on the gaily-lit and Westernized streets of Yokohama, Enma rested his chin in his hand and stared idly out the window.

He could see a police station diagonally across the way, through the lattice-work of the window. In front of it stood a young girl. She'd been trying to tell a cop something for a while now, but he seemed unmoved by her plight. Still, she wouldn't give up and stood her ground, continuing to plead. Enma kept his eye on what was happening. It had nothing to do with him, but he was curious. She was just a kid, maybe thirteen or fourteen years old. What could have happened?

Thick clouds hung in the sky, making the day much darker than normal. If she didn't hurry home, she was going to get caught in the rain.

The restaurant owner was glaring at him as Enma nursed his one bowl of soba, but he didn't notice it. He had plenty of time to kill. There was no need for him to hurry for anything.

At last, the clouds could hold their burden no longer. Countless raindrops began pelting the ground and rooftops. He figured the girl would run off somewhere to seek shelter, but she didn't move. She didn't even run under the eaves. She just stood there, facing the building in front of her. His *kosode* was instantly soaked, and her braided hair thrown into disarray.

Enma paid for his noodles and left the restaurant. He walked over to the girl, opened his umbrella, and held it over her head.

"Thank you..." she said, not turning to face the man who'd offered her such kindness.

"Let's get under the eaves there," he coaxed.

"I don't care if I get soaked. Please, don't worry about me."

Not the sort of answer he expected from a young girl.

"Then use this."

Enma offered his umbrella, but the girl didn't take it.

"My father will scold me for taking charity," she said.

"And he won't scold you for wasting a favor from someone?"

This was more a case of him butting in than doing her a favor, and Enma knew that perfectly well, even as he said it. The girl grew flustered, caught between the two truths being thrust at her so suddenly.

"Well, if that thing's a bother to you, you should throw it away! Good day, sir!"

Putting the umbrella over his head, Enma turned to leave. Suddenly, the girl turned to look back at him.

"Wait, please!" she cried.

Her eyes met his, then widened for an instant. She was clearly surprised when she looked at Enma. While his face still looked only twenty years old, there was a sadness to it that revealed his true age to be far older. Enma steeled himself, wondering if this child was able to sniff out that he was different from other people.

"Are you... Are you related to a man named Amane Ichinose?" she said, seemingly astonished.

Enma paused, then asked, "Do you want some soba or something to eat?"

It seemed he needed to have a little chat with this girl after all.

Her name was Natsu Hisaka. She was thirteen years old, and while her true physical beauty was yet to blossom, he could already sense a great dignity and cleverness within her.

"It'll warm you up," he said.

Natsu wouldn't touch the steaming bowl of buckwheat noodles in front of her at first. Then, little by little, at Enma's urging she began to slurp them down. She must have been starving, because she didn't leave a drop behind.

"I'll pay you back," she said.

"You can pay me back by telling me about yourself," he replied. "It's not like I'm going to make the child of an acquaintance of mine owe me for some soba." The truth was, Enma didn't know anybody named Hisaka, but she knew his real name, so they may have shared some sort of connection.

Natsu silently regarded Enma, then blushed.

"My father has a photograph of a man who looks a lot like you," she finally said. "He said that the man's name was Amane Ichinose."

Enma had only been photographed once in the past. When he'd enlisted in the Shinsengumi, he'd been invited by three other new recruits to have one taken to commemorate their joining up. He hadn't refused, but being a spy, appearing with them in a souvenir photo had been awkward, to say the least. That meant this girl was the child of somebody who'd survived being in the Shinsengumi. He didn't see any hostility in her face, so Enma decided that she must not have heard yet that he'd been a Choushuu spy.

*Who is this girl...?*

Enma repeatedly stroked the palm of his hand, now covered by fingerless leather gloves.

"So, are you related to Mr. Ichinose?" she asked.

He paused a moment before answering, "Yeah, pretty much." He could have simply told her that the resemblance was accidental, but he was also interested in why she'd been in some sort of dispute in front of that police station.

"Is your father well?" he asked. Natsu nodded that yes, he was. "But I'm afraid something awful is happening to him," she continued, scowling at the police station through the window. "The police came and took my father away a few days ago. I think he's still being held in there."

So, her father had been arrested. That meant she'd probably been there trying to get the cops to let her see him. Enma dug through his memory, trying to think of who he'd been photographed with that time. It'd been Osanai, Saki, and...

"My father's name is Seinosuke Hisaka," she said. "But his surname used to be Okazaki."

Enma covered his face with his hand.

The end of the Shinsengumi had been a tragic one.

One group died with the Shogitai, a group of Tokugawa retainers who opposed the new Meiji government. They fell at the battle of Ueno. Yet another group of them perished at the battle of Aizu, and a great number of their regimental soldiers fought to the last man at Fortress Goryoukaku in Hokkaido. As one might expect, there were survivors. Afterwards, they joined the government forces, and it was said that former Shinsengumi members participated in putting down the Satsuma rebellion, settling their old scores with that clan.

Till that moment, Enma had no idea what had happened to Okazaki, and he was genuinely happy to hear that he was still alive. Their time together had been brief, but Okazaki was one of the very few people with whom he could share his feelings. But now Okazaki was being held by the police, and here Enma was in his home, having walked Natsu back from the soba shop.

"Here's the photo I told you about," she said, handing it to him.

He took the photo and looked at it a while, motionless. Amane and Okazaki stood side by side in the front, seventeen years in the past. In contrast to the slightly worried expression on his own face, Okazaki looked proud, his gaze fixed straight ahead. He remembered very well how tough it had been to hold that pose for such a long time. Amane had owned his own copy of the photo, but was forced to leave his belongings behind in the barracks when his cover had been blown and he'd been forced to flee.

He must have treasured his memories of being a soldier in the Shinsengumi to have held on to this, even though he must also have wanted to tear up and throw away a photograph in which he was standing next to a traitor.

"You really do look just like him, don't you?" Natsu said, sounding very impressed. Even having the exact same scar under his eye must have made the resemblance all the more remarkable for her.

Okazaki's home was a big old house surrounded by fields that stood one *ri* (about two and a half miles) from the police station. From its setup, it looked to have once been the manor of a village headman. It was a lonely place for a child to be living all by herself.

"You think so?" he answered. The face of the man in the photo was the same as his, but looking at it, he felt as though it was a distant memory of an existence now past. For nearly twenty years, he'd been dreading something like this.

"Father treasured this photo. I've heard him murmur about how those were the best days of his life."

Guilt stabbed at Enma's heart. And here he was, the man who'd trampled those memories.

"Your father didn't happen to mention what happened to the other men in this photo, did he?"

"No," she replied. "All he ever told me was their names."

"I see... So, do you have anyone else in your family, Miss?"

Natsu shook her head.

"I don't have any brothers or sisters. Mother died when I was four, so it's just been Father and me ever since."

Just the pair of them, father and daughter, all this time. It must have been a lonely existence.

"Father, being the third-born son in his family, got himself adopted into the Hisaka family and ended up inheriting this farm. He farms and also teaches the children in the area how to read and write on the side."

Even though there was now a nationwide system of primary schools established, it was common to find children whose families were too poor to afford the commute they might have to make to them. Apparently, Okazaki had been teaching them.

"Father never hid the fact that he used to be a soldier. In fact, he boasts about it."

Enma unconsciously nodded in agreement. That was just the sort of man Okazaki had been.

"That's why some of the police thought he's up to no good. Especially one officer named Kawamura, who's from Choushuu. He would just straight out call Father a rebel."

Many of the police were former members of the anti-shogunate faction.

"A few days ago, one of the children Father teaches was accused of stealing. Father went to the police to protest. That was three days ago, and he hasn't been back since."

He saw her hands, folded onto her lap as she knelt on the floor and balled into tight, hard fists as she spoke. Enma sighed. As stouthearted as she seemed, she was still just a kid. The worry she felt looked like it was crushing her.

"They told me he needed to be investigated for being against the government. It's an awful, trumped-up charge."

He may have been a stubborn, straitlaced man who hated Enma's guts, but he didn't deserve the rough treatment he was suffering.

"Please, won't you help me?" the girl asked. "Won't you go with me tomorrow to help negotiate his release? They won't even talk to me if I go by myself."

The police were people that Enma tended to avoid, and if these cops were as overbearing as Natsu said they were, it was likely that he'd end up getting interrogated by them as well. If that happened, he'd only end up making things worse for Okazaki.

The Family Registration Law had been inadequately enforced up until now and he'd been able to take advantage of that, but it was going to get harder and harder to keep hiding his identity. The Meiji government needed to increase tax revenue and set up a military conscription system, and an accurate census was vital for that. They wouldn't be overlooking him much longer.

"Look," Enma began. "I'm a tattooist. I don't think I should go trying to mess with the police." He couldn't explain his actual situation to Natsu, so this would have to be his answer. Tattooing was banned for now under the Meiji government, so it was true that he was hesitant to tell the police what he did for a living.

At first glance, Enma just looked like some sort of poor houseboy. Natsu took his excuse as a declaration that he didn't want to get involved in her troubles. As she stared at the floor, tears welled up in her eyes. She hastily wiped her cheeks, embarrassed that she was crying.

"Excuse me," she said. "It was selfish of me to have asked."

Enma scratched his cheek, wondering what he should do.

## —2—

The following day, as he was cutting through the line of cherry trees at the side of the road, Enma looked up at the sky. He spied blue peeking through the gaps in the overhanging branches.

In the end, he had decided to go to the police station. Natsu walked at his side, her eyes downcast, looking apologetic at having imposed on him. The girl was showing remarkable self-control, a testament to how Okazaki had raised her.

"Is your father a gentle man?" Enma asked her. He was curious about what sort of parent Okazaki made.

"Yes," she replied. "He always tells me that a person shouldn't stray from their path and that they should always do what they feel is right. He's strict, but he's a good father."

Enma felt happier, glad to hear how typically Okazaki that was. He was thankful that the man hadn't changed.

"You said your mother passed away. What was she like?"

"I was so little when it happened that I don't even remember her face," she said, shaking her head sadly. "All I can remember was standing in front of her grave, crying, and an angel appeared and comforted me." Her gaze was distant, filled with wonder, as though she were looking at one of the *yasha*, the guardian deities of Buddhist lore. She then looked down, embarrassed. "I may have just dreamed it, but a person suddenly appeared behind me. The angel was pretty and kind, and said that if I was that sad, he could take me to where my mama was."

A lot of Christian-themed artwork was starting to appear recently. Natsu must have seen a children's Bible or something.

Except… Enma's brow furrowed. He didn't know whether it had been an angel or not, but something seemed fishy about this person who'd comforted her.

"I don't know why I thought that way about him. I can't even remember if it was a man or a woman, but he looked like an angel from heaven, like I'd seen in a picture book. Like big white wings on his back wouldn't have been out of place…"

It was the sort of vision you'd expect a young girl to have. Enma decided that she must have been romanticizing the memory.

"I don't really remember what else he said, except that he'd come back for me when I grew up."

Natsu smiled slightly as she recalled it.

"Oh, yeah. When I told Father about it, he had a fit. He said that the man might have been trying to kidnap me and forbade me to ever go with him."

That made him sound like a parent who doted on his child. Enma found himself smiling too at how charming it sounded. Still, this whole "angel" business had piqued his interest. It was possible that it was all just a child's dream, but there were people out there who'd kidnap girls from the country to be sold overseas.

"Even so," she went on, "I don't think anyone would want to kidnap a girl who was as plain as I am."

"What, somebody told you that you're plain?"

"People say that I'm not very pretty all the time. It's true, so there's not much I can do about it. I can see that just by looking into a mirror."

She may have been acting like it was no big deal to her, but Enma was shocked that anyone could say something so cruel to her.

"Well, those people are wrong," he said. "From where I'm standing, you're very pretty, and you're going to be even prettier when you get older. Anyway, your dad was right. If that person ever shows up, stay away from him. He sounds like trouble."

Natsu looked up at Enma, surprised. She then nodded yes, looking pleased with his compliment.

Arriving in front of the police station, he took a deep breath. He wasn't looking forward to the game he was about to play.

Who was it that once said the authorities didn't exist to protect citizens from crimes, but rather to remove people who were inconvenient to the government?

Still, no matter what he did for a living, there must be somebody among the cops he could reason with. Thinking that, he went inside.

The self-important bearded officer he found himself confronted with couldn't have been more than thirty. He figured it had to be that Kawamura fellow who had declared himself to be Okazaki's enemy. He was from Choushuu, but thankfully he wasn't anyone who might have recognized Amane. He scowled suspiciously at Enma.

"Hisaka again, huh? So, who are you?"

Yeah, this cop was full of himself. Enma answered that he was a relative, thinking that would be the easiest way to talk to this man.

"Look," he said. "Their family is just him and his daughter. You can't leave the girl to fend for herself. Please, let her father come home."

He thought he'd made a polite and impassioned plea, but the cop looked up at Amane like he was a child who'd spoken out of turn.

"You're another one of those traitors, aren't you? One of the shogun's dogs? You piss me off just to look at you!"

Even Amane was irritated by how open this man's contempt was for him. Now he could see that there was no reasoning with a guy who'd leave a young girl to live by herself.

"Can you call another officer over here?" Enma asked. "I'd like to speak with someone who will take this seriously."

"How dare you!" Kawamura screamed back, his face turning bright red. "Get out of here till you learn how to speak to your betters, you little punk! We aren't finished investigating Hisaka!"

He must not have liked how the "little punk" was taller than he was. The man didn't have a leg to stand on. You saw these sorts of cops all the time, and Enma was fed up with how common they were. Oh, how he wanted to tell this little twerp how much older he was, just once!

"What investigation?" Enma said slowly, ignoring Kawamura's insults as he turned away. He pressed Natsu's back and they began walking in the direction away from her home.

"Um, where are we going?" she asked.

"To see somebody important."

Natsu opened her eyes wide and looked up at Enma.

"I've got a trump card to play," he said.

After nearly an hour of walking, they arrived in front of a magnificent Western-style home. Even the normally stoic Natsu faltered in its presence.

"Don't let it scare you," Enma told her. "Most of the rooms inside have tatami mats, like regular houses."

With the birthing cries of the Meiji era, many of the nation's wealthy had embraced the new age by building grand Western-style mansions. Even so, they couldn't completely let go of traditional touches, so they ended up being halfway affairs, Western in construction with Japanese interiors.

"This is Lord Muta's house, isn't it?" she asked.

"Oh, you know this place?"

"The Black Mansion is famous."

A Western mansion with a jet-black outer wall was, indeed, an unusual sight. For that reason, it left a slightly odd impression. Still, with its broad lawn and garden boasting flowers in full bloom, it sparkled like some sort of pleasure garden.

"A black house certainly carries a lot of different meanings to it," Enma said.

"Do you have some sort of an appointment here?"

"Nope," he replied.

Genzo Muta, the previous head of the family, was a well-known success story who had made his fortune in food stalls over a lifetime. Once the Meiji period had started, his assets bought him a wife from the family of former cabinet minister Shinomiya, linking his name to the highest levels of nobility. The Muta family was one of the wealthiest and most powerful in the nation, and ugly rumors about them abounded.

A man who absorbed the darkness of the last days of the shogunate, swelling his true nature all the more. That was Genzo Muta. He was a monster who no longer haunted this world.

"Um… Are you sure about this?"

"No, I'm not. He may not be home."

Heedless of Natsu as she began to say that wasn't what she'd meant, Enma called out to an old man who was tending the garden.

"Is Lord Nobumasa Muta in? Could you please tell him that we'd like to see him?"

The old man looked dubiously at this youngster in his worn-out *hakama* asking to see the elder brother of the head of the family.

"Just tell him it's Enma Houshou. He'll know who I am."

"I hope," he added under his breath. It'd been six years, after all. He wasn't sure if the man would remember.

Unable to simply reject him outright on the off chance he really was an acquaintance, the gardener gave a curt nod and walked into the mansion. A short time later, a young woman wearing a dark blue *kosode* with a Western-style apron over it appeared and bowed to Enma.

"The master will see you," she said. "Please, come with me." Following the maid inside, Natsu looked almost overwhelmed by the grand staircase that confronted them. It was like they were on the stage of a theater, and they felt as though, at any moment, a grand dame from some foreign land would descend it, holding the hem of her gown in hand. They were finally led into a tea room, wherein a man wearing a kimono sat cross-legged on the floor, waiting for them. He rose as they approached. He was young and tall, about six feet, and while on first glance he seemed quiet and composed, there was a dark, shrewd glint to his eye.

"Well now," he said as he got a good look at Enma, "if it isn't the tattooist who was of such great assistance to me."

Nobumasa Muta extended his right palm in front of Enma. On it was tattooed a six-pointed star. He quickly returned his hand back into his sleeve and pressed his thin lips into a smile.

"I've been a sober man ever since, thanks to you," he continued. Enma didn't return the smile. "I must apologize about the payment. I meant to send you the money, but I lost track of where you lived."

"I'm sure," Enma replied. "I had to move right after I helped you."

"Then you should have come here sooner. You must have heard that my father had passed on."

Nobumasa wisked tea in a bowl. The sweet scent of green tea powder hung in the air.

"I heard you were working as a policeman. And since, unlike your father, I knew you wouldn't stiff me on a bill, I decided to hold off on coming until I needed the money."

"So, you're having money problems then. Very well. I'll pay you double, to make up for the long delay. This has been weighing on me for quite some time, after all."

Enma shook his head.

"No, never mind about the money. I'd like to ask a favor instead."

"Oh...?"

"It should be a simple thing for you."

Nobumasa placed a bowl of tea before Natsu.

"Might I assume it has something to do with this young lady you have with you?"

"My name is Natsu Hisaka, sir," she said, keeping her eyes cast respectfully downward as she knelt.

"Her father is being held by the police. Could you have him released quickly?"

"You want me to let a criminal go free?"

He'd said it as though it were a joke. Natsu's eyes burned with anger.

"Father did nothing wrong. He's being held unjustly by a puffed-up, idiotic policeman."

Even Enma was shocked by what she'd dared to say. "Stop that!" he hissed. "He may be young, but this man is a police superintendent!"

"Then that's all the more reason I have to say it to him. Please, sir, release my father Seinosuke Hisaka."

He eyed Natsu with interest through the semi-circle lenses of his spectacles.

"Very well," he said. "I'll order his release at once. Soukichi!"

As quickly as he agreed, Nobumasa ran his writing brush over a piece of paper, which he then handed to a servant.

"He'll be released before the day is out."

It seemed to be a letter for the chief of the police station. Bowing once, the man named Soukichi quickly left the room.

"Shouldn't you have confirmed this first?" Enma asked. "What if he really was a criminal?" He felt a little let down by how easily this had gone.

"I can tell he isn't just by looking at her. He probably irritated the police officer by making an entirely justifiable argument in that furious tone she just used."

Natsu hung her head, her cheeks bright red with embarrassment.

"It seems what I just said is disturbing you. That's inexcusable," Nobumasa said, bowing his head. "I apologize for my rudeness. Please forgive me."

Natsu hastily bowed her head as well, not expecting this important man to speak to her like this. Her heart, nearly in pieces from worry and frustration, seemed to finally be regaining its composure. She smiled broadly, a look of relief spreading across her face. Finally wearing an expression more appropriate for a girl her age, she looked surprisingly adorable.

"Um," she stammered. "I'm going to go wait for my father to come out. Master Houshou, Superintendent… Thank you so much!"

Unable to contain herself, Natsu dashed out of the mansion.

"What a fascinating child," Nobumasa said admiringly, watching her go.

"Yeah."

"Shouldn't you go to meet her father as well?"

"I don't think he'd be able to stand the shock of seeing me," Enma replied, draining his now cold tea in a single gulp.

"Oh…?"

"Besides, he'd just as likely kill me on sight," he continued, gulping down some sweet bean jelly as well.

"That girl's father must be much older than you," Nobumasa said. "What sort of quarrel could he possibly have with you?"

Enma scratched his head.

"It's complicated," he replied. "But I'm the one to blame."

Nobumasa reached out and seized Enma's hand.

"Show me Lord Enma."

As quickly as he nodded yes, Nobumasa stripped the glove from his hand.

"What sort of oni did this character put inside of you?" he asked, his sharp gaze searching for an answer.

"You know that. It heals any injury quickly. The worse the injury, the more it hurts."

"And that's all that it does?"

"Pretty much," Enma replied, quickly recovering his hand.

"I don't know how old you are," Nobumasa said, "but you haven't changed a bit since I last saw you."

Amane had to turn his eyes away from the man's probing gaze.

"You don't age that much in just six years."

"You think so? I think I've changed."

"Of course you have. You used to be a drunken rag of a man."

Enma remembered him clearly: the young man glaring out of the corner of the dark room. Terribly thin and sickly, body trembling, with wounds all over. He'd screamed obscenities at the tattooist who suddenly appeared before him.

"I was an animal back then," Nobumasa said.

He was eighteen years old and drowning in liquor, poisoning himself into sickness. He was constantly hurting himself, and it was just a matter of time before he'd either die at his own hand or from a complete breakdown. The doctors could do nothing, and so in the end Nobumasa's father Genzo had to rely on a shady tattooist who had earned the nickname of Ura-Enma: Enma's opposite. The man who would deny the lord of death his prize.

"The only thing I should be grateful to Father for is his bringing you to me. With that one exception, the man was a piece of garbage."

He wished he could object to the way this son talked about his father, but unfortunately Enma couldn't disagree. He'd basically forced Enma to do what he did and then chased him off without paying for it.

"He died about a year later. Just when he thought he had the world by the tail."

"You really hated him, didn't you?"

"The man was filthy rich, but he wouldn't even pay a tattooist's fee?"

Enma remembered what Genzo had spat at him: how Nobumasa being cured of his drinking problem had been a coincidence, how he wasn't going to pay for it, and that Enma should be thankful he didn't call the cops on him.

He'd had some nasty customers before that, but it was the first time he'd ever been treated that badly. The man had a round body like a greasy *daruma* doll with sunken eyes. He was farsighted, and his pitch-black eye sockets gave him a skeletal appearance.

"Back in the Tokugawa days, he came to Kyoto to do business. By the time he went back, he had more gold than he could carry. And if you looked really closely at it, you could see blood on it. I didn't know at the time, but years later he let it slip when he got drunk. He'd talk about how he'd attacked a money lender and stolen it like it was some great war story."

There were many people like that in Kyoto back in the closing days of the shogunate. Genzo Muta must have been one of them. He'd been a real scoundrel who used his stolen funds to bankroll a big new business which was so successful, it took him straight to the top. He'd probably overheard talk of oni-gome when he was there.

Except for the forbidden uses, Baikou had never been particularly discreet about it.

"Was that the reason you started drinking?"

"It doesn't matter at this point, does it? I can't really remember, anyway."

He seemed to avoid talking about these ambiguous things because he didn't want to remember them. He probably really didn't care about the past now. That was how completely this man had recovered.

"In any case, I'd like you to have this."

Nobumasa placed a bulky envelope in front of Enma.

"I don't want your money. Doing me that favor was enough."

"Take it. Otherwise, it's going to look like somebody bribed the police for a favor. Besides, the one at fault here was a policeman performing an unjust detention. In that case, it's my duty to make amends for it."

He had a point. Enma gave a quick nod, then put the envelope in his breast pocket without looking inside.

"I'd better go. Your being so reasonable about this really helped me out."

"Come to me any time if you have a problem."

That was an odd thing to say. Enma turned to look back as he was leaving.

"Why?" he asked. "You've paid your debt. You don't owe me anything now."

"Because you've seen me at my worst and know me better than anyone else."

The smile Nobumasa showed him was disturbing.

"That was the alcohol making you do that, wasn't it?"

"I was just thinking that a man who always looks so young may have some troubles he'll need help with."

Damn, Enma thought, he's figured it all out. Even so, he couldn't lose his cool that easily.

"You're right. All right then, have you ever heard of a tattooist named Yasha Houshou? He may be living under another name now, though…" Enma asked, not really expecting an answer.

"You don't have a photo of him, do you?"

Enma shook his head. The man he sought lived in similar circumstances. At a moment's notice, they might have to leave and leave no records behind. That wasn't even getting into the fact that he'd become immortal before Enma had, and it was doubtful that any cameras had even existed in the nation then.

"No, he's sort of an elder colleague of mine. There may be unexplained murders in which the victim's heart is torn out when he's around. He's probably a young man, with a tattoo of a *yasha* on his lower back and a crescent moon on his palm."

Nobumasa pondered it for a moment.

"Corpses missing their hearts, you say? Now that you mention it, there was a murder like that last year in Kisarazu."

"…Kisarazu."

If it was last year, he doubted Yasha would still be in the area. If he'd murdered someone, it'd be only natural for him to get out of there.

"The victim was a plasterer whose wife had died recently. He was so depressed about it that when his body was found, people first thought it was a suicide. But I don't think you can kill yourself by ripping your own heart out."

Nobumasa summoned his maid and asked her to bring him his newspaper clippings from November of last year. It seemed he kept clippings of interesting cases from outside of his jurisdiction.

"After removing the heart, the killer apparently replaced the clothes neatly on the corpse and then arranged it cleanly, face up. The face of the corpse had been wiped clean of any blood spatters and there was no sign of enmity on his face."

Enma's breath caught in his throat. It was exactly like what had happened with Sawa. The front of her kimono had been stained with blood, but she looked as if she'd died in her sleep.

"And the cause of death?"

"Probably asphyxiation. There were no strangulation marks on his neck, so I expect the killer did it by pressing his hand over the victim's nose and mouth. But there were no signs of struggle, either. It was a very strange killing, and the murderer hasn't been caught yet."

Nobumasa must have had a personal interest in the case, since he recited its details without needing to check the newspaper article. Enma was disturbed by how many details this killing shared with his sister's. He didn't want to think that a man he'd even jokingly refer to as a colleague was a monster who ate flesh and blood.

"You think your colleague committed the murder?"

"Maybe..."

Enma prevaricated a bit in his answer. He had to be the one to take care of Yasha.

"In any case, this guy sounds really dangerous. Even a policeman would have to be careful with him. I'll investigate whether there are any similar cases."

If Enma found him alive, the first thing he'd have to ask was whether he'd ever been to Choushuu. He needed to know if this man had eaten his sister.

"So, you finally came," Nobumasa muttered to himself as he saw the young tattooist off from the window. He watched the back of the man he wished to see again recede until he was out of sight.

"Isn't it time that you got changed, Master?" called out the meddlesome head maid.

It was true. He'd been invited to dine with an older widow that evening. Of course, it was a clandestine meeting some might call a rendezvous. She had her quirks, but the woman was beautiful. She would torment men in the way she treated them, sweet as honey, both playful and serious. Truly, she was a formidable opponent.

"It's still early," he replied. "I'll wait until Soukichi returns."

Soukichi was a clever man, and he had no doubt he'd return once he'd confirmed that the girl's father had been released. Nobumasa looked at the oni-gome on his palm, scratching it in irritation as he thought about the past.

"He's a monster," his father Genzo Muta had told his son after he'd driven Enma away without paying him. "Have nothing to do with him."

"What do you mean 'a monster?'"

"I heard things in Kyoto, about a person in this world who never ages, never dies. I think it may be that man..."

At the time he'd thought it nonsense, although it was clear that Enma possessed an uncommon power. But having seen what he looked like today, he wondered again about what his father had told him. Enma didn't look like he'd aged at all. Still, six years wasn't that long a time, so it was possible that was why he seemed unchanged.

And even assuming that Enma was a man who couldn't die, to Nobumasa at the time, his father seemed to be a far worse monster. Even when the wife for whom he caused so much grief was stricken with an illness, the man was too stingy with his money to summon a doctor to examine her. He'd take advantage of illiterate employees, lending them money at usurious interest rates that would drive them to suicide. To an awkwardly earnest youth like Nobumasa, there was plenty for him to find unforgivable. It was what had made him the cunning man he was today.

His father had driven the tattooist away without paying what he'd been promised. The son quickly sent his manservant to run after him with the message to come back later so that Nobumasa could pay him directly. When he didn't return, he'd considered hiring people to search for him, but never went that far. Still, he had a feeling that they'd meet again sooner or later.

Returning to school, he studied economics. And, perhaps because his antipathy for his father had grown stronger, Nobumasa joined the police force upon graduation. He would have had Genzo arrested if he could, but by that time his father was already dead.

He would never forget the strange atmosphere when the oni-gome was applied, the feeling of something manifesting. As their surroundings had grown hazy and dark, a whiteness had lightly floated up around his right hand only. For some reason Nobumasa, realistic in the same way that his father was, didn't have the ability to sense things that weren't of this world. Even so, he knew that he'd set foot into the spirit realm. His blood had roared within him, although he still felt chilled. He had the impression of the demon embracing him from behind.

Amidst that, the face of the young tattooist had seemed like that of the Buddha. His face, still holding traces of boyhood, had looked not so much like the stern King Enma, but rather like the anguished King Asura, guardian deity of Buddhism. The technique of oni-gome seemed to wear on his very body.

Nobumasa would get back on his feet, no matter what. Every time he saw the mark on his palm, he would swear that to himself. The tattooist had given him the strength to do that.

One could say that the man was an embarrassment who went around making people indebted to him to extract favors later on. But, in truth, Nobumasa felt nothing but genuine gratitude to Enma. If the tattooist was in trouble, then he wanted to help, no matter what sort of monster he might be.

*Besides...*

As he watched the tattooist walk away, Nobumasa smiled.

More than anything else, he liked unusual people.

Enma left the Muta estate.

As he trod the long path from the front door to the gate, Enma could feel Nobumasa's gaze upon his back. He wasn't just seeing a guest off. There was no doubt in his mind that the man was looking for something as he watched. There would be no hiding anything from him, and it would probably be best to keep as far away from him as possible. Even so, Enma had a foreboding that they were locked together in an inseparable relationship.

The truth was, in the last six years, he'd been itching to see Nobumasa again. Who could have imagined that the boy with the sunken, scowling eyes, so thin and wasted he looked like a ghost, would have matured into such a man?

He remembered finding him sitting on the floor in the corner of that dark room, hugging his knees to his chest and biting his nails. The light cotton *yukata* kimono he wore was open, and Enma could see his ribs practically sticking through, his limbs stretched out like dead twigs. The room stank from the earthenware sake jars scattered around the floor, and just his entering it seemed to have put the boy in a bad mood. Looking at Enma, Nobumasa had screamed, "Kill me!" That had really angered him. If he wanted to die, he could just die. He could expect to die. To Enma, who was prevented from even killing himself by the oni within his body, all he looked like was a spoiled child.

If he wanted to be saved, he just had to say it. Enma bore the blows and bites the boy inflicted on him, then showed him how the wounds from them would heal. Genzo Muta, who was there in case something happened, was dumbfounded by the sight. After doing that, there was no going back.

"You see," he'd said. "That's my power. I can make it so that just the smell of liquor will make you puke. How you live your life after that is up to you."

Nobumasa had then quietly held out his right hand.

That was what the dignified Nobumasa had originally been. His height didn't differ that greatly from Enma's, but his body had grown twice as stout, making Enma seem like the youngster now.

For seventeen years since the day of oni-gome, it had been like this for Enma. Seventeen years, and he was getting sick of it.

*I should go home*, he thought.

Kuro was there waiting for him. The cat was a selfish creature, and it was common for him to not come home for a month at a time. Enma told himself that he needn't worry about him, but the cat was very old now and he couldn't help it. Kuro may have just been an animal, but he was also the only family Enma had. It was amazing that a cat could live so long, but they say that pets took after their owners. On that point at least, he had to agree.

There was one possibility that occurred to him…

Maybe it was just a trait that came from being an animal, but he recalled one time when Kuro had been bitten by a stray dog. The cat had stalked off to hide itself for a while, but when he returned, he was so healthy again that you could scarcely tell he'd ever been injured. Enma didn't know how bad the original wound had been and hadn't paid it much mind at the time, but was it possible…?

*He belonged to the old man, after all.*

Well, he'd get an answer to the mystery of the little monster someday. No point in worrying about it now.

He thought about making sure that Okazaki had been released unharmed before he went home. But how could he see him, looking the way that he did?

Watching the wind rustle the cherry blossoms, he suddenly wished he could be a tree. This tree had stood unchanged for decades and it would stay that way for decades to come.

Enma hung his head as he walked along the damp road.

Every time he attracted people's attention, he would move. How many times would he have to keep doing it before he could stop? Just the fact that he couldn't imagine it was awful in itself. If he just had someone to confide in, it would make him feel a bit better.

The face of Nobumasa Muta floated up in his mind. Could he trust him, though? Should he really rely on him?

Nobusmasa may have been a police superintendent, but his roots were as suspect as Enma's. While he was the eldest son of the Muta family, he hadn't succeeded his father as its head. That position was held by his younger brother Atsushi. Nobumasa's mother had come from a peasant family, while Atsushi's mother had come from the imperial court. Their father Genzo had only been able to obtain his position in the nobility on the condition that Atsushi be the one who would succeed him as the leader of the Muta family.

Nobumasa's mother Toyo had supported her husband as any wife should, but in the end the hardships he caused her were too much to bear, and she died young. Meanwhile, Genzo's second wife could be said to have been more like a mistress. It was possible that, having finally joined the nobility, his father just saw Nobumasa as an embarrassment.

Fortunately, Atsushi was a goodhearted boy who loved and respected his older brother. They shared their estate, neither having married. When Enma had gone to the Black Mansion six years earlier, their mother had still been alive. He remembered how cold her eyes had been as she'd looked at the young tattooist. To a princess who'd been bought for money, everything she saw must have seemed filthy to her. Even now, as he thought about it, he couldn't help but pity her.

It was possible that seeing Nobumasa having given in to despair while still so young had deeply affected him as well.

Once he'd abandoned his drinking and recovered his health, Nobumasa had returned to his studies and eventually joined the police force. He was probably on course to be a high-level official. His skills had led him to solve a few difficult cases, apparently. The fact that he could get a prisoner released with just a short letter to the station chief meant that he was shameless in how he used his authority and family connections. It was probably for the best that his younger brother had been made the head of the family instead of him.

The oni-gome was a spell, but he could see no bad effect on Nobumasa. Enma always hesitated whenever he applied one, wondering if the oni taking up residence in their body would end up devouring their host. The fear wasn't without some basis. There'd been times when he'd had to extract an oni from a client who'd been driven to the brink of madness. The oni hadn't allowed Nobumasa to ever drink alcohol again. He'd suffered a while, writhing in pain, clutching at his throat. The suffering of its host was the oni's favorite thing to eat. But Nobumasa had overcome the pain, and Enma was relieved that the oni-gome had set him on the right path.

As he trudged along the wet ground, he came to the police station. He couldn't see Natsu anywhere. She and her father had probably gone home by now, he thought. Well, if he'd been returned unharmed, that was all that mattered.

Ducking under the eaves of the soba shop, he listened for what was going on in the station, just to make sure.

"Father!"

A voice that was practically shrieking brought Enma running. The one he'd heard inside of the police station could only have been Natsu.

"Father! Oh, Father, what have they done…?!"

Entering the station, Enma couldn't believe what he saw.

"Okazaki…"

The man being supported by the police officers, his head and hands wrapped in bandages, could barely stand. His lips were split and caked with dried blood, while his eyelids were bruised and swollen. Natsu trembled, speechless with horror at the sad sight of her father.

"Oh, this?" Kawamura said, bold as brass. "The man just fell down the stairs."

"So," Enma said, casually stepping in front of Kawamura, "that's why you wouldn't just let him go. You didn't want people to know that you'd practically beaten a man to death in your investigation." He had been an assassin once. The rage in his eyes was enough of a threat to make the police shrink back.

"Wh-What are you saying?"

Enma wanted to give this cop a taste of his own medicine, but Okazaki came first.

"Natsu," he said, calmly. "Go get a doctor. I'll bring him to your house."

Snatching Okazaki from the police, he carried him out of there. The exhausted man was exceedingly heavy, and he had a fever which Enma could feel practically burning through his clothes.

"You read the letter from Superintendent Muta, didn't you? Now get the hell out of my way!"

Carrying the man to whom he had once sworn his friendship, Enma left the police station.

## —3—

Two of Seinosuke Hisaka's fingers and one of his ribs had been broken. Besides that, there were bruises and cuts all over his body.

But those injuries weren't the real problem. His body was wracked by convulsions, bending in pain. It was most likely tetanus, the doctor had said. He believed that the wounds the police had inflicted on him had become infected.

"They injured him this badly and gave him no treatment at all? How could they?!" asked Natsu, her voice trembling as she knelt at her father's side.

He'd last maybe three more days. Even the doctor Nobumasa had sent, who had studied in Germany, had given up hope. He was sorry, he'd said. Maybe if they'd called him sooner, but now...

The next day, Okazaki suddenly opened his eyes. The painkillers seemed to be making him feel a bit better, but they'd also fogged his brain.

"Amane... Is that you?"

The immature youth had grown into a man with a tender gaze. Those eyes now regarded Enma.

Enma said nothing and simply nodded. How must he look to Okazaki now? The traitor who had not aged in seventeen years.

The only sound in the room was the crackling flame from the paper lantern.

"You're alive."

"And you're going to be, too."

Enma jerked his head towards Natsu, who had fallen asleep at the low table behind him. Don't go leaving this girl alone, his eyes pleaded.

"Having a ghost of the Miburou ronin for a father has caused her nothing but pain..."

"Not half as much as your dying would."

Okazaki laughed at that. He was having trouble opening his mouth. Just doing that caused him pain.

"Remember Saki? He died at Fortress Goryoukaku. I should have died there with him..."

So, that frail slip of a boy had gone down fighting. He wouldn't have guessed that. Not that apple-cheeked kid. He'd been eighteen when he'd enlisted, but had looked barely fourteen or fifteen.

"Looking at you now makes me remember it all so clearly..."

"Yeah, I'm sure."

Time for Enma had stopped when Tokyo had still been called Edo.

"I'm the one who's the ghost here," he whispered, almost too soft to be heard. "I'm not...human anymore."

Okazaki gazed gently up at him.

"Oh? I've never met anybody that was more human than you."

"Okazaki…"

"I didn't get to die as a samurai…"

"No," Enma said, shaking his head. "That isn't true. You'll be a true samurai till the very end. That girl behind me could only be the daughter of one. She's the proof that you lived, so don't you dare deny her."

He took Okazaki's right hand, staring at his palm.

Was there still time? Could he do it? He'd never made an oni-gome for immortality.

Okazaki moaned, his body writhing in pain. Enma brought his leather bag over at once and laid it down. Inside was a complete set of the tools of his trade. If it worked, he could save Okazaki. Natsu didn't have to be left an orphan.

But in return for his life, he'd be forcing a cruel existence on him instead. Enma hesitated.

*What should you do?*

The oni within him seemed to enjoy his discomfort as it asked him that question. Guessing at what was about to happen, evil spirits began to surge forth and watch from the darkness. From here and there, insects began to crawl out, white serpents entwined themselves at his feet…and from the heavens came a woman's head, long hair dangling down.

They were all there, eagerly awaiting the moment when a man would cease to be a man. This wasn't like any of the other times he'd made an oni-gome. Enma felt the darkness crushing him. He wiped the sweat that was dripping down his jaw.

"I must be close to the end," Okazaki murmured. "I can see an oni."

Before Enma could say otherwise, Okazaki stopped him with a single look.

"Take care of Natsu."

It wasn't a request. It was an order. In the face of a glare which wouldn't take no for an answer, Enma could only meekly nod.

"I want her to have a happy, ordinary life…"

In his haze of consciousness, it was unclear just how much Okazaki really understood what Enma was considering, but at the very least he could tell that his situation was hopeless. Maybe that was why Enma could feel the weight of what he'd been burdened with.

"Take care of Natsu…"

Repeating his order as though to emphasize it, his voice now terribly weak, Okazaki closed his eyes and immediately fell back asleep.

*I was about to rob Okazaki of his right to die as a human being.*

Okazaki's rugged palm was already covered with cuts and blisters. What could he have possibly tattooed on top of that? His own self-serving hypocrisy made him sick.

Returning Okazaki's right hand back to the futon, Enma went outside.

The strong wind whipped at his hair, furling it out. The surging spirits sounded disappointed and angry. A branch caught in the wind hit his cheek, opening a thin wound, but he didn't even notice it. He staggered over to the big cherry tree, unaware as he trampled tiny imps which gnawed at his feet. The tree swayed grandly in the pitchblackness of the night.

It seemed to be doing some mad dance, its blossoms scattering to paint the darkness. Enma crouched down and vomited a bit.

The sleepless night finally lightened into dawn.

Was the medicine still working? Okazaki was sleeping quietly and didn't seem to be in any pain. Since there was no hope of saving him, the doctor had left a supply of strong painkillers meant to keep him only half-conscious.

Even looking at his face as he slept was painful, so Enma got up to look for Natsu. There was no sign of anyone in the deserted house; Natsu's clogs were missing from the entryway. She was a strong girl, but seeing the terrible state of her father yesterday had left her shaken. He had a feeling she had gone someplace to cry. He went outside to make a quick walk around.

The spring morning was pleasantly cool, prickling his skin. The cherry blossoms blown down by the night wind lay on the ground, wet with morning dew.

He quickly found Natsu behind the house, crouched before a small shrine to the bodhisattva Ksitigarbha, hands clasped as she prayed for guidance.

She turned as Enma approached.

"Master Houshou..."

Judging from how red her eyes were, she mustn't have slept much either.

"Please, enough with the 'master' stuff."

He couldn't help but be a little creeped out by it.

"Well, what would you like me to call you?"

He started to say "just Enma," then stopped to think it over. This was Natsu, after all. She'd probably still put a "master" on his name, and he didn't relish the idea of being addressed like he was the king of hell.

"Father called you Amane, didn't he?"

He had the same face and the same name as the man in the photo from seventeen years ago... A smart girl like Natsu was probably wondering what it all meant, but she didn't pursue it any further. This wasn't the time for that.

"I was praying to Lord Ksitigarbha, but... Father isn't going to live, is he?"

He wondered how he should answer her. She was smart, so she'd probably see through any lie he told without a problem. He could offer her no peace of mind.

"No, I'm afraid not," he replied.

Natsu's mouth clenched as he told her. She looked so sweet and vulnerable that Enma instinctively embraced her tiny shoulders. She grasped his sleeve, her body trembling. It looked like it was all she could do to keep from crying.

"I have no way to help him," she said. "Just relying on gods and buddhas doesn't mean anything in the end. I want to save Father myself…"

He could only think what a strong girl she was. Even now, she wouldn't give in to grief.

"I'm going to be a doctor. Women can be doctors too, can't they?"

Her gaze was so direct and earnest, Enma had to turn away. He felt as though he were witnessing a miracle. In the midst of despair, Natsu was searching for the path she had to follow.

"I know you will," he said at last.

He had no doubt in his mind that there was nothing this girl couldn't do.

It had been three days since they'd returned from the police station. Okazaki was dead.

Natsu had knelt before his body, weeping. Enma didn't think there were enough tears in anyone to cry as much as she had. He hadn't shed a tear since the day that Baikou had died, and he'd almost forgotten that they even existed.

For an assassin, death was a fact of life. For a man doomed to immortality, death was something to be envied.

As her tears fell rapidly, one after another, he realized that this was the first death Natsu had ever mourned. The people of the village performed a modest funeral service, and after the body had been interred, Nobumasa Muta appeared, dressed in mourning clothes.

"The chief of police will be coming tomorrow to apologize," he said.

This incident was now making front-page news, and it looked like it was causing trouble for the entire police department. There were some attempts to cover it up, but Nobumasa wouldn't allow it. Officer Kawamura and the others who'd been involved had been dismissed and were awaiting judgment.

"As far as the student who'd been accused of theft, we arrested a pickpocket who'd drifted up here from Kyoto who confessed to the crime. It was all too late to matter, though."

"No. Okazaki would have been glad. Now that child won't have to suffer his name being dishonored."

Isn't that right, Enma said to the grave stone. Under the humble grave marked by a stone on the rich soil, Okazaki quietly returned to the earth. Her hands clasped together as she knelt before the grave, Natsu listened to the two adults as they talked. She was crying so hard that it was impossible to read her expression.

"Does the girl have any relatives?" Nobumasa asked.

Enma shook his head. Her father had been the only family young Natsu had in the world.

"Then would she allow me to adopt her?"

It was a magnificent proposal. As the daughter of a filthy-rich noble family, Natsu's future would have been assured. But, again, Enma shook his head.

"She's a little too old to be your daughter."

Natsu stood up and looked up at Nobumasa with her earnest eyes.

"I'm thankful for your kindness," she said, "but I think I want to honor my father's last wish."

Nobumasa looked to Enma to confirm this.

"Seinosuke Hisaka asked that I take care of her," he explained.

"But there's certainly no way she could pass for your daughter, despite how old you really are."

Nobumasa had a vague suspicion of the truth now.

"Then she can be my little sister. Anyway, we'll just let nature take its course."

He may not be able to be a father for her, but he could look after her until she was grown. The oni who dwelt within him would no doubt make it difficult, but Natsu was going to honor her father's dying wish.

"I see. Well, I hope it works out for you."

Clapping Enma on the shoulder, Nobumasa then bent down before Natsu and looked into her eyes.

"Miss, your father did nothing wrong. We are entirely to blame for this. I'm truly sorry. There's no way I could ever apologize enough for this…"

He bowed his head deeply.

"The words of a policeman apologizing from his heart will live on in mine," she replied.

Hearing such forgiving words from the lips of one so young, Nobumasa furrowed his brow, looking like his own heart would break as well.

Natsu bowed and went back into the house. Even if she wasn't going to lock away her anger and grief in her heart, they must have felt as heavy as mud to her.

"Why does a child trying so hard to be brave seem so much more pitiful?" Nobumasa murmured.

"Because she is the proof," Enma replied.

How she would live her life would be the proof of her father's goodness. Enma understood that was what Natsu was thinking. And for that reason, she couldn't just keep crying, because somebody would criticize her for being childish.

*Take care of Natsu.*

Enma sighed as he realized the real meaning of Okazaki's words. He had entrusted his daughter to Enma to stop her from torturing herself with standards that no one could ever meet.

"Easier said than done," Enma grumbled softly at the grave.

## Chapter 3

# The Yokohama Ripper

*A.D. 1890 (Meiji 23)*

## —1—

*I hope the weather hasn't been too hot for you.*

*Have you been well? Have you been eating properly? Combing your hair? Occasionally taking your futon out into the sun to air it out? I've heard that awful murderer has claimed another woman in Yokohama. I beg you, please be careful. You have a knack for getting yourself caught in strange situations. Please, try not to do anything rash.*

*I worry so much about your living all alone. Yokohama is barely an hour from Tokyo by train, but I haven't heard from you in such a long time.*

*I study diligently every day to become a doctor, but not being able to be with you is as lonely as can be. I sometimes find myself growing a bit resentful, wishing that you might come to visit me.*

*The weather's grown hot now, and I'll be coming there soon. I should be able to stay for a short while, so I hope you won't mind my visit. In my heart, I still consider myself your daughter or younger sister, even though I look like your older sister now—*

Natsu stopped writing the letter and put the writing brush down. She feared that she'd end up revealing what had to remain hidden in her heart if she was as obvious as this.

She took the piece of paper she was writing on and crumpled it up into a ball. If she lost the bond of family between them, she would also lose any chance of being involved at all with this man named Enma Houshou.

Biting her lip, she arranged the books on the writing desk and wrapped them up in a cloth. They were doing a cadaver dissection today, and being too cheerful wouldn't be very appropriate. If she ended up feeling faint the way she had last time, the male students would never let her hear the end of it.

"There, you see?"

"That's why women are no good for this."

She never wanted to hear criticism like that again. She didn't want to bring shame to Enma and Nobumasa Muta for allowing her to go to medical school. Ever since she'd become determined to be a doctor, she'd been prepared to overcome any obstacle that might stand in her way. Facing an autopsy with a cool expression might lead to the others calling her an ice queen behind her back, but she'd be proud of insults like that. She hoped that would start happening soon.

The iron wind chimes hanging in the window that faced south tinkled coolly. Closing it, Natsu left the boarding house. The sun burned white hot. The cicadas were out in force today, buzzing away so loudly that the sound itself seemed to scorch the ground.

Yesterday, Natsu Hisaka had turned twenty-one years old.

Time for Enma had stopped when he was twenty. She was now a year older than the man she called her big brother.

*August 1890 (Meiji 23)*

This had once been called Yokohama village. They say it was so far off the beaten path, not even the birds would bother flying through it.

One after another, the enormous foreign ships came to the village. And, seemingly in the twinkling of an eye, Western-style buildings of red brick sprang up, lining streets through which strode foreign people with red hair while steam locomotives belching black smoke ran to and fro.

Yokohama had become an odd place indeed, where topknot and blond hair passed each other on the streets while the sound of steam engines and the ancient calls of street vendors echoed in the air. Edo was a distant memory now, the samurai having vanished like the morning dew. This place was on the forefront of the future. Yokohama greedily absorbed foreign culture, seeming to, at long last, consign all the troubles of the past to the stuff of bad dreams.

On his way to a client's house, Enma turned to look back.

The sunset faintly colored Mt. Nogeyama as it stood watch over Yokohama's past and present. There were some things which never changed.

Some people, as well…

"Yokohama really is an odd place, isn't it?" murmured the woman seriously, having moved there from Tokyo six months before. She seemed to be talking more to herself than to Enma at her side.

"It has a magnificent railway station, the homes of fashionable foreigners, but if you just wander away from the streets a short distance, you're back out in the boondocks."

She was talking a lot to distract herself from the pain.

While she couldn't see him as she lay face down, Enma was sincerely nodding as she talked. He didn't make much of a conversation partner as his work demanded his attention, but the least he could do was listen. But then, Enma wasn't much of a talker even when he wasn't working, so he was rather grateful for people who liked to monopolize conversations.

"It's an odd mix of a hick town and a city from the West, isn't it?"

He could detect a trace of her northern accent in her complaints. Its roughness didn't seem to quite fit the half-naked woman who lay sprawled out before him, her skin dimly illuminated by the light of a paper lantern.

"Still, for all I say about it, it's not as if I don't like it. The city, I mean. It's just that I find it kind of amusing."

He agreed. This was a city which could accept its share of oddballs.

"There's nothing strange at all to see foreigners walking around. Them and their giant beards. And now our stupid politicians are copying them. Can you imagine?"

It was rare to see a man with whiskers back in the Tokugawa days. However, as they entered the Meiji era, more and more men were growing beards in an attempt to look dignified. There were not a few overbearing policemen with mustaches which tapered to sharp points.

The woman lay silent for a moment, and he heard a faint rustling sound. A brown moth was beating its wings against the corner of the ceiling, searching for a way out. It might have been attracted by the flowers on the woman's back.

"Well?" she asked. "Is that peony blooming nicely back there?"

She knew the answer without needing to see the nod. She smiled and said that she was looking forward to seeing it.

He was tattooing an enormous blossom across her back. The brilliantly blooming flower was beautiful, and he was almost done with it.

"Lord Enma never makes mistakes in his work, does he?" she merrily laughed. "You know, you've never told me how old you are. Twenty? Twenty-one?"

"Dunno," Enma muttered bluntly back.

"You're so slender and your skin's like white porcelain, so I'd think you were young, but your eyes don't have a young man's sparkle."

Maybe they had exactly the sort of sparkle you'd expect of someone his age.

"But those eyes make me feel relieved. The bastard I have to sleep with gets a nasty gleam in his that's just unbecoming of a man his age."

She'd been a prostitute a few years before, but had been redeemed by a man who ran a building materials factory to supply all of the foreign houses that were springing up in the city. He was the one who had wanted the peony on her back. In truth, he'd pretty much ordered her to do it.

"Still, you gotta admit, he's pretty sharp. Having his concubine get a tattoo on her back so he can show her off to foreigners."

All too often, men would sacrifice the bodies of their concubines in order to attract foreign clients. By making this peony bloom on her back, he was just being an accomplice to the crime, Enma thought. His heart ached for her.

"Oh, don't take it like that," she said. "You aren't the one who's causing me all the grief here. Actually, you're pretty good, it hardly hurts at all. And every minute I'm getting tattooed by you is a minute I don't have to be sleeping with anyone."

A film of pyrethrum smoke stretched across her back. Enma coughed a little.

"Nice, isn't it?"

She pointed to a white parasol which had been left open on the floor.

Enma had been wondering about that ever since he'd come there that evening. The parasol on the room's tatami floor fluttered in the breeze coming through the window.

"I bought that myself yesterday. It's not new, but the quality's fantastic. It's the first time I've ever indulged in such a luxury, but the real reason I wanted it was because it was so pretty." The way she said it, sounding almost embarrassed, was charming. Even Enma found himself smiling without realizing it.

"It's not something a concubine would walk around in public with, though."

"I don't agree."

"Oh?"

"It suits you."

The woman blushed. From her cool demeanor, he'd thought her to be close to thirty, but she may have been younger.

"All right, then!" she said. "At some point, I'll take my parasol with me for a stroll down by the bay."

Her face, looking so happy in profile, made her seem surprisingly young, indeed.

"Look at me here with my parasol, getting to chat with you here. I'm a lucky gal, aren't I?"

"You must think I'm really dull," he replied.

He doubted that people had much fun with him. It's not that he was particularly or especially taciturn, but he just wasn't good at making clever small talk while he was working. Some of his clients complained about having to endure his long silences, wondering if he was a little stupid or whether he preferred to let them suffer in silence.

"You don't say much, but you listen well. And you really pay attention. Besides, listening to me bitching about things is boring, as well. I appreciate that."

And he appreciated her for saying it. A girl who was merely young wouldn't say such a thing, but a woman who had suffered repeated hardships and given up on something could accept a man's fragility and pathos.

"My master won't be home for another three days. I've been very lucky lately."

Resting her chin on her folded arms, she narrowed her eyes like a cat lurking on a porch.

"I'm originally from Aizu, up north. After what happened there, my parents brought me to Tokyo when I was still little."

Aizu had resisted the new government to the very end. Many lives were lost.

"But then they both ended up dying, and what else could a fifteen-year-old girl left on her own do but start selling herself on the streets?"

Once the Meiji era had begun, there'd been talk of equal rights for women, but it would be a long time before that became reality. To Enma, who'd known life when

Tokyo was still called Edo, male chauvinism still seemed to be as strong as ever.

Her expression darkened, and her downturned eyes seemed to cloud over.

"Have you heard? A streetwalker got herself killed in the alley behind the French Hall."

Six days ago, a woman had been killed behind an antique shop.

"The body had been hacked to pieces. As if she hadn't been human, just because she was a prostitute..." the woman murmured regretfully.

The wound on the murdered woman's head had been so deep that it had exposed bone, and there were also signs that she'd been eviscerated after being laid open from breast to belly. She'd only just arrived in Yokohama from the rural village of Kofu, near Mt. Fuji, so it was doubtful she'd even had time to make any enemies here.

Another prostitute had been killed about two weeks earlier. The gruesome remains had been found in a grove of trees, although it looked like the dogs and crows had gotten to them first. Having lain out there for three days after death, the body had been badly chewed up.

The appearance of a serial killer had all of Yokohama on edge.

"It's beyond cruel. Those poor girls..."

Because even whores were human. They laughed and cried and the blood flowing through their veins was the same as anyone else's. That was probably what she wanted to say.

Enma was silent. His expression was hard, but he understood the woman's pain.

The killer was likely making himself out to be a client so that he could murder them. There was no doubt he was targeting these women who had no choice to earn a living except by trusting their customers. Enma clenched the hand in which held his needle.

"Ow!"

"Sorry."

Blood ran across the woman's back, right from the dead center of the flower petals. Tattooing always drew a bit of blood, but a blossom dripping with blood just looked pathetic.

"It's all right," she said. "Anyway, show me the Enma mark on your hand. I love seeing that."

He couldn't understand what was so fascinating about it.

"It's just Sanskrit."

"No, it's more than that."

The great skill and craftsmanship Baikou had demonstrated in that Sanskrit character was as beautiful as something out of a story, and it inspired strangely powerful feelings in those who saw it.

"But I wouldn't want to meet Lord Enma face to face," she added. "He'd probably just say that I'm a criminal and then cast me into hell."

She chewed her nails.

"I often dream of my hands being stained red. In my dreams, I seem to kill many men. The men who bought me for money. First, I cut off their filthy hands, then their greedy tongues, their yellow eyes… Aren't you sick of me? I'm probably not much better than a murderer."

Her sadness not completely dried up, a blue fire seemed to dance in her eyes.

"You haven't killed anybody."

Dreams were dreams. Everyone had dreams like that.

"Yeah, well, nobody's perfect," the woman chuckled. Then she stared at her own palm.

"Blood wouldn't look good on a hand like that," Enma said.

The woman looked up at him.

"A flower would suit it more."

He looked down at the floor, as though embarrassed by what he'd just said.

"I'm flattered," she said, smiling nervously. "I don't know how you could say that with a straight face. Anyway, it doesn't hurt so much now. You can go ahead."

He had made a promise to get this job finished today. Not with the woman, but with her master. Even while he was forcing her to have this done, he probably couldn't stand the thought of her exposing her skin to another man. Apparently, he never expected that such an accomplished tattooist would also be so young.

"If you don't finish soon, my master will probably start quibbling over your payment. He can be a real cheapskate," the woman giggled. She was silent a moment. "Honestly, I wanted to talk to you more, though."

This young woman was the concubine of a sixty-year-old man. It was a relief for her to associate with someone closer to her age, as Enma apparently was.

"Although I seem to be the one doing all the talking here," she added. "You probably do all the talking usually. Don't you have a family of your own?"

Enma hesitated a moment before answering. "I have a little sister."

Natsu was already older than he was now, but he kept calling her his little sister because he preferred to. He'd probably have to start referring to her as his older sister now, but part of him still resisted doing that.

"Oh, really? I can imagine a little sister of yours must be lovely."

"Dunno. I haven't seen her in six months, but I wonder if she's gotten a little more refined now. She's in Tokyo, studying." He tilted his head as he recalled the face of that overly serious young girl.

"A student? Well, now I'm jealous. I've always wanted to go to school, even once. Maybe if I'd just learned to read, my life could have taken a completely different path," she said, a tinge of regret in her voice.

"Was there something you wanted to be?" Enma asked.

"Anything other than a whore or a concubine. Something where I might occasionally buy myself something good to eat with the money I earn."

It was such a modest wish, but for her, it was probably a dream that seemed almost heavenly.

"All finished."

Enma wiped the sweat from his brow and let out a long breath.

"Really? So, that's it, then?"

"The true colors won't appear until the swelling goes down and the ink settles into your skin."

It would be a few days before that peony fully bloomed.

"I know that already. Wow, it's practically midnight."

The woman looked tired as she moved her body.

"It'd be best not to move yet," Enma warned.

She stopped herself just as she looked like she was about to stand up.

"I just wanted to walk you home, kid. It's dangerous out there."

"I'm not some kid who needs to be seen home by his customer," he replied.

To a worldly-wise woman like her, the scrawny, tongue-tied Enma must have seemed like he was still wet behind the ears. In fact, he was likely fifteen years her senior.

She laughed. "I suppose you're right. It probably would look strange for you to be seen home by a woman on the streets at night."

It had taken him months to complete this epic work. In all that time, they'd talked about many things. About the foreign vessels which adorned the harbor, the picture book she'd gotten from a foreigner, her memories of Aizu. She was a clever speaker, able to talk about even painful or sad things with a smile and without any hesitation.

"It's a shame I can't see my back very easily," she went on. "I'm sure that flower looks lovely."

"It's no flower. It's a disgrace. All I've done is given you an unwanted scar on your beautiful skin."

He'd enjoyed their time together, but had been saddened by having to scratch ink into her skin.

"Any scar from you is a treasure. I'll cherish it."

The woman smiled.

"Chie-san…"

It was the first time Enma had ever called her by her name. Up until now, he had stubbornly referred to her as "okyaku-san": his honored customer. As a man who couldn't form any long-term associations, he was normally careful not to have any relationships with his customers outside of business. However, his feelings for this woman had grown.

Chie reached out and took hold of Enma's hand.

"Thank you. Truly."

The evening breeze stirred weakly, carrying the humidity that hung in the air.

Enma took a deep breath as he left the home of his client. The air smelled of salt water. The fragrance of the woman's rouge and powder was pleasant, but he preferred the scent of the sea. He uncovered his hand in the moonlight. Even Enma on his palm seemed to be in an usually good mood tonight.

Business had picked up since he began amusing people by saying he called the tattoo Enma because it meant he held the king of the underworld in the palm of his hand. Thanks to that, he was now in a position where he could choose which customers to serve.

He pulled the fingerless leather glove back over his right hand.

His ankles peeked out from under his slightly too short *hakama*. His small face with its air of detachment from the mortal world might have been better suited to Western-style clothing.

Enma rolled his sleeves up to his shoulders and began walking, his wooden clogs echoing into the humid air. Frogs and insects vied for supremacy in the chorus of croaks and buzzes which sang into the night. The foreign residences weren't far from here, but the area he was in now was a mass of farms. The Meiji era may have seemed to be sweeping everything into the future, but the hold of old Edo wasn't quite dead yet. Despite the cries for Japan's Westernization, people's lives prolonged the past.

Relishing the salt air, he headed for his roost. The row house in which he lived wasn't far if he hurried, but Enma was in no hurry. Except for his work, he took things as slowly as possible. After all, he had no reason to rush.

Enma suddenly stopped.

There was a smell in the air which didn't belong. There was no mistaking it. It was the smell of blood.

Maybe a dog had died somewhere. Enma looked around. Stepping into the bushes at the side of the road, he felt something like a cloth cord tangle around his ankles poking out from under his *hakama*. When he looked, he saw it was a woman's waistcloth. It was light pink, but stained darker, here and there.

"It's blood," he said to himself.

There was no way he could leave without making sure of this. Enma pushed deeper into the brush.

He spotted something that looked like a white stick. Drawing closer, he saw that it was a woman's leg. Two pale legs sprawled out, gleaming bewitchingly under the moonlight.

*Shit...*

There was a naked woman lying in the grass, her black hair spread out like a fan.

Her belly was torn open, one eye was gouged out, and her head had been nearly hacked off. Her skin was still warm when he touched it, meaning she'd been killed only a short while ago. Her remaining eye was wide open, seeming to stare up into the starry sky.

The moon reflected in it was trembling.

## —2—

He couldn't just ignore what he'd found and went to the police to report it. As expected, he earned himself an unpleasant interrogation for his trouble.

In addition to being the discoverer of the body, the fact that he had knives among his possessions and was engaged in an illegal occupation left a somewhat shady impression. Perhaps suspicion was unavoidable for someone who had no real relatives, but having them look at him with such obvious doubt in their eyes was getting a bit tedious at this point.

When asked if there was anyone who could positively identify him, they rejected his suggestion that they ask his sister. It would be too much trouble to contact her at her school in Tokyo. Enma felt rather relieved when they said that. But if nobody came to take custody of him, they would have to hold him there as a suspect.

With no other choice, Enma gave them the name of the one man he could call.

Nobumasa Muta appeared that evening.

When Nobumasa, the older brother of Viscount Muta and superintendent of the Tokyo police, came expressly from Tokyo, the kowtowing by the Yokohama police couldn't begin fast enough. Luckily for them, they hadn't mistreated Enma, and so nobody would be punished for this.

"The police nowadays don't even cut their own members a break when it comes to this. They really didn't do anything unreasonable?" Nobumasa said as they stepped out of the police station.

Enma hadn't slept since yesterday, and the setting sun was too bright for eyes weak from a lack of sleep. "I suppose," he answered halfheartedly, trying to shake the buzzing out of his head.

In all honesty, Enma didn't want to see this man again. Now in his thirties, Nobumasa made for an impressive figure. All it did was serve to remind Enma of how he still looked like a beardless youth no matter how many years had passed. But, worse than that, it was pathetic how he had to call upon Nobumasa for help all the time, like the fox who borrowed his influence from the tiger.

"Sorry for causing you any trouble."

"No, I'm grateful that you reported this so quickly."

Walking alongside Nobumasa, whose solid frame was dressed from head to toe in Western finery, only exacerbated Enma's feelings of inferiority.

His fortieth birthday had passed long ago, and yet his scrawny boyish body practically swam in his worn-out *hakama*.

*Ow!*

He must not have been paying attention, because he'd just run straight into another man coming the opposite way.

"Excuse me. Are you all right?"

The man spoke with some difficulty. Looking up, Enma saw a sandy-haired foreigner standing in front of him.

"I wasn't paying attention, so..."

It was hard to judge how old foreigners were, but he looked to be around thirty. He wore round glasses and a few freckles were scattered around his nose.

"I was the one who ran into you. I'm in a hurry, you see."

As he said this, the foreigner pointed to the police station. He bowed his head awkwardly, then started running again and vanished into the brick police station.

"As you can see, these incidents are so heinous as to attract the attention of foreign reporters," Nobumasa said with a bitter smile.

Enma nodded in understanding. That must have been a foreign newspaper correspondent. He'd come running for an interview, now that another victim had been discovered.

"This is turning into a national disgrace, so the police in there are under orders not to leak any information about the case. He won't be getting anything from them."

"Every country has murderers. That's ridiculous."

They even had murderers back in Hagi, where he'd come from... Enma grimly pressed his lips together as he recalled the dead girl's face, drained of blood and growing cold.

"Certainly," Nobumasa replied.

Since the murder had occurred in Yokohama, Nobumasa was in no position to have any say in the investigation. Even so, he took an interest in it and had a number of questions for the coroner's office. One of them concerned whether or not the victim's heart remained in the body. Without missing a beat, he confirmed the matter of most interest to Enma.

The body was in a gruesome state, but they confirmed that its heart was still there. That was the one piece of good news in all of this.

"I think it was the year before last. In England, there was an incident in which five prostitutes were hacked to death. This case bears a striking similarity to that one."

"Did they catch the guy?"

When Nobumasa replied that no, they hadn't, Enma frowned.

"Well, keep up the good work, *Nippon Porisuman*."

Raising his hand to wave goodbye, Enma crossed a small bridge over the open sewer trench. From that point on, the neighborhood turned to lines of filthy row houses. It was no place for a man of Nobumasa's breeding to come.

By proclamation under the Peerage Act of 1884, which established the five official ranks of nobility, Nobumasa's younger brother Atsushi had been granted the title of viscount.

Being the older brother of a viscount was a strange position for Nobumasa to be in. "The curtain rose on the Meiji era under the banner of equality for all classes, and then, instead, they took the absurd step of creating a whole new class system," he'd laughed. He didn't seem to mind it too much, though.

"I'll be staying at my place in Motomachi for a while. Come and visit sometime."

The Muta family still kept an old residence in Yokohama. Apparently, they still used it for business dealings and the like.

"I'd rather not."

Nobumasa's eyes narrowed as he watched Enma turn and smile hello at a passing pretty girl. He wondered if something was on his mind as he watched Enma walk away.

Smoke from grilling fish rose from the row houses as wives busied themselves preparing dinner. Children dressed only in *haragake* bibs ran around them.

The sheer commonness of the scene made Enma feel relieved.

"What happened? You didn't come home last night. Did you manage to get laid?" said Masa, the lady who lived across the way from him, a sly grin on her face. "I'll bet you did. What woman would pass up a fine specimen of man like you? If I was just a little younger, you know…"

The other wives laughed uproariously. Women couldn't help but tease a young bachelor like Enma.

"If a gal could support me, I wouldn't care how old she was."

Enma was used to this, and gave as good as he got.

"Well, that'd be a problem, then. I don't have any cash socked away for that. Anyway, hurry up and get inside. Natsu's home!"

Why didn't you say so in the first place, he thought. Enma hurriedly threw open the door.

Natsu was kneeling on the tatami floor, waiting for him. The narrowed eyes on her usually impassive face made it clear she was angry with him. Her lips were pressed stiffly into a thin line.

"It's been a while, big brother."

Natsu bowed her head. No matter the situation, she never forgot her manners.

"Uh… Yeah. So, you're home."

This was beyond embarrassing. Kuro, who was sprawled out on the floor next to her, let out a yawn as if to ridicule him. How old was this cat, anyway? At this point, Enma was going to have to admit that the cat was afflicted with the same curse he was. If he wasn't, then Enma expected his tail to split in two and reveal he was an enchanted *nekomata*: a forked-tail monster cat.

"Yes, since yesterday."

Which meant he'd left her waiting for an entire day. Natsu only came home from medical school in Tokyo to visit for New Year's and the summer O-Bon festival.

"I sent a telegram that I was coming home yesterday, didn't I?"

Yes, she certainly had. He hadn't forgotten, but finding those grisly remains had blown all of that.

"Yeah, I got it. Yesterday was kind of…interesting for me."

There was no need to scare her, so Enma didn't elaborate on the exact circumstances beyond that.

"I came back from visiting my parents' graves for O-Bon memorial holidays. I was very much looking forward to seeing you."

Yeah, she was really angry with him. It looked like that had come through loud and clear when she'd talked to Masa and the others.

"You can imagine my surprise when I arrived and found out my brother has been out carousing…"

"Do I look like I'd ever do that?"

Jokes like that didn't really work on someone as serious as Natsu.

"Sorry… I'm tired. I'm going to bed."

He should talk about something else with her, shouldn't he? Like medical school, her studies. After all, he was "big brother," wasn't he?

Whether it was out of habit or because she didn't know what else to call him, Natsu called him big brother. There still wasn't an obvious difference in their appearances, so calling him that didn't seem that strange. But what about as more time passed? His heart sank as he thought about it.

By now, he was used to having people overtake him as they aged, but how could he explain this to Natsu? Lately, the anxiety he felt over it was making it impossible for him to accept even the kindest words from her. It wasn't that long ago that they behaved like a real brother and sister.

*Am I jealous of her?*

Of Natsu, and all of the mature self-confidence she'd accumulated?

"I see… Then please, go get your rest."

She sounded so lonely.

Even so, he hadn't had a wink of sleep since the day before yesterday. The demon deep within his body demanded deep sleep. It was exceedingly strict about maintaining the health of its host. Enma was so tired he was practically ready to fall unconscious where he stood.

When the next day came and Enma showed no sign of waking up, Natsu left him to do some shopping.

Just as she'd feared, his clothes were practically rags. His teacups and bowls were so chipped that you could almost cut your lips on them. Enma's cavalier attitude about these things annoyed her. It was like he needed someone to help him with every detail in his life.

Did he still spill his miso soup? Did he still get those little fish bones caught in his throat? She let out a long sigh, thinking how she had to worry about what should be the most trifling of matters.

After buying some necessities for Enma, Natsu headed for a foreign bookshop she was familiar with. She hoped to examine some dictionaries and medical books, since Western books were more easily available in Yokohama. Every time she went there, she would inevitably end up buying several new ones.

At that moment, Natsu was the only woman in her medical school. There'd been two others at first, but they'd quit, unable to stand the strict regimen. But, no matter what happened, Natsu was determined not to give up. She was despised by the others there and treated badly. All because she was a woman. Because of that, she always needed to get the best grades. She couldn't give the men there any opportunities to drag her down. No matter how much she studied, it was never enough. Well, if this nation hated having educated women, she was going to make them hate her as much as she could. It was in that spirit that Natsu dedicated herself to her studies.

Since the money from the sale of her father's house had run out long ago, Natsu depended entirely on Enma for her tuition and living expenses. Since they weren't really family, there was no way she could go on living off of his generosity. She wanted to start earning a living as soon as she could. She convinced herself that she didn't deserve to let him know her special feelings about him so long as she remained dependent.

Two years ago, Natsu became a medical student and began to live on her own in Tokyo. At the same time, Enma moved from Osaka to Yokohama. Natsu had grown up, and living in the same place for five years was truly the limit. The neighbors had grown suspicious, and so he'd found a new home, as though he were running away.

To be honest, she hadn't immediately believed him when he'd shown her the Enma mark on his hand and told her about oni-gome. Until he'd gotten stabbed in a fight and she saw the wound in his chest close up as she watched, she'd thought it was just a story he'd told her. The wound had been bad enough to freeze Natsu's blood in terror.

"It's nothing," he'd said. "Unless somebody cuts off my head or stabs me in the heart, I can't die."

Instant death, which didn't even give the demon a moment with which to heal him. Anything short of that wouldn't kill him, he said with a wry smile that was full of self-derision.

The blade had just barely missed his heart, and the wound was over three *sun* (three and a half inches) deep. Normally, death would be certain. But then the wound began to heal before her eyes. She saw blood vessels reconnecting, muscle rebuilding, flesh closing up as perfectly as it was before. As graphic as the scene was, Natsu had choked down the scream that was rising in her throat. If she allowed herself to be frightened by this, it would only hurt Enma. She was desperate to avoid making a scene.

She had no choice but to believe him…

Because, even more than that, Enma had not changed at all since the day they'd first met. Even though she had grown from a child into a woman.

Eventually, she would overtake him, and she had long been frightened of the unacceptable future they faced.

That time had come so easily, but it did nothing to ease her anxiety. The difference between them would only continue to grow. If Natsu continued to live with him, the fact that Enma strangely never aged would become too obvious for their neighbors to ignore.

Natsu needed to live on her own.

Adjusting the collar of her *kosode* and straightening up her back, Natsu strode through Yokohama. Though worn down by the influences of the West, traces of Edo still remained mixed in to the look of the streets, giving them a fantastic atmosphere. Gaslights and tiled roofs. Blackened teeth and ice cream. Anything and everything. It was the perfect place for an eccentric to live.

She entered an alleyway set back a bit from the main street. Next to the shop that specialized in imported goods, she spied a stylish sign which identified its shop as

"Mikazuki-Doh"—Crescent Hall. It was Natsu's favorite imported bookshop.

Originally built as a warehouse, Mikazuki-Doh had a rich assortment of books, from ones dealing with rare European folk remedies to complex works dealing with the science of the human mind. Natsu wanted to be a surgeon, but she found these just as fascinating.

"Anybody home?"

Was that kind, funny shopkeeper in today? She peeked inside.

"Welcome, please," a voice said in English.

Not expecting to be greeted in another language, Natsu stopped just as she was about to step into the store. A large foreigner with red hair and a beard stood inside. She could spot red chest hair as well peeking out of his wide white shirt collar. There were Western instructors in medical school as well, but even for someone used to dealing with them, like her, this enormous bear of a man was intimidating.

"Well now, if it isn't the young lady medical student."

Natsu was relieved when the casually dressed young man with his lovely, familiar voice came in from the back of the store.

It was him, the one and only owner of Mikazuki-Doh. The word that came to mind when looking at him, with his gentle demeanor, was "elegant." He was a real lady-killer.

"Oh, thank goodness. For a minute there, I thought I was in the wrong shop."

"Heath here may look scary, but I can assure you, he's a fine man."

The foreigner named Heath nodded, then held his thumb up and smiled.

"I beg your pardon. You're Mr. Mikazuki-Doh's friend, then?"

With his graceful, almost androgynous looks and strangely unearthly air about him, it wasn't surprising that he'd be acquainted with strange foreigners.

"Not so much a friend. Heath here is the joint-manager of Mikazuki-Doh."

"Only recently started," Heath added.

Natsu thought that was surprising. She'd never seen anyone else working in the store before.

"I see. Oh, and thanks for the help last time."

He'd come to Tokyo last month on business and had stopped by to say hello.

"That *kusa manju* bun you gave me was delicious."

Living with Enma had caused her to avoid forming relationships as much as he did. At long last, she'd finally made a friend.

"If I keep bringing things like that, can I expect to see you and your pretty smile in here more often?" he said with a grin.

"There he goes again," said Heath, shrugging his shoulders. If there was one thing Mikazuki-Doh was good at, it was flattering ladies.

"I had enough, thank you. Once I'm a doctor, please come to see me any time you need help."

Mikazuki-Doh thought it over for a moment, and then murmured: "Can you examine a wound in my heart?"

Natsu's eyes widened. The fields of psychology and psychiatry were still fairly unknown in this country. It hadn't been covered much in her lectures.

"I don't know about that. I'm planning to become a surgeon, so… I'm sorry. But if you're ever injured, I'll do everything that I can to cure you."

Mikazuki-Doh smiled a strange, wistful smile.

"Injured… Yes, of course."

She'd seen that look before. Enma sometimes smiled just like that.

"There's something I need to tell you, Miss Natsu. Within the year, Heath will be taking over the store and I'll be leaving Yokohama."

Natsu was shocked.

"The name may change to Crescent Hall, since an American will be running it, but as things stand, I'll be handing over the store."

She showed no sign of appreciating his little joke.

"I see… That's a shame."

As much as she liked this shop for its wide selection, she always looked forward to seeing its owner, as well.

"I hope we can count on your continued patronage here."

"But, once you give the store away, where will you go? What will you do?"

The question may have been a little rude and prying, but she was curious.

"I haven't made up my mind yet. I'll just go wherever the wind blows me."

He had the air of being as lost as a child, with eyes that looked as resigned to fate as an old man's. The same sort of feeling she'd always gotten from Enma, as well.

"You smell like ink…"

"Pardon?"

Natsu, wondering aloud if maybe she'd spilled some India ink on her kimono, hastily sniffed her sleeve.

"No… That's tattooing dye."

Startled, Natsu looked up. It was the lingering odor of ink that Enma used. Before she'd left that morning, she'd tidied up some of his work implements.

"My older bother is a tattooist."

Natsu didn't hide it. It wasn't considered a respectable profession, but Enma had raised her by doing it. She felt no shame about it.

"I don't know much about tattoos," she said, "but the ones my brother makes are very pretty. Prettier than any painting…"

She felt that way from the bottom of her heart. There were times that she envied Enma's clients. Until the day they died, they would carry his passion with them.

"I see… I'd like to meet him," Mikazuki-Doh muttered.

"He has a prejudice against men," Natsu chuckled.

"Sounds like my kind of guy."

That was because he was such a "ladies first" sort of guy, unlike most Japanese men, Heath teased. His Japanese was quite fluent.

"Oh, yes. I have a gift for you, as thanks for being such a good customer."

He held out a thick medical book to her. The cover had "Psychiatry" written on it in German.

"But…"

Books were expensive. She appreciated it, but didn't feel she could accept such a thing.

"It's not one of my products. It's from my private collection. Please, take it, if you like. I don't need it anymore."

She was surprised to hear it was his personal property.

"You've read it?"

"I managed with the help of a dictionary. I have lots of time on my hands, so it was a nice diversion."

He pressed it into her hands. Natsu bowed repeatedly, grateful for his kindness.

"It must be hard for a woman who wants to be a doctor. I hope you can put it to good use."

"Thank you so much!"

The pain in her heart seemed to lessen. She truly was thankful to hear someone say those words to her.

"You have a lot of bags there. Need any help carrying them?"

"No, no, I wouldn't think of it. I used to live on a farm, so I'm pretty strong. Besides, I don't live too far from here, so I'll be fine."

To Natsu's eyes, Mikazuki-Doh's owner seemed weaker than she was. He looked particularly pale today.

"It's no trouble," he said. "Are you sure you aren't working yourself too hard?"

"I'm fine, really. It's a row house just back of Motomachi, right near here."

"The Densuke houses?"

Natsu blushed at the mention of the of the two-story row houses that had been built only ten years before. She didn't live in a palace like that.

"No, a little further back than that, near the sewage ditch… Um, really. I'm fine. Thank you so much."

Natsu hurried out of the store, and then stopped suddenly. She realized that all she'd ever called him was "Mr. Mikazuki-Doh."

"Um… Could you tell me your name?"

For some reason, the shop owner tilted his head and seemed to think it over before answering.

"It's Onitsuki," he finally said, a gentle smile lighting his pretty face.

After Natsu had left, Heath turned to him and grinned.

"New name?"

"Yeah."

Leaving Heath to mind the store, Mikazuki-Doh's owner Onitsuki strode out onto the main street, still dressed in his casual outfit. It was sunny, but not too hot that day, so the going was easy. She shouldn't have too much trouble, even carrying those heavy bags.

The tree-lined carriage road was beautifully maintained, and passers-by could look at it and temporarily imagine themselves seeing exotic, foreign sights.

"Natsu Hisaka…" he murmured to himself.

Her eyes shone with such vibrant life, as though this girl had never once in her life ever wanted to die. Full of wit and righteousness, one look from them made him want to cling to the strength he saw within.

When she asked him his name, he'd immediately chosen Onitsuki: Oni Moon. He'd had many aliases before that, but he was happy now for the chance to use Onitsuki.

This tattooist brother of hers interested him.

The smell of that ink was similar to the ones used by the man he'd once called his master. He heard that the old man had died long ago, leaving behind a young apprentice.

Considering he'd been cut off as unworthy, it didn't surprise him that his master had sought a more suitable successor.

*Is it possible?*

The thought crossed Onitsuki's mind, then was quickly dismissed.

He strolled through the street and bought a newspaper. Walking slowly, he noticed a woman just up the sidewalk making a spectacle of herself as she picked up the packages she'd been carrying. Sure enough, it was Natsu.

"You sure you don't want me to help you with those?" he said, rushing over to help pick up a pot and some chopsticks. The household goods she'd purchased looked heavy.

"Th-Thanks, but really, I'm fine. My hands were just a little sweaty and they slipped," Natsu said, apologizing for any trouble she'd caused him.

"Then why not catch your breath, at least? I feel like chatting with you a bit more. That place over there is pretty good, and they even sell *ramune*."

He was pointing at a fancy Western-style restaurant. Natsu was so thirsty that the offer of the new soda drink was too tempting to pass up. She didn't hesitate to accept. Blushing, she quickly nodded.

Picking up her packages, they went inside. It was hot inside, but just being out of the sun made it seem cooler.

"Would you like some ramune, Natsu?"

"Yes, please… I'm really thirsty. I may have overdone it with the shopping today."

Despite her wanting to maintain some decorum, she definitely needed something to drink. He would have given her some water back at his store if she'd just asked, he said. She may have been a thoroughly modern woman who was studying medicine, but she also seemed to be quite the *yamato nadeshiko*: the very embodiment of old-fashioned Japanese feminine virtues.

They sat down and ordered some coffee and ramune from the waiter.

The headline on the folded newspaper proclaiming "Yokohama Lady-Killer

Strikes!" leapt out at her. Now that a third victim had been found, you couldn't avoid hearing people discussing it.

People always relished even the bloodiest of stories, as long as it didn't directly involve them.

*A third victim...*

A dangerous light tinged Onitsuki's eyes.

"Awful thing, isn't it?" Natsu said, looking at the headline, her expression stern.

"Yes... It is."

"I think it's unforgivable."

Her tone conveyed just how much the crime galled her. There wasn't a particle of gossipy fun to be had in discussing this. Her lips were drawn tight in sheer rage.

Her looks were somewhat plain, but there were times when Natsu seemed absolutely beautiful. It must have been a technique that came from having a noble soul.

The ramune and coffee they'd ordered soon arrived. Downing her drink quickly, Natsu heaved a sigh of relief.

"That probably wasn't very ladylike..."

"You seem to be feeling better now."

Onitsuki drew a small glass bottle from his breast pocket. Inside, it was half-filled with a black powdery substance.

He held it up to the sunlight that streamed in through the window. The black grains inside sparkled slightly, like iron filings.

"Oh, is that medicine?"

"It's the potion of immortality."

As he answered, seemingly ready to laugh, Natsu's eyes widened. Nobody would believe that, of course. Onitsuki couldn't possibly be serious.

But he wouldn't let it go...

"If there ever was such a thing in this world, you shouldn't drink it," Natsu answered, her expression serious.

"Why not?"

"Because you'd never be happy if you did."

There was no hesitation in her answer. She knew exactly what she was talking about.

"Yes, of course..."

He wanted to ask this young woman who spoke with a wisdom that belied her years just how one would cope if they'd already made that mistake.

"I didn't think you looked well at all today. You aren't sick, are you?"

Natsu leaned forward, concern showing on her face.

"It's just heat exhaustion. I'll be fine once I drink this."

He uncorked the bottle, then scooped up a bit of the powder inside with the spoon that accompanied his coffee. At first glance, it seemed to be some sort of herbal medicine, and even Onitsuki seemed unsure of how much he should take.

His right hand was throbbing. *Go on, swallow it,* whispered the oni inside of him. *Do it, or you will die,* it laughed. And even though he wished that he could, he obeyed.

He put the spoon in his mouth, filling it with a taste like ashes. Looking like he would vomit at any second, Yasha quickly drank some coffee. The dark, fragrant drink seemed to help the "potion" go down.

It spread deep into his body. As he felt the now-sated demon quiet down, his breathing eased. The pain in his right hand subsided. Wiping the sweat from his face, he exhaled a long, thin breath.

"Does your medicine taste that bad?" Natsu asked.

"I don't think there's anything in the world that tastes worse," he replied.

As a doctor in training, Natsu seemed genuinely concerned about him.

"Do you have any family?" Translation: Do you have any relatives who can take care of you?

"I have no family. I've been on my own since I was nine, when my mother died."

Natsu looked down.

"I didn't mean to be rude."

"Please don't worry about it."

"Judging from you, your mother must have been lovely."

Was she, Yasha wondered to himself. He couldn't remember much about his past.

"Her face was beautiful in death. She was smiling, as though she was happy..."

He hadn't thought about it in a very long time.

"She was probably smiling from dreaming about being with you."

He was bringing the coffee cup to his lips, but stopped before taking the drink.

"My mother was...?"

"Yes. My father told me that once, long ago. My mother would sometimes smile in her sleep. He asked her about it later, and she was a little embarrassed to admit that it was because she was dreaming about holding me. So, I think it may have been the same for your mother, too."

Small ripples seemed to spread through a heart he'd thought had dried up long ago. Still, he wasn't so childish as to tell a young girl straight out that her fancies were completely wrong.

"Perhaps you're right," he replied with a smile. He may have not managed to do it well enough, because Natsu's expression clouded.

"Did I say something wrong?"

It must have shown on his face. That wasn't like him to do.

"No, not at all," Yasha smiled as he shook his head. "It's just that you remind me of someone I once knew."

* * * * *

It had been a very long time ago. The times were changing even as he did not. Maybe it had been during that period where he'd been a bit depressed. He'd not been doing anything, just staring out at the sea, when a young woman had rushed up to him.

"Are you... Don't do anything rash."

He had to laugh, because there'd been that other time a woman had said the same thing to him. Did he really look that desperate to die?

"Your mother went through a lot of trouble to give you life. If you throw it away over something trivial, heaven will never forgive you."

She was the daughter of the impoverished village headman, who you'd always go to for advice when things went wrong. Her husband was also a good man, in that he seemed to do no harm. He preached a philosophy of living an unpretentious, straight-talking life. The woman was also very pregnant.

"Here. Eat this and you'll feel better."

She took something from the basket of vegetables she carried on her back.

"It's ripe, so you can eat it just as it is."

He'd seen one of those before. He'd heard they were ornamental. Could you really eat one raw? Thinking that, he'd taken a bite.

The unusual vegetable from far across the sea smelled like grass and tasted of the summer sun.

* * * * *

Thinking back now, it still gave him a strange shiver.

"Was it someone you loved, Mr. Onitsuki?"

Natsu seemed interested.

"No. This story isn't nearly that romantic. Just somebody I met by chance and talked to. She was married, and seemed so happy as she rubbed her round belly."

She seemed to be enjoying the act of bearing a child from the bottom of her heart. To this day, Yasha had never seen anyone look as happy or alive.

"Since it's going to be born in the summertime, I was thinking of naming it Natsu if it's a girl," she'd said.

Natsu... It was a good name, he'd thought. It sparkled. Perhaps, at that moment, the still unseen child had already become special to Yasha.

"Did she look like me?" Natsu asked.

"Well, a bit... Maybe it was you who was in her belly at the time, Miss Natsu."

At that, Natsu burst out laughing.

"You're not *that* much older than me, Mr. Onitsuki! Just how long ago was this?" She wiped a tear from the corner of her eye, seeming to find the thought hilarious.

"You know, you remind me of somebody. I've been thinking that for a while now. Not your face, but... How do I put it? The mood you give off. It's my big brother, though."

His interest in this tattoo artist brother of hers grew even stronger.

"Could you tell me your brother's name, please?"

Natsu hesitated a moment. "He doesn't like too many people to know about his work. So, could you promise not to tell anyone else his name?"

"Of course."

Natsu lowered her voice, not wanting anyone else to hear. "It's Enma Houshou."

He couldn't help but gasp. That name filled Onitsuki with a delirious joy. He had to fight the urge to start laughing.

"Have you heard of him, by any chance?"

"No... But the name Houshou has a familiar ring to it."

"I think he inherited it from the master he apprenticed under."

Oh, what a strange fate he had. It was as if everything were being directed according to some unseen being. As he realized it yet again, Yasha was filled with wonder.

"Looks like another streetwalker's been killed."

"It's an outrage, is what it is."

He could hear them talking at the seats behind them. Two men in Western clothing were having an animated discussion about the so-called "Yokohama Lady-Killer" as they greedily filled their bellies with roasted meat.

"It's because all these uneducated hicks from the countryside are flooding into Yokohama. Most of them are probably criminals."

"But stripping them naked? Hacking them up and tearing out their entrails? It's disgusting. I heard he's even hacking up their faces!"

"Yeah, exactly."

Natsu balled her hands into fists. Onitsuki rose from his seat.

"Why don't we leave?" he said.

Natsu, who seemed uncomfortable, nodded silently.

"Thanks for everything today," she said after they'd left the restaurant, bowing politely.

"Don't you want me to help you with your bags?"

"Please, get some rest. I'm about ready to offer you a piggy-back ride back to your store," Natsu laughed. She lifted her bags with both hands to prove she was all right.

"Well then, say hello to your brother the tattooist for me."

Seeing Natsu off, Onitsuki sighed. The glare of the sun made him dizzy.

A thought suddenly crossed his mind. What was more truly disgusting: something human, or something inhuman?

## —3—

The sun beat down on the row house by the sewage trench, making it stifling inside.

Was there an older or dirtier tenement in Yokohama today? Its close proximity to the main street made it an excellent location, but one little tremor from the earth would probably reduce the entire structure to a pile of splinters.

Since the inside of the apartment was so gloomy, Natsu went out. She carried a small barrel to a grassy area near the row house, then sat down upon it to read her book.

The realization that she no longer had the jewel on the ornate hairpin that her mother had left her was now sinking in, and she was not in a good mood. Sitting outside and reading would be just the thing to make her feel better.

But even wearing her wide-brimmed French hat pulled low to her eyes, the sun's glare was terribly strong. She didn't think the hat really suited someone as plain as her, what with its lively arrangement of bird feathers and artificial flowers. She hadn't worn it before, but the glaring sun demanded otherwise.

It had been given to her by one of her fellow students when he'd heard Natsu had turned twenty-one. It seemed it was the custom overseas to celebrate one's birthday every year, he'd said. The young man, the son of a doctor who was studying at the same medical school, was the only one there who showed her any kindness.

She was happy to have gotten it, but also shy. Even Natsu, who had devoted herself so exclusively to her studies, was now belatedly approaching the age when marriage would be demanded. She knew that Enma would never have given her a fashionable gift like this. He'd probably just give her money and tell her to buy what she wanted.

There was nothing she could do about his not seeing her as a woman, but she wondered if Enma's attitude might be different if she was prettier.

*You're being foolish...*

Ever since the day they'd met, she'd yearned for this lonely man. She'd been in pursuit of those lonesome eyes. She'd longed to feel even a bit of the warmth of his body. And if she ever admitted this, it would just be one more burden for him to bear, she thought.

The only way she could live was to keep those feelings hidden. To do otherwise would lead to ordeals that the young Natsu could scarcely imagine. She just wasn't ready to commit to that.

Natsu went on reading her book, trying to shake off these thoughts within her. It was the German medical text that she'd been given by Onitsuki the day before. She found reading and writing German to be surprisingly difficult, and even the normally confident Natsu was having trouble with it. She regretted not bringing a dictionary with her, as well.

If Mr. Onitsuki could read and understand this, he must be quite the intellectual, she thought. He had the appearance of a wealthy and idle young dilettante, but who was he, really? Inside of the book she found a Western picture postcard, like a bookmark. Printed on it was a snowy scene with a circle of holly branches. A picture to celebrate the birth of the Messiah.

She found what was written on the page it marked to be most interesting.

It concerned the case of a man who had become convinced that he was a blood-sucking vampire, who would attack people night after night in order to suck their lifeblood. In Japan, this would have been dismissed as a case of spirit possession by a *mononoke*, but the book wrote about it from the point of view of it being a disease of the brain and mind.

So, had Mr. Onitsuki had an interest in the case described? Or had the card simply gotten trapped between those pages by accident? As she pondered this, she spotted a foreigner standing opposite of her, mopping sweat from his face.

Spotting Natsu in her conspicuous hat, he waved and shouted something to her. It was hard to make out, so Natsu approached him, book still in hand.

The eyes behind the round glasses he wore had a look of relief in them.

"May I…help you?" Natsu asked, although she knew her English was still quite clumsy.

"Oh, thank goodness. I finally got someone to talk to me," the relieved man replied in fluent Japanese.

"Everyone else I called out to would just run away, and I ran out of places to turn."

He smiled gently at her, and Natsu couldn't help but smile back. Even the people here in Yokohama had little patience for dealing with foreigners.

"What seems to be the problem?" she asked.

"I'm looking for someone. Do you know a tattooist named Enma Houshou?"

He'd still been asleep when she'd left the house, but maybe he was up by now.

After his long sleep, he awoke to find himself covered with sweat. Things were still dim for him, but he was met with an unfamiliar foreigner standing in front of him. A customer, Enma wondered, scratching his head.

"Well, well," the foreigner said. "It's you. We met in front of the police station."

Now he remembered. The foreign man with the round glasses who'd run into him.

"Yeah. You're the reporter from then, right?"

Surprised that the two of them already knew each other, Natsu went to make some tea. The room was oppressively humid, with a unique aroma that was a mixture of sweat, mold, and ink, but the journalist didn't seem to mind it too much.

"Oswald Ray of the *London Weekly*. And you are Enma Houshou, the practitioner of irezumi, I presume."

"Horimono, actually. There's a big difference. So, what can I do for you? Do you want to hire me?" Sitting cross-legged on his futon, still barely awake, Enma was blunt with his question.

"No, but I was thinking of doing a story on Japanese tattooing for my newspaper. I'd like to interview you."

"Why me?"

There was a questioning light in Enma's eyes. There were plenty of other tattooists out there. He couldn't see why he'd specifically seek out a youth who lived in a broken-down back alley tenement.

"A French acquaintance of mine got a tattoo from you. It was a particularly impressive one of a devil."

Yes, he had tattooed an oni on the shoulder of a foreigner not too long ago.

"Foreigners can be tough to deal with, since they raise hell over the smallest pain. Even though they're so big, too."

"Well, he really liked the finished product you delivered. He was showing off his fascinating devil and recommended that I look you up if I wanted to do a story for my paper."

Since he wasn't able to practice his craft in public, he'd normally be grateful for a customer's word of mouth drumming up some extra business for him. However, it brought him uninvited guests as well. That part was always a headache for Enma.

"I'd like to get a tattoo before I return to my country."

"Don't ruin your skin for this. You're some kid from a rich family in Britain, right? This'll just make your parents cry."

Not the sort of thing he'd expect a younger man to say, let alone a tattooist, Oswald thought with a bitter smile.

"My parents are dead. Nobody will cry over this."

"Then you'll make your god cry," Enma said, his disinterest now obvious.

"Well, now… I don't personally know God, so I couldn't say."

That shocked Natsu. She'd never heard a foreigner say anything like that.

"I suppose you wouldn't," Enma replied. "But wouldn't the Yokohama Lady-Killer make a better story?"

The Yokohama Lady-Killer was the name the local newspapers had given the killer in their headlines. The discovery of a third victim had rocked the city.

"Actually, I was hoping to get some information on that, as well. It was you who discovered the third victim, wasn't it?"

Startled, Enma looked up. This was the first that Natsu had heard of it, and her eyes widened in shock.

"How do you know that?"

"Because I'm a reporter, amateur that I am. As they say in this country, 'serpents travel their fellows' paths.'"

A policeman must have let it slip. Only the cops had known that. Enma pondered what to do.

"I have nothing to say," he finally answered.

As he realized that the object of his interview was growing more cautious, Oswald gave a bemused smile.

"Figured you'd say that. Well then, the tattoo story would be good enough for me, so just hear me out. I want to introduce Japanese culture to the Westerners living in Yokohama."

Enma just shook his head. It was risky to be photographed or even remembered by others. Having a newspaper article written about him was completely out of the question.

Natsu quietly set the tea out in front of them, paying close attention to how this situation was developing.

"I couldn't care less about culture or all that. Find someone else. There are plenty of others who'd be glad to do it."

Oswald kept his eyes fixed on Enma as he spoke. "The singer at Reggie Hall was most grateful to Ura-Enma. She seems to be completely cured."

Enma looked up at the ceiling. Somewhere along the way, he'd picked up the name Ura-Enma, which was used only when he was performing an oni-gome. It was never used in public.

"All I gave her was a regular good luck charm. To give her some comfort."

It had been an American woman who'd been performing at the foreigners' private theater. She'd been hopelessly addicted to cocaine and had come to Enma in tears by way of a mutual acquaintance. He'd placed the oni into her with a tattoo of a teardrop on her palm.

"I'm sure. Faith would allow one to be healed by a sardine's head, as they say. Perhaps that's what did it. But my readers love to hear stories about the mysteries of the Orient, and this would be perfect for that."

In other words, this man didn't believe in it at all. If they were looking to put things like that into print, then it couldn't have been a very reputable newspaper.

"Please, don't take this the wrong way. I think anyone would find a tattooist who has two sides to him to be interesting. By all means, I'd like to interview you. And I think it would be good publicity for your business."

He may have had a gentle face for a Westerner, but he seemed to be fairly stubborn as well. Still, it appeared that he didn't understand exactly what the other face was that Enma was hiding.

"I told you no. Now, if you're not hiring me, get the hell out of here!" Enma thundered at the man before rudely turning his back, his patience now exhausted.

"I understand. I'll leave, then. Actually, I've heard there's another man who'll tattoo a charm onto your dominant hand, but he seems impossible to find. That's why I was so eager to interview you. It's a shame."

Enma's head suddenly jerked around.

"What did you just say…?"

"What's wrong? Oh, is that man an acquaintance of yours, by any chance?"

Enma chewed his nails as he pondered what he'd just heard.

"I'm not sure… What's his name?"

"Sorry, I don't know. It's just a rumor I've heard. He doesn't seem to be in the tattooing business lately, so I can't find him. Apparently, he charges an exorbitant fee to do one. All I know is that he seems to have a crescent moon on his palm."

Enma gasped. There could be no mistake.

"Is there a tattoo of a yasha on his waist, as well?"

Oswald tilted his head, looking unsure.

"I couldn't tell you that, I'm afraid."

"Where is he? Yokohama?"

Oswald shrugged. He clearly didn't know.

"It's just a rumor. I could do a little more checking into it, if you like. But, in return…"

Oswald's eyes lit up as he realized he now had a bargaining chip for getting his story.

"You know, you'd better just leave," Enma replied.

This would just buy him trouble he couldn't afford, he thought. He couldn't ask favors of some foreigner he'd only just met. Any person in the world would see immortality as a wonder to be sought. Who knew the risks of having this guy learn the truth?

Enma crawled back to bed, making it abundantly clear he wasn't interested in listening to anything more he had to say.

"Mr. Houshou?"

Oswald was dismayed by his childish attitude.

"Um…" Unable to just watch anymore, Natsu interrupted. "As you can see, he's very picky about who he works for and doesn't want much publicity. Would you please excuse us now?"

Oswald stood up, acknowledging the inevitable. Natsu bowed as he walked to the door.

"I'm sorry we treated you so rudely after you took the trouble to come here," she said. "However, my brother won't change his mind."

"I'm a stubborn man as well. I'll be back."

Natsu gave a wry smile.

"Then I'd better take this opportunity to apologize to you now. I'm afraid that won't be of much use to you."

Her tone made it clear that any more visits would just be a waste of time.

"Ha ha. I've been posted here in Japan for a year and a half, but you're the first woman I've met who's shown such a charming wit. Well, if you'll excuse me, then. Once the Yokohama Ripper case has been solved, I'll be back to negotiate for an interview. Good day to you."

A year and a half. Natsu was stunned. His Japanese was already that good?

## —4—

There were no signs that the Yokohama Lady-Killer would be caught any time soon.

This sort of case was unprecedented in Japan, and the police were probably as bewildered as anyone. Enma was depressed as he left his home that day. The fact was, Natsu had wanted to get the place thoroughly cleaned up and had thrown him out in the meantime.

"Why don't you take a stroll up the carriage road? The ice cream they sell over there is delicious," she'd said, but he honestly didn't like places thronging with pedestrians.

"I need to go see how my last customer is doing," he'd replied, as though remembering he had to.

"I'll be late. Don't wait up for me."

The real plan was to do some night fishing and not come home till morning. The apartment was a single room only six tatami mats large, so they had to sleep with their futons side by side. To say quarters were close hardly described it, and his roommate had grown up quite splendidly. He couldn't just sleep in there with her as he had when she was a child.

"See you later," she called as he left.

The slight chilliness he heard in her voice was probably just a reflection of his own guilty conscience. This distance between them might be proof that they weren't really family.

While she'd appeared to be his younger sister, the truth was that Enma was old enough to be her father. While they were living together, he'd thought of her as a child, no matter how much time had passed. But now that they lived apart and only occasionally saw each other, he couldn't maintain that illusion. Now that Natsu had grown into an adult woman, he couldn't bear to face her.

*Dammit, I thought I was prepared for this...*

From the day they'd met, he'd never thought of her as a woman. He could never entertain those sorts of feelings for Okazaki's daughter. Even if he couldn't raise her as his own daughter, he'd tried his best to treat her as a younger sister. They'd laughed and cried together, and he'd supported her dream of becoming a doctor. They'd been happy years. At least, he thought so.

If he let the feelings drain away from the relationship he had built, from the memories he had, he felt like he would lose everything.

He let out a long sigh.

Enma headed straight for Chie's home.

The peony he'd tattooed on her back should be settled in by now. Tattooing wasn't something you should do in the summertime; the sweat and heat made it more likely to fester. It was even more likely on something as large as the one he'd done. He'd tried to talk Chie's master out of it, but he hadn't listened. If Enma refused to go through with it, her master would just hire another tattooist, so Chie had asked him to see it through. He'd agreed to do it only at night, since it would be a little cooler.

A flower that bloomed on the beautiful skin of a concubine, all to make her an exhibit for foreigners. Apparently, that was the artistic value that this country's tattooing rated. To hell with that. Tattooing should only be the secret hobby of the one who got them.

The picture he was engraving into Chie's back was not horimono. It was irezumi. Chie herself might deny it, but it was true.

As he passed by the place where he'd found the body, Enma crouched down and clasped his hands together.

He didn't know if there was a God or a Buddha in this world, but he could be sure that there was no shortage of murder in it. He too had been a killer once, but he couldn't comprehend what would drive someone to kill a defenseless woman simply for pleasure.

He found Chie watering flowers in front of her house. The water droplets catching the light of the setting sun as they scattered from the dipper made for a very refreshing sight.

"Oh, if it isn't you, Enma."

Since every meeting they'd had consisted of him looking down at her back in a dimly lit room, this was the first time he'd ever seen Chie standing up in the light of the sun.

What he saw was neither a whore nor a concubine, but simply a woman. It pained him to think that removing one piece of clothing would reveal the gaudy tattoo she'd been burdened with.

"Your back doesn't hurt, does it?"

"Not at all, thanks to your skill."

"I came to see how it's turning out."

Chie smiled happily.

"Thank you, but the streets are dangerous these days, and you should go home before it gets dark. You shouldn't be wandering around outside."

Even now, Chie insisted on treating him like a child.

"I don't think some pervert who gets his jollies out of killing women would have the courage to attack a man."

"But the last killing happened so nearby… Oh, it's awful. How could anyone do something like that? What trouble does a streetwalker cause anyone? If you don't like them, you can just ignore them, and that's that. If you think they're dirty, then either keep away from them or ask them to keep away from you!"

Chie bit her lip. She didn't seem to know that it had been Enma who'd found the third victim. Of course, there was no need to tell her that.

"Come in. You can take a look."

Enma followed after her. The pale nape of her neck seemed even more dazzling than usual.

Leaving the windows open, Chie opened her *kosode* and exposed her back. Her white skin was in full, horrid bloom. Colored by the light of the setting sun, it looked even more unearthly. There seemed to be no sign of festering. The colors had settled in, and the skin was now used to them.

"It's all right. Even if your master comes." Meaning, she could sleep with him now. That was still Chie's job, after all.

"Dear me, I don't know if your skill was a good thing or a bad thing in this case." Her laugh was tinged with bitterness as Chie covered herself again. "I wanted to have a little more time off."

"Sorry about that."

Chie's eyes widened as Enma apologized, like she found it funny. Then her eyes narrowed, as though it was too heartbreaking to stand.

"Really," she murmured.

Chie threw her arms around his neck and pressed her lips to his.

This wasn't love.

She was probably just looking for someone, anyone, before once again submitting to the disgusting old man's touch. And Enma was a suitable man who just happened to be in front of her at that moment. A young, lonely, attractive tattooist.

Accepting all of that, Enma embraced Chie.

The sun was high in the sky by the time Enma set out to return home the next day.

He'd passed a long, gentle night with Chie. It had felt so cozy and comfortable that it nearly frightened him. But they would never meet again, not as long as that peony bloomed so brightly on Chie's back. All he could do was pray that the flower would become her guardian angel.

Despite this unexpected development, he'd told Natsu that he'd be home late, so he had no worries about that. He gave his clothes a cautious sniff. Just to be safe, he'd let them air out a little before he went home.

Several cops were wandering around the infamous clump of bushes. They were back to reexamine the scene of the crime, and from the looks of things, they'd reached an impasse.

One man among them wasn't in uniform. Heavy set and dressed in Western finery, it was Nobumasa Muta. He didn't seem to be investigating anything in particular, but he didn't appear to be directing operations, either.

Noticing Enma, he waved him over.

"Coming home from work, or from a woman?"

There was no note of sarcasm in his voice.

"Never mind that, what are you doing here? Is the superintendent making an inspection?"

"I took a vacation, but I'm curious about this case."

It probably would have been more accurate to say he had taken a vacation *because* he was curious about this case. Most likely, he was using it as a fig leaf to avoid the appearance of invading another department's jurisdiction.

"Aren't there any clues?"

"No witnesses, no evidence, no way forward."

Nobumasa's lips were bent in frustration. His sense of justice as a police superintendent made the thought of a criminal wandering free unbearable to him. As calm as he appeared, he was a man of fiery passions.

"Aren't you looking for a guy in Western clothes?"

"What do you mean?"

Enma scratched under his ear.

"Because there was a mark on her, right here. Something round… I think it was a sleeve button."

"News to me. That wasn't in the report."

As Nobumasa glared, Enma shrugged his shoulders.

"Maybe it had faded by the time the police came to investigate. It was dark and I couldn't see very well, but I thought it felt like the mark of a shirt button when I touched it."

He was the only one who suspected this. He hadn't mentioned any marks on the back of her neck because he honestly hadn't remembered it until now.

"Perhaps the murderer grabbed her from behind and throttled her…"

Even in Yokohama, not many men wore Western clothes. Still, if you got every foreigner in the city into one place, you'd have a fair number of them. That wasn't even getting into how much trouble it would cause if the murderer was a foreigner.

"With three prostitutes killed so far, there's been a big drop in their trade lately. The police here are hoping that it may wipe out the business completely, but I doubt that."

"Maybe they're not in any hurry to arrest this guy."

Nobumasa glared sharply at him. He could tell it was just a passing burst of anger, but something had clearly struck a nerve.

"That's not true. What's wrong with you? You angry about something?"

"I woke up on the wrong side of the bed. I'd better just head home."

The dead woman had been crying. The moon had been reflected in her remaining eye, and her eyelashes and face had still been wet. He didn't care who it was; nobody deserved to die like that.

"You'd better watch what you say in front of other people. You still look like a kid who's barely twenty."

Some of the investigating officers who'd heard a snatch of their conversation were staring at him in shock. Being seen as some good-for-nothing punk trying to pick a fight with the nobleman police superintendent would be trouble.

"If you'll excuse me, Mr. Superintendent, sir. And from the bottom of my heart, I hope you solve this case soon."

Speaking with excessive politeness and bowing his head deeply, Enma beat a retreat from the scene.

Nobumasa was helping him quite a lot. Natsu had been accepted to medical school at the behest of the Muta family. No matter how genuine her love of learning was, just being a woman would have been enough to disqualify her. The younger sister of a tattooist would never have been accepted otherwise.

Had Nobumasa not recommended her, it all would have remained an unattainable dream. There'd be no way that she could finish without their continuing to rely on him.

And that, for him, was pathetic.

Even now, when he'd been totally honest in speaking his mind, he had no sense of them being intimate. The last thing he'd ever wanted to become was some rare specimen for Nobumasa to keep in his collection.

As he expected, Natsu wasn't in a good mood when he returned home. Her intuition was sharp enough to know when she was being avoided.

"I'll go back to Tokyo tomorrow."

Enma looked visibly relieved.

"That's for the best."

It'd be better if she left this dangerous city. His mind would be much more at ease if she was in Tokyo now than Yokohama. He didn't intend to be unkind, but Natsu's eyes trembled as though he'd physically struck her.

"You can read newspapers in English? That's amazing," he said. Trying to change the subject, Enma picked up a newspaper lying on the low dining table.

"It's the paper that British reporter we met writes for. I picked up one to study. I'm more comfortable reading a foreign language than speaking it, and it's full of details about the murders."

He recalled the bespectacled sandy-haired man with the affable smile.

"City of Terror… Murder… Yokohama Ripper, huh?"

"Oh, you can read it?"

"A little. When you get foreigners as customers, you can't help but learn some. Even when they come to Japan, they never bother to learn how to speak Japanese."

Natsu snorted with laughter without thinking.

"But Oswald spoke very fluent Japanese, I thought."

Ah, that was why she had such a good opinion of the man. It was also probably what had interested her in getting the newspaper.

"All the more reason not to trust him."

"You can be so difficult sometimes!"

Did he really need to be so prejudiced? Natsu stood up, shocked at his reaction.

"Don't wander off by yourself. Be back here before it gets dark."

"You're the one who should be worrying, big brother. Were you ever planning to tell me that you were the one who found that dead woman's remains?"

Natsu was so upset about not being told anything that she was actually letting her irritation show in her speech. Enma rubbed his hands through his bristly hair as he thought of something to say.

"Well… I didn't think there was any need to scare you."

"I'm a medical student. It takes a lot to scare me." She seemed angry, practically lunging at him.

"You should be a little scared," Enma retorted. "Because, unless I'm mistaken, there's a murderer stalking this city!" The thing that worried him was that Natsu's natural courage would override her sense of danger.

"On the off-chance anything happens, regardless of how embarrassing it might be, I'll scream my head off. I'll scream for help in my shrillest voice. While I'm at it, I'll scream where I am and a description of the criminal, too."

Natsu shot Enma a look that told him she was serious.

"Relax. I'm just going outside for some fresh air. Somebody in here smells like face powder."

Enma hurriedly sniffed his sleeve.

"I knew it," Natsu sighed, then went outside.

She got him. Enma grabbed his collar and, opening his kimono to get the breeze on his chest, he lay down. There was no smell of powder, but he thought there might have been the faint scent of camellia oil.

As night fell, Natsu began studying by the light of a paper lantern.

She spread the incomprehensible book out in front of her and glared at it with a perplexed look on her face. German, it seemed to her, was a language very similar to muttering. Enma had gone outside to sit on the barrel so as not to disturb her.

The air resounded with the noisy chirps of insects. He could hear the boastful sounds of a cricket right at his feet.

"Oh? What's with you? There's a terrible murderer wandering Yokohama. You shouldn't be out at this hour."

The lady who lived across the way had called out to Enma from her house. She was wearily dumping out some water from a bucket. The murderer seemed to be the only topic of discussion in Yokohama these days.

"You should be careful too, Masa. That nightgown of yours leaves nothing to the imagination."

Her enormous, melon-like breasts were half hanging out of the front of her nightgown, but she didn't seem to care.

"You're a good man. My husband hardly even thinks of me as a woman anymore. Calls me an old hag. What's wrong with looking my age? Anyway, ol' baldy's hardly one to talk!" Masa said with a hearty laugh.

"Yeah, looking your age is the best," Enma whispered earnestly. Each and every one of Masa's wrinkles seemed to shine in the darkness. Hell, she and Enma were probably the same age.

"Definitely. You should set him straight. I think he'll be coming home soon."

Masa's husband had apparently gone out to drink. Since all of the victims had been women, none of the men around there were particularly scared of the killer. Some others were just so annoyed at being scared all the time that they walked around as an act of defiance.

A man with the butt of his kimono tucked up came jogging up towards them. It was Masa's husband Suekichi. His face was red and twisted with the effort, his forehead bald.

"What's yer problem? Wipe that smirk off yer face!"

Looking completely disgusted, Suekichi grabbed his smiling wife's arm, spittle flying from his mouth as he shouted at her.

"What the hell are you thinking, walking out of the house dressed like that?! Another woman's been killed! The Yokohama Lady-Killer's struck again!"

Enma's eyes widened.

"What? Where?!"

"Oh, you're the tattoo guy. It was some concubine in a home near the meadow where the third girl was found. I don't know the details, but the whole town's in an uproar."

The row houses were cheap and flimsy, and the sound carried into them. Natsu, looking worried, appeared at the door.

"Big brother, please come inside."

She was probably going to try warning him not to do what he was about to do. It would have been a waste of time.

"Natsu, under no circumstances are you to leave that house!"

With those words, his face twisted in anger, Enma tore off into the night.

*No…*

His blood was boiling. Now free of any of Natsu's restraint, he ran through the nighttime streets.

It can't be her, he kept telling himself. Chie wasn't a prostitute. She wouldn't be a target. But even as he tried to convince himself, he could feel an unpleasant trickle of sweat pouring down his back.

He was getting close to the commotion. There would probably be a crowd of onlookers around the body. His legs were a tangle. His lungs, at their limit, seemed to beg him to slow down, but he had no thought of rest. He couldn't stop his legs until he could see that Chie was all right.

The woman had fallen face down in the entryway of the house.

Her face, bleached in the moonlight, had been brutally hacked up, its owner no longer identifiable. But one glance was enough for Enma to know who it was. A white parasol, looking so incongruous in this place, was still open on the ground, swaying in the breeze.

"Damn it…"

Her back had been left untouched, as though specifically for Enma to see. A peony bloomed bewitchingly, seeming to float upon the surface of her pale skin.

It was the flower which he had engraved into her. The chain binding this unfortunate woman.

He seemed to be losing his mind. His throat ached. He couldn't hear the uproar around him. All he could do was stare silently down at the cold, fallen body of the woman.

She'd been so sweet. A warm, passionate, but sad woman. The warmth of her arms still seemed to cling to him. He couldn't comprehend how she was now a bloody corpse lying at his feet.

Other than the flower on her back, she'd had no value. The manner in which she'd been killed seemed to say that.

He couldn't even embrace her, since doing so might have torn her head from her body. Enma merely touched her pale white fingertips with his trembling hands.

*Who did this to you...?*

Perhaps the dead offered no answers because finding them was the task of those who were left behind.

At last, the police came running and began kicking the rubberneckers back from the area. Enma, his legs unsteady, left the scene.

He was left with one inescapable thought... The killer somehow knew him.

## —5—

Now that four women were dead, they couldn't sell the newspapers fast enough.

This time the victim wasn't a streetwalker, but a woman who'd been killed practically in her own home. Now the people of Yokohama were really nervous. Thanks to that, the main street had been practically deserted for the past few days.

Seemingly unconcerned by the lack of customers, Onitsuki and Heath passed the time leisurely drinking coffee and perusing the newspaper in front of the store.

"This fellow's looking more and more like Jack the Ripper," Heath muttered seriously.

"Ah, you mean that lady-killer in London?"

Having read the English-language newspapers aimed at foreigners living there, Onitsuki was familiar with the case as well. It had caused quite a stir not only in Great Britain but across all of Europe as well.

"Yes, the technique this guy's using is very similar. The criminal in London also goaded the police there, though," Heath continued, fanning himself with a paper fan.

"Yeah. Scotland Yard's honor was nearly destroyed because he made the police look like fools. This criminal still hasn't gone that far."

According to the papers, only the tattoo on her back had been left untouched. Had the killer done it to provoke the tattooist, or had he spared it simply because he'd liked it? In any case, the culprit seemed to have something to say to the man who'd inked her, not the police.

"There's a funny rumor going around that the cops knew who'd been doing it, but wouldn't arrest him because of some complicated circumstances."

"Circumstances?" Heath replied, lowering his voice.

"The Queen has a great number of children. Apparently there was a prince among them who pulled out all the stops when it came to bad behavior," Onitsuki continued with a smile that was pregnant with significance.

"You're saying the prince was the murderer?"

"It's just an irresponsible rumor dreamed up by the public at large. Interesting, isn't it?"

Interesting or not, Onitsuki thought that it made a certain amount of sense.

"If you're interested in Jack, I have an acquaintance I should introduce you to. He's a correspondent for the *London Weekly* who knows all about the royal family."

He really wasn't that interested in the London killer, but asked for the reporter's name, anyway.

"Watch the store for me."

Tying his long hair at the nape of his neck, Onitsuki left his redheaded successor in charge as he went out.

While they said that the world was basically unfair, at least the sun over their heads beat down on everyone equally. It was hot today.

The fourth woman had been killed on the doorstep of her home. That was a big difference from the previous three murders. With Yokohama on alert, it was now difficult for criminals to find victims walking on the road to prey on. Even the prostitutes had cut down on their roadside business of late. That, the police reasoned, had caused the killer to change his tactics.

He walked straight along the carriageway, emerging onto a wide lane next to a meadow. Watching the foreign boats coming and going, he headed for the home of Chie Matsui, the latest victim. He'd heard she was the concubine of the owner of the business next door to him, a man who'd made his fortune running a brickworks.

They might be holding the funeral now, but it wouldn't be considered impolite to pass by while out for a stroll. As he neared the house where the murder had taken place after nearly an hour's walk, he heard some sort of argument going on inside.

"What?! You just put her in a pauper's grave without even holding a funeral?!"

It was the voice of a young man, and he sounded angry.

"I don't owe anything more to a dead concubine! It's not like she ever bore me any children. Agh!"

A man who looked to be about sixty years old came flying out in front of Onitsuki.

"Wh-What's the big idea?!"

The young man had probably hit him. The old man's nose was bleeding, and his knees shook in terror.

"Cut it out! C'mon, calm down!"

The younger man now emerged as well, grabbing the man dressed in Western clothes from behind and putting him into a Full Nelson.

"Lemme go! You're killing me!"

It wasn't rage that had transformed the younger man's face. It was a look of absolute, inconsolable grief from one whose heart had been broken. It was an expression Onitsuki found impossible to ignore.

"You're just a tattooist! I'll sue! You see, Mr. Superintendent? This guy's a violent nut case!"

The Western-dressed man he identified as the police superintendent gave a hint of a smile as he shook his head.

"Is he? All I saw was you slip and fall."

"What? Goddammit, you two are in cahoots, aren't you? Hey, you over there! You saw what happened, right? This kid here knocked me down!"

Onitsuki's eyes widened. This was an odd turn of events, considering he'd just intended to pass by.

"Old man, you need to watch your step, or you'll trip again," he said with a gracious smile. The beaten man's face was now red with anger. But, his clothes now spattered with mud and nose still bleeding, he saw that he was at a disadvantage here. He quieted down and, holding his nose, retreated back into his house.

"Thank you for your cooperation," the superintendent said to him. Onitsuki gave a quick nod and then continued on his way as if nothing had happened.

*That was the tattooist...*

He seemed awfully young.

And he wore a fingerless glove on one of his hands.

That interested him. Onitsuki turned around and headed back towards the house he'd just passed. He then secreted himself behind a hedge so that they wouldn't notice him.

"Truly, the judgment of Lord Enma is severe."

That was the voice of the superintendent. Teasing the other man by calling him Lord Enma meant that his companion must be Enma Houshou, Natsu's older brother.

Well, well, this was getting better by the minute.

"Knock it off..."

"Oh, don't be angry. Even if he'd given her a funeral, that guy wouldn't have held a memorial service for her."

"If you want to honor her memory, then catch the guy who did this. The cops act like they're so great, but this is the best they can do?" The tattooist still seemed to be pretty pissed off.

"Well then, do you have an opinion on why your tattoo was the only part of her that was left untouched?"

"They keep asking me that like they think I did it and didn't want to harm my own work. If it wasn't for you, they'd be treating me like a criminal again. Yet another thing I owe the great Superintendent Muta."

"The girl didn't know about you, did she?"

"I told you, no, she didn't. Besides, why would I suddenly start killing people? I never even met the other three women. You think Chie was murdered because of me?"

He couldn't take it. Enma's voice was so full of bitterness. A prickling pain stabbed at his heart. What a fine voice he had.

"You don't look so good. Have you not slept since it happened?"

"Like I'd be able to sleep after that?"

"Did you fall for her?"

"It wasn't like that. It was more like us licking each other's wounds..."

He'd muttered that last bit, sounding strained, then had lapsed into silence. A steam whistle, maybe from some foreign ship leaving the port, echoed in the distance.

"He'd apparently shown the tattoo on her back to some foreigners that day."

There was hesitation in the superintendent's voice. Perhaps he paused to wonder if it was a good idea to tell Enma this.

"That son of a bitch…"

That would no doubt be in reference to the elderly man that he'd knocked down before.

"They all complimented you on your skill as a tattooist."

"Tell me their names, and don't leave a single one out."

There was a bloodthirsty menace in the tattooist's voice now.

"To do that, I'll have to bribe the cops here even more…" the superintendent complained.

*Interesting guy, this one.*

Onitsuki thought about the young tattooist as he strolled along.

Was he young or just passionate? And yet he could see a sort of resigned air in him, as well.

Natsu definitely had a good head on her shoulders. Enma and Yasha. She could detect the same scent upon them both.

On the way back, he sat down under a tree and lit a pipe. He smoked a bit as he looked out to sea. He had succeeded in meeting the tattooist. Now there was one other man he wished to meet that day.

Following the road along the coast, he headed for the neighborhood lined with the foreigners' offices.

Engraved upon the iron nameplate of a Western-style house made of brick were the words "*London Weekly* - Yokohama Branch."

The windows and door were thrown wide open, perhaps owing to the heat. Inside, a voice was shouting in English, "Another Yokohama Ripper interview, Oswald? Aren't you carrying that story a little far at this point?"

"Is there a better story anywhere out there for me?"

"Granted, it's all we've got at the moment. And I'll admit, your Ripper articles are stirring up the readers, too."

That was the gist of the conversation he could make out. It was much easier to follow than Heath's English, with its strong Chicago accent.

"By the way, you know a lot about Jack the Ripper, don't you? Tell me what sort of profile you've worked out on the criminal in this case."

"Right, yes. Somewhere in his twenties or thirties. I think he may also be a loner and an intellectual, possessing a unique aesthetic sense."

Onitsuki tilted his head. Wasn't it a little unscrupulous for a newspaper reporter to make up such a flattering image of a criminal? There was no aesthetic sense in murder, Onitsuki thought to himself as he studied his reflection cast in the window panels of the building he faced.

This murderer was a real monster. His killing methods were in extremely bad taste, but a killer as nasty as he might have what it takes to kill an immortal man.

He was thinking that as he opened the door to the building.

The sun was beginning to sink into the west. He may have overdone it a bit with the walking today.

When he dragged his exhausted body back to the store, Heath was looking glum. He was fiddling with a red ball between his fingers as he appeared to be lost in thought.

"What's that?"

"Oh, I found it while I was cleaning up. I wonder what it is."

Onitsuki picked it up, then nodded in recognition. "It's a jewel off of an ornamental hairpin. Possibly coral. It's nice."

A customer had probably dropped it. But female customers to a foreign bookshop were rare. The most recent one had been Natsu Hisaka. Now that he thought about it, there had been a hairpin in her neatly arranged coif.

"Maybe I should go over to her place later and give it back."

If he just went further back behind the Densuke row houses to the ones near the sewer trench and then asked around, it shouldn't be that hard to find her.

"You really have a soft spot for the ladies, don't you?"

"What's got you in such a bad mood? Wisdom teeth bothering you?"

Heath shook his head weakly. "It's not that. I was just feeling depressed right now because I was thinking how I'm like an accomplice of the Yokohama Lady-Killer."

Onitsuki's eyes widened in shock. "That's the most ridi—"

"I was invited to go see a tattoo before. A woman with a huge flower blooming on her back. It was the lady that was killed."

Onitsuki tilted his head in thought as he regarded his friend scratching his unruly red hair. Lots of foreigners went to view tattoos. He'd even heard of occasions where "salons" for them would be held.

"And how does that make you an accomplice?"

"She...just looked so unhappy, like she really didn't want to show her skin in public. But it looked like she didn't fight back. It makes my heart ache just thinking about it."

How very like Heath, Onitsuki thought in admiration. He might look like a red devil, but in this respect, he was quite sensitive.

"If she was that unhappy, maybe she preferred to be dead. It's nothing you should bother yourself over."

"There comes a time in everyone's life when they think they want to die. That doesn't mean anyone has the right to make that happen. God would never forgive such presumption."

As Heath grew more excited as he talked, Onitsuki offered him some coffee to calm him down.

*Presumption?*

Now that he mentioned it, Onitsuki had a feeling he was right.

## —6—

Enma ran.

He'd nearly narrowed the suspects down to one person. But for now, it was merely a guess. In any case, he needed to get Natsu out of Yokohama. She was worried about how depressed he'd been of late, and so had delayed her return to Tokyo.

Today, at last, Nobumasa had shown him a list of the men who'd participated in a "tattoo salon." The moment he'd found that name, he'd felt every hair on his body stand up.

He still hadn't gotten caught up in anything. He wasn't directly connected to it. But that name was causing alarm bells of suspicion to ring wildly in Enma's head.

He couldn't shake that feeling that he was running headlong into trouble. When he got to the front of his row house, there was Masa to accost him, as usual.

"What's wrong? What's got you in such a rush?" she asked.

She seemed concerned, but there was no time for this. Enma opened the door to his home without answering.

The room was empty. Natsu's luggage was still there, meaning that she still hadn't returned to Tokyo.

"If you're looking for Natsu, she went out."

He turned his head back towards Masa's voice.

"Where to?"

"That I couldn't tell you, but she was with a foreigner. It may have been that newspaper man who came here before..."

"Oswald!"

His blood froze. He'd sweet-talked Natsu into going with him. Chie hadn't been enough for him; now he was after Natsu, as well. It was the situation he feared the most.

"I knew that guy was bad news. Go look for her. I'll go tell Master Muta about it."

Enma broke into a run without another word to Masa. However she knew about Nobumasa and where he lived hardly mattered now.

Be that as it may, he headed for the district which was lined with the foreigners' offices. The sight of a man tearing through the city in a dead run must have drawn some odd looks. His breast heaving, almost ready to burst from anxiety, he drove himself to the limit.

Even if he had to endure the flames of hell a hundred times over, he could not allow Natsu to die. It had nothing to do with the promise he'd made to Okazaki. To Enma, Natsu had become someone irreplaceable in his life. If she died, he had no doubt that it would drive him to madness.

Spotting a building with a "*London Weekly*" nameplate on it, he burst in, demanding to know where Oswald was. He only succeeded in scaring the young, clueless clerk inside out of his wits. No matter. It was clear that Oswald wasn't there.

After half-threatening physical harm to the poor kid in the office and learning both Oswald's home address and about an old warehouse down by the harbor that the newspaper rented out, Enma resumed his mad dash through the city. The kid would most likely go and report this to the police. Well, that would save him the trouble. He didn't care if the cops chased him through Yokohama. The authorities all bent over backwards for the foreigners in the city, and they'd come running to protect Oswald from some suspicious character.

His home or the warehouse? Enma figured a guy like that wasn't the type to dirty his own castle. Without any hesitation, he headed for the harbor. Rows of identical brick warehouses stood next to each other. It was lunchtime, so not a soul was around.

His legs were starting to cramp up from all the running, but Enma didn't stop. He wouldn't stop until he'd found Natsu. He checked nameplates in a variety of languages and peered into windows as he checked the warehouses one by one.

"There!"

But the warehouse had a huge padlock hanging outside on the door. He doubted that anyone was inside. Even when he peered through a small window, all he saw were some huge barrels. Had he made a mistake? If Oswald was at his home, it'd take him nearly an hour to run there. Just as he was about to sink into despair, Enma's eye fell upon a pretty-colored gem.

*That's…!*

In front of a black brick warehouse set further back lay the decoration off of an ornate hairpin. He remembered that Natsu owned one that same color. And there was no padlock on that door, either.

Enma immediately threw himself at the heavy door and heaved it open.

"I'm surprised. You got here even sooner than I expected."

There in the dark room were Oswald and Natsu. The killer held a knife in his hand, while at his feet lay Natsu, her mouth gagged, arms and legs bound.

"Natsu!"

Before he could rush over to her, Oswald stepped in his way. He pinched the knife's hasp between two fingers of his right hand, pointing its blade downwards. Right beneath it was Natsu's breast.

"You ready to see if jumping at me will make me drop the knife?"

Natsu gazed at Enma, her eyes as firm as ever, but he could see blood dripping from her forehead and lips. The sleeves of her *kosode* had been torn off. It was clear this man showed no mercy at all to any woman.

"The Yokohama Lady-Killer, I presume."

"I don't care for that nickname. Could you call me the Yokohama Ripper, instead?"

That sealed it. He felt his blood rise in rage.

"Shut up, asshole."

There was no way he could ever forgive this man for hurting Natsu.

"It's so bright. Lovely weather, isn't it?" Oswald's eyes narrowed as he looked at the sky and sea visible through the open door. "The air in London is awful. There are advantages and disadvantages to industrialization."

"And now it's exporting murderers?"

A smile came to Oswald's thin lips, as though he found Enma's remark amusing. "Will you just shut the door, please? I have a lamp already lit, as you can see."

On a wooden box was placed a stylish lamp. But shutting the door would close off his one avenue of escape. Enma hesitated.

"Hurry up!"

Oswald pushed down on Natsu's abdomen with the sole of his shoe. She gasped behind the gag in her mouth.

"Stop it…"

He shut the door with both hands. The room immediately dimmed, with only one source of light now.

"I figured you'd find the paper's warehouse quickly enough, but you found this vacant one so readily."

"So, you reveal your true nature now."

Even though he was smiling, he scarcely seemed human. "Everybody has more than one side to them. The face of the mild-mannered reporter is also my true nature." Still clutching the knife, Oswald lifted it up in front of his face. "Nice knife, isn't it? It cuts very well."

The blade shone silver above the ornately carved grip.

"Is that what you used to kill Chie?"

"Yes. I've killed three women with it, including yours."

Enma started. "*Three* women?"

Hadn't there been four victims?

"I don't know who killed the first whore. But that was what inspired me…"

Why would he be lying now? But, if he wasn't, that meant there was another murderer out there. An old anxiety began to rise within him.

Oswald stared at his eyes reflected in the blade. "It's hard to quit doing this once you've started."

"Is it possible… Are you the lady-killer from London, too?"

Oswald smiled inscrutably. "My father wondered that very thing about me. And thus I was banished to this oriental Eden."

This guy was a hardcore monster. Enma's breathing became ragged. "So, your father was an awful person, too, I see."

"I heard he suddenly passed away in the spring."

Hadn't he thought to accompany his murderous son? Did he think he could just send him to another country till the heat of the crimes had died down? That was ridiculous!

"I want so badly to return to my country to claim my share of his fortune. The food here just doesn't suit me."

He looked down at Natsu. She looked nervous, but didn't lose her cool.

"Your little sister looks worried. When I told her that you'd been injured and were being treated at my office, she came at once. The young lady certainly seems to care about her big brother, doesn't she?"

That would have been about the only thing he could say to get her to rush out with him. She wouldn't have been worried about the injury itself, but people couldn't be allowed to see his wounds healing instantly. He could see her saying "I'm sorry" with just the look in her eyes. No, he was the one who needed to apologize here. Enma shook his head.

"Your sister didn't seem to understand her position here when she got angry and started lecturing me. She's stubborn, so I punished her a bit."

Natsu must have been holding back when she did that. If it had been a full-on argument, Enma doubted that this man would have emerged in such high spirits. At any rate, this man certainly did like to talk. It was almost like he was telling Enma everything so that he could take credit for his glorious crimes.

Should he stall for time?

*Nobumasa…*

Should he expect him to help? Would he gallantly appear as he always did, in that way which so irritated Enma?

It was like a steam bath in the warehouse. Wiping his sweat away, he began inching closer to the killer.

"So why provoke me like this? Is it because I refused to let you interview me?"

Oswald chuckled. "You were the one who found that woman's body in the bushes. I was actually nearby when you did. I'd dropped my pocket watch and returned to the scene to retrieve it. I thought that you might have picked it up, so I used the interview as an excuse to sound you out about it. I'd done a story on tattooing before, so I knew a little about you."

Enma's face stiffened.

"You do have my watch, don't you? What's your game, not turning it into the police? But I'll wager you thought about doing it."

"I have no idea what you're talking about."

Had he approached him because he'd thought Enma was going to blackmail him?

"You must have guessed that the criminal was a foreigner because you picked up that pocket watch. It was given to my father by Her Majesty the Queen. It's not something any Japanese would own."

Telling him that he didn't have the watch would just be a waste of time. Even if he had it, handing it over to him here would have sealed both his and Natsu's fate.

"No, I had a suspicion that the killer was a foreign man dressed in Western clothing because there was a mark shaped like a button on the corpse's neck. Men in this country didn't use to really have much scorn for women who engage in prostitution. I thought it seemed strange that they'd turn so formal since Meiji took over, so I figured that anyone who so obviously despised the women who were being killed must have been a foreigner. I also recalled that there'd been a similar rash of lady-killings in London. I wasn't certain that it had to be a foreigner doing it. It was more a matter of likelihood. I have no idea what happened to your damn watch."

Oswald nodded in understanding. "Homosexuality, mixed bathing. This country certainly has no morals as far as sex is concerned."

"It's called being tolerant!" Enma shouted, then froze. "You son of a bitch. Did you kill Chie just to threaten me?"

Oswald nodded. "A message, so to speak. I wanted to convey to you that I wouldn't submit to blackmail if you had the watch. Trying to humiliate a proud member of the British aristocracy would carry a severe penalty. Of course, there was also the pure desire to kill on my part. She wanted to die so badly, I could practically smell it on her."

Enma's fist trembled as he thought of Chie's pathetic mangled corpse. "How dare you… Chie was…"

Oswald shrugged his shoulders, seemingly unable to understand Enma's rage. "Why are you so upset? Whores aren't people. They're nothing but miserable playthings."

Enma's eyes widened in horror.

"Your customer was formerly a whore. Being a man's concubine is no different. But that flower you tattooed into her… That was a true work of art. That was the only thing on her I couldn't bring myself to cut."

No, Enma thought. His burdening her with that worthless tattoo had been a far worse crime.

"Do you think anyone becomes a streetwalker by choice?!"

Oswald's brow furrowed slightly, displeasure showing on his face. "That doesn't matter to me. All I care about is my desire to kill. It's as natural to me as breathing is to you. And if these women are in such unfortunate situations, aren't I showing them compassion by ending their suffering?"

"You arrogant—"

A gunshot rang out. At the same time, Enma collapsed, his face contorted in pain. A vast gush of blood was now pouring from his thigh.

"If you thought I was armed only with a knife, you're sadly mistaken. Naturally, I can kill men as well."

Oswald leveled a pistol at the fallen Enma.

"I do so hate the noise they make. It's such an unrefined weapon. But no British gentleman would ever let a commoner like you insult him in such a manner. You should know when to hold your tongue."

He pressed his heel down as hard as he could on Enma's left hand. There was the crunch of splintering bone, and Enma couldn't help but scream in agony.

Natsu struggled desperately, as though trying to rescue him. But the ropes were tied too tightly, and she couldn't break free.

"Your sister's very brave. If she's so eager to not see her big brother die, I can just kill her first."

Enma lifted his face. He was dizzy, most likely from losing so much blood at once, as he dragged himself over to Natsu and threw himself over her body to shield it.

"I won't let a monster like you..."

He had no idea how he would protect her. This man wasn't going to just stand there doing nothing while his wounds closed. Behind her gag, Natsu was begging him to stop. She shook her head, practically in tears. Funny, the thoughts that crossed your mind in these situations. He suddenly realized he'd never seen her face from this close before.

He whispered to her in a barely audible voice.

"He... He's coming... I know he is... Just hang on."

He wanted to tell her not to lose hope. She knew he was talking about Nobumasa. Natsu answered with a barely perceptible nod. If help was nearby, they would have heard the gunshot.

"I won't...let him...kill you..."

He loved her. He loved her so much. He drew close and hugged her head close to his. He now clearly realized the feelings he'd hidden so deeply inside.

"The great affection of a brother for his sister. Yes, yes, I understand. Since you're willing to go that far, I'll kill you first."

Oswald squatted down. He placed the knife blade on the back of Enma's kimono and cut a neat line through the cloth. A line of blood oozed out.

"You'll be much more satisfying to kill than your stouthearted sister. You're like one of those whores. Your eyes have that disgusting look in them, like you want to die."

Enma regretted that they appeared that way.

*Natsu...*

He wished they could have talked longer. He wanted to tell her to be careful not be taken in by bad men, that studying was all well and good, but to take care of herself and become a fine doctor... Anything at all. But, in the end, he said nothing.

Oswald was shouting something in English. He seemed drunk on his own deeds, talking faster and faster.

He thrust the knife deeply into his side, near his shoulder blade.

Enma grunted in pain. He doubled over in agony as he wondered if the blade had pierced his lung. There was a sound inside his chest like blood being regurgitated. His moaning ceased.

That moment sharpened his senses. As Oswald ceased his gloating to silently indulge himself in his victim's death, Enma vaguely heard the sound of footsteps. Somebody was running outside of the warehouse.

It's Nobumasa, he thought. It was more hope than certainty speaking, but it was all he had to wager at that point.

The knife pierced his back over and over. Oswald was probably missing the heart with each thrust in order to prolong his enjoyment.

As Enma still held Natsu protectively, he tried to untie the ropes that bound her. But the knot was just too hard, and in his state, it was too much for him. Feeling as though he was praying, he worked the gag loose.

"Scream..." he whispered to Natsu with his failing breath.

Enma felt her tremble beneath him as she took a deep breath. Then she let loose with all she had.

"Lord Muta! Anybody! We're in the black warehouse! Hurry! He's killing my brother! Help us!"

The building trembled. Her scream had been terrific. It must have penetrated through even the warehouse's thick brick walls.

"You bitch...!" Oswald hastily clamped his hand over her mouth, brandishing the knife.

Suddenly, light flooded the warehouse as the door was thrown open.

"They're here!" It was Nobumasa's voice.

With the sudden appearance of the enemy, Oswald let loose a torrent of profanity in English. As he raised his gun at Nobumasa, Enma kicked his hand with the last of his strength.

The last thing Enma saw was Nobumasa disabling his assailant with a shoulder throw. Then a wave of agonizing pain swept him into unconsciousness.

## —7—

There was a word in Choushuu dialect: *sennai*.

It meant "unavoidable." He'd completely forgotten it till now.

The pain had subsided and his wounds closed of their own accord, but Enma did not get up.

He stared dully at the ceiling of the row house, then grew tired of that and switched to staring at his right hand. There was still a scar, but no longer any pain. He suddenly felt a rough tongue licking his hand. It seemed even his cat Kuro had been worried about him.

"How could I have trusted a man like that?" Natsu muttered, her eyes clouded.

"Hey... That was a hell of a scream. You might have the makings of an opera prima donna."

Even with danger literally pressing at her, she'd screamed without any concern for appearances and had even shouted where they were, just as he'd reminded her to do.

"In the end...I was saved...by you."

There was a painful-looking gash on her forehead. He prayed that it wouldn't leave a scar. "You found me, big brother. And you protected me."

Of course he had. Enma laughed. "If you disappear, I'd search the ends of the Earth for you."

Tears fell from Natsu's eyes.

He should have been the one crying. He wanted to live to protect Natsu. It had been a long, long time since he had actually wanted to live. If he'd been a normal man, he'd be dead now. Right now, he felt a bit of gratitude to Baikou for giving him this accursed body.

"I could spend a lifetime and never describe my feelings for you… But as long as I live, these feelings will never change," Natsu blurted out, as though it was something she couldn't contain any longer.

Enma's heart shook. Natsu seemed amazingly beautiful to him. He wanted nothing more at that moment than to take her in his arms and feel her lips upon his own.

"Oh, pardon me. Am I interrupting?"

Hearing Masa's voice as the door opened, Enma and Natsu jumped and then came to their senses. They hastily rubbed their eyes.

"It's all right. Tears of joy shouldn't be held back. I'm so glad to see you're better now." Sounding unconcerned, she peered at Enma's face. "You look much better today. Get well soon."

"I owe you a lot too, Masa." If she hadn't summoned Nobumasa, he and Natsu would both be dead now.

"What are you saying? We're neighbors, aren't we? Of course I'd do that for you."

*Neighbors…*

They couldn't have ended up living in the same row house by chance. She probably also knew about Enma's strange healing power. Even so, Masa didn't seem at all concerned about it. She'd probably been placed in the apartment across the way to keep an eye on him.

As long as nothing happened, it would be okay. But if anything ever went wrong… Well, he'd seen what she was to do.

*Like a damned babysitter!*

Unavoidable.

Competing against Nobumasa all the time had just gotten to be a pain. He had to recognize the fact that he couldn't live without somebody else's help. He had become such a creature.

*Am I making a virtue of necessity?*

His eyelids, puffy from too much sleep, felt so heavy they seemed to close of their own accord.

"Oh, is this the ornament off of your hairpin? Oh, good. You found it, then?" Picking up the gem from the low dining table where it had been placed, Masa squinted at it.

"Yes, he found it in front of the warehouse where I was being held. I wonder why. I lost it days ago."

Enma also found the business of finding the gem to be very odd. If it hadn't been there, he probably never would have found Natsu.

Someone had placed it there. But who?

The next evening, Nobumasa Muta called on his injured acquaintance, bearing Western confections in one hand.

"How are you?"

At the sight of his nonchalant face, which hadn't sustained even a single injury,

Enma couldn't help but be a little irritated. There he'd been, close to death, and then Nobumasa had swept in at the very end to play the hero.

"I'm fine now. Thanks to you."

Hearing Enma's gratitude brought joy to Nobumasa's dark face. "And because of you, we were able to catch the Yokohama Lady-Killer. I should be thanking you."

Another great achievement by the talented superintendent. The world really was an unfair and irrational place. It was irritating.

"Well, you can thank my attentive neighbor and a sister whose lovely voice carries well, too."

"It was thanks to you, Lord Muta." Natsu bowed her head, addressing Nobumasa in an uncharacteristically quiet voice.

"I'm glad you're all right now. Well, I may have gone out of my way on all this, but he is your only family, Miss. I can't let him get killed, can I?"

Natsu's father had been beaten to death by police. Even now, Nobumasa felt a need to make up to Natsu for that.

"I'm truly, truly grateful to you." Her feelings at last set free, Natsu was moved to tears.

"Is he acknowledging the crime?"

Nobumasa nodded yes to Enma's question. "He confessed to all four murders without any hesitation."

Four murders…

"What's wrong?" The almighty superintendent did not miss the slight change of expression on the injured man's face.

"He told me that he didn't know who killed the first woman. He said the first murder was what had inspired him."

Nobumasa's eyes narrowed, as though he couldn't believe it. "Really?"

Natsu turned pale as she replied with a question of her own: "Speaking of the first victim, her body was badly devoured by crows and stray dogs, so you couldn't confirm if she'd been killed the same as the other three, could you?"

"What about her heart?"

"It was gone. But that could have been because of the animals. We don't know if the murderer had anything to do with it."

Enma squeezed his eyes shut.

"I assumed that the crimes were growing increasingly extreme, but if there was a different killer in the first place, then…" Nobumasa muttered pensively to himself.

Enma fell silent. There was another murderer at large in Yokohama, and it could be the man with whom he shared the name Houshou. Just the thought of it made him irritated and sick.

"What's going to happen to that British reporter?" Natsu asked, her brow furrowed. By all rights, he should get the death penalty, but Natsu worried about whether a Westerner would be charged with the crime.

"Well, about that…" Nobumasa was prevaricating. "He'll be deported to England in seven days."

Now it was Enma's turn to furrow his brow. Natsu looked stunned.

"But why? He killed all those innocent women," she protested, drawing closer.

"Considering our relationship with England, deportation is the best we can do. Even though the suspect has admitted to the crime, he's making a big deal that living in an unfamiliar country warped his mind."

"That's unacceptable! Will he be punished back in England?"

Nobumasa shook his head, as though saying that was too much to ask. "Evidently, he's the son of a nobleman. He'll probably be hospitalized for a while when he returns. The ship to England leaves in seven days, and that's all there is to it."

Natsu bit her lips, looking in utter despair.

"I want to see him," Enma whispered. He slowly turned his head towards Nobumasa and fixed a gaze full of menace on him. "Take me to him, Superintendent."

"What do you plan to do?"

Enma began stuffing the tools of his trade that were scattered about into his leather bag, then rose impassively to his feet. "Isn't it obvious? I'm giving him a souvenir."

His right hand throbbed in anticipation.

Oswald Ray was being held at the British Consulate.

The room was plain with a barred window. Seated on the bed, Oswald welcomed the tattooist.

As he looked into the bold eyes which sparkled with a dark light, Enma gave a slight click of his tongue. Chie and the others now lay in the cold earth, and yet this man was given a soft bed to sleep on.

"I'm surprised. You're looking much healthier than I expected you would." Oswald's surprise was natural. After all, the man he'd stabbed in the back multiple times only two days before had just strolled into his room. It was amazing that he was still alive.

"I'm not."

The most life-threatening wounds tended to heal first, so his left hand was still impaired. The wounds on his back hadn't healed completely, either. Just breathing was painful.

"Why did you confess to all four of the murders?"

"Four, three, like it'll make any difference? Who cares?"

Just the answer he'd expected. He wouldn't be executed even if he'd killed a hundred women, so why not just say yes?

"I hear you'll be going home soon."

"Too bad about that. I had a fine time here in Yokohama."

Enma raised his eyebrows as Nobusmasa and a consulate staffer looked on worriedly. "How about a souvenir tattoo from the great Ura-Enma? A special one. No charge."

Oswald's thin lips stretched into a leer. "Ura-Enma, you say? What a fascinating proposal. But can you tattoo with your injuries?"

"As long as I can move my dominant arm, I can manage."

Enma grabbed the glove on his right hand with his teeth and quickly drew his hand out. He showed him the Sanskrit tattoo of Great King Enma on his palm.

"This is the king of hell, who judges all criminals."

"I see. That's where your name comes from."

Oswald stood up.

"Let's get this over with."

Sitting in a chair, he placed his right hand on a desk. As he sat face-to-face with him, Enma opened his bag. Nobumasa silently watched the scene. Noticing the edged instruments in the bag, the consulate staffer observing the procedure softly laid his hand on the gun hanging at his hip.

"The really scary part comes after the verdict."

"I've seen images of hell in temples. They were amazing."

He probably wasn't interested in the religious beliefs of other countries. In the end, it was all just somebody else's problem. "What do you want to put into it? Do you have a wish?"

"You can put your own wish into it, if you like."

Enma took that to mean he should try and stop Oswald's urge to murder. "Unless you wish to not want to kill anyone anymore, the oni won't take up residence within you."

That was the rule of oni-gome. Unless the recipient truly accepted it, it was nothing more than a normal tattoo. All the tattooist did was grant the other party's request.

"That's going to be difficult," Oswald shrugged with a smile.

"Well, how about this, then? When you want to kill anyone, you'll kill the person who's closest and most important to you," Enma proposed, his face an expressionless mask.

"Only kill the one I love, you say? In other words, if I want to kill, I'll start with my own relatives? Fine with me. I find my brother and grandmother to be tedious. I doubt that I love them, though."

He'd likened this to a "sardine's head" before: an object of faith. He didn't believe in the power of oni-gome, figuring it to just be the product of a personal delusion. Oswald thought of it as a game, which was why he'd accepted it so casually.

"What shall I tattoo?"

"Good question… A knife would be good. Sadly, the police saw fit to confiscate mine."

Enma picked up his line-drawing needle. There was no need for a rough design. He intended to tattoo it in one go.

"It doesn't matter. I can remember it."

It would be most appropriate to tattoo the silver knife which had drawn so much blood into this man's hand.

"How effective the oni-gome is will depend on you. Now don't run away."

"That's why I have to truly desire it, right? The person closest and most important to me, huh? Very well. Show me the power of the shamans of this country."

He thought it was just a good luck charm or something like that. Then it would behave like one for him.

Enma set to work, cutting into the surface of the palm. It probably hurt, but Oswald betrayed no weakness and voiced no complaints. Instead, he began to talk in detail about how he'd killed the women.

He talked about how he'd cut out the mouth of one woman who'd begged for her life. How he'd gouged out their breasts, torn out their intestines... The consulate staffer turned pale, his mouth drawn into a thin line. He probably didn't want to believe that his fellow countryman could be such a monster.

Oswald was so intoxicated by his own blather that he didn't even notice the demons around them as they crowded and squirmed. As a two-headed snake twined itself around him, the consulate staffer felt nothing. He merely leaned against the wall, scratching his head.

This wasn't a taboo oni-gome, but it was possible that Enma's dark thoughts were summoning more specters than usual. Nobumasa's mouth was drawn into a thin, tense line as he watched.

The night grew long and dark.

When Oswald finally ceased his self-satisfied prattling, his hand sported a beautiful tattoo of a knife.

The skies in the east had begun to lighten by the time they left the consulate.

Enma walked out at Nobumasa's side, the fingerless glove back on his right hand. Oni-gome was a tiring process. It felt like something scraping at his body's core.

He watched the sun rise over the sea. The heartless sea that would carry the killer away.

"Having a murderer escape from under your very nose... It's hard to do." It was rare for Nobumasa to say something so typical of the police superintendent he was.

"He won't escape."

"The oni-gome? But..." Nobumasa pessimistically shook his head. "I don't think there's anyone that man loves," he muttered, and Enma nodded in agreement.

"Perhaps."

That was a man who hadn't loved anyone from the day he was born. A love of killing wasn't love, after all.

"But there is one I can think of."

There was someone a man like that would hold dear, precisely because he was a man like that. Enma turned to look behind them.

*Isn't that right, Jack?*

## —8—

As he tidied up the rear room of the store, Onitsuki wiped the sweat from his face.

The home in which he'd spent the last three years as a mere shopkeeper after losing interest in tattooing was a jumbled mess, seeming to tell the tale of how comfortable his life had been.

"You still feeling down?" he called out to Heath.

The American was watching the store. He really was an adorable man, Onitsuki thought as he smiled pleasantly.

"It's not like it was your fault that the Yokohama Lady-Killer was an acquaintance of yours."

A moan floated back to him.

It hadn't been published in the papers yet, and the police didn't seem to be making any announcements, but the Yokohama Lady-Killer had been captured. And it had turned out to be Heath's British reporter friend. The rumors had swept through the foreign residents of the city first.

"Oswald… I can't believe it."

According to Heath, he was an intelligent, soft-spoken gentleman. Or, at the very least, he had appeared to be one.

"It seems I was sending you to meet a real cad. But you never went to see him, did you?"

"Unfortunately, we never met."

That was a lie.

The day he'd seen Enma, he'd also gone to visit the office of the man to whom Heath had referred him. He remembered the face of the foreign reporter who'd talked in such glowing terms about the Yokohama Ripper.

The man who'd hacked up that woman in the meadow.

After the first woman had been found dead, a series of copycat murders began. There was no way Onitsuki could ignore that. And, as though drawn there by the smell of blood, he'd encountered the scene of one of the murders. The killer was so busy gleefully hacking up his victim that he never noticed the witness to his crime. He'd then fled so quickly that he'd dropped his pocket watch.

He'd been surprised that Heath's acquaintance had turned out to be the killer he'd seen. When the man had come out of his office, he'd struck up a conversation and given him a welcome tidbit of gossip.

"There's a tattooist who suspects it's a foreigner," he'd said. "He has evidence, too. I imagine he'll be going after the criminal soon, so you're sure to get a scoop if you stick close to him."

He figured the tip was worth some money, and Oswald had rewarded Onitsuki for his trouble.

Oswald kidnapped Natsu the day after making contact and then had tried to finish her off with her brother. This was a man who'd had no compunctions at all about killing an innocent woman as diversion even when he wasn't sure if the tattooist had the watch that would act as evidence to his crimes. It was almost impressive, how quickly he'd acted.

The pocket watch and the jewel off of the hairpin. He'd managed to put both lost items to good use.

It had been Onitsuki who'd purposely laid Natsu's lost jewel in front of the warehouse, figuring it would serve as a guidepost to finding her. If Enma managed to save her, then he figured it would make up for his selling her out to the killer.

It was clear that there was only room in her heart for Enma. There was no way she could ever be his companion through life. He hadn't any feelings to spare to form an attachment to a stubborn woman like her.

Of course, some feelings just couldn't be explained logically. Despite everything, he still truly desired her.

Even so, that man had protected her…

Enma Houshou. There was no doubt that he had been a disciple of Yasha's master. If he had an oni-gome under that glove of his, then that would mean they were both burdened with an identical fate. He'd heard that his master had died twenty-five years earlier. That man looked to be twenty years old at most.

*That crafty old fox…*

Without him thinking about it, a smile came to his lips.

After warning him not to practice the forbidden technique, the old man had done it before he'd died. It was just the sort of selfishness he'd expect of his old master. Now the memory of the old man, his face looking as angry as a real oni, casting him out didn't seem so bad.

At the very least, the old man's worries had been justified. He knew what sad fate awaited a man who tattooed an oni-gome of immortality onto himself…

Even so, the oni made things complicated. The man who'd stolen Natsu from him was his brethren.

They may call themselves brother and sister, but the reality was that their ages made them closer to father and daughter. The age difference was only going to widen as time went on.

It was going to be interesting to see what they would end up doing about it.

Thinking that, he began tidying up the room again. He wanted to be able to leave at any time.

He found running his foreign bookstore to be interesting work and would have preferred to keep doing it a bit longer. However, it was a business that made it easy to draw public attention to himself. He figured three years was the limit for doing that. He'd only partnered with Heath on the condition that he'd turn over the store to him when the time came.

As he dusted a chest of drawers, a yellowed old newspaper fell out from behind it. It was from last year, so it had no articles about the Yokohama Lady-Killer. An article proclaiming the Constitution of the Empire of Japan took up one entire page.

Underneath, he read with great interest an article on a man named Kaidou, who had been named as an advisor to the Privy Council. Shigekiyo Kaidou was way over seventy years old, but he seemed to be a leader in the Meiji government whose name had been raised as a candidate for prime minister.

*Hmm…*

As he was generally uninterested in politics, this was the first time Onitsuki had heard about this. It had been decades since he'd made the trip to distant Choushuu to find him.

*He's an important man now…*

He tore out the newspaper clipping by hand, then folded it away into his pocket.

The image of a young woman who'd rushed out onto a stone bridge with him suddenly flashed into his mind. The autumn twilight, the pampas grass swaying in the breeze… He couldn't remember it very well, but it had something to do with his visit to Choushuu. But just as quickly as he'd recalled the fragment of memory, he cast it away. There was something about it that he didn't want to remember.

"Heath, the shop is now yours." Saying that, Onitsuki set down a large bag upon the chest.

"What? What do you mean?" Heath said, rushing to him.

"I'm leaving. I've found something else that I'd like to do." Wiping the dust off, he began packing his things into the bag.

"But, you can't! I thought there was still time before you'd do this."

"It's in your hands now."

Heath was fluent in Japanese. He was in love with the eldest daughter of a pharmacist on the carriageway and was prepared to have his bones be buried in this country. He'd be a fine owner for the shop.

"You always make these sudden decisions. I thought you were going to teach me a little more about running the shop."

The man with a face like a red devil now wore an expression like an abandoned puppy.

"Heath, you're perfect," Onitsuki replied, clapping him on the back.

He enjoyed seeing people like Heath, who lived their lives overflowing with energy and innocence. At the same time, it was also true that he felt uncomfortable being around them.

Onitsuki continued his travel preparations in silence. He packed a rectangular bag with the bare minimum of supplies, then placed a straw boater hat upon his head. His casual dress coupled with a Western-style hat and bag made for a queer sight.

"You're going now?"

"I'm feeling a bit rushed, which is rare for me." He smiled as he stood up.

"Come back and visit some time. Promise me you will."

Heath was moved to tears. Even as he nodded, Onitsuki knew better than anyone else that he would never see his friend again.

If they were to meet again in a few years or decades, even this kind man would call him a monster. That would probably be more than he could stand.

That was why it was best to just break things off like this. Onitsuki gave his red-nosed American friend a beatific smile and then walked out of the store.

It still wasn't public knowledge that the Yokohama Lady-Killer had been caught.

The guy was some sort of troublesome Westerner. He'd probably be deported, but the truth was hard to discern. It would probably be something like that. The tattooist was probably gnashing his teeth in frustration over that by now.

Now that O-Bon had passed, the twilight brought with it the sounds of insect chirps from everywhere. Evening had fallen, so the street in that neighborhood was deserted. Normally, there'd still be some pedestrian traffic, but publicly the murder case was still ongoing. The effect of that was to cast a shadow across all of Yokohama.

He took out the pocket watch to check the time, then quickened his pace. He wanted to catch the six o'clock train. He'd been walking a bit too leisurely, and now he would only just barely make it in time. Still, the train always ran late. He wasn't that concerned about it.

He spied the roof of the British Consulate. The killer was probably being held there.

A woman's scream pierced the twilight. Onitsuki ran towards the alarming cry.

On a lane that led to the ocean, a woman was sitting on the ground. She was shaking like a leaf, looking up at a foreigner standing in front of her.

The man was raising a knife in his right hand. But the blade was directed, not at her, but at himself.

His eyes showed that he had no idea what was happening, that he didn't believe it was happening. Panicking, he had grabbed his right hand with his left, trying to hold it back. But the strength of his dominant hand was winning out, and the tip of the knife was drawing closer and closer to his throat. The man shook his head, practically weeping with fear.

The scene was like a bizarre one-man show. People were gathering to watch.

As Oswald Ray's right hand battled his left, he was screaming something in English.

*I can't stop my hand! Damn it, that tattooist...* He let loose a flood of curses directed at him.

Ah, now he saw. Enma Houshou the tattooist had delivered a judgment worthy of his namesake.

"H-Help me!"

Oswald pleaded tearfully as his eyes met Onitsuki's.

He took the gold watch from his pocket and swung it in front of the pathetic man's face.

"You...!"

Oswald suddenly realized that the man who had told him the tattooist had the evidence needed to trap him was the one who had taken the lost watch from the scene.

"Hell is waiting for you."

It could have been the voice of a demon lurking in Hades. Oswald's expression froze. His left hand seemed to lose any strength it had to hold back his right. The knife glinted as it caught the moonlight.

The blood spouted like a gory fountain. He fell back, his eyes still wide open.

Oswald Ray had torn his own throat open. It was clear to anyone who had seen that he'd gone mad and killed himself.

The weapon slipped from his right hand, revealing another knife shining upon it. Onitsuki, the man who once went by the name Yasha Houshou, could see at a glance that he bore an oni-gome.

It was pandemonium all around him, shrieks and shouts of anger mixing together.

They must have been people from the consulate, talking excitedly in English.

*Wasn't he under heavy guard? Who had been watching him? Where did he get a knife?*

*Still, since it was a suicide, there was no problem, was there? In fact, it was rather convenient. The man was a disgrace to England.*

It was hard to make out, but he got the gist of what they were saying.

Great…

He'd set this man after Enma to see if he could kill an immortal man, but Oswald hadn't turned out to be much of a murderer after all.

He heard a rumbling of something large moving across the ground. He turned to see the train moving out through the darkness.

That was the last train to Shinbashi in Tokyo. Now, of all times, it had to leave right on schedule. Onitsuki heaved a tired sigh.

Going back to Heath now would just be embarrassing. Besides, some of that blood had sprayed onto his own kimono. Maybe he should get a room near Yokohama station to change his clothes.

Perhaps, he thought, it might be nice to try wearing some Western fashions for a change. He wasn't even looking at the dead man's body anymore as he walked away.

The moon shining overhead lit the way.

## —9—

It was a hot day, despite the rain. It was noon, but the day was still terribly dark.

The normally jam-packed Yokohama station was comparatively quiet, with few passengers, perhaps owing to the weather. Though trains had been brought to the country eighteen years ago, even the lowest fares were still pricey, so they couldn't yet be called a means of transportation for the masses. It was less than an hour between

Yokohama and Tokyo, but the trains still ran infrequently.

"I won't see you again for a while, will I?" Natsu murmured sadly. She couldn't help worrying about her "big brother," who was somewhat childish and unreliable, despite his age.

"Study hard."

All those things he'd wanted to say to her while Oswald was killing him, yet here he was, face to face with Natsu, and this was all he could say.

"...I will."

Natsu looked down.

Feeling a little awkward, Enma changed the subject. "Looks like Mr. Superintendent isn't coming."

He'd said yesterday that he'd be taking the train back to Tokyo with Natsu, but there was no sign of him.

"He might be busy. It sounded like there was some sort of trouble last night."

He'd heard from Masa that morning that someone from the British Consulate had committed suicide last night. He didn't bother to ask who it had been. It seemed that the man never even got a chance to take his souvenir oni-gome back home. The guy was a fool, he thought. If he'd just been quiet and not tried to kill again, it would have just been a normal tattoo. And yet he hadn't even tried to stop.

"Doesn't he have a woman in Yokohama? Maybe that's why he's taking a little extra time."

"No. The only woman Lord Muta associates with is a lady in Tokyo. Haven't you heard? She's some sort of older widow. He's not some philanderer who carries on with lots of women."

That was news to him. Seeing how she lived in Tokyo, Natsu probably knew more details about Nobumasa's life.

"It seems to have been going on for years. He told me it's a casual, non-binding relationship."

How typical of that man, Enma thought.

"I wanted to thank Lord Muta again in person, but I suppose I can do that when I get back to Tokyo."

"You're too polite."

"I still get shivers thinking about how you nearly died because of me. I can't thank him enough."

"It'll take more than that to kill me."

Natsu shook her head. "That's what scares me the most... You don't value your life at all, big brother."

*Don't throw your life away. You'll probably do something reckless.* He remembered what his older sister used to say to him.

"I'll be careful. I have to see you become a full-fledged doctor, after all."

"You will, because if you ever think that it's okay to die, I'll never forgive you."

As Natsu stared silently at him, Enma nodded again. He thought there was something he wanted to tell her, but his natural awkwardness just got in the way. Nobumasa would probably have had something clever to say at a time like this.

A station attendant announced that the train was about to depart. Several passengers hurried to catch it. One of them ran into Enma.

It was a man, still young. He must have gotten caught in the rain, because the Western fashions he'd taken the trouble to wear were a bit soaked.

"I beg your pardon. Are you all right?"

The young man had a delicate, almost pretty face. Enma had a feeling they'd met somewhere before, but he couldn't place it.

"Well, if it isn't Mr. Mikazuki-Doh!" Natsu happily exclaimed.

"Ah, the young lady medical student. What a pleasant surprise."

"Are you on a business trip?"

"No, I quit the store. Heath's running it now."

Natsu looked surprised. "I didn't think you'd be quitting so soon."

"I'm not the type who stays in one place for very long. By the way, who's this with you?" He turned to Enma with a smile.

"This is my brother."

"Ah! The tattooist you mentioned." He fixed a searching gaze on Enma. "How do you do? My name's Onitsuki. She talks about you all the time. I'm glad we could finally meet."

Onitsuki… Oni and Moon. He thought that would be a fitting name for a man with tattoos of a crescent moon and a demonic warrior on him. Even if it wasn't, the man had given Enma a strange feeling of unease since the moment he'd laid eyes on him. He needed to ask this guy to show him his palm. Just as he was thinking that, the train whistle sounded a shrill blast.

"Oh, dear. We'd better hurry."

He stood aside, waiting for Natsu to board first. The gesture was so refined as to be almost annoying.

As the two of them boarded the train, the mass of iron belched black smoke and began to slowly roll out.

*Maybe I'm overthinking this.*

He doubted that the delicate-looking man was a murderer who devoured the hearts of his victims. But, even as he watched the train pull away, he couldn't shake the uneasy feeling he had.

Just as the last car rolled by, Enma looked up in shock.

Onitsuki stood on the rear deck of the train, smiling and waving his hand. There was a tattoo of a crescent moon on it. He had let Enma see it on purpose.

"Wait, you goddamned…!"

Teeth clenched, Enma ran after the train.

"Hey, stop! You want to kill yourself?" the station attendant yelled, but Enma couldn't let that man get away now.

*Yasha Houshou… So, that's him.*

He was probably the other Yokohama Ripper.

Enma's hand was almost on the railing of the rear deck. Just a little more... Yasha stood there, watching the scene curiously.

He just barely grasped the railing. For a moment, it looked like he'd be shaken loose, then he managed to find a foothold. The train was now pulling away from the station.

"You know how dangerous that is?" Yasha said. Enma just hung there, huffing and puffing, unable to answer. "You know you could die. The two of us aren't completely invulnerable."

So, this guy had figured out who he was, as well. He hung onto the railing from the outside and glared daggers at the other man.

Just as he tried to climb over the railing, his opponent moved to push him back. For now, Enma was stuck where he was, the rain making his precarious footing even more slippery. There was no hiding the naked animosity Enma was projecting.

Yasha held an umbrella in his hand.

"Yasha Houshou... The foolish apprentice Baikou cast out."

Yasha laughed. "What a wonderfully dramatic way to put it."

"Shut up! You were the one who killed the first woman, weren't you?!"

Yasha looked a little sad when he heard that. "She told me that she wanted to die."

"Bullshit! You killed her and then ripped her heart out!"

"Give and take."

Enma felt his blood rise in rage. If he hadn't been hanging on with both hands, he would have leapt at him.

"You're just like that Englishman. You make me sick!"

Yasha furrowed his brow as he considered that. "I don't want to think that I'm like him at all..."

There was a question that needed to be asked.

"My older sister died when I was thirteen."

Yasha looked suspicious, but said nothing.

"She was murdered, and her heart had been ripped out of her. It happened in the autumn of Ansei 6 in Hagi in Choushuu. Do you know anything about that?"

Yasha once again looked lost in thought.

"Perhaps."

"What do you mean, 'perhaps?' Don't you remember?!"

This bastard was playing with him. Enma's hands were now trembling with rage as he gripped the railing.

"I visited Hagi once... And I believe I did kill someone there."

Yasha thrust the tip of his umbrella at Enma's chest when it looked like he was about to climb over the railing.

"You're in no position to be attacking anybody, so why don't you just stay where you are?"

Enma hung on for dear life. To be so close to his adversary, and yet unable to do anything...

"Ah, yes," Yasha sighed, seemingly lost in his memories. "It's always stayed with me. I remember it now. It was on the bridge at sunset. She was a pretty girl, with such sad eyes. I see... That was your sister."

"You killed her because it looked like she wanted to die?"

Yasha nodded. "Yes. From the very beginning, I was never bold enough to just kill. Maybe I needed to make up an excuse for myself. That I was doing them a favor by killing them." He seemed to be analyzing his behavior as he talked.

"My sister caught a disease when she was a child, and a doctor told us she might never be able to bear children. Nobody would marry her then. It's not strange that she'd get tired of living a life like that, but still..."

Enma looked up, his face stained with rage.

"Feelings like that don't last long. My sister wasn't a weak woman. She would have gotten back on her feet and found some way to find happiness for herself. But you stole my sister's future from her! Not just from her. From every person you've ever killed!"

He was wasting his time shouting. The only feelings the word "future" held for this man were ones of melancholy and regret. Even so, he couldn't help but shout.

"Say something!"

Was he just going to let that hang in silence?

"If you can't forgive me, then by all means, take your vengeance," Yasha said at last. What was he thinking by saying that? Enma couldn't read his intentions.

"Don't jerk me around..."

He never thought he'd want to kill someone this badly. Hatred seemed to flood his brain. But he would not kill another person. The moment he'd taken the name of Enma Houshou, he'd left his days as an assassin behind. He had decided then to never take another human life.

Not even the life of this son of a bitch.

Just then, the door to the train slid open, and out came Natsu, holding her hair down with her hand.

"Big brother?"

She could scarcely believe what she was seeing: there was Enma, just barely hanging on to the handrail at the back of the train.

"Keep back, you fool," Enma shouted, but all Natsu could do was stare in bewilderment.

"I thought I saw you chasing after us, but I didn't think... What's wrong? For heaven's sake, climb—ah!"

Just as she was reaching over to help Enma into the train, Yasha grabbed her from behind. He clamped his right hand over her nose and mouth. Before long, Natsu's body went limp.

"Natsu!"

"Whoops, careful now."

Yasha smiled as he held onto Natsu by her kimono sash, threatening to send her tumbling over the railing.

"You…!" Enma's lips trembled.

"Relax, she's just fainted. But one false move, and I let go."

The only things supporting her were a railing that barely came to thigh level, and Yasha's left hand.

"This method is convenient. If I just press down on their mouths a little longer, they die without any suffering. That's why everyone who falls into my hands dies as if they're dreaming."

Enma recalled how peaceful his sister's face had been in death, and shook with rage.

"Get your filthy hands off of her!"

"Why are you so concerned about her? She's not your real sister."

"Shut up and take her back inside!"

Natsu wasn't moving a muscle. He noticed how white the nape of her now soaking wet neck was.

"Nobody else is going to come out here in this rain. The only one who can save her is you."

Enma held his tongue.

"Hmm… She's precious to you?"

"Of course she is! Natsu is like a daughter to me! Like a little sister! Like a—"

"Like a lover?" Yasha asked as though he already knew the answer.

"That's not…!"

"You're so easy to see through. It's all there, written on your face. I'd never guess an ageless immortal man would be so sensitive and naive."

Enma grew even more indignant as Yasha laughed at him. But saving Natsu had to come first. He had to keep reminding himself not to lose his head.

"Natsu has nothing to do with this… Now stop it and put her back inside."

"Oh, but she has a great deal to do with this. We never would have met had it not been for her."

The rain was coming down even harder now.

"How old is she? Twenty-one? That's a good age to make her immortal. You must have considered it, surely."

"The hell I have! Who would do something like that?!"

Yasha tilted his head, his expression blank.

"I just don't get what you're after here."

"I don't have to explain myself to someone like you!"

The man who'd killed his sister was now threatening Natsu's life. What could he understand about the relationship Enma and Natsu shared?

"What do you plan to do?" Enma asked. "We'll reach the next station soon. Or the conductor may come back here."

Yasha nodded in agreement. After a moment of hesitation, he smiled broadly, as though he'd come to a decision.

"Jump off."

Enma didn't immediately understand what he was saying.

"Disappear, and I'll spare Natsu's life. Well?"

Enma gulped and glanced over his shoulder. Two iron rails stretched back out of sight. On one side of the gravel-lined track bed was the ocean, and on the other was a steep cliff. There was a good chance that he'd die instantly if he jumped. And, if he fell into the sea, he might die by drowning. Even the demon inside of him couldn't supply him with air under water.

"You might die. Scared?"

For Yasha's part, he had just let him see the crescent moon on his hand to provoke Enma. He'd never expected him to leap onto the train like this. He also never expected to get into an argument with him here. If the police got involved, it would be bad for both of them. That was why he was telling Enma to just leave.

However...

"I can't trust you. I have no guarantee that you won't tear out Natsu's heart and eat it."

Yasha shook his head. He drew a glass vial out of his pocket. "I just have to kill one person a year. I simply burn the heart to ash and then eat it bit by bit."

The bottle was filled with a black powder. Was that the heart of his victim? Enma regarded it with disgust. "Ashes..."

Yasha nodded. "Yes. I don't really like it raw."

"Don't play games with me!" He was so angry it felt as if his hair was standing on end. Yasha's light tone was severely pissing Enma off. It set his teeth on edge to think that he had to share the world with a man like this. No matter how many people Yasha killed, it'd never be enough.

"The oni inside of my body hurts me as it rages. If I taste this, the pain subsides. You can try it, too."

"I endure the pain. Baikou warned you. Whoever tries to tattoo immortality into himself won't just become the host for an oni; he becomes an oni himself. It's not the oni going crazy inside of you. You're the one who's choosing to devour people!"

A bit of that seemed to get through to him, as he stopped laughing and fell silent. After a short pause, he opened his mouth. "You want to eat me, though. I want to see you drunk on my flesh and blood."

The figure of the gentle man in front of Enma merged with that of a demon. It wasn't like the oni had said something and then turned back to a human.

"Baikou asked me to kill you."

"I hope you can." He didn't seem to be taunting him. He really seemed to want to be killed. Maybe to make up for all the people he'd killed up until then.

"I will not kill anyone," Enma replied.

Hearing that, Yasha's face crumpled in disgust. "Then you're no use to me. Now, time to fly. I don't think I'm that strong, and holding a person up like this is tiring me out."

Enma made up his mind. He couldn't just let himself die. The oni within him would never allow him to commit outright suicide. If he tried, he'd lose control of his own body. Besides, he'd just promised Natsu at the station that he wouldn't. He couldn't die when his promise not to was still barely out of his mouth.

*I will live. I'll live, if only to kill this bastard.*

He glared at Yasha, as if looks alone could kill.

"I'll jump a hundred times or a thousand. Just keep your hands off of Natsu."

And with that, Enma let go.

The young man fell from the train and vanished in an instant. Yasha thought he saw the body bouncing along the track bed, but he had no idea what happened to him after that.

*Amazing.*

Yasha was shocked. In the fifty years he'd been alive, he'd never seen such a fool.

Pulling Natsu's body back, he held her in his arms as he slid the door open. Fortunately, the car was empty, with nobody there to focus suspicion on him. Setting Natsu on the rearmost seat, he gently wiped her wet hair dry. She still showed no sign of coming to.

"Sorry."

Had he killed the man she loved, he would have been truly sorry. But he had a feeling the man was still alive.

"Natsu..."

She hadn't changed since she was a small child.

How old had she been when he first met her? Four? Five?

He'd been coming back from a job when he suddenly remembered the woman and her basket of tomatoes. He was passing by the village she'd told him about.

If the child had been born healthy, how old would it be now? As he was wondering that, his feet took him towards the home of the village headman.

There, under a cherry tree, a little girl had stood sobbing in front of a grave marked only with a stone.

"What's wrong, Natsu?"

When he called her name, the child raised her tear-stained face.

"Mother died."

He recalled the face of that woman, happily rubbing her belly. So, she was dead. Then this really was the child she'd been carrying.

At the time, Yasha had felt terribly envious of that unborn child. Once again, he was jealous.

What could be more wonderful than feeling so sad? Where did all those tears keep welling up from?

"If you're that sad, I can send you to your mama, if you like."

The child had just looked up blankly at this strange man who said strange things.

But, even as she continued to cry, she shook her head vigorously.

"No! Mother told me to live a long time and be happy," the tiny girl emphatically replied. She looked at him like he was a filthy monster, trying to lure her into temptation.

I want that, he thought. He wanted that strength to help him bear what he'd become.

"Then why don't I let you live a long time?" the monster murmured.

"Can you?" she asked. Her eyes went wide and round, and she looked adorable.

"I can. If you let me put a charm on this hand. But it has to be when you're a little older. I'll come back for you."

He wanted to kidnap her right there and then, but leaving her in a child's body for eternity would have made it hard for her. Best to stop time for her when she was an adult. He made his decision.

When he'd gone back to see her a few years later, Natsu was gone. The old woman next door told him that her father had died and that she was living with a relative now. However, she came back occasionally to visit his grave. She was attending medical school in Tokyo now, and the girl was headed for great things, the old woman had boasted as though talking about herself.

Female medical students were rare enough, and he knew her name, to boot. It wasn't hard to track her down. He tried to find a way to approach her. He even indirectly tempted her. But he immediately realized that only one man held a place in Natsu's heart.

That it was the disciple of his former master, burdened with the same fate as he, must have been karma at work.

Having jumped from the train, he'd be in considerable agony for a while, but that was a trifling revenge at best. It wasn't nearly enough.

He'd taken his older sister. He hadn't taken the younger. Enma's hatred would be considerable.

Yasha stood there a while, silently regarding the palm of his hand. Each time he looked at the crescent tattooed on his right hand, his heart grew a little sicker. It looked so crude, engraved into his flesh with his left hand in a way that would be an embarrassment to any tattooist's pride. To think that it controlled him, even to the point of making him kill and then devour the flesh of his victims!

Was killing an act of his own will? The way that not killing was of Enma's?

*Well, I can't let that go on, can I?*

He wanted there to be even more killings. So long as he bore the oni's mark, saying you didn't want to kill anyone was a sad joke. He doubted it was true. Deep down, he knew that Enma wanted to kill.

He just couldn't bring himself to accept the simple truth.

In any case, he'd defended Natsu. On that point, Yasha had to give the guy credit, and so he hadn't harmed her.

He was also interested in what Enma planned to do with Natsu. Would he just let her live on without giving her immortality? If they lived together, he'd have to be prepared to watch her grow old and care for her as she approached death, no matter what. Yasha would keep an eye on how this would turn out. Until the day that Enma killed him, at least.

After putting Natsu back in her seat, he returned to the rear deck. The rain had stopped at some point. Rays of sunlight streamed from between the clouds, creating glowing shafts that connected sky and sea.

Yasha took the small bottle out of his pocket again.

It was the chain that never let him forget about evil. When he killed a person and devoured their corpse, his mind and body could feel at peace. And as he repeated the ceremony which let him forget that he was human, he assimilated a bit more of the oni's wiles.

Or, perhaps he'd already assimilated them completely. The impulse to put this theory to the test suddenly ran through him. His hands trembling a bit, his heart pounding, he uncorked the glass bottle, held it high over his head, then inverted it. The black powder sparkled as it was carried off on the wind. Then he let the bottle drop as well.

*That wasn't so hard.*

He was still able to resist. It seemed he hadn't completely been taken over by the oni yet. But that wouldn't be true forever. He knew that much, and no doubt the oni lurking within his body was laughing at this small act of defiance by its host.

Even so, his body did feel a bit lighter now.

The train soon arrived at Kanagawa station, and Yasha got off as though nothing had happened.

For the first time in ages, he felt like tattooing again.

## Chapter 4

# Daydream

*A.D. 1895 (Meiji 28)*

### —1—

It had been twenty years since the game called baseball had arrived in Japan.

It was mainly played as a novelty by students and the children of wealthy families, mostly because of the expense involved. Despite that, baseball was beginning to spread beyond the privileged classes to become a more mainstream pastime.

It was a sunny day in June when the Ikkou High School and Shirogane ball clubs met in Yokohama for a game.

Natsu had never seen a baseball game before she had accepted the invitation to see this one. She'd been working in a Yokohama hospital for three years now. She was still only at the beginning of her medical career, so there was lots to do and little time for herself.

Since she was earnestly devoting herself to her career, today was the first day in a long time that she had taken any time off.

"Whew! Just looking at the sun is making me dizzy!"

Natsu shaded her eyes with one hand. She'd figured that opening a parasol would block somebody's view of the game, so she hadn't bothered bringing one. She was wearing her best *kosode*, which was just a bit too heavy for such a warm day.

"That's because you keep yourself locked inside all the time. Please, drink in all the sunlight you can today," Kakei chided, prompting a smiling nod from Natsu. He was a short young man, about the same height as she, and his eyes always seemed to project a gentle gaze as he spoke.

They'd attended the same medical school and had become doctors together. None of her other school friends showed as much trust or respect for her. It was impossible to say how important she found his support to be.

Even so, what had happened came as a complete bolt out of the blue for Natsu. She hadn't been expecting Seijiro Kakei to propose to her.

"Where's your little brother?"

She reflexively looked down when he asked that. Her "little brother" was Enma, of course. Natsu was twenty-five now, and there was no way they could pass for "big brother-little sister" anymore. It was hard on her to play the big sister role now, but if she didn't, she'd have to give up his relationship as family, too. There was really no choice. Of course, when the two of them were alone, she still called him big brother.

However, she'd had few opportunities to do that of late.

"I asked him to come join us, but he may be busy with work."

There was no other explanation. Why wouldn't he come, she wondered, feeling a little irritated. She'd sent a card to him five days ago. She hardly ever asked him for anything, so she'd really hoped he'd come this time.

"I see."

Enma's excuse was that he was a tattooist, and that it wasn't a good idea from the start to associate with a man who'd probably be uncomfortable with him. The thing was, that didn't especially bother Kakei at all. He liked to say that, when it came to occupations, how highly or lowly they were didn't matter. He really was a fine person, Natsu thought.

This was the man who had asked for her hand in marriage, and she wanted Enma to meet him, if only once. She'd told Enma that a month ago, and he hadn't even tried to hide the displeasure on his face. She'd expected him to be happy for her, so she was surprised by his reaction.

For the last year, all Enma seemed to ever talk about when they got together was when she was going to get married. Those words hurt Natsu to hear, but at the same time, she had resigned herself to it.

She'd been entrusted to Enma by her father. "Take care of Natsu," he'd said. Enma probably felt that his promise wasn't fulfilled so long as she remained unmarried. He wanted to be free of the burden at this point. And really, could she blame him? Marriage wasn't such a bad choice if it would bring him some peace of mind. As long as they couldn't walk through time together, they'd have to part eventually. This was better for both of them, Natsu convinced herself.

Once this game was over, she'd give her answer. And yet, despite that, Enma wasn't here. She couldn't ask him his opinion about this.

"It's about to start. Let's go."

Following Kakei, they headed for the guest seating, taking their seats on the benches on Ikkou's side. Ken had apparently reserved seats for both Natsu and her younger brother.

Kakei had graduated from Ikkou High School and also acted as the team doctor, so he'd been able to reserve some choice seats for them.

The umpire yelled "Play ball!" The Ikkou players scattered to take up their positions on the field.

They looked funny in their baggy white uniforms, but the players were taking their game very seriously. Dust flew, and a little white ball soared into the sky. This being the first baseball game she'd ever seen, everything was unusual to Natsu.

The players seemed to be having a fine time as well. They were living in good times, she thought. On the other hand, war was brewing with China. Natsu herself wasn't quite clear on what the reasons for it were, but she hoped that war might still be averted.

It was hard work keeping people alive. Compared to that, killing them was a simple thing.

*There's no such thing as a good war...*

If she ever dared to say such a thing out loud, she'd only end up hearing the usual nonsense about how women were naive. Natsu wasn't in the mood to go picking fights with any polemicists she might run into.

All she had to do was what she was able to do. Save the lives of the people in front of her. That was her job.

And she had honestly tried to find a new love for herself, but it wasn't easy to erase the burning feelings she'd had since she was a young girl. The ones she kept hidden in her heart still smoldered. They were harder to cure than any disease she knew of.

"So, once they get three outs, the team in the field gets their turn at bat. Now, watch this. These kids from my school are terrific batters," Kakei happily explained.

He was the second son of a man who ran a large hospital in Tokyo, and he worked there as a doctor. There was nothing to criticize about his personality, and he was a fantastic physician as well. There'd be no better man for her to marry than this one, Natsu thought.

She'd never been particularly interested in marrying into a wealthy family, rather thinking that it would be more trouble than it was worth. Still, Kakei made up for that by being a good person. He'd most likely be a wonderful husband.

"What I love about you, Natsu," he'd told her once, "is how you seem to shine as a doctor. So please don't ever stop, even if we get married. I'll always be there to support you."

They both lived in a world where male chauvinism was a matter of course. She could confidently assert that a man who said things straight out of her dreams would never appear again. Aside from that, she was no great beauty. She tended to be stubborn and inflexible. And she was a doctor, to boot. In all honesty, she thought there was almost nothing appealing to her as a woman.

*I'm really lucky, aren't I?*

Marrying Kakei would carry no disadvantages whatsoever. But what about him? Would he be happy marrying an insincere woman like me?

There was nothing worse than a woman who'd choose a man she didn't love, just so she could forget the one that she did.

A mighty crack resounded into the air, and the little white ball flew skyward. While she was pondering her options, Ikkou scored a run.

* * * * *

While Natsu was enjoying herself at the baseball game, Enma was lying half dead.

A strong breeze blew in through the window. It'd been windy outside since yesterday.

Enma lay face up on his bed, staring dully at the ceiling. He'd been locked in a room here in the Jujo estate without food or water for six days now.

He'd come there, telling Natsu that he couldn't meet her suitor until he'd finished a big job and collected a correspondingly large payment. Now look how he'd ended up. He couldn't help but think of this as some kind of divine punishment.

She was a strong woman. She had saved so many, and was loved by just as many. He was the one who just couldn't stay away from her. Time had stopped for Enma, and Natsu was the only thing keeping him anchored in the present.

Was she all right? He hoped she was having fun with that fellow Kakei, watching the baseball game in Yokohama. Maybe this thing happening to him was a blessing in disguise. There was no telling how he might have spoiled the mood by going there and ending up moody and sulky.

*God, I'm pathetic…*

He'd finished all the water that had been in the flower vase. He'd smashed the chair to pieces trying to break through the heavy oak door, but it remained unmoved. He'd broken the window glass, but the iron bars over it kept him from slipping through. Even as he knew it was useless, he'd tried shouting for help, but any cry from the isolated house would vanish into the wind to be soaked up by the dry wilderness outside.

He may have been harder to kill than anyone else, but he was so dehydrated now that he could barely move.

There may have been limits on just how immortal Baikou had made him. He never said if the oni really would get tired of possessing him and leave, or to what extent the oni itself had a limited lifespan. The oni inside of him didn't seem ready to leave or die, and as long as it remained, Enma wasn't going to die unless someone killed him properly.

"Water…"

Even the oni couldn't do anything when there was no water to be had. He'd probably die eventually. He touched his parched lips with his finger.

Enma reached out for a piece of broken glass and placed the point of it to his throat. He knew that he couldn't die, but where was the harm in trying? He figured he might die if he slashed his carotid artery, but his hand wouldn't move no matter how much he tried. Was the feeling of the oni holding his wrist back just an illusion?

Blood dripped from the palm of the hand with which he'd grabbed the glass shard. Without thinking, he began sucking his own blood. It smelled like rusty iron, but it slaked his thirst for the moment.

"Why…?"

The palm he'd cut on the glass hurt no more than usual. And yet he knew that the skin and blood vessels which had been violently cut were regenerating. He'd cut his hand deeply, so it should have been burning like fire.

"Damn it…"

Was it because he'd sucked his blood? He gulped down saliva that wouldn't come.

If this was the same as when Yasha killed a person and ate their heart, then maybe he wasn't that different from him after all. The thought froze Enma cold.

<That's right. You're a ghoul who craves blood and flesh.>

The oni sneered at him before his eyes.

*It's true. I am a ghoul…*

He was a monster now. He no longer had a human heart. By doing this, he was taking another step in that direction.

<Just devour the dead flesh of the one you kill, and any pain you have will be transformed into ecstatic delight.>

As he teetered on the brink of insanity, Enma could swear he heard the oni's mocking laughter in the sound of the wind.

He sucked at the wound for a while, then rose to his feet and wiped his mouth.

Would the lady of the house's determination win out, or would death? Even in his half-conscious state, he felt like taking the bet.

Ashen skies, withered plants. Not even a bird in sight. Grasping hold of the iron bars on the window, Enma cried out. Anyone who heard his howl might think it was a wolf in its death throes. But, somehow, Enma managed to stay on his feet and look outside.

Walking away from him down the path that led to the front of the mansion was the butler. No matter how Enma screamed, he did not look back. Enma beat at the bars in frustration.

The butler was moving off further away. Was he headed somewhere? He seemed to be a man who'd dedicated everything to serving his mistress, which apparently kept him very busy.

He'd also seen the maid and cook leave together just before noon. They probably weren't back yet, which meant that, right now, Yoshiko was the only one in the house.

If he could just get the door open…

As he glared bitterly at the immobile door, Enma dimly recalled the day when he'd come to this estate.

That had been the start of his days in hell.

## —2—

It all began a month ago.

The clouds hung heavy and low, and it was dark despite it being midday.

The ground was sticky with mud, making it hard to walk, and his leather shoes were now soaked and discolored. Enma was wearing Western-style clothes today at his client's request, which was why he wasn't wearing the wooden *geta* clogs he was more accustomed to.

"I've got a bad feeling about this," he muttered to himself.

He thought he'd understood what he was getting himself into, but Enma still found the gloomy appearance of the Jujo estate to be odd.

The mansion which confronted him was as creepy as the black mansion of Viscount Muta seemed like a normal Western-style home. Iron bars covered its windows. The building's walls were so covered with vines that it was impossible to tell what color they were. The plants were withered to the point of petrification, such that one could scarcely believe it was only the beginning of May. It all had the atmosphere of a decaying cemetery. Enma gulped.

He wouldn't have had to take this job if his home hadn't been robbed while he was out. They'd cleaned him out, taking his household goods, his money, even the precious tools of his trade. That was when this juicy job had fallen into his lap.

The extraordinary advance they'd offered was too good to pass up. Just that alone had enabled him to buy new tools. He'd been more than happy to agree to their conditions to wear Western clothing, that he stay at their estate till the job was complete, and that he tattoo what they told him to. He'd actually been thankful that he would get to stay there. It gave him an excuse not to meet Natsu's suitor.

He now regretted jumping at this job so easily. He shivered and his head began to hurt. He dug his fingers into his hair and pressed them to his skull, but there was no sign that his headache was letting up.

"I want to go home," he muttered without thinking.

As he'd spent his advance, there was no backing out of this now. He buttoned up the front of his shirt which he'd left sloppily open.

He'd do the tattoo, and then head straight back home. Convincing himself that was all that was required of him, Enma knocked on the front door.

It wasn't as bad inside as he'd feared. A bit dreary, perhaps, but neat and clean. The walls were papered with a feminine flower pattern, and it was extremely stylish, with its French doors and ornamental paintings. Unlike the Muta estate, with its mixture of Japanese and foreign design, this place was completely Western.

"Madam eagerly awaits meeting you. She tells me she wishes to do so at once."

Enma nodded hurriedly as the old butler led him on. So, it seemed that his client was the lady of the house. The air of old Edo had vanished completely, and while there was now a hint of decadence in the world, he never expected that the wife of a nobleman would let her skin be polluted in such a manner.

"This way, please."

As they entered a room, a woman sat facing him. She was reclining on a large couch, dressed as a lady might have in Europe. She smiled when she saw Enma.

"So, you are the tattooist."

Her large, sleepy eyes seemed anxious. While she was elegant, the woman gave the impression of being on the verge of collapse. In any case, she was most definitely possessed of a beauty which Enma rarely saw.

"Thank you very much for your invitation. I'm Enma Houshou."

Normally, Enma didn't bother to moderate his natural insolence, no matter what social status his client might have held, but he was relatively polite to the elderly and to women. It was getting so that there were very few people who were older than he was, so at this point, it was a level of courtesy he reserved for ladies.

"I am Yoshiko Jujo," she said. "I am sorry to have troubled you to come to this remote place."

As elegant as her manner of speech was, she didn't sound particularly sorry to him. Yoshiko waved Enma over to a chair in front of her.

"An acquaintance of mine tells me that you are a skilled tattooist. You really are quite young, aren't you?"

This acquaintance of hers was probably a former customer. As someone who couldn't operate openly, he was glad for the word-of-mouth business. However, he had a suspicion that working on a woman of her high class may cause him trouble in the future.

"Do you really wish to have your skin inked?" he asked.

"That was why I summoned you here."

He usually had no second thoughts about practicing his craft when asked by the person to be tattooed, but when it was a woman, he had to be extra sure about it.

"It'll never come off, you know."

"I desire it."

It couldn't be helped, then. Enma opened the sketchbook he used to hash out his ideas. Since he'd been out sketching plants and buildings when he'd been robbed, his sketchbook and pads had been spared the theft.

"I was told you had something in mind, but I brought these for reference."

Yoshiko gave a charming smile.

"Oh, are there any restrictions on what Ura-Enma might tattoo?"

There it was. Enma removed the glove from his right hand and showed her the character on it which represented Great King Enma.

"Yeah, there are," he replied. "It's gotta be on the palm, you see."

Yoshiko's eyes widened at the sudden change in his manner of speech, but she seemed amused by his rude behavior and revealed her white teeth as she smiled.

"There's not much space to work with, so you can't do something like you could on your back."

Yoshiko inclined her head.

"That won't do. I want both sides of my hand covered with roses. Yes, like I was wearing gloves of roses."

Now it was Enma's turn to widen his eyes. The shelves behind the woman were decorated with so many roses, it would take both hands to hold them.

"Are you serious?"

"Of course. And I'd like it to be done by Ura-Enma. Would that be possible?"

An oni could only be placed in the middle of one's palm. Anything aside from that would just be normal tattoos, but as he'd never done anything like that before, he had no idea what would happen.

This woman wasn't sane...

"Could you call your husband?"

He needed to persuade this lovely, mad noblewoman not to do this.

"Unfortunately, my husband passed away. It's been about thirteen years now."

Enma was stunned. How old was she? She only looked to be in her thirties.

"I know I look young, but I'm thirty-eight," Yoshiko said with a sweet smile.

They said that it was hard to grow old for those who didn't carry the scent of life, but she was still fairly young.

"Your parents, then."

"Long dead. I have no children, nor any relatives, either."

She smiled, as if to say that there was no one to dissuade her from having her gloves of roses.

"It becomes hard to perspire once you have ink in your skin, so I don't recommend doing it on your hands and fingers. Besides, it hurts a lot just to tattoo the palm. A woman could never stand the pain of having it done all around her hands. Please, just don't do this."

"Gentlemen always assume that ladies are fragile things. Even though they say women can bear far more pain."

Enma gave up on his half-hearted persuading and looked at the roses behind her. He'd done cherry blossoms and peonies, even lilies, but never roses. It intrigued him.

"And what sort of oni do you want among these flowers?"

Yoshiko suddenly looked down. She clutched her hand to her chest, and looked as if she was in pain.

"I want to forget. To forget the one I cannot help but love."

Enma chewed the back of his pencil.

He didn't want to make an oni-gome for love or passion. He wanted to tell this woman to just deal with what she was feeling on her own.

It wasn't because of the advance he couldn't pay back that kept him from kicking over the chair and leaving. Neither was it because he'd been moved by the tearful eyes of a beautiful widow. No, he'd started work when the butler who'd been watching the exchange had pulled a gun on him. As he watched Enma with a stern expression on his face, Yoshiko had smiled slyly.

Swords had been banned shortly after the world had changed so precipitously, but small firearms were to be had easily from the shops in that area. Occasionally, this kind of contradiction would cause trouble like this for Enma. He'd had dangerous sorts force him to tattoo them before, but this was a noble household. He hadn't been expecting them to go this far.

Enma reluctantly began tackling the rough sketch for the roses. He'd tattooed designs completely around arms and legs many times, but around all ten of those slender fingers as well? That was going to be daunting.

The bedroom he was in was decorated with roses as well. Enma lay on his bed, drawing roses. He erased what he was doing, then redrew it. He'd never had a job this difficult. Baikou might have wept with joy to have gotten it, but Enma didn't share his old master's whims.

Roses were rare and expensive things. How much money was she spending on all these? What was really odd was that, by comparison, the garden had practically fallen to ruin.

There was a knock at the door as the butler brought him some black tea.

"Have you made any progress?" he asked.

Enma sat cross-legged on the bed and took the teacup. "Can I assume this isn't poisoned?"

"Don't be absurd."

It was true that there'd be little point to killing the tattooist at this point. Enma drank the tea.

"Sugar?"

"Don't need it. Sweet tea makes me sick. Anyway, are you sure you want to go along with this?"

"Whatever do you mean?" the butler replied with an emotionless smile.

"Unlike the back or the leg, the hands stand out for everyone to see. If a lady gets a gaudy tattoo like this on her hands, she'd never be able to go out again."

"Madam has not stepped outside of this house for almost two years. I doubt she was planning to go out after this."

Now he understood why her skin was so pale. "Once she forgets about this man, she'll probably feel like going out again. I imagine that'll make you happy, since you're like a stagehand in her little drama."

The butler shook his white head. "Just please do as Madam desires."

That was an order, not a request.

The butler left the room, leaving Enma to resume his worried pencil-chewing.

He picked up one of the roses in the room and held it in his hand. One of its thorns pricked him, drawing some blood.

That was when the idea hit him.

After staying up the entire night sketching, Enma met again with Yoshiko the next morning.

She gazed languidly at the picture he handed her. The fingers that held it seemed like white serpents, her wrists so slender that they seemed ready to snap off of her arms.

"We'll have two rose tendrils loosely entwining your wrists, with buds on the back of your hand, and culminating in a large blossom on your palm. It'll be a symmetrical design, the same on both hands. What do you think?"

"It's a bit different from what I had imagined." She'd probably planned on her skin being so completely covered that you'd no longer be able to see its texture.

"This would be using your skin to the best advantage."

It was his honest opinion. All he wanted at that point was to finish the job and get out of there, but he also wanted to create as fine a tattoo as he could. No tattooist would ever be stupid enough to completely ink over skin like hers.

"I'll trust your skills for this. Please begin doing it at once."

"Very well, then."

Enma made a great show of laying out his tools on the table. He decided to forgo the rough sketch and proceed straight to tattooing her. However, there was something he needed to be sure of before he could begin.

"Are you sure that you want to forget about this man?"

"What are you saying?" There was a severe gleam in Yoshiko's eyes.

"Do you really want to break off all of your feelings for him?" He asked because people tended to cling to memories of lost love. If there was any part of Yoshiko which was doing that, then the oni-gome wasn't going to work.

"Of course I do."

But even as she answered him, Yoshiko seemed to lose her confidence and pondered it for a moment.

"Take it all away... I'm sure that I want it gone."

The way she said it made her seem like a fragile young girl.

Enma had a brand-new needle, but it didn't fit his hand quite right. Once again, the seriousness of losing the tools he was used to was driven home anew.

"Sorry, I'm so tired that I can't concentrate. Can we start on it this evening?"

"I suppose it can't be helped."

His eyelids drooping, Enma stood.

"If you change your mind before then, don't hesitate to tell me. The advance you gave me... I can pay it back in installments."

Returning to the bedroom on the second floor, Enma collapsed into bed. Hugging the pillow to him, he seemed about to fall asleep, but there was still one thing that he needed to do.

Sitting up, he rolled back the cuff of his pants and then pressed the new needle into his own calf. Having skin which could heal any wound without a trace was convenient for doing test tattoos. Enma continued tracing lines on his skin in this manner until he was used to the new needle. After enduring the lingering pain that accompanied the action, he finally surrendered to exhaustion.

He'd been doing this job for nearly thirty years now, but there was always a tension he felt whenever he first inserted the needle into a woman's skin. He couldn't help but feel guilty, as though he were committing an act of violence.

He began by drawing buds on the back of her left hand. Working just by lamplight made him uneasy.

Yoshiko's beauty in the meager glow was enough to shake the heart of anyone who chanced to see her. The little grimaces that she made as she endured the pain were sensual.

After an hour, he took a break. As he sank into the chair, Yoshiko let out a long, tired sigh.

"So, what was he like?" He was curious about this man who tormented her so.

"A bad person."

"I can imagine."

Yoshiko chuckled. "No. Actually, he was mature in both the good and bad sense of the word. We knew each other for more than ten years, and yet I never really knew him."

"You saw each other all that time and there was never any talk about marriage?"

Studying the outlines of the roses on her hand, Yoshiko shook her head. "There were circumstances which demanded that he remain unmarried. And besides, I was quite disgusted with marriage at that point. That was due to just how awful a man my late husband was."

The butler who had brought them tea interjected himself into the conversation. "The master hit Madam hard enough to break her bones. Truly, he treated her terribly."

So, the master of the Jujo estate had been an abusive one. That was surprising, since Enma had heard that he was from a family related to the imperial line.

"He was a man who just lived off of his inheritance without earning a living of his own, not to mention abusive, as well. If the master had any sense of decency, he showed it by dying quickly."

That may have been going a bit far.

"You shouldn't speak ill of the dead. Thank you. That will be all for tonight."

The butler looked a bit disappointed, then bowed and withdrew.

"Did your husband die of an illness?" Enma asked.

"No, he slipped on the stairs. He must have been a little drunk."

There was a huge stairway in the entrance hall at the front of the mansion. It split off to the left and right from the landing, like something you'd see in a theater.

"On those stairs."

"Those were difficult days for me, and I'd be lying if I said I didn't wish for my husband to leave. But if you suspect that I killed him, you'd be wrong."

Enma felt ashamed. "I never implied that."

"It's surprising how easily a person can die," Yoshiko said with a bewitching smile that left Enma at a loss for words.

"Should we continue?" he asked at last.

Being the first day of work, he really should have stopped after an hour, but he'd changed his mind. He had to get the hell out of this mansion as fast as he could.

Tattoo, sleep. That became his routine, day after day.

Even for someone with an endless amount of time on his hands like Enma, the hours had never weighed on him so heavily. He no longer had a sense of what date it was, or even when it was day or night.

Rubbing his eyes, he put the needle down.

"I'd like to go back to my home for a bit," he said. "Could I just have a day or two to rest?"

Yoshiko looked up at him. "Oh, dear. Do you yearn for your big sister?" That she was saying something so provocative showed him that she had no intention of letting him leave the estate. "Your sister's a doctor, isn't she? She must be a very level-headed person."

So, she'd done some checking up on his background.

Except for when Natsu had been a child, he'd mostly lived on his own. He hadn't seen her in six months. She now worked as a surgeon in the big hospital in Yokohama. At the moment, she knew neither that he was practically penniless nor that he was here.

Calling himself her younger brother hadn't been his idea. In fact, their change in social position had practically seemed like a disgrace to him. However, Natsu had readily taken to the swap from younger sister to older. She didn't have any trouble at all when she'd first introduced him as her "little" brother, but it was hard for him.

"Or perhaps there's someone else you wish to be with."

Enma frowned at the meaning loaded into that question. "Just leave it."

Enma didn't expect that she would, despite his plea.

He continued to work his needle in silence, making it clear he was refusing to say anything more. Two roses twined around the woman's hand.

There were some foreigners who praised tattooing as an art, but Enma had never once felt that way himself. So far as he was concerned, it was still an injury. But this time, as he looked at the roses he was tattooing into Yoshiko's hand, he could trick himself into believing it was an expression of art. Yoshiko's white hand was like a piece of ivory that was just waiting to be carved.

The more he scratched into her, the more he felt a sort of tepid poison flow through his needle from her. This woman was dangerous. He could understand why that man had left her. He'd likely endured her poison for ten years. Enma wiped away the sweat that was crawling down his neck.

The left hand was finished.

The roses decorating Yoshiko's hand, having gorged themselves on Enma's vitality, now bloomed in full.

He felt no sense of accomplishment. He let out a sigh. The job was only halfway done, and there was so much left to do. Without any concern for the feelings of the tattooist, Yoshiko stared at the roses on her hand, as though transfixed by them.

"They're magnificent."

"Thank you."

"Let's celebrate the completion of this half of your task. I have a fine wine to drink."

It was late at night, the butler having retreated to his quarters long before, and so Yoshiko prepared the glasses herself. She proudly poured out the crimson spirit.

Urged into joining her in her toast, Enma brought the wine to his lips. Its rich aroma and sour taste filled his mouth.

"Is there a lady you keep company with?" Yoshiko was in high spirits this evening.

"No."

"Oh? But why? Girls today are so bold, I can't imagine they'd just leave somebody like you alone."

One-night stands were about all he'd ever had. They were the only sort of relationship he could manage. "There's no reason for you to tie yourself down to one man, either. You could have your pick of suitors if you wanted, couldn't you?"

"I've never wanted another." A blush of red came to the pale woman's cheeks.

"Was this guy really that great?"

"Yes. He really should have been a viscount, but he ended up turning the title over to his younger brother. Noble rank didn't mean anything to him."

Why did that sound so familiar to him?

"He's been very successful in business since he retired from the police force. He really is the sort of man who succeeds at anything he tries."

Nobumasa...

It was possible that he was the only man who could have been a match for this woman.

I'll get him for this.

Destiny had really thrown him for a loop this time. He chewed his thumbnail nervously.

Enma stood up, leaving his wine unfinished.

"I'm going to bed."

He staggered out of the living room. Never had a job so exhausted him like this.

The roses decorating his bedroom must have been changed, because they seemed to always be fresh. Their scent hadn't seemed very strong at first, but now it was choking him.

The door in the main entryway was locked from the inside, and there were iron bars over every window. The whole house was a prison, and having nowhere to run was driving him mad.

He dove into bed face down and pressed the pillow on top of his head. This mansion and its mistress were both poison. It had so permeated his body that even the oni inside couldn't work fast enough to make him recover, and so he couldn't help but feel sluggish all the time. He was getting sicker and sicker as the days passed.

He couldn't bring himself to eat more than half of the meal that had been brought up to him, although that may have been because he'd eaten nothing but Western cuisine since arriving here. It wasn't so much a matter of his liking or disliking it, but rather that he'd just gotten sick of eating it. He'd asked the cook directly to make him some rice balls, but the man had refused. It had been decided that only Western cuisine was to be served in this estate, and he'd be sacked if he broke his word, he'd said. The cook, the butler, and the maid all wore Western clothing, no doubt due to another of their mistress's decrees.

In a way, he was rather impressed by how far she'd taken her attempts at Westernization.

I hope Kuro's all right, he thought.

This was no time to be worrying about that monster cat of his.

The days passed in a blur.

It had to be June by then. The spring rains had left a chill in the air, so he hadn't felt the change in seasons.

The tattoo was nearly complete. He doubted that it was painless for her, but Yoshiko seemed to have grown used to it readily, and her expression didn't change a bit. He could imagine that a great many senses within this woman weren't working entirely right.

The daily grind had worn Enma out, but it only seemed to sharpen his sensitivities.

The texture of the petals, the luster of the leaves, the sharp brilliance of the thorns all seemed to pierce the viewer. Yoshiko's skin drew the needle into itself. It was dyeing the inks with its own colors.

Almost like a love affair. Like it was lusting for it.

Perhaps this devilish power of hers was what had driven Jujo to abuse his wife, if he had actually abused her. Yoshiko was a woman who drove men to madness. An ordinary man would drown in her poison, his body falling to ruin because of it.

"Oh…" Yoshiko twisted her body slightly. Pain had already become a source of intoxication for her.

"Should we stop?"

"It's all right. Keep going…" The words seemed to leak out of her in an orgasmic sigh. "When he used to come visit me here, the garden would be full of blooming roses."

Yoshiko glanced at the window. Even though it was summer time, dead leaves whirled in the air outside.

"I haven't cared about my garden since he stopped coming. I ended up letting the gardener go." The desolate appearance of the mansion's exterior reflected its mistress's heart. "He told me we couldn't be together anymore. I'd sensed the end was near, but actually hearing him say it was over was still hard… I never got over it, and haven't left the estate since."

It was the way of men and women. He couldn't put all the blame on Nobumasa.

"It's my own fault. I was so worried about not being young anymore that I just gave in to jealousy. Just his standing next to a young, beautiful woman was enough to make me feel like my body was on fire. It's no wonder he finally ran out of patience. Please, feel free to laugh at the foolish woman you see before you."

Enma shook his head. A person who recognizes their own foolishness wasn't a fool, he thought.

Just a little bit remained to be done. Her right hand was now completely covered with roses. Yoshiko no longer looked like a human being. She was now the very image of a rose fairy.

"There's something I'd like to ask you." Enma laid his needle down with a sigh. "Who was it that told you about me?"

Yoshiko kept her gaze fixed on the unfinished rose on the back of her hand even after he asked the question, but the slackening in her mouth told him that she'd heard it. "A colleague of yours," she replied.

Not a client, as he'd assumed, but another tattooist. Enma didn't know many others in his trade. He certainly didn't know any well enough to call an acquaintance.

"He gave me a tattoo in a more inconspicuous place before." Yoshiko got to her feet and then, without a moment's hesitation, pulled the hem of her dress up.

"Wha..."

"Right here."

A single crimson rose bloomed on the inner part of her left thigh. Coupled with her soft alabaster skin, no rose could have seemed more beautiful or more obscene.

"You, madam, are no lady."

"All I am is a pathetic woman. I heard about them a long time ago, about these mysterious tattoos engraved onto the palm of the hand. I finally found a man who could do the deed, but I couldn't go through with it. In the end, I just had him give me a regular tattoo."

Enma's eyes widened. A tattooist who could perform oni-gome. There was only one other man he knew of aside from himself who could do that. He imagined the beautiful widow, her white leg stretched out and exposed on a couch to the immortal tattooist with the elegant profile... The spectacle was so obscene it made him dizzy just thinking about it.

"Just before he left, he told me something. That there was another man who could perform this technique. If I ever found the resolve to go through with it, I should seek out Enma Houshou, he said."

Letting her dress fall back, Yoshiko once again languidly took a seat in her chair.

"He was a young man with a pretty face. And like you, he kept one of his hands covered. Perhaps he too had a tattoo that carried a wish in it."

Enma paused. "And what was his name?"

"He called himself Onitsuki."

As he thought. He could practically hear the grinding of his own molars. What was Yasha playing at? Why would he have mentioned Enma's name to this woman then? Enma lapsed into silence, unable to guess Yasha's true motives.

"He showed me the yasha tattoo he had on his lower back. It was an oni that was both beautiful and frightening. The eyes on it looked like it had just devoured a person."

He recalled Baikou's tattoos, and how intensely they portrayed beauty in sadness and gloom. "Did he mention anything else to you?"

"He was a most fascinating person. He'd wandered all over Japan and could speak on any number of topics. A gentleman as intoxicating as sake." Yoshiko seemed intoxicated just talking about him. "Oh, yes. He said that, if he were to go to a foreign country, he'd be called a vampire. He told me that with a smile."

"Vampire?"

"Apparently, it's a monster which lives by drinking human blood. When I asked if he wanted to drink my blood, he answered with a charming smile that he would if he ever grew weak, but that I didn't have to worry since he was healthy now."

Yoshiko smiled ecstatically, as though she wanted to be killed by the man. Yasha had once charmed Natsu when he ran a bookshop called Mikazuki-Doh, so he may have had a talent for manipulating women.

"When I asked if he had a lady friend, he told me that he didn't know how it felt to yearn for someone."

Was it that he didn't know or that he didn't want to know? As a man who shared a similar fate as Enma, there was no way Yasha couldn't avoid learning what it was like. Once it had hit home, his body would writhe in despair.

"Except, he did mention that he'd once met a little girl who was crying for her dead mother, and that he'd come for her once she was fully grown. Isn't that a wonderful story? It's like something out of *Genji.*"

Enma couldn't say that for sure, since he had never read the *Tale of Genji*, but it reminded him of something he'd once heard somewhere.

"He said that when he came back to visit her once, she was gone. His junior colleague had come and brazenly stolen his Lady Murasaki-no-Ue from him. Isn't that an awful story?"

Enma's eyes practically bulged from his face. Had Yasha met Natsu before he had?

*I can send you to your mama, if you like.*

Enma's body shook as he recalled what he'd heard from Natsu. Natsu could have been killed by Yasha then.

That man...

The thought that he'd go so far as to lay his hands on a little child filled Enma with an almost mindless rage.

Natsu had probably refused him outright. That was why she was still alive. He'd never thought that her strength was as magnificent as this.

So, he not only took my sister, but tried to take Natsu, too? Unforgivable!

He hugged his arms tightly to himself. If that man took Natsu from him as well... He couldn't even bear thinking about it.

"But why are you asking me about all of this? Isn't he an acquaintance of yours?"

Yoshiko smiled syly at him, with a look on her face that said, "Do you know what I know?"

"The two of you are struggling over someone you both treasure... That's what he told me. That sort of relationship is like a dream."

He'd taken Sawa from Enma, and Enma in return had taken Natsu from him. That was how Yasha saw this.

He had to be kidding. Could anyone really see it in such a twisted way? Enma wanted to shout out in indignation, but somehow kept his cool. Yoshiko was still talking.

"That's why he says he won't mind if you kill him. But, in return, he's going to take back what you took from him."

Enma's blood froze as he bolted up from his chair so fast that it fell over backwards. Enma's obvious rage didn't go unnoticed by the eyes of the butler standing in the corner of the room. "Meaning what?"

"I imagine it means he's coming to take her back. And since you are an obstacle to him doing that, he apparently wants me to keep you locked up here for a while."

In other words, Yasha had asked this woman to hold him prisoner. And she'd managed to do it for nearly a month now. What had happened to Natsu? What did she mean by "he was coming to take her back"? Was it to kill her or, else… To make her immortal?

"Damn him to hell!" Enma yelled, dashing from the room. He ran into the entryway, but the heavy doors remained shut despite all his efforts. "Unlock them! Give me the key!" he yelled back over his shoulder, but the butler merely cocked an eyebrow and shook his head. He held a gun in his hand.

"Please come back in here. Your job isn't finished yet."

Enma didn't even look at the gun barrel pointed at him as he flung himself at the half-crazed butler. "Shut up! If anything happens to Natsu, I'll kill you both!"

The butler, not expecting to be immediately attacked head on, had no time to pull the trigger. Enma knocked him back, sending them both down to scuffle on the floor.

In this case, Enma's youthful body gave him the upper hand. He prized the gun out of the butler's hands and then, sitting on his back, pressed the barrel to the other man's forehead.

"I don't have time to worry about you people. Now give me the key!"

The butler didn't answer. He betrayed no sign of fear at all, practically telling Enma to shoot if he was planning to shoot him.

"Oh my, how violent." Yoshiko peeked her face out of the room. It was irritating how there was no hint of tension in her voice.

"Open the front door, or I'll kill him!" Enma screamed.

Yoshiko's only response was a small, sad shake of her head. "I'm sorry, Murota."

"Don't trouble yourself over it, Madam," the butler replied casually.

Their exchange horrified Enma. These people weren't normal… He'd understood that, but hadn't realized they were willing to go this far.

"Did you arrange to have my home robbed, as well?" Now he understood why his old work tools had been taken.

"You can have everything back once this is all finished," Yoshiko admitted frankly. Make a man penniless, then make an offer he couldn't refuse.

Had Yasha suggested that to her, as well?

"Why don't you kill us and set fire to the mansion? You might be able to get out if you did that." It was like she was sneering at him, not caring if he killed her. "Go on, then. Feel free to kill us."

Of course. Yasha must have told her. That he didn't kill people. And yet, he didn't think they'd even care if he did. Even as he thrust that gun's muzzle at them, Yoshiko and the butler still had the upper hand.

Maybe he could shoot the door's lock out. Stepping away from Murota, Enma placed the gun's muzzle to the keyhole and pulled the trigger.

No bullet fired.

"That gun isn't loaded. It was strictly for intimidation."

Looking back, he saw that Murota had another gun in his hand. Apparently, he had two of them at the ready.

Flame spouted from Murota's gun. The bullet grazed Enma's temple and embedded itself in the door behind him.

"That man wants you to kill him. To do that, you'll have to hate him more. That's what he told me. That much, I can help him with."

He couldn't understand any of this. Even so, he managed to ask a question. "Why does it have to be me? If he wants to die, there are other ways he can do it."

Was it misplaced resentment for his taking Natsu from him? Or was it out of some deep-seated delusion towards him as a junior practitioner of their common trade?

"You'll have to ask Mr. Onitsuki that yourself."

And what did this woman stand to gain by being Yasha's accomplice? This didn't seem like something the idle rich would do.

"I'll give you your oni-gome right now. That will be enough, won't it?" The tattoo itself was mostly finished. The oni-gome would take less than an hour to do. That was more certain than this awkward standoff.

However, Yoshiko seemed disturbed by the proposal. Getting the oni-gome would mean her forgetting Nobumasa completely. As far as she'd come, it seemed she still hadn't made up her mind about that.

"Well..."

"He made up his mind that he wasn't coming back to you, didn't he?" Once that man decided something, he would never go back on it. Yoshiko's lingering affection for him would never be repaid.

"That's a cruel thing to say." Yoshiko glared at Enma, tears coming to her eyes.

"You called me out here and kept me locked up because you wanted to forget him, didn't you?!" Enma shouted without realizing. It was June already. In all that time, he hadn't been allowed to set one foot outside of the mansion, and he was at wit's end. All he wanted was to leave at once and protect Natsu.

"You've wanted to run away that badly?"

What was this woman saying? Enma couldn't understand why he was being criticized like this.

"You ran away, too. With that person." Yoshiko was screaming as she cried, seeming to confuse Nobumasa and Enma. Her Western hairstyle was now all askew, and she clawed at her breast as though she couldn't bear what she was feeling anymore.

"He left because he said it was all over. It's time you accepted that. That man's never coming back here. He's never going to hold you in his arms again!"

Yoshiko pressed her hands to her face, let out a voiceless scream, and fell to the floor.

"Madam!"

Shoving Enma aside, the butler ran to her. Holding her carefully, as though she might break, he carefully carried his mistress to the couch and laid her down.

"Please return to your room."

He pointed the gun at Enma again. This man would kill him easily if it was necessary. Even seeing the wound heal wouldn't matter to him. His expression would remain unchanged as he shot Enma again and again until he was finally dead.

Natsu…

He couldn't die yet. With a silent nod, Enma dragged his heavy body to the second floor.

He listlessly sank into the bedding. His head was numb. He couldn't think. As consciousness receded from him, he heard a rattle from somewhere.

"Wha…" Enma sprang up and grabbed for the door handle. "What are you doing?! Open this door!"

It had been locked from the outside.

"Please remain in there until Madam has made up her mind," the butler softly said.

"You've gotta be kidding! And when is she gonna make up her mind?!"

"I do not know."

He heard the butler walk away from the other side of the door.

"What do you mean you don't know?! Hey! Lemme out!"

Enma continued to beat at the door, until at last he sank to the floor.

Now he really was locked up. He hugged his head to his knees and tore at his hair in frustration. Nobumasa had broken off all contact with this woman.

He could expect no help from him this time.

* * * * *

The door remained locked for six days.

The baseball game would be ending soon. Was she still safe? Even in his hazy half-awake state, Enma unconsciously called out her name.

"Natsu…"

## —3—

Feeling as though someone had called her name, Natsu looked back over her shoulder.

She was a little ashamed of herself for still hoping that Enma might show up. Perhaps she hoped that he'd object to her getting married, or that he'd tell her not to look at any other men. Even though, to her, he was like both a father and an older brother. The self-loathing she felt was ripping her heart to pieces.

"What's wrong?" Kakei peered worriedly at her face, wondering why she was hanging her head down instead of watching the game.

"Oh, no. Sorry, I think I need to find a toilet."

Kakei bowed his head as he apologized for prying, his face turning red.

Of course, it was a lie. Thinking of Enma even while she was here sitting next to Kakei was making her disgusted with herself. After she made her way from the guest seating and the cheers had grown distant, Natsu let out a long sigh.

"Well, if it isn't Natsu."

Natsu looked up, startled by the voice. There in front of her stood an imposing figure dressed from head to toe in Western finery.

"Lord Muta."

She never expected to run into him in a place like this. She worried that he'd seen she was on the verge of tears.

"I didn't know you had an interest in baseball."

"Oh, no… An acquaintance of mine invited me."

Nobumasa smiled, a knowing look in his eye. "Oh? And what's he like?"

Natsu's face immediately reddened. Flustered, she asked how he knew it was a man without her having mentioned it.

"Because I imagine it would usually be a man who would invite someone to watch a baseball game. Besides, you're dressed up more than usual."

She was starting to see why Enma always felt at a loss whenever he dealt with Nobumasa. "You're right, as usual, Lord Muta. Yes, it's someone I went to med school with. We might even be getting married," she answered frankly. Nobumasa Muta was her patron. There was no need to conceal it from him. Besides, at that moment, Natsu wanted to talk to someone about it.

"I take it by your saying 'might' that you haven't decided on it yet."

"I'm going to give him my answer once this game is over."

Nobumasa nodded. He seemed to understand what was troubling her. "And what has Enma to say about all this?"

"Nothing. I asked him to meet him here today, but he hasn't shown up."

Nobumasa grunted, an annoyed look on his face. "Well, then… It can't be helped, can it?"

She wanted to ask him exactly what he'd meant by that, but she figured it would only trouble Nobumasa unnecessarily. Better to leave what was hard to say unsaid.

"Did you hear about that man Yasha Houshou?"

"Yes. Mr. Mikazuki-Doh, you mean. Honestly, the fact that he's a murderer seems like a bad dream, even now."

She knew without being told that he was immortal as well. That was probably what she had sensed in him that reminded her of Enma. But never in her wildest dreams did she think he was a monster who killed people and devoured their hearts.

"I wonder what happened on that train five years ago. Big brother refuses to tell me. Surely he told you, didn't he, Lord Muta?"

When she'd regained consciousness, both he and Enma were gone. All she could do was return to her boarding house without a clue as to what had transpired.

"If he hasn't told you, then it's not my place to do so."

It seemed that the men shared a special bond, even though they didn't particularly like each other. Natsu couldn't quite understand it, but decided not to press the matter. "You remember Kuro, don't you, Lord Muta?"

"That cat? What about it?"

He looked confused as to why she'd suddenly bring up the subject of their old black cat.

"He's at least thirty years old. Big brother told me that he thinks it may be like him."

Nobumasa seemed to understand what she was getting at. "The cat's immortal too, you mean."

"And when he told me that, I let it slip. That I was envious of Kuro."

Even while Enma himself saw little appeal in eternal youth and immortality, Natsu truly envied that cat, because he was able to live in the same time as Enma. But Kuro was a loner. She'd never seen him with another cat. The others probably feared the oni inside of him; animals were far more adept at sensing these things than humans were. Kuro likely stuck with Enma because he sensed that they were both of a kind.

"He scolded me for saying it. After that, every time I saw him, he'd tell me it was time I got married."

"He feels he owes it to your father, and certainly because you have a future which he doesn't think he can share with you."

Natsu nodded. Her father, who had died worrying only about his daughter's welfare. He'd probably left some sort of instructions to Enma. So long as that wedge existed between them, Enma would never consider getting involved with her, or look at her as a woman.

"You worked hard to be a doctor, after all."

"All thanks to you, Lord Muta."

"Being a surgeon suits you."

Of the few women who were doctors, most put their skills to work in obstetrics and gynecology. "I suppose I inherited my father's tendency to be unconventional."

Seinosuke Okazaki had been a man who'd maintained his honor even as he defied the changing times. A man who had died preaching justice to the policemen who'd beaten him to death. Nobumasa smiled wryly.

"He would have liked the idea of me mercilessly cutting into people who were afraid of being operated on by a woman, and then making them better for it."

"I see. That sounds like fun."

Natsu suddenly looked up into the sky. "But seeing him makes my being a doctor feel like a waste of time. After all, any injury he gets will just heal on its own."

Enma's existence lay beyond all known medical science.

"What he has is a disease, a sort of incurable illness."

"Yes, of course..." Curing his immortality would mean death for him. He was an extremely burdensome patient to have.

"He knows the depths of the darkness he carries within him... It's bottomless, a darkness which he could never invite anyone else into."

Nobumasa's words pierced her heart, adding to the ache she felt there. "I know..."

The cheering grew louder. Someone must have scored a run. "The truth is... I, too, said something that I shouldn't have, and it made him very angry." Nobumasa smiled. "I told him that, if he got lonely after you married, he was welcome to move in with me, that I would gladly provide a place for him."

"Oh, my!" Natsu could just imagine how Enma had reacted to that.

"He demanded to know why I was trying make him into my pet dog, in a tone so sharp I thought it might stab me to death."

Enma had a terrible inferiority complex when it came to Nobumasa. Poking at what little self-respect he had, it was no wonder he'd gotten angry.

"We both need to watch what we say around him. He's more fragile than he looks."

Natsu and Nobumasa looked at each other, then burst into laughter. Being able to talk and laugh like this had lightened Natsu's mood considerably.

"By the way, were you here to see the game too, Lord Muta?"

"I know someone in the Shirogane ball club in Tokyo. I owed it to him to show up."

Nobumasa had quit the police force three years earlier, retiring as soon as he'd determined who would be promoted to replace him as police superintendent. He could see what was coming. In the police force, there was only one position higher than superintendent.

He was now managing a trading company, and business seemed to be going exceedingly well for him. The word "multitalented" seemed to have been made for him, Natsu thought.

"Are you here with your lady friend?"

The woman had managed to monopolize a man like this for more than ten years. She was interested in meeting her if she could. Even Natsu was curious about what she was like. But her question only elicited a worried expression on Nobumasa's face.

"We broke up two years ago. At the moment, I'm a lonely man who only has his work to occupy him."

"I see…"

Naturally, she was polite enough to refrain from asking why they'd broken up.

Nobumasa had turned over his family inheritance to his younger brother. It seemed that he'd decided to forgo having a wife and children in order to spare himself any anxiety about the future. Perhaps having a relationship that might lead to that had been too big a problem for him to handle.

"Well, getting married is something you should decide for yourself. Whatever decision you make, know that you have my blessing."

Yes, this really is my own problem, Natsu thought. It was wrong of her to want Enma to make the decision for her. It wasn't fair to Kakei, either.

"Yes. I'll make the decision."

Thanking Nobumasa, Natsu returned to her seat.

Someone else had silently observed the scene.

His eyes were squinted, as though he was looking at something dazzlingly bright, and when the woman finally took her leave, he called out to an old man standing nearby. "Say, isn't that Lord Muta?"

The old man looked up, straining eyes that were buried in wrinkles on his face. "Ah, yes, so it is."

The old man grabbed his cane and stood up. It was only early summer, but the sunlight was intense. He'd come to see the game with a friend, but had ended up spending it resting under a tree. Still, Nobumasa Muta was already known for his brilliant exploits as police superintendent, and his name was now gaining fame among the wealthy families who dealt with foreign nations. This would be a good chance to become a bit friendlier with him.

So thought the old man, for although he'd retired from the world of politics, he liked to demonstrate that he still held some influence.

"Well-spotted, Onitsuki."

"He's a famous man," Yasha replied with a smile.

The old man's name was Shigekiyo Kaidou. He was a former retainer from Choushuu and a man who knew the dark side of the Meiji government. Yasha had re-assumed the name of Onitsuki and was employed as the old man's private secretary.

"I say, Muta!" Kaidou called out. Leaning on his cane, he slowly tottered over to meet him.

"Master Kaidou, what a surprise. You're looking well, sir." Nobumasa bowed politely to the old man wearing *hakama* marked with his family crest.

"Because I'm a bad boy that has power in this world. I'm not going to die that easily," Kaidou laughed, showing the gaps where his front teeth used to be.

"And who's this with you?" Nobumasa's gaze was drawn away from the old man to Yasha.

Well, that was only natural, Yasha thought. He'd met the man once before. Five years earlier, in front of the house of a victim of the Yokohama Lady-Killer. He may not recall where he knew him from, but Yasha couldn't afford to let his guard down around a man as keen-eyed as this. It was clear Nobumasa remembered meeting him somewhere.

Even if he did remember, there was no way he'd know of his relationship with Enma.

"I'm just here to assist Master Kaidou. I'm nobody of any note."

That was an extremely modest way of talking. Something about it didn't sit quite right with Nobumasa, but he didn't pursue it any further.

"Still single, aren't you? How about letting me introduce you to my niece?"

"You must be joking, sir. There's no way someone like me could get along with your family, Master Kaidou."

"Can't say I can see why. Ah well, I doubt women will be able to resist a man like you."

They continued their light banter, smiling as they did.

This man knew nothing. Nothing about what the woman he'd once loved was doing to the tattooist.

Speaking of which, Yasha wondered if Enma was still alive. It depended on the widow. She might surprise him by killing Enma. Well, that would probably please the younger man. After all, he would never be able to die unless he got someone to kill him.

After saying goodbye to Nobumasa Muta, Kaidou announced that they were leaving.

"The game's still in the fourth inning."

"I've paid my favor to the president of Ikkou High School. Enough, already."

He'd put his social discourse to practical use. There was no longer any reason for him to remain here. As far as Kaidou was concerned, baseball was just some silly game.

Naturally, Yasha didn't protest. He'd lived here only five years ago, and there were still plenty of old acquaintances around. Running into one would just raise uncomfortable questions.

He called for a rickshaw and helped Kaidou aboard. He had a secondary residence nearby, so they'd be spending the night there.

"You must be tired."

"Yes. Terrible thing, getting old."

As healthy as he appeared, he was nearly eighty. He probably didn't have much longer to live.

But would he remember while he was still alive? That incident which could only be described as a youthful indiscretion.

The time when he'd been barely twenty years old, and had gotten a girl pregnant...

## —4—

Yasha had a mother up until he was nine years old.

She'd been pretty, as far as he could remember.

What he remembered clearly was that her face always looked sad. She was kind to him, but he never saw her smile. Even as a child, he thought that his mother was an unhappy person. Unfortunately, the presence of a son brought her no comfort.

They had no relatives, and she had worked her way up from prostitution to working as a maid in an inn that catered to sailors. She would set out serving trays, dust, fold the bedding away, and occasionally submit to the innkeeper's unwanted advances. In that endless cycle, his mother had never displayed even a hint of happiness.

His father had apparently been a young retainer from Choushuu. In the end, he'd just been toying with his mother, and didn't seem to think that he could have a child with a former prostitute. When Yasha once asked what his name was, his mother had stabbed him with a nail, telling him to never think of him as a father.

And yet, despite all that, his mother's face had seemed peaceful when she died.

One morning, his mother simply never woke up, and on her face was that calm smile. It was the first time he'd ever seen an expression on her that seemed happy. She looked like she was having a pleasant dream, and so he thought that he'd just leave her alone to enjoy it.

Eventually, there came an uproar. He heard someone tell him that his mother's heart had stopped while she was asleep.

Was death really that pleasant? Only the dead knew, and they never answered that question.

Or perhaps she'd been smiling as she dreamed about being with her son, as Natsu had once said. Had it made her happier to do that?

After that, he did whatever he could to survive. Not a day went by when he didn't steal something. Not until he reached the age of eighteen, and became Baikou's apprentice.

The day he met that man, Baikou had suddenly said, "Let me give you a tattoo!" At first he'd thought he was some guy who was into sex with men, but he wasn't. He was something much more bizarre.

At that time, Baikou had injured his finger and hadn't been able to tattoo anything for a long time, so the desire to do so had built up in him. Once he'd willingly let himself get tattooed and Baikou had offered him an apprenticeship, there was no reason to say no. He spent five years living with Baikou, learning the trade. He never expected his master to disavow him.

When he'd admitted that he'd made himself immortal, Baikou had nearly worked himself into a fit of apoplexy. Forgetting that he could extract the oni if he wanted to, Baikou grabbed a knife from the sink and rushed at him screaming, seemingly intent on lopping his apprentice's arm off. Even knowing full well that cutting the arm off would make no difference.

And on that note, they ended their association.

"Onitsuki, put some tea on, would you?"

Yasha rose in answer to the old man's muttered request.

Was this tendency to think about the past of late a result of age or from his being with this old man? Either way, it was depressing him. He didn't have many pleasant memories to recall.

"Could you make it a little sweet today?"

Yes, he answered. They'd just returned from the baseball game, and he was probably tired.

"For pity's sake, thanks to you, I'm reduced to having these little tea parties," Kaidou grumbled as he stretched out on his bed. The old man had been a heavy drinker in his day, and his liver had been completely wrecked. Doctors had warned him to give up alcohol completely, but he hadn't been able to do it.

Of all the requests he'd heard for oni-gome, abstinence from alcohol was the most common. It was also the one which was most likely to result in good fortune for the client. Five years ago, shortly after his leaving Yokohama, this old man had contracted Yasha for an oni-gome. He'd remained at his side ever since.

When the old man's mood was good, as it was today, serving him was easy. Occasionally, he'd grow terribly obstinate. He'd always been a forgetful and moody man.

"There you go." After letting it cool a bit so as not to scald him, Yasha passed the cup to the old man.

"You seem to be staying away from home more often these days."

"Because I have my main business to attend to." Tattooing was his main business. He would brazenly declare that being Shigekiyo Kaidou's private secretary was just a hobby.

"For pity's sake, you don't have to spend all of your time caring for me. You're a foolish man, aren't you?" the old man said, amusing himself. "Still, you're an interesting guy, and good-looking. And nobody makes a better cup of coffee or tea. So fine, do what you like."

"I'm grateful, sir."

Finishing his tea, Kaidou stretched out on the bed again. His breathing soon changed to the soft rhythm of sleep.

Yasha could relax for a while. He settled back onto the couch by the window and shut his eyes. The ball game was probably still going on.

It had been easy to get the old man to like him. He'd done nothing so far to inspire any hatred. Yasha thought of himself as a seducer of people. The only exceptions to this were Enma and...his own dead mother.

That's why he wondered about it all the more. Why hadn't his mother loved him? Would the world really have been that much more beautiful without her son in it?

His inability to resist the temptation of the oni-gome of immortality, as well as his need to show up anyone bearing the name of Houshou, didn't arise from a simple desire to test himself.

Perhaps what he desired was to conquer death itself. That was why he had tattooed himself rather than another person. As the oni had penetrated his skin and run through his entire body, he'd known that he was no longer human, and had changed into a monstrosity.

There was no turning back. He'd sensed that. He'd crossed a line he shouldn't have crossed, and was dyed with darkness as a result.

Occasionally, he'd run into a monk or some such who could perceive that and hunt him. Apparently, the ugliness of the oni who lived beneath his skin was plain to see.

He now understood. He hadn't conquered death at all. He'd been rejected by it.

Not having to devour people anymore could be seen as a sign of some progress. Getting the heart required not only killing someone, but also mutilating the body. From the very start, that hadn't been something that Yasha liked doing.

The ordeal he'd suffered getting to this point had been awful. Writhing and crawling around in agony from pain which spread through his entire body. Falling into a madness beyond even an oni's ability to endure. He'd even once smashed his right hand into a shapeless pulp with a rock in order to stop it from taking a heart without his controlling it.

Eventually, the oni had given in.

If its host body was driven completely insane, the oni would no longer be able to control it. Insanity was the triumph of ego over everything else. The oni probably feared that.

It had been five years since he'd dumped out those ashes from that speeding train. Since that day, even when he'd taken a life, he hadn't devoured the body. Nobody was more repulsed by the act of eating a heart than Yasha himself. He considered it a victory just being able to resist doing it.

Perhaps, one day, he wouldn't have to kill anyone at all.

Be that as it may, since becoming Kaidou's right-hand man, he'd forgotten all about Enma and the others for a while. Having stumbled so close to political power greatly stimulated Yasha after a lifetime of idleness. Trying to influence the world from behind the scenes might be a good way for him to pass the time. At least, it seemed to be.

His spotting Natsu by chance in the hospital earlier that year had rekindled an interest in his young colleague.

Natsu had clearly aged. Doing her gallant work as a lady doctor had erased the last traces of girlhood from her.

Didn't that guy want to tattoo immortality into her?

<Why hadn't he?> the little oni within his heart had fussed.

Take a hand in this, he thought. You haven't gotten enough. Yasha Houshou can't help but kill. This time, just accept it.

He wondered if he could get Yoshiko Jujo to corner Enma for him.

"There's someone I wish to forget," she'd said.

With that request, she'd invited him to that obscene mansion of hers about two months earlier...

Not having left the estate in such a long time had given the woman almost sickly pale skin.

The truth was that she was probably ill. Both in body and mind. She'd gotten dizzy the moment she'd stood up. As her butler waited on them, she'd regarded Yasha with an anxious look in her eyes.

"I've been looking for you for a long time," she'd said. "For the person who can save me."

"I'm a tattooist," he'd replied. "I doubt I can offer any comfort to your heart, Madam."

The large shadows cast in the flickering candlelight upon Yoshiko's melancholy features fascinated Yasha.

Here was a woman very close to his own soul. Both beautiful and ugly. She probably didn't realize it, but even without an oni-gome, there were already ghastly shadows wriggling around her.

"When I heard that you'd given old Mr. Kaidou a tattoo that had cured his drinking habit, I knew that you were the man I was looking for. The same technique helped the man I love to get himself on the right path years ago. I've finally been able to find you."

"Oni-gome, you mean?"

With her slender neck, she nodded. "Yes. The miraculous technique which saves people from their inescapable karma."

"All it does is trap your karma with another. You may find that it only leads you to hell," he cautioned her. This high-born aristocratic widow seemed to have overly romanticized illusions about what he did.

"It couldn't be any worse than the hell I find myself trapped in now. Day after day, my body burns with feelings which I cannot forget."

"But an oni-gome won't work unless the one receiving it truly desires it to. If there's any hesitation there, there's no point in attempting it. And I beg your pardon, but it seems to me that you still haven't made up your mind about this."

Yoshiko practically swooned at his words. It was a gesture so melodramatic that, normally, it would only have come off as hilarious. But she played her role of tragic heroine so well that he was sorely tempted to leap to his feet and applaud her.

"What a wondrous man you are. You see through me, sir. Yes, you're right. The desire to forget and yet not forget him struggle within me."

While she hadn't been able to make up her mind, Yoshiko had still asked him to tattoo a rose somewhere people couldn't see, and so he'd given her one on her left inner thigh. She had fine skin. Baikou might have screamed and fought to have a chance to work on skin like that.

Yasha sympathized with this woman whose soul so resembled his own. When he'd noticed it, he told her about his mother. Tears came to Yoshiko's eyes as she heard the tale of the woman who was saved by death.

He had to repay her for shedding tears for his mother. He would present to her the best sacrifice he could think of.

"If you ever do make up your mind, please ask a tattooist named Enma Houshou to do it instead of me. He was the man who saved your love from the ravages of drink. Lord Muta guards the tattooist carefully these days, though. It's all right. I'm sure this king of hell will be able to save you."

He'd then told her Enma's address.

Even in her hollow state of mind, hearing the name Muta seemed to grab Yoshiko's attention as she looked up at him.

"Nobumasa…?"

"Yes. Your beloved." He didn't know just how far Yoshiko could understand his intentions. Even so, he could see murderous intent in her mad eyes. "This…would make the two of us accomplices. Would you do me a favor in return?"

Yoshiko nodded.

This woman was more than he'd even hoped for. She'd motivate Enma more than enough.

If Yoshiko managed to kill him, he wasn't a man worth bothering with anyway.

It all depends on you…Enma.

With a slight moan, Kaidou turned over in his sleep. Yasha laid a thin blanket on the old man.

The position of being Kaidou's private secretary made it very convenient for him to investigate things in absolute secrecy. He'd even checked up on Nobumasa Muta, learning about his long-running relationship with that noble widow and even his patronage of Enma.

Yoshiko had thought she'd found him, but naturally that was only because he'd let her do that.

He couldn't understand why the oni within him was so obsessed by that man. However…

Lately, his right hand had started to ache.

For the first time in five years, he could once again hear the muted whispers of the man-eating oni within him.

## —5—

It was the final inning. Just two more outs and it would all be over. Ikkou High School was ahead by two runs. Even Kakei was on the edge of his seat as he watched, as though he might leap up at any moment.

A runner, tagged out as he slid into home plate, punched the ground in frustration. The cloud of dust he'd raised drifted over to them, eliciting some light coughs from Natsu.

"Are you all right?"

"Yes. It must be hard on those boys, it being so dusty. But it makes me feel better to see kids like them sweating out there." Just looking at the players perform was dazzling.

"Well, that's not something I like to hear. They're not that much younger than we are, you know. You're acting like they're children."

Natsu's face reddened as Kakei laughed.

As she watched the game, an old thought occurred to her: decades after she was born, even Enma and her father, who'd once tried to kill each other, might have sat here together like this to enjoy a baseball game. It was a flight of fancy both pleasant and heartbreaking.

One more out and the game would be over. She would have to give Kakei his answer.

When she ran it through her mind, marriage wasn't such a bad way to go. Kakei was planning to study abroad in Germany next year. He'd said that he hoped she would join him. They'd be learning advanced medicine together. She'd probably be too busy to even think about Enma.

Kakei's kindness had seen her through a lot of trials back in med school. As the other male students had unfairly slandered her time and time again, Kakei was the only one who'd always be there to lend a hand.

Natsu really did love him, but not in the same way she felt about the man with so many faults with whom she'd lived.

The field erupted in cheers. The game was over. The players rushed out. Even Kakei had jumped up next to her to applaud them. As she watched the young players embrace each other in delight, she felt ashamed of her own indecisiveness. Even as, five years before, she'd told Enma after he'd risked his life to save her.

*As long as I live, these feelings will never change.*

With the excitement of the close game still reverberating in them, the spectators began to make their way home. There were only a few people left in the corner of the playing field.

Standing under a large oak tree, Natsu faced Kakei. The short young man was rigid with tension.

"Thank you for everything today. I had a lot of fun watching the baseball game." A word of thanks before she proceeded to the question at hand. She could feel her heart racing in her chest.

"Will you be my companion through life?" Kakei repeated the words of his proposal.

She had to tell this sincere man how she felt. She took a deep breath to calm herself, let it out, and stood still as she faced her suitor.

＊ ＊ ＊ ＊ ＊

The high ceiling swam before his eyes.

"Natsu..."

Saying her name, Enma closed his eyes.

All he could do was pray that she stayed out of Yasha's reach.

Once Natsu married, he would be alone once more. There would be no need for her husband and children to know about his immortality. The ideal solution would be for him to go off somewhere far away and never be seen again. In short, to sever all contact. That would do nicely.

But he remembered how he'd shuddered when faced with the reality of the situation.

He realized once again that, as much as Natsu needed him, he needed her even more.

Even though they lived apart, she'd been the only family he'd had for a long time. To break that bond and go back to being a lone, rootless man frightened him more than he could bear.

She'd gotten very pretty of late, Enma thought. She'd always had a terrible inferiority complex about her looks, but it wasn't true. Her eyes sparkled with wit and determination more than anyone else's, and her round, pink face was full of vitality. They probably didn't notice it immediately, but as people got to know this woman named Natsu, they were amazed by the dignified beauty she possessed.

Natsu was his pride. As a child, she'd been so pretty he'd been hesitant to even lay a single finger on her. No matter what decision she made, his feelings for her would never change, not for the rest of his life.

His life...

What was he thinking? Enma found it funny. Just what sort of future does a dying man have?

As long as Natsu was safe, he could ask for nothing more.

He was nearly finished now, and had suffered a lot. His throat was swollen shut, and he could barely breathe. In his dreams, rose vines were tangled around his neck, strangling him.

They were the roses that he had tattooed. Tinged with their fragrance, letting out a sigh, they had come to him, having taken human form.

Feeling a drop of water fall on his face, Enma's eyelids opened.

"I see..."

A pale white woman's face floated before his eyes. Her long hair hung down, and her half-opened lips were wet and red. Tears were falling from eyes which looked worn out from crying.

She hasn't made up her mind?

Unable to either forget or to hold on to her memories, Yoshiko had both hands around Enma's neck as she strangled him.

"I wonder what nirvana is like..." the woman asked, as if dreaming.

So, after five days of anguished crying, this was the conclusion she'd reached.

The lamp above his bed cast the shadows of the two of them on the wall. The figures of a woman who had climbed on top to strangle him and of a dying man flickered there.

"Don't…drag me into…a double suicide…"

With one hand, he pushed Yoshiko back. He tumbled from the bed, gasping for breath. He probably should have been gentler, seeing as she was a woman, but he wasn't softhearted enough to get himself killed.

"There's nothing left here for me to do… I'm leaving." Adding that he'd have a glass of water before he left, Enma crawled across the floor and out of the room. Despite it only being twilight, the inside of the house was dark.

"Where do you think you're going?" Yoshiko muttered. Standing there, her frail body covered with a nightgown like a white dress, she looked like a ghost. She'd probably sent the servants out on errands so that she could take care of him. "Are you running to him?"

"What are you talking about? And why do I have to die with you? It's the other guy you want, isn't it?"

Yoshiko gazed at Enma with a look so heartbreaking it was almost too much to bear. "I won't let you touch him anymore."

She was talking about Nobumasa. Enma opened his eyes so wide, it almost hurt. "You mean you knew that I'm…?"

She'd summoned Enma because she'd known that Nobumasa was an acquaintance of his. He had a tattoo on his right hand. He may have told her about the oni-gome as well.

"So, you weren't doing this for Onituski. You intended to kill me from the start."

"I don't know… I don't know what I wanted."

Perhaps that was true. She hadn't decided to do this until she'd reached her conclusion.

"But when you came here and I saw you, I was astonished. Because I remember you."

Yoshiko leaped onto his back and began strangling him from behind. She couldn't squeeze very hard, but her fingers were as thin as silk floss and still effective.

"Has it really been more than ten years now? Since the day I saw the two of you together. You were angry and he seemed to be trying to calm you. I'd never seen him enjoying himself so much."

That must have been after Okazaki had died. After that, his chances of running into Nobumasa had exceptionally increased. So, this woman had seen him that long ago?

"You haven't changed at all. You're just as young and brilliant as you were then. Even as I've grown older. Old enough to even be jealous of a young man like you!"

He wanted to tell her that she was wrong, but he couldn't speak. And as she was strangling him from behind, he couldn't push her away, either.

"You couldn't have not changed… It must be because I'm mad. Now I see. He won't come back to me because I'm old and insane!"

He managed to loosen the fingers entwining his neck. Gasping for breath, he raised his body. Grasping the stairway bannister in the corridor, he struggled to his feet.

Once he'd gotten out of this mansion, and made sure that Natsu was safe, he would bring Nobumasa back here. Even if he had broken things off with this woman, there was no way he'd just ignore her when she was so clearly ill.

You aren't crazy, he thought. I'm just not human, and I'd cut my own head open to prove it if I could.

Coming to the stairs, Enma looked down to the landing below. It wasn't that far, but it was so dim downstairs that he couldn't see clearly. As he climbed down while clinging to the railing, Yoshiko approached unsteadily.

"I can't be with him anymore… So, I'll kill the both of us. Then… You won't be able to be with him, either!" She reached out with her rose-emblazoned hands.

"That doesn't mean…we have to die!"

All these people. All of them, wanting to die, like fools. One might be charitable and say that it was only human, but it irritated him.

They scuffled as Yoshiko tried to wrap her hands around his neck.

Her foot slipped, and Yoshiko teetered on the edge of the stairs. Enma reached out to grab her, but he was too late. The sound of her tumbling down the staircase seemed to shake the mansion. Her long hair and white nightgown splayed out, like a flower in bloom.

"Don't die!" Enma screamed as he practically threw himself down the stairs after her.

Her lips were red from the blood she'd spat up. Her breathing was shallow, but she was still alive. Yoshiko looked up at Enma with vacant eyes.

"Keep still. I'll get a doctor right now."

Natsu might be able to save her, he thought as he unlocked the front door.

"Madam!"

The butler had returned from wherever he'd gone to. Seeing Yoshiko lying bleeding on the floor, he ran to her side and cried out.

"What on Earth…?! You did this!"

He looked back over his shoulder at Enma, his face twisted in rage. Before Enma had a chance to explain, the butler had his hands around his throat. He squeezed with a strength Yoshiko could only dream of having.

"How dare you! How dare you harm her!"

There was no reasoning with him. This man was even madder than Yoshiko.

"Murota… Stop…"

Hearing Yoshiko's weak voice from behind him, the butler let him go.

"It's all right… He didn't push me…" Her voice was faint, but calm, as though the demon possessing her had fled. "You needn't worry. Mr. Onitsuki told me… He won't touch the one you treasure so… Because he has…" The rest of what she was saying trailed away into a muttering sigh.

"I'll get a doctor." Leaning against the wall, Enma rubbed the finger marks that still bruised his throat.

The butler shook his head. "Madam is dead."

All Enma could see from where he stood was Yoshiko's arm peeking out from behind the butler. The hand tattooed with roses was no longer moving. "Dead...?"

"Your work here is finished. Please leave," the butler said without turning to look at him. There's nothing more for you here. Leave us alone, he was saying. This man had sacrificed his entire life for the sake of his mistress.

Yoshiko's husband had met his end on these same stairs, and perhaps that had been the butler's doing. Maybe that was why he had immediately assumed Enma had pushed her when he saw Yoshiko lying at the bottom of the stairs.

His body battered, Enma stood up and silently left. He couldn't think of anything. He was saved, but he took no pleasure in it.

Baikou, Okazaki, Chie... Why was he never able to save anyone? Why was he so powerless?

The area was already quite dark, and a cold, wintry wind was blowing. He never would have guessed it was June.

He staggered onward. After a while, he heard a crackling and a sound like a tree splitting open.

"Did that madman..."

Looking back, he saw smoke rising from the Jujo estate.

Murota the butler had set the place on fire. Enma ran back along the path he'd taken. His legs were a tangle, and he fell along the way, but he kept on running.

"Hey! Open the door!"

The front door appeared to have been locked from the inside, and didn't budge. Enma pounded at it, but there was no answer. All he heard was the sound of the house collapsing inside and of the fire spreading.

Flames erupted from the windows. People from nearby arrived and pulled Enma back as he tried to force the door open.

"Careful! Get back!"

"There are people inside...!"

"There's no saving them now. Hey! Somebody, get this guy out of here."

With the men offering their shoulders for him to lean his thin body on, Enma was led away from the estate.

Everyone had to die some time, so why were people in such a hurry to rush through their lives?

He started to fade out. The last thing he remembered seeing was enormous flames, fanned by the wind, licking into the sky.

## —6—

Four days had passed since the Jujo estate had burned down on the outskirts of Tokyo.

Two bodies were recovered from the wrecked house, and the press reported their deaths as being the result of an accidental fire. The deceased were Yoshiko Jujo and her butler Murota. The name Enma Houshou wasn't mentioned anywhere in the newspaper articles.

As there was no evidence that he'd returned to the row house where he lived, the only place the badly wounded Enma could have gone to stay was with Nobumasa Muta. As bad as his wounds had been, they should be healed by now.

It didn't take too much to imagine what had transpired that would end with Yoshiko and Murota's deaths.

Yoshiko had probably tried to bring down the curtain on this drama herself. Well, she'd certainly played the role of tragic heroine to the very end.

"What should I do to make a man who has vowed never to kill so angry that he would kill anyway?" Yasha had asked.

"I'll have to let you know."

That was all he'd asked Yoshiko to do. He didn't know exactly what she'd done. At her root, she was a weak woman. Someone like her, living on in agony over her lingering regrets, probably hadn't been able to stand being tattooed.

He'd killed yet another unfortunate woman. All he'd done was change the method that he used. He was wound up, and the great clock that had been stopped began to move once more.

His right hand ached now. It was already past the throbbing stage.

He glanced at the old man's face as he slept. His neuralgia had grown worse lately, and he needed pills in order to fall asleep. He was growing even more forgetful, and Yasha doubted that Kaidou even remembered his mother now.

There was no point in staying here any longer. He'd been a fool to have expected anything to come of it. Tomorrow, he'd leave.

"O… Onitsuki," the old man moaned.

"Are you awake?"

As he drew near, the old man glared at him with his rheumy eyes. His pains were probably acting up, and he was in a bad mood.

"I was having a bad dream, dammit."

"A dream, sir?" He wiped sweat from the old man's brow.

"I saw a man I let die long ago stand up, all bloody."

"That you let die?"

The old man nodded. "It was some kid from a Choushuu samurai family. He was an assassin. We had him infiltrate the Shinsengumi, but he was discovered and I heard he'd been killed… This was about thirty years back. In the end, he was just a pawn we sacrificed. I'd forgotten all about him. Why would I be having a dream about him now? Damn, it pisses me off."

Ah, now he saw. The old man had done all sorts of things like this. He'd betray others, stepping over them to survive. There probably wasn't a fragment of a memory left in him of the woman he'd impregnated in his youth.

"Water."

As ordered, he filled a glass with water and handed it to him. He tried to help hold it to keep it from spilling, but the old man pushed him away, saying he could damn well drink his own water.

"Goddamned quack. He should've given me better drugs to take." He sipped his water as he cursed, then suddenly frowned. "It's warm."

"It's boiled water. I let it cool."

"Oh, you useless… Get me some cold water, dammit!" Kaidou's temper flared. His face looked like a demon from hell.

"The doctor said that you shouldn't." The doctor had warned him not to drink any cold or unboiled water. He was old, and prone to diarrhea.

"Don't talk back to me, you monster!"

The old man threw his glass at him, striking Yasha in the forehead.

Yasha regarded the old man silently.

That's right, he was a monster. The old man's words had made him remember a fact he'd half-forgotten. He didn't even notice the line of blood that was dripping from his forehead.

"That little cut will just heal soon, anyway. Why am I the one who has to be stuck in such agony? Ah, dammit all! It hurts!"

Grumbling and moaning, Kaidou lay down. He might have still been mumbling something, but Yasha couldn't hear anything anymore.

His right hand pressed down on the old man's face, precisely covering his nose and mouth. Kaidou's eyes were wide with terror, seeming to beg for his life. His stringy hands clawed at the air, searching for something to grab onto.

Yasha's blood roared. His heart exulted. It wasn't just the oni. His own body rejoiced in doing it. Yes, he thought. This is my true nature. The murders he'd committed before this were done because he'd enjoyed doing it. He could pretend to be human for a little while, but it wouldn't last very long.

How irritating.

The face of his younger, impudent counterpart floated up through his mind. What was the difference between one who'd tattooed immortality into himself and one who hadn't?

"It's your fault, because you wouldn't remember," he muttered accusingly at the old man.

He could send a person painlessly to their death, but Yasha didn't do that. He wanted this man to suffer and then be cast into hell. He looked down with dead eyes at the old man who writhed in agony, seemingly pleading not to die. At last, the old man's arms fell limply to the futon, and Yasha removed his hand.

"Goodbye, Father."

As though satisfied, his right hand no longer throbbed.

The breeze blowing in from the window felt pleasant. The sky was blue everywhere.

Where would he go now?

Some place as far from here as possible.

* * * * *

Enma was at the Muta residence. Rather than the Black Mansion, this was a house Nobumasa had built for himself a few years earlier.

How many times had he cheated death by now?

Even so, this time he still hadn't fully recovered even after four days. His wounds had healed, but he'd gotten a fever right after.

The fever had to be due to Natsu, Enma thought. Just when he thought he could relax at seeing her healthy and unharmed, she told him the news.

"I turned down the proposal."

As dumbfounded as Enma was, Natsu managed to smile and maintain her composure.

"It seems I didn't have the audacity to marry Kakei. Since I doubt someone as fine as him will ever propose to me again, I guess you're stuck with me."

Enma's eyes went wide. "You… You're a fool!"

"Yes, a very big one." But this was for the best, Natsu added. "In a few years, I'll probably go from being your older sister to your mother. I get depressed thinking I'll have to be your grandmother at some point, though. But, it's all right. I want to keep helping you until I no longer can, big brother. That's all."

When she saw the conflicted expression on Enma's face, she continued, "I know this is a losing game, but it's something I have to do. It can't be helped." There was almost a singing tone in her voice, then she was back to being the same old Natsu. "I mean, look at you. I take my eyes off of you for a little while and look what happened. While I was thinking you didn't want to come to a baseball game, you were dying. Honestly, I'd be too worried to ever leave you to get married."

Natsu placed some wild chrysanthemums in a vase as she fussed. She'd spotted them growing by the roadside. The simple white blossoms calmed Enma.

Thinking that he and Natsu could still be family made him sincerely happy. There'd certainly be more troubles for him ahead. The day would come when he'd have to play her son, and finally her grandson. But as she'd said, things were best as they were now. Besides, this was the daughter of Okazaki, and once she'd made up her mind, there could be no deviation. It was pointless to try and talk her out of it.

Enma covered himself with the futon.

It seemed Yasha hadn't shown up for Natsu. Had Yoshiko been lying to him, or had Yasha told her to tell him that lie? He could imagine that either case could be true.

Nobumasa had come running out there as soon as he'd heard that the Jujo estate had burned down. That was when he'd learned that Enma had been taken to the hospital. While he didn't know Enma's connection to the fire which had killed Yoshiko and the butler, he quickly had him taken to his home before his strange secret was discovered.

If his immortality ever became public knowledge, even Nobumasa would be helpless to protect him.

"Lord Muta agrees with me. He said you need a good talking-to." With Nobumasa playing backup, Natsu had given him a good piece of her mind. She seemed satisfied and told him that she was returning to Yokohama today. "You may heal on your own, but my patients won't without treatment, big brother."

There was no point in playing nursemaid for him, she went on, scolding him. All this nagging may have been springing from newfound confidence, having finally scaled the mountain of doubt that had been growing inside of her.

It was true that Enma didn't need a doctor. However, he needed Natsu. Even though he couldn't admit it, those were the feelings he couldn't fake. What he felt could genuinely be called love, and while his real age was a little too advanced, that didn't take away from what it was.

"All right, all right. Get going back there. You're going to miss the train to Yokohama."

As Enma urged her to go, Natsu got a slightly sulky look on her face. "You're always driving me away, big brother."

"Unlike me, you lead a busy life. Oh, besides that, if that Onitsuki bastard shows up, stay away from him. Don't let him sweet talk you, just tell me or Nobumasa right away."

Natsu meekly nodded. Learning that the "pretty person who would have looked good with white wings" that she'd met as a little child had actually been Yasha had shaken her severely. It must have been horrible for her to think that, had she given the wrong answer then, she might not be alive today.

"He said he was coming for me. What would he want with me?"

"Perhaps…" Enma began. "Perhaps he wants to burden you with the same fate that he has. There are times when you want someone who can walk through eternity with you. Very much."

And he'd want a strong girl like Natsu all the more, he thought. Someone to support him where he was weak, who could walk with him in the same flow of time, no matter what… Enma bit his lip as he considered the implications. While he couldn't forgive Yasha's madness, he could understand it. And he was annoyed with himself for it.

"My heart will always belong to you, big brother," Natsu declared with dignity, a refreshing look on her face. "I'm leaving. Masa can handle the rest of what needs to be done."

She quickly began getting ready to go.

After Natsu had departed, Enma lay down on the couch and wiped his eye with the back of his hand.

She made me cry…

He wasn't going to hand Natsu over to anyone. Not anyone.

Clean bedding and warm meals. The Muta residence didn't skimp on creature comforts. If he didn't leave soon, he really was going to end up as Nobumasa's pet dog. That wasn't a joke.

After today, he decided that he'd thank Nobumasa for everything and then go home.

"Oh, dear. You haven't finished it again. You have to be sure and eat it all." Seeing the rice gruel left in his bowl, Masa was raising a fuss.

"My mistake. I'll eat it up right now." He was glad to see that his former neighbor was as healthy as ever. As he'd thought, she was in Nobumasa's employ, and was in charge of all the household duties here.

"You'd better. You're not going to get well unless you eat your meals. I don't care how tough they say your body is, you can't push yourself too far."

"I think you look tougher than me, Masa." Maybe it was due to her wearing an apron over her kimono, but Masa was about twice Enma's girth.

"Not really. I have back trouble. My husband finally passed away last year, that good-for-nothing."

A slightly sad smile came to her face as she mentioned her late husband. Her children were all grown and on their own now, and Nobumasa was clever at everything, so he needed little caring for. Masa always seemed like the type who took pleasure in taking care of someone else. And she was even more stubborn than Natsu.

"Now, eat every last drop."

He didn't have much of an appetite, but the oni within him was definitely telling him to eat it. The oni may have been similar to Masa in some ways. He picked up the bowl and slowly began spooning the gruel into his mouth.

"Oh, by the way, the gardener gave me something for you before. From a friend of yours?" She produced an envelope from her breast pocket and handed it to him. A piece of paper was folded inside.

"A letter?" Nobody knew that he was here, save for Natsu and Masa. Thinking how strange this was, he unfolded the paper.

Yasha…!

He crumpled the letter in his hands as he unsteadily got to his feet.

His body was still sluggish, but if Yasha said he wanted to meet, then they were going to meet. There was too much bad blood between them to ignore this.

"Oh? Are you going out? Don't push yourself too hard yet."

"I'm just going for a walk around the neighborhood." He ran his fingers through his hair and fixed his open kimono.

"The master will be back soon. Why don't you leave it for later?" Masa's round face clouded, as though she had some vague sense that something was wrong.

"I'll be back soon."

The ashen skies were truly dismal, the clouds looking terribly oppressive. The damp chill air of the rainy season made Enma cough a bit.

There was a grove of bamboo just behind the Muta residence. It had grown lush, thanks to a long rainy spell that seemed to specifically target the imperial capital. The bamboo seemed to stab at the sky, having grown green and thick, swaying in the breeze.

He was waiting in the grove back there, just as his letter had said. He hadn't signed his name, but he'd drawn a simple crescent moon on it instead. Of course, Enma would have figured it out immediately even without that.

He could feel the sweat welling up in his clenched palms. Part of him wanted to scream at Yasha and punch him out, but if he lost his cool, he'd likely end up murdering him.

Pushing his way through the grove, he spotted a tall, slender man dressed in Western clothing.

"Hello. Has it really been five years?"

The man Natsu had mistaken for an angel when she was little still had an ethereal quality to him. His feet almost seemed to float above the ground.

"You're so late, I was thinking of leaving."

"What's your hurry? You have all the time in the world, don't you?"

Yasha motioned that he'd hit back if Enma got too close, so he stopped about seven or eight shaku (approximately feet) from him.

"I'm leaving this country. Ships have schedules and such to keep. I'm glad we could meet before I left."

Seeing the oddly sad look on Yasha's face, Enma frowned. "You're going overseas?"

"A little vanishing act till the heat dies down."

He must have done something. "Are you still after Natsu?"

"Not so much these days. I have you now. Like it or not, we're joined by a common destiny."

Enma nearly spat in disgust at what he said. So, to fill the loneliness of eternity, Yasha's companion would be someone he treated like a younger brother but who also hated his guts. Was it tied to this man's desire to be killed? In any case, it seemed that Yoshiko had been lying when she said that Onitsuki wanted him confined so that he could go after Natsu.

"Why did you set Yoshiko Jujo on me?"

The memory of her weeping as she tried to strangle him was still fresh in his mind. The woman bound by a chain of roses had lay down in the coffin she lived in, both of them consumed in flame. Along with her devoted companion.

"Because I thought it would make you hate me. Enough to kill me."

Enma raised an eyebrow in surprise. "What the hell is that supposed to mean? Do you… Do you want to kill me, or be killed by me? Which is it?"

Yasha considered it for a moment. "Maybe… Seventy percent to be killed by you and twenty percent to kill you."

"Your math's off."

Yasha gave an embarrassed smile, as if to say he couldn't account for that last ten percent. "People's hearts are like the world at large. They very rarely follow exact calculations."

As always, all he did was speak in riddles. Still, everyone had times when they themselves didn't understand how they felt. Besides, he and I both have to live as monsters, Enma thought. Maybe it was impossible not to go mad.

Were the whispers he heard coming out of the darkness himself? The oni? There were times when it was hard to be sure of even that. They could resemble the nonsensical ravings of a ridiculous madman.

"Whatever. But I warn you: never get an unrelated woman mixed up in this again. And of course, stay the hell away from Natsu."

Saying "or else I'll kill you" would only have pleased Yasha. There was no opponent harder to deal with than someone with nothing at all to defend.

Could that be what he regrets the most?

He stopped considering it immediately after the thought popped into his head. Yasha wouldn't want his pity, and Enma didn't want to give him any clumsy sympathy, either.

"I killed people, before I got this body. I'm through with that now." If you don't change, you can't live, Enma thought. For all the resentment he felt for Yasha, he earnestly kept it under control. It was partly willpower.

Yasha shrugged, as if to say that was too bad. "You don't have to worry for now. It's not like I can do anything from overseas." He drew out a gold pocket watch and checked the time. "I have to get going. I'm sorry we couldn't have more time to talk."

"Is that watch…" Enma felt a sensation like his blood was flowing backwards as goosebumps rose on the back of his neck.

"Yes. The one the Yokohama Lady-Killer lost. I've grown quite fond of it."

Yasha grasped the chain between his fingers, then suddenly twirled the pocket watch around. He grasped it tightly for a moment, then tossed it to Enma.

"Keep it. Goodbye, until next time."

And as soon as he'd uttered his parting words, he was on the run, vanishing deeper into the thick bamboo grove.

"Why, you…!"

Still holding the watch, Enma ran after him. If it hadn't been for this watch, Chie wouldn't have been murdered. And Natsu wouldn't have been kidnapped and threatened.

Yasha had been behind all that. The one who had led the killer on and turned his bloody assassin's blade on them had been him.

Enma ran through the bamboo grove, the stalks rustling around him. Sliding down a steep hill and emerging on a road, he couldn't see Yasha anywhere.

As he stopped, wondering which way he'd gone, Enma saw a man dressed in a black *hakama* approaching from the right. It was Nobumasa, returning from the funeral service of an acquaintance of his.

"What's wrong? Shouldn't you be in bed?"

He was surprised to see Enma there, gasping for breath, his thin kimono open.

"Did you see a young guy dressed in Western clothing? It was Yasha."

"He grabbed the rickshaw that just dropped me off. That was Yasha?"

Nobumasa turned to look back.

"Wait!" He seized Enma's wrist to stop him from giving chase. He pointed to the blood dripping from his toes on his sandal-clad feet. Enma hadn't even noticed the bamboo splinters he'd stepped on.

"Never mind! Lemme go!" I'll kill him, I'll kill him, I'll kill him… Enma's eyes were red, as though the blood in his body was seething with rage.

"You can't chase after him on those feet. Let's go back." Trying to calm the enraged Enma, Nobumasa patted his back. "That was Master Kaidou's private secretary. So, he was Yasha, huh?"

"Kaidou?"

"A former member of the Privy Council who died the day before last. He was an old man with a lust for power and an inexhaustible supply of nasty gossip. I'd heard that there were some questions about the cause of death, but if that man was involved, then…"

Kaidou… Enma thought he'd heard the name somewhere before, but he wasn't interested enough to try to remember any more. He was now ruled by his anger towards Yasha. Now, at this moment, there was no doubt that the devil had taken possession of his heart. He was no different from the sinner, except that the man he had to kill wasn't standing in front of him.

If Yasha had killed an important politician and had to flee overseas, he wouldn't be back for a while. Enma's shoulders shook with frustration. He threw the pocket watch down and smashed it to bits with his foot.

Enma returned to the mansion and began to get ready to go home. He folded his clothes, unable to conceal his frustration.

Nobumasa watched Enma silently. In addition to the wake for the old man Yasha had killed, he'd attended the funeral service for Yoshiko and her servant, attended to the Jujo family legacy, and generally settled their affairs. These last few days had been exceedingly busy for him.

Yoshiko had left a will stating that her estate was to be used for charitable activities in the event of her death, and she had named Nobumasa as executor. Even after they'd broken up, having no relatives, Nobumasa had been the only person she could rely on.

"The police is closing the case on this, calling it an accidental fire caused by a fallen candle."

"I see…" Enma was being taciturn, probably because he worried about what he'd have to say if Nobumasa asked him any questions. As long as the other man didn't bring it up, Enma wouldn't have to tell him.

"Was it really just a coincidence?" At last, the subject was broached. "That you were there when it happened?"

Enma had tried to conceal the truth. It wasn't out of consideration for Nobumasa, that knowing everything would only hurt him, but rather simply because he hadn't wanted to talk about it.

"How many times do I have to say it? I happened to be walking by, saw the house on fire, and just ran over to help." Enma heaved a tremendous sigh. "I'm sorry… For not saving them."

Nobumasa shook his head. "No. The one who didn't save Yoshiko was me." He let out a weary sigh as he looked at his right hand. "Yoshiko was interested in the tattoo on my palm, and I told her about the oni-gome when we were in bed one time. I didn't mention you by name, of course, and I tried to make it sound like I was kidding, but she kept asking if there wasn't a way to use it to keep from getting older. I laughed and kept telling her that, no, there wasn't. Why was she so obsessed with youth?"

Enma had a feeling he knew. Nobumasa was the sort of man who only grew more attractive with age. Perhaps his keeping company with an older woman like Yoshiko made her insecure.

Enma scratched his head and looked up at Nobumasa. "Probably because she loved you, that's all."

"I wonder about that. The last time I saw her, I said I didn't want to be with her anymore. I couldn't deal with it anymore." He may have been a man who was like a mass of mature dignity, but he seemed surprisingly oblivious of her love for him.

"Maybe that was more than she could deal with." Despite the hell she'd put him through, Enma looked back on Yoshiko with pity.

"You seem to know a lot about how she felt."

Enma rose from the bed, looking amused. "Despite appearances, I'm fifty years old. I've learned a few things about life, in my own way."

He may have been free of any wounds, wrinkles, or blemishes, but that didn't change the fact that he was older than Nobumasa. He had the right to lecture this snotty kid once in a while.

"Despite your exceptionally long association with her, she may have been more unstable than you realized. Maybe you could have reassured her a little more. Because, believe it or not, you dolt, neither women nor the world revolve around you."

Saying that much was the best punishment he could manage in that woman's place.

His fever had dropped. He was well enough to leave. He changed into the kimono and *hakama* that Natsu had brought from his home.

"Goodbye, and thanks for your hospitality."

Thanking him bluntly, Enma turned to leave the room, but Nobumasa seized his arm.

"What happened with Yoshiko? What did she say to you?"

No mere accidental acquaintance would talk about a dead woman that passionately. Of course Nobumasa had taken notice.

"Nothing. You're imagining things." He shook off Nobumasa's hand. I won't let you touch him. He remembered Yoshiko saying that. "The police say it was an accidental fire. Leave it at that."

He didn't want to see the scandal that would play out in the papers about the unnatural death of the beautiful widow. How she'd killed herself in her longing for a lost love and how her butler then set her estate ablaze. The common people loved to sneer at the love affairs of the rich and powerful. The more it was written about, the more that would come to light. If he wasn't careful, Nobumasa's name would get mentioned as well.

"All of your money was stolen. What are you going to do?"

So, that secret was out, too. He couldn't help but gasp. "Shut up, I'll manage."

"Why didn't you tell Natsu?"

"Because if I did, she'd just complain and say how this was just like me to do. I don't want her to worry..."

Nobumasa shrugged in resignation. "But they stole your tools, too. How will you earn a living?"

The new ones he'd bought with Yoshiko's advance had been lost in the fire. This really was a crisis.

"Look, if you need money, I'll just—"

"No, I don't need it! Who the hell needs to borrow money from you?!" With an enraged shout, Enma stalked out into the entryway. He was angry enough about Yoshiko, and now Nobumasa was pissing him off even more.

"Come on, at least take this!" Nobumasa held out a small package wrapped in a cloth. He smiled wryly at Enma's suspicious look, and added, "They're rice balls that Masa made for you. If you don't want them, you can return them to her yourself. I'd be too scared to."

Enma was speechless. Of course, there was no way he could do that, either.

He silently took the package. He felt a surge of anger as Nobumasa stifled his laughter, but there was no way to win when he had Masa on his side.

"I loved Yoshiko, although I doubt I loved her more than Murota did. There was never another woman for me, before or since."

"I see. Then that's good."

Nobumasa's words were probably a fine tribute to Yoshiko's memory.

As Enma stepped outside, his body trembled. The chill, rainy sky seemed leaden and oppressive.

In his weakened state, it seemed even colder. It was a little hard for his *geta*-clad feet to walk on the damp ground.

He'd borrow money from somewhere, get new tools... As he thought that, he was thankful for the rice balls. He hugged his arms tightly to his chest.

He heard a crumpling sound. When he touched the rice balls, he felt they weren't wrapped in bamboo skin. With a sense of foreboding, he unwrapped the package.

"That son of a bitch..."

There was a bundle of bank notes under the rice balls. Nobumasa had known Enma would never have simply accepted the money outright.

Jerked around, yet again...

He thought it over, then stuffed the bills into his breast pocket. He'd pay it back. With a lot of interest. By hook or by crook, he'd pay it back. Swearing that to himself, Enma set out once more.

There was no time to be depressed. Tomorrow, he'd have to get back to work right away.

## Chapter 5

# The Dawn of a New Century

*A.D. 1945 (Showa 20)*

### —1—

Like a sign of the times, he'd seen the name "Onitsuki" crop up again and again.

There was that newspaper account detailing the signing of the Treaty of Portsmouth which ended the Russo-Japanese War, which mentioned an interpreter named Onitsuki. And then there was a businessman calling himself Onitsuki who'd made a killing during the reconstruction following the Great Kanto Earthquake of 1923. The name Onitsuki even popped up regarding the killing of military personnel in the Mukden Incident. Of course, there was no way to know for certain if it was him.

The man had a death wish, and it seemed to be his fate to throw himself into dangerous places.

As the Meiji era became Taisho, and Taisho became Showa, the world seemed to grow darker and darker. At the dawn of the Meiji Restoration, most people viewed the Tokugawa era as a dark night. But as it receded and became the stuff of childhood memory, it seemed more like a lively moonlit night in its own way. The nights of the Showa era weren't like that at all. The way ahead seemed to be only one of inky blackness. People suffered in a darkness that would cause even the creatures of the night to flee in terror.

It was 1945, the twentieth year of Showa. The month of March was nearly over, and Enma Houshou lived in the bombed-out ruins of Tokyo.

The world had gotten tough to live in.

"Forward! One Hundred Million Burning Souls!" proclaimed the disgusting propaganda poster. Enma eyed it wearily. They'd been at this for three years now. When the hell was this war going to end? The city had been practically leveled by large-scale aerial bombardment, and yet, ironically, this poster survived unharmed.

He emerged onto a road which had escaped the bombing, passing by a row of cherry trees. Looking up, he saw the clear sky peeking through the spaces between the flower petals. It was hard to believe that, somewhere in that same sky, yet more meaningless killings were taking place.

A young girl dressed in *monpe* work pants turned and stared at Enma like he was some sort of curiosity. There weren't that many young men around these days. The fact he was also walking along in the middle of the day holding a cat in his arms must have made him an especially odd sight.

Kuro slept a lot these days. Nothing seemed to be specifically wrong with him, but he was definitely getting weaker. Since the monster cat with the oni-gome of immortality showed no signs of recovery, this wasn't a trivial matter.

He recalled something that Baikou had told him. It was idle talk about whether an oni would lose interest and leave the body, or whether they had a limited life span which nobody would likely ever be able to practically confirm.

He imagined an oni leaving would be the same as extracting it. Considering Kuro's true age, he'd most certainly die at once, and yet that wasn't happening. What that meant was that the oni inside of him was growing gradually weaker, and vanishing bit by bit, didn't it?

So, was it coming to the end of its life span?

The words "life span" were tinged with both hope and unease. It meant that a day would finally come when he would die. There could have been no better news for Enma than that. However, it also meant that he'd be losing Kuro soon.

The frail, purring Kuro he carried in his arms looked like an ordinary cat. At one time, you could sense something supernatural about him. Not anymore.

He'd heard there was a veterinarian somewhere around here, and had scooped Kuro up to see if he could get him some medicine, but he soon ended up having to retrace his steps.

He saw a child's bones buried in the rubble along the way. The air raids had taken a terrible toll, and Tokyo was now awash with injured people. How many tens of thousands of people had died so far?

There was nothing more cowardly than dropping bombs from the sky, he thought. You couldn't even see the people you were dropping them on as they fled from you. It made the act of killing too easy. Lots of blood had been spilled in the upheaval towards the end of the shogunate, but it was mostly from people fighting each other with swords. They would feel the flesh splitting open, the blood spraying on them, and see their opponent die before their eyes.

"There was a morality to killing, back then…" Enma grumbled to the cat asleep in his arms, like an old man might. He never thought he'd ever miss those days.

This was no time to be wasting effort on examining one cat. Every vet, dentist, or anyone with any medical knowledge at all was busy examining people these days.

Even Natsu was hard at work, treating the injured.

Enma and Natsu had arrived in Tokyo ten days ago. From the day they'd arrived after the two-day trip from Kyoto, Natsu had been working as a doctor. After hearing about the raids, she'd specifically rushed here to help with the relief efforts.

It went without saying that there was no call for a tattooist anywhere. The closest he'd come to doing that was applying ointment to scraped skin.

This was a time for life and death, not for tattooing anyone.

I want to tattoo something…

An image of the four heavenly kings, or perhaps one of the Buddha of Transcendent

Wisdom. Even a scene of cherry blossoms falling like a blizzard... He hadn't tackled a really big project in years, and now had an inkling of how Baikou had felt so long ago. It was worse for Baikou, since the oni inside of him raged to make him tattoo till the day he died. He probably didn't fight it at all.

But a war was on, and some people had a need for the skills of Ura-Enma.

He'd been arrested by the so-called Special High Police, also known by the more sinister moniker of the Thought Police. Their job was to investigate political agitators and traitors. He wasn't really involved with any anti-war activities at all. He was a tattooist, open for business that wasn't really coming his way. At first, he wondered if they'd discovered an irregularity in his draft exemption. Enma had been labeled a Class D: mind and body unfit for military service. Being branded like that was like revoking his manhood. People saw him as a good-for-nothing disgrace.

However, what the Thought Police had been after was the "mass production of super soldiers." They wanted him to tattoo oni-gome into their men that would make them unafraid of death and fight for their country. That they were discussing this idea in complete deadly seriousness convinced him that they were about to lose the war. Still, how had they found out about oni-gome? Well, although he swore his customers to secrecy, he supposed it was hard to hide a tattoo that was on such an easily seen place as the palm of your hand.

There was no way he could turn people into weapons. Naturally, he'd refused. And naturally, they made him sorry that he had.

The Thought Police specialized in torture. They beat his entire body continuously, not giving it any time to heal. Since his toenails grew back by the next morning after they'd been torn off, Enma had to keep tearing them off again himself. He knew that if they learned the secret of his oni-gome, their next demand would be for him to make them soldiers who couldn't die.

After four days of this, Enma was released. Natsu had made a direct appeal to Nobumasa Muta. She was in her mid-seventies at this point, and just finding Enma had been difficult enough. Fortunately, Nobumasa had been searching for him as well at the same time.

"We have to save Enma at once," the young girl had told Nobumasa.

Even at the age of eighty-five, Nobumasa still possessed considerable authority. The Thought Police normally let nothing stop them, but even they didn't dare keep torturing the man who had Lord Muta as a patron. Despite the tremendous pain, Enma was still able to move a bit, and so he paid Nobumasa a visit. How many years had it been? He didn't want to see him, and it wasn't because of a childish inferiority complex as it had been before.

Even for a man who was skilled at using age to make himself seem even more majestic, old age had him firmly in its grasp. It would be tough seeing him now, after ten years. Still, he had to thank him. Natsu would never let him hear the end of it if he didn't.

The white-haired old man was asleep when Enma came for his long-awaited reunion. His deeply wrinkled and stained face, his body now so frail it seemed to be just skin and bones, left Enma at a loss for words.

"I told him that Enma was coming today, and he said he'd stay awake and wait for you, but…" the girl at Nobumasa's side said.

* * * * *

Keiko Muta. Nobumasa's adopted girl. She was from his mother's side of the family, a blood relative, but just barely. He'd adopted her after her parents had died years ago. She was a young girl with a pretty face and eyes which always made her seem vaguely annoyed by something. Her hairstyle suggested that of a traditional Japanese *ichimatsu* doll, but her pale eyes were more like those of a Western figurine.

She'd still been a child the last time he'd seen her, but now she had blossomed into young womanhood. One thing that hadn't changed about her was the informal way she called him just plain Enma, with no mister, master, or lord in front of it. He doubted that she disliked him, but she always seemed to look a little angry whenever they met.

"You saw me coming?"

"Yes."

He'd expected her to say that. Keiko was clairvoyant, he recalled Nobumasa telling him. Naturally, he hadn't doubted him. Compared to immortality, clairvoyance was just a personality quirk.

"By any chance… Did you know that I'd been arrested by the Thought Police?"

"I didn't know that it was the Thought Police specifically, but I knew you were in a situation where you had to be rescued. As soon as I told grandfather, he made arrangements to look for you."

Ah, so that had been it. Good thing, too. Had the torture gone on any longer, they likely would have discovered his true nature.

"You saved me."

While his wounds weren't completely healed yet, a normal man would most likely have died from their torture. There were all sorts of ways you could torture an immortal man if you just thought about it. You just had to keep it up at a level which didn't kill him instantly. He'd have fallen into an endless hell, kept just short of death. The Thought Police were the worst opponents he'd ever faced.

"I wish we could have rescued you sooner," she murmured with regret, reaching out to touch his face. Some burns still showed where they'd stubbed out their cigarettes on it.

"Don't you know when the war's going to end? I'm sick and tired of the whole thing."

"This summer. Or maybe by autumn."

Enma whistled in amazement. "Well, that'll be nice. Is that your clairvoyance?"

"No, grandfather estimated it from the war situation and his own guesses. I can't see the future." Keiko couldn't make predictions. What she saw was vague, and limited to what was happening in the present.

"I see… Then it must be true." He felt a little relieved that he just needed to be patient a bit longer.

"Is Dr. Natsu well?"

"Yeah, she's doing fine. She had patients to see, so she couldn't come today."

That wasn't actually true. Lately, it was getting harder for her to carry out the physically demanding tasks medical treatment required. It had been eight decades since time had stopped for him. Everyone that he'd known had left him behind and grown old. Masa, who'd been the same age as him, had died nearly twenty years before. Even so, he was told that she had lived an exceptionally long life.

"Nobumasa's asleep. Please thank him for me. I'll leave now."

"Grandfather was really looking forward to seeing you. Won't you wait a little longer? It's cruel to just leave like this." She stepped in front of Enma as he prepared to go. Nobumasa was so old now, and there was a war on. If he didn't see him now, he may never see him again. Keiko must have been thinking this as well.

"It's still too soon for him to be meeting the king of hell… Tell him not to get senile."

He didn't think he could talk to Nobumasa now. When Enma left, he felt like he was almost running away.

That had been two months ago.

He wondered how Nobumasa was doing.

Everyone was dying.

He hugged Kuro to him. His only compatriot. If he died, Enma didn't know what he'd do. The plague of death spreading through this nation frightened him like nothing else ever had.

That was why he wanted to tattoo. When he was doing that, he could forget about everything else. He thought about going home and tattooing his own leg, then reconsidered at once. That might as well have been masturbation.

He was losing it…

Kuro suddenly meowed, his gaze fixed at one point.

"You see it too, huh?"

He wished he could have passed right by and pretended not to have seen it.

The young man lying under the cheery tree seemed to notice the cat's meows and lifted his head slightly. When they inadvertently made eye contact, Enma was confused.

"Saki…?"

It couldn't have been him. That kid had died decades before at the siege of Goryoukaku. Even now, he could still remember his face, uncertain and looking like he was about to cry. Enma walked up in front of the figure who'd been passed out on the ground. He had the bristly hair of one whose head had been shaved bald and then allowed to grow out. Tall, thin, and baby-faced, he had a nametag on the breast pocket of a national service uniform, and puttees on his legs.

The more he looked at him, the more he saw the resemblance. Even so, it was a memory from back in the days of Edo. Until he'd seen this boy, he'd honestly forgotten what Saki had looked like.

Ichinose-san, it's morning.

The fragment of memory popping up in his mind made Enma dizzy as he remembered it.

"Um…" The boy hesitantly addressed the man who was staring at him silently. "Could you help me, please?"

He probably couldn't figure out if Enma wanted to help him or not. Enma scratched his head, looking a bit embarrassed now. "A bit, I guess."

"I'm really hungry, so… Could I please…"

Begging for food from a complete stranger in the burned-out ruins of Tokyo might have been a little over the line. But how could he ignore this boy who looked so much like Saki?

Laying Kuro down, Enma produced two steamed sweet potatoes from his pocket. Two almost impossibly expensive potatoes he'd bought from a vendor along the way.

"Thank you so much."

The boy began wolfing it down, not even stopping to unwrap the newspaper around it.

This doppleganger of Saki was named Hiroaki Takami. He was eighteen, he explained, and had come to the capital to study at an art college. Even though he'd prepared himself for it, the ruins of Tokyo were worse than he'd imagined. The school building itself had been spared by the air raids, but many of the teachers and students had been killed, and there were no prospects of it reopening. But then, most schools had lost their original function long ago as a result of students being called up to serve in the military. While he was still technically a student, he'd been mobilized to help make weapons for the army. He'd finally gotten a day off, had headed off in high spirits to do some sketching, and then had collapsed from hunger.

"You're not a little kid, you know." Enma couldn't believe his ears. The youth was like a little child who, heedless of the fever it had, ran around and around until it had collapsed.

"I was engrossed in sketching. Then, when I got up, my legs just wouldn't stand straight." Takami blushed. Sitting there on his knees with his legs splayed out to either side made him seem even more childish, and he looked fourteen or fifteen at most. As he stroked Kuro, who'd climbed onto his leg, he smiled apologetically.

"I suppose, being a poor student, it couldn't be helped. Have you got any money?"

"I think I still have a little left in the bank, and I was going down there to withdraw it."

"Best to do that now, before a bomb falls on it," Enma said, nodding.

"I'm really such a fool. I forgot to even drink any water since the day before yesterday."

Was there anything left in Tokyo worth looking at that would so engross this boy? As far as the eye could see, there was nothing but depressing ruins all around them. "May I see?" asked Enma, eyeing the sketchbook to his side.

"They're not good, but… Sure."

Taking the shyly proffered sketchbook, Enma looked inside.

"Wow…"

There was a radiant young girl looking up at the sky from the rubble, an old rice gruel vendor, smiling brazenly, a woman with imposing breasts nursing her baby… Every manner of person, overflowing with vitality. All sorts of facial expressions, strong, but with a feeling of gentleness, rendered with a sentiment that came from the artist's hand.

"Amazing. These pictures are fascinating."

Takami looked surprised. "What do you mean?" he asked.

"I mean what I said, these are fantastic. No, I'd never be able to draw anything like this. The scales have fallen from my eyes. They're amazing. Really impressive." Enma was being completely sincere. It was praise from the heart to a dazzling young talent who sat before him. Looking at drawings like these made him see how dark and obscene the stuff he did was.

"Pardon, but do you draw, too?"

Enma smiled wryly at how expectantly the boy looked at him. "My canvas is the human body. I'm a tattooist."

"A tattooist…"

He seemed a bit put off. Perhaps that was the natural response of a decent person. The only people getting tattoos during wartime were unpatriotic low-life.

The times being what they were, his walking around dressed casually probably made him seem like one of those people. Just one look at a Class D like Enma drove home just how sick he appeared to be.

"Excuse me. I've never seen one, so I don't know what they're like."

"There's no need for you to know. Anyway, goodbye, kid. Keep studying."

Takami didn't respond immediately to this guy who didn't look much older than he was calling him "kid." As Enma picked Kuro back up and turned his back, the boy stammered, "Y-Yes, sir. I'll do my best." He stood up and bowed deeply.

"The Kumegawa clinic is up ahead. If you feel like you're going to collapse again, ask for a lady doctor there by the name of Hisaka. She'll take care of you."

Military drills and mobilization must be hard on a frail body like his. People didn't all have the same physique or physical prowess. The guys in charge could rile them up all they wanted, but guts and patriotism only got you so far.

With Kuro in his arms, he headed home.

He no longer had the potato he'd gotten as a gift for Natsu, but he was glad he'd met the boy who looked like Saki. It filled him with such nostalgia, his eyes seemed to burn inside.

## —2—

They said the death toll was in the hundreds of thousands. The number of injured was many times that. Natsu had no time to rest.

No matter how many people she treated, there was no end to them. There was never enough medicine, never enough of anything. In all her long years as a doctor, she'd never felt so helpless.

Natsu Hisaka was now seventy-five years old.

She wanted to practice medicine until the day she died, and so when she'd heard about the air raids on Tokyo, Natsu had rushed here to help. After two days on a train that didn't move nearly fast enough, she arrived in Tokyo to help out a junior colleague in her clinic and had immediately began treating people.

Ever since he'd been arrested by the Thought Police and then gone to see Nobumasa Muta, Enma had been acting oddly. He'd been taciturn and distracted. She'd been shocked by something he said during one of the air raid warnings.

"I hope one of those bombs falls right on my head."

Saying that Enma shouldn't be left alone in his state, Natsu had half-dragged him to come work with her.

In fact, Enma did quite well. He aloofly helped out with everything from work at the hospital to the household chores. When all was said and done, she was old now. The reason she'd managed to survive in the ruins of Tokyo so far had been through Enma's efforts.

Her hair might have been white, but her skills as a physician hadn't diminished. Physical strength aside, Natsu possessed a wealth of experience. Even so, old age had definitely crept up on her. In a few more years, she'd no longer be able to stand, and then she'd no longer be able to work.

How must this old crone look to a man for whom time had stopped when he was twenty? Just thinking about it made her feel faint. Feeling as though she were drowning, Natsu fell to the floor, still holding her medical charts.

She wasn't sure how much time had passed, but when she opened her eyes, Enma was standing nearby. His eyes were a little bloodshot as he stood there looking at her.

"Big brother…"

It would have seemed a bizarre sight to any stranger. An old woman calling a young man her big brother. Fortunately, she realized that she was resting in their home. The only other one there aside from Enma and her was Kuro.

"Do you hurt anywhere?"

"No, I was just a little tired."

Enma let out a sigh. She could see how worried he'd been, how his heart had nearly been crushed with dread.

Neither Lord Muta nor I must have much time left.

Enma feared that more than anyone else.

"It's because you spend all your time just helping others. You need to rest occasionally."

Thinking back, she'd never been much of a sleeper. She'd always been worrying about Enma and treating people's illnesses and injuries, and never been taken care of the way she was being now.

They said doctors often neglected their own health, but that was really because they kept running nonstop. It was no wonder that their bodies would raise a fuss once in a while.

"Was Lord Muta well?" Nobumasa was about ten years older than she was. She wondered how much trouble his body was giving him.

"He had Keiko there with him."

Natsu let out a long sigh as she recalled Keiko and her doll-like beauty. "Keiko really is lovely, isn't she?" she said. She wished she had been born with those looks.

"Is she? She looked as grumpy as ever to me."

Natsu wasn't sure if it was just the usual moodiness that came with adolescence, but Keiko was definitely a girl who never smiled. Any contact with Enma especially irritated her. Even Keiko would eventually figure out why that was.

The power Keiko possessed had saved Enma from the Thought Police. Perhaps she would be the one to help out this lonely immortal man from now on.

"Oh, yeah. Would you like some rice porridge?"

"Did you make it?"

Enma nodded proudly. "Yup, and it turned out pretty well."

"Then by all means."

In short order, a steaming bowl of porridge was placed before her.

Enma's cooking, like nearly everything else he tried aside from tattooing, wasn't that good. Still, Natsu had never eaten a bowl of porridge prepared with such tenderness.

She rested for three days. It was simple exhaustion. Even though she honestly could go back to work at that point, having Enma caring for her was so pleasant that she took an extra day off.

Enma's lips tightened a little when she said that she'd be going back to work the next day.

"You said that you'd rest a little longer. You're as bad at taking it easy as I am."

In many ways, she was glad to have Enma waiting on her and caring for her. But the experience had given Natsu a bitter premonition that it could eventually turn into her reality.

There were limits to everything, and she might be approaching hers.

Even Natsu was something to worry about now. She actually intended to go back to work tomorrow.

That woman just wouldn't listen to reason. He knew it was useless to try and stop her, but this one time, Enma argued loudly for her to rest some more.

"Don't push yourself too hard. You're not—"

You're not young anymore.

He bit his tongue just as he was about to say that. Enma was the last person who should talk to anyone about age. He especially didn't want to talk about it regarding Natsu.

Even if Natsu didn't mind it, he did.

To him, no matter how old she got, she was still that same obstinate young girl who gave everything her all. He needed to face the fact that she had gotten old without him.

It was too much for him to handle, so Enma went outside.

He heard sobbing coming from the apartment across the way and a few doors down. The people from the neighborhood were gathered at the entrance, whispering about what had happened.

"Those poor people. He was their only son."

"Only nineteen, wasn't he?"

Enma soon realized what it was about. This family's son had been killed in the war. Enma may have only just arrived here, but this was still his neighborhood. He'd have to go offer his condolences and it wouldn't be any trouble to show up for the dead boy's wake. All the more so because he'd been so young.

"Oh? Who's that?"

"Ah, the guy who lives with Dr. Natsu. The Class D."

"Looks healthy enough to me to serve. What a disgrace."

Enma instinctively started coughing. What he really wanted to do was yell at them, but he thought about Natsu's situation and pretended to be an invalid.

I'm gonna be a hundred years old next year, he grumbled as he walked away. He wouldn't have minded enlisting if he knew for sure that he'd be killed. What he worried about most was getting injured and then having someone see him healing quickly from it.

Nobumasa did all he could behind the scenes to keep Enma shielded from the world. It was thanks to him that he could live as openly as he did. If it hadn't been for Nobumasa and Natsu, his true nature would have been exposed long ago and he'd certainly have ended up on the run.

He lived his life fairly isolated now. But he wouldn't know true isolation until both of them were gone.

Feeling depressed, he took a little walk and ended up in front of the Kumegawa clinic. This was the hospital where a younger colleague of Natsu's practiced. Natsu had been working there free of charge since they'd arrived in Tokyo.

Isn't that…

Enma waved to the boy walking shamefacedly from the hospital.

"Oh, thank goodness."

"What's up? Feeling sick? Natsu—Dr. Hisaka, I mean, is taking the day off. Well, I suppose the doctors here still checked you out."

Takami ran over to him, shaking his head no. "I wanted to thank you for everything. I realized that I forgot to ask you your name. I'm really sorry about that."

Enma was amazed that he'd come here specifically just for that. "That's really conscientious of you. My name's Enma Houshou. It's a pleasure."

It wasn't his real name, but he didn't go by any other at this point. Even if he met someone who might remember it from the past, all he had to do was claim to be his grandson and he'd have a fairly effective deception.

He'd once lost his cool when an old man surprised him by saying, "You look exactly like your grandfather." He'd gotten very serious, saying he heard that all the time, to which the old man had just laughed. He knew the face, but couldn't place him at all till the guy had shown him the tattoos on his upper arms. He'd been a yakuza customer of his a very long time ago, although now he was a fairly genial old man.

Occasionally, the time which had stopped only for him would launch a surprise attack to even the score.

"That's a fantastic name."

"My old master gave it to me. I think it's kind of silly, myself," he casually dismissed what appeared to be his real name. Being such a serious boy, his companion immediately became embarrassed.

"You don't have your cat today?"

"He's at home, asleep." He'd been sleeping since he last saw the boy, neither eating nor drinking. "Anyway, what happened to your face?"

There was a bruise just beneath Takami's eye.

"My drill instructor hit me. I'm…clumsy."

Yes, he was clearly clumsy, but Enma didn't see why that was any reason to hit him. "That's awful…"

"No, really. I'm terrible at anything I try."

Enma patted him on the back. "Wanna go get some rice stew? My treat."

"No, I really…"

"Stop that and just come with me. I hate eating alone. After all, I'm a useless Class D. It's not like people usually like being seen with me."

As he walked at Enma's side, Takami glanced up at him and asked, "Um… What's wrong with you?"

"Yeah, well… What I have is sort of an illness. My body's actually a lot healthier than most."

Takami tilted his head. "Huh…"

Around there, the best they could do for eating out was a rice-stew shop operating on the side of the road. They served the sort of stuff that one might complain about for being too watery, but Takami's eyes lit up when he saw it, and he immediately set about to transferring the stew from the bowl into his stomach. Enma offered him his still-untouched portion of stew as well. Takami politely refused at first, but his manners were no match for his growing appetite, and he wolfed it down in the blink of an eye.

"E-Excuse me." His face reddened as soon as he'd finished.

"Had you eaten since yesterday?"

"No..."

Enma turned around and ordered another bowl from the man running the shop.

"I'm fine now, really."

"Be quiet and eat."

It was mostly liquid. He'd have to eat bowl after bowl to fill his stomach, but it would have to satisfy him for now.

Takami used his left hand to hold his chopsticks. That was another way he was just like Saki, and Enma was moved even more.

"I really appreciate your help..."

Finishing his third bowl, Takami let out a long, satisfied sigh.

"Thank you. Thank you." He insisted that he hadn't intended for Enma to do any of this as he bowed his head over and over.

"I wish I had more to offer you than rice stew."

"Don't be silly. Thank you, really. But why are you being so kind to me?"

Enma scratched the back of his neck, looking embarrassed.

"This is the first time anyone's treated me this well since I came to Tokyo."

"Well, Tokyo doesn't have a lot of hospitality to spare these days."

He'd known this town longer than anyone, and Tokyo was a fairly hospitable place. All the same, these days, it had trouble showing it.

"Didn't you withdraw your money from your bank account?"

"There was never much in it to start with. I don't get an allowance. I planned to work my way through school, but being mobilized for service means I have no time for that. I thought I could come to Tokyo and somehow make it work, but I guess I was being naive." Takami smiled bitterly, as though ashamed of his own unworthiness.

"So go home. The war'll end soon, and then you can start over. You're still young, right?"

Takami hung his head, saying that he couldn't do that. "My parents are dead, so I was staying with my older brother's family, but I didn't feel comfortable there. My brother and I have different mothers, and he's so much older that he's never thought much of me. I don't know if I'd even be welcome there if I went back... Besides, I don't have the money to get home, so it's pointless talking about it." Takami's circumstances bore a remarkable similarity to Enma's boyhood.

"It's hard to go back, huh?" The kid had Saki's face and his own life story. He couldn't help but think that their meeting each other had some significance.

"I'll stay here a little while longer and try to make it work. If the college reopens, I want to draw as much as I can. I want to draw so badly, it almost drives me crazy."

Enma knew only too well how Takami felt. More than anything, he wanted to tattoo someone.

The gears of war would easily grind up even this sort of passion. It frustrated Enma to think of it.

"Use this." He took a wallet out of his pocket and handed it to Takami.

"Um…?"

"There should be about 500 yen in there. Take it."

As soon as he'd said it, Takami handed the wallet back, his face bright red. "I can't! I'm not a beggar. You have no reason to give me that money."

Maybe he had been a little too forward there, Enma thought. He remembered how Nobumasa would offer him money, and how he'd get irritated and return it. "Call it a loan, then," he said.

"I can't repay it." If he was in any condition to repay him, he wouldn't be having such trouble, Takami pleaded with tearful eyes, and Enma had to admit that was true.

"Okay, then I'll commission a painting from you. This is my payment for it."

"A painting?"

Yes, nodded Enma. "I know. Do one of Kuro. You remember the cat, right?"

"A picture of your cat?"

Enma once again handed the wallet to Takami. "Right. And make it one of your best, Maestro Takami."

"But, this much for it? I'm still just a student."

It wasn't much money to Enma. He'd earned a considerable income from a big job before the war. Because he'd been so eager to work to repay the money that Nobumasa had lent him, the fame of Ura-Enma had spread from mouth to mouth. As a result, after a few dangerous jobs, he'd amassed substantial savings.

"It should be done by somebody who deserves to do it." And, telling him to get to it, Enma turned to leave.

"But…"

"Draw the cat as you remember him. If you've forgotten what he looks like, then come to my place. There's a dirty little tobacco shop up ahead of here. I'm in the broken-down house next to it."

Takami chased after him as he walked away.

"Why are you doing this?"

Enma turned to look back.

"Because you remind me of someone a lot. Someone who died a long time ago."

He stopped and regarded the boy silently, then added one more request.

"Stay alive."

## —3—

The cherry blossoms had begun to fall, and Kuro was no longer eating or drinking very much. He'd gotten very thin, and there were times when convulsions would wrack his body. His once-brilliant black fur had lost its luster, turning dull and dry.

Doubt had become certainty. Enma had no idea how long Kuro had lived. It might have been several spans longer than Enma had.

If the death of the oni within meant death for the immortal, then…

Then when am I going to die?

Had he not lived even ten percent of his time? Or had he long ago passed the halfway point? The limited life span was his salvation, but not knowing what to expect made things chaotic.

There was no point in thinking about it now. The problem at hand was that Kuro was dying. He'd lived with the cat even longer than he had with Natsu. Losing him would be like having a part of his body torn away.

"Don't die… You stupid little monster."

Enma stayed at Kuro's side throughout the day, silently watching him, stroking his body, letting out pathetic sobs.

The cat was a selfish loner, who'd often stay away for long periods of time. This may have been the longest they'd ever spent together. That was how sick he'd become.

He walked unsteadily to drink some water, then fell back asleep. Even Kuro seemed to be tired of his irresponsible life.

Enma had no idea what this cat thought or desired. All he could do was stroke his body, as if that might take the pain away.

Natsu was worried about Enma.

No matter how much he'd remind her that he was a hundred years old, from her point of view, he still seemed barely a child. Most people matured inside as they grew older, but that was necessary to match how they looked on the outside. People became what they appeared to be.

Of course, there were times when she'd sense Enma's maturity as well. But, at heart, he'd always be a young man. No matter how long he lived, he'd always be a stubborn, idealistic kid.

It was because of this that she'd never left him. Natsu's feelings ran quiet and deep. They had to be family first, rather than man and woman. And though she'd prepared herself for it, this was hard on her.

Even though she was old, now, her feelings for Enma hadn't changed a bit in the last fifty years. She had no regrets about going to her grave with them still nursed in her heart.

But, as she went on her rounds, she realized that was just another way of saying she had surrendered.

She hurried around, encouraging a child who was in pain, then pounding on an old man's back as he coughed. She felt a little awkward leaving those two pathetic monsters alone so she could work, but Natsu was a doctor. She couldn't just ignore her patients.

She walked among the teeming casualties, choosing her battles, determining who was hopeless and had to be left to die and who she might be able to save. There was no time to waste on hopeless cases. That wouldn't be changed by one old surgeon who wasn't long for this world.

Even though she was a doctor, she still felt helpless.

As evening came and she finished her examinations for the day, Natsu was shocked to return home to find all the tatami mats in their home overturned.

"What..."

It didn't look like they'd been robbed. Just as she was thinking how odd it was, Enma came up out of the crawlspace under the floor.

"What's wrong?"

"The little monster's gone." Enma looked deathly pale. "He must have left when I dozed off..." He opened a window and looked around outside. "Kuro can't move very well in his condition. He couldn't have gotten far..."

She held Enma back as he was about to dash outside. "Big brother, please! Calm down."

He must have turned their home upside down looking for Kuro. With a little sigh, Natsu fixed one of the mats and then knelt down.

"Just sit."

"But..."

Natsu, her face twisted with grief, looked up at Enma. "Kuro is an animal."

Enma's eyes went wide.

"And animals can sense when they're about to die. That's why he's left: to find a place where he can die. Let's leave him be to do that." It was hard for her to see Enma as upset as he was.

"Yeah," he said at last. "You're right."

Enma squatted down. Lips trembling, he held his head.

Not wanting to see Enma so distraught, Natsu went to the sink and began preparing their dinner. The only sound was the echo of her knife on the cutting board.

This would be a wound that would take a long time to heal. Kuro was no ordinary cat. To Enma, he was a unique and special being.

Though there was one other man who was burdened with the same fate...

Yasha Houshou—Enma still burned to take vengeance on Onitsuki for the death of his sister. The man who'd nearly killed Natsu when she was but a child. The man he hated more than any other, with whom he was doomed to walk through eternity.

Before coming to Tokyo, Natsu had met Yasha once, in Kyoto...

It must have been around the end of January.

She'd just finished a house call and was on her way home. Her reunion with the beautiful, unearthly creature had occurred as she approached a bridge, shivering in the cold.

"It's been a long time. I see you haven't changed, Natsu."

The man who stood before her, breath steaming white as he talked, hadn't changed a bit in the fifty years since she'd last seen him.

"Mr. Mikazuki-Doh..."

"How nice to hear that again. You were the only one who ever called me that."

Leaning against the railing on the bridge, Onitsuki was still the same young man with the elegant face. She was used to this with Enma, but seeing another person displaying the strange power was shocking to her.

"I'm glad I ran into you. I have a little business to conduct here. I'm sorry I couldn't bring you something tasty as a souvenir."

His manner was as light as ever. She saw blood dripping from his left hand.

"You're hurt."

When she pointed it out, Onitsuki licked it with his tongue.

"It'll heal soon. Surely you know that." Just like your "big brother," he laughed. "I unexpectedly had a kitchen knife thrust at me just now. It was some man, selfishly saying I had to give him my money, so I escorted him out."

From this life. Natsu drew a sharp breath as she realized that was what he'd meant. She fearfully looked down at the water flowing beneath the bridge.

"He's not there anymore. The river's great for that. It just washes everything away."

Despite the terrible things he was saying, she didn't find it at all strange or shocking. Maybe it was because none of what was happening at the moment seemed real.

"Aren't you frightened of me? I'm a cannibal, after all. The man who once thought of killing you when you were little."

"I've seen a lot of things in this war… At this point, it hardly matters."

She doubted that Onitsuki wanted to kill her now that she was an old woman. And there was no way he was going to tattoo immortality into her to make her like him. And even if he was a monster, all he inspired within Natsu were feelings of pure nostalgia.

"I suppose that's true. I really envy you, Natsu. Looking at you now makes me think that the phenomenon of aging is the most beautiful thing there is."

Onitsuki bent down a bit, looking Natsu in the eye. She shivered in Kyoto's twilight winter chill. The man dyed red in the dark setting sun seemed ephemeral, as though he kept one foot in the next world.

"Have you come here to tease an old woman?"

"Heaven forbid! I'd still have you as my partner if you'd let me."

Natsu shook her head. "The only person I'd allow to stop time for me is Enma Houshou."

"And yet he didn't… Such a waste."

Even as old as she was, her feelings about that were complicated. Part of her still had the desire to share his destiny, to overcome it. But she yearned for Enma precisely because he was the sort of man who hadn't done that.

"Is it true? Did you really…kill his sister?" Even if she could forgive what he'd almost done to her, she could never forgive that.

"Yes. I killed her." Onitsuki looked at the sky in the west. "I'd met her on a bridge, much as we're doing now. A girl who was lovely in her overwhelming grief. I still dream about her occasionally, even now. Maybe I was slightly smitten with her when we met."

Natsu looked puzzled. "You killed someone you were smitten with?"

"I had the arrogance to think that I was putting her out of her misery… An old friend once lectured me about that."

What he was saying disgusted her. Even so, he didn't seem to be a madman. "Then please, some day… Apologize to my brother."

"Would he forgive me if I did?"

"No, I don't think that he would. But… It may bring him some closure. Maybe he won't hate you anymore." Just that would make an apology meaningful, she pleaded.

"But I want him to hate me so that he'll kill me. Would you tell him that for me?"

Natsu wasn't surprised. She figured it might have been something like that. Onitsuki's interests had long ago moved from her to Enma. "My brother still regrets what he did in the past. Please don't make him kill a person again."

"He doesn't have to think of me as a person. He'll be able to do it if he thinks of it as an oni extermination."

"You're still a human being," Natsu replied, indignantly.

Onitsuki sank into silence. Perhaps the old woman's words had struck a chord in his heart. Looking disturbed, he changed the subject. "I heard he was arrested by the Thought Police. They didn't beat him up too badly, did they?"

Surprised, Natsu looked up at Onitsuki. "You're well-informed. If I should accidentally let slip to them about your oni-gome, it'd cause trouble for you. What do you think?"

No matter how much they may have hated each other, the two men were in the same boat. The thing they feared most was letting the world find out that they were beings who were beyond human. Because of what that meant, they couldn't live their lives unaffected by each other.

"They tore off his nails and smashed his fingers, but he told them nothing. He was so afraid that they'd force him to create unkillable soldiers that he even kept tearing his own nails off to keep his secret."

Enma was off seeing Nobumasa Muta, and she was glad he wasn't present. His wounds still hadn't healed completely. If anything happened with Onitsuki, he wouldn't be able to fight him.

"Good for him."

Onitsuki smiled, renewing her conflicted feelings about him. How could a man with such a lovely smile be a villain who was rotting from the oni inside of him? Even now, she couldn't believe it.

"Would it be possible for me to see him?"

"He's gone out today."

He looked dubious, but didn't press the matter. "Oh, well. Kyoto in winter can be tough, can't it? I'm living in Kyushu now. In a nice town. Anyway, until next we meet."

Twilight had turned to night. Onitsuki suddenly vanished, like a specter returning to the dark.

She still hadn't told Enma about her encounter with Yasha. She had a feeling that it was best not to in his current fragile state. Occasionally, a thought would come to her. Perhaps her father hadn't entrusted his daughter to Enma's care, but rather had entrusted Enma to his daughter.

Enma and Yasha's relationship would continue even after she was dead. It would be wonderful if they could learn to support each other. From the bottom of her heart, Natsu regretted that they didn't.

The character on his palm had never faded.

He wondered just how long Kuro had lived. He wondered when King Enma on his palm would lose his power.

Alone in the room, Enma stared absentmindedly out the window.

What exactly was the oni-gome of immortality, anyway? Even an animal like Kuro was endowed with the instinct to survive. Maybe the immortality oni-gome was the only one that would work on an animal. All the other types involved reinforcing a person's will. In short, they pushed a person to make themselves better.

Even Baikou wouldn't have been able to top the number of oni-gome he'd done in his lifetime. However, Enma hadn't yet broken the greatest taboo of all. Of course, he had no intention of doing so, because immortality was a curse.

But he still had the power to make someone like himself. How long could he resist the temptation to do so? The hole that had been punched through his heart was awfully cold.

Enma was stricken with such a feeling of loss that he didn't hear the voice asking over and over if anyone was home.

"Mr. Houshou? It's me, Takami."

Noticing him at last, he crept out to the entryway, where Takami bowed his head repeatedly. He was wearing a white shirt and pants in lieu of his national service uniform today.

"Ah, you've finished the painting? Come in."

Takami seemed to have gotten even thinner in the two weeks since he'd last seen him. He carried something wrapped in a cloth. From its shape, Enma could tell it was a canvas.

"Um, where's Kuro?"

"Gone. I think he might be dead by now. I'll warn you right now: I may cry when I see your painting." As Takami stared at him, speechless, Enma scratched his head nervously. "I'm kidding. He was just a cat. Come on, let me see it."

Takami unwrapped the cloth, revealing the canvas. It still smelled strongly of paint.

"Wow..." It wasn't just a picture of Kuro. There stood Enma on the canvas, smiling and holding Kuro in his arms.

"You haven't been crying, have you?" Takami must have seen his eyes tearing up.

"No... But I might." Kuro was a stubborn, selfish cat who lived for himself and then blew away like the wind so he could die, but there the little monster was, in his arms.

"I'm sorry. The picture isn't really done yet."

Enma looked to see what he meant and saw that the background had only been half-painted in.

"I have to go back to Nagasaki tomorrow... This was all I could paint in time." Takami chewed his lip nervously. His fists trembled as they lay in his lap.

"Has something happened?" Enma looked up.

"I've been called up for duty."

His eyes wide, Enma felt his body stiffen. He stopped breathing as his throat went dry.

"I'm not very healthy, so I got graded as a Class C on my physical exam. That's why I've been working in the labor force till now... But it looks like they can't afford to keep me there anymore."

He'd heard that Class C's were usually assigned to the transportation corps, but the entire nation seemed to be resigned to fighting to the last man. There was no point in holding anything back now, and it was very likely he'd be sent to the front lines. Takami himself seemed resigned to that.

"I'm sorry that one painting can't repay all the kindness you showed me. There were all sorts of places I wanted to go see after the war. I wanted to draw people from all different countries. I wanted to, but... But I guess I never will, now."

Enma said nothing. Every possible angry word he knew was gathered at the base of his tongue in a formless mass.

"I'm going off to die honorably for our nation. Take care of yourself, Mr. Houshou."

A smile came to his young face.

That was when Enma's feelings exploded. "Bullshit! I told you to live, didn't I?! I refuse to just let you die for the sake of this idiotic war!"

Takami, his eyes wide, shook his head. "Don't! Don't say that, not so loud."

"I don't care who hears me! Is it a crime to yell that I want you to live?!"

His fists gripping the sides of his pants, Takami hunched his back.

"I'll take care of this painting. Come back here alive and then finish it."

Why did this frail child have to go to the battlefield? Enma would have taken his place if he could. He'd have gladly died to spare him.

"But, I'm... I'm weak and clumsy. I couldn't kill anyone. I just..." He didn't think he could survive, Takami stammered.

Enma's right hand throbbed. Something whispered in his heart.

Don't you have the power to see that he does?

<Use it. Save the boy. If you hesitate, he'll die> it urged.

Even though it was the middle of the day, the denizens of the night grew excited, salivating at the chance to see the birth of a new monster.

Even as he struggled in his heart, Enma took hold of Takami's hand.

"You're left-handed, aren't you?"

He mustn't do this. He knew that. Even so, he didn't want to let the boy leave without doing something for him.

Some people became ambidextrous in order to correct their left-handedness. An oni-gome might not take in that case. But he couldn't not do it now.

"I'm going to give you a farewell gift. A good luck charm, so that you'll come back alive."

The creatures of the night rejoiced at his words. They jeered at Enma's failure.

*Now, you are truly a Houshou.*

*Oh, how long it's been... How we've longed to see this. Nothing is more beautiful than a new monster.*

The voices of the oni were no longer confused.

Judge me, Great King Enma upon my palm, he screamed within his heart, mete out whatever punishment you see fit.

Even though he'd steeled himself for it, breaking the taboo had been harder on Enma than he'd expected.

More clearly than before, he could see how he'd been corroded from within by the oni. It was like the time when he'd sucked his own blood. If he broke the taboo again, he had no doubt that he would lose the last of his humanity.

To be honest, Enma didn't even know if it had worked. This was the first time he'd ever done it. He had only a vague memory of what Baikou had taught him. It was possible he hadn't remembered how to do it right.

No, he probably had. Once the oni-gome of immortality had been put on his body, he'd never forgotten it. He had no right to.

Aw, kid...

Not a day went by without him thinking about Takami.

After joining his hometown company and being trained, Takami had been sent to the battlefield. With the capital city being bombed as much as it was, defeat was near. He'd overheard that their forces were in shambles from Manchuria to the southern fronts.

Even though he'd tattooed immortality into him, it'd be all for nothing if he was killed instantly. And it'd be bad for him if he healed completely while those around him still had their wounds. Still, he thought, if it increased his chances of survival, it'd all be worth it.

If he came back, Enma could extract the oni from him. Once he did that, he'd be able to die like a normal person. And if... If that boy wanted to live in the same time as he, then he'd...

Was he just looking for a replacement for Kuro? Just doing what he couldn't bring himself to do to Natsu? Over and over, he asked himself that question, never getting a clear answer. His right hand had throbbed ever since that day, as though King Enma himself was blaming him.

And like that, spring became summer.

It was a summer of sweltering heat which felt like the screams of the entire nation.

Enma received a letter from Nagasaki. It was from Hiroaki Takami.

*Dear Mr. Houshou,*

*It's been a while since I last wrote. Has anything new happened to you?*

*I'm embarrassed to say this, but I got wounded at the front and have been sent back to Nagasaki to recover.*

*After achieving every boy's dream of being seen off by a cheering crowd waving little flags, I was sent off on an expedition. I know you told me to live, but I knew I was being sent into battle. I was prepared to die.*

*While I wasn't terribly good as a soldier, I did my best as a member of the Imperial Army to help defend Okinawa. However, on a certain day in June, just before the end of the battle, I lost my left eye to an enemy shell. Since I was to be discharged as a wounded soldier, they just slapped a bandage over my eye without any proper treatment and shipped me back to Kyushu. I was shipped out and left in that unsightly state for days, without any place to go.*

*All that time, I had no idea what was happening to my left eye. I'd just abandoned all hope of there being anything but a gaping hole where it used to be. But then, something amazing happened. When I gingerly removed the bandage, there was my left eye, like nothing had happened to it. It was a little sensitive at first, but I can see with it just fine.*

*When I think about it, all sorts of wounds I received on the battlefield have completely vanished from my body. I'm sure it's all been thanks to that farewell gift you gave me. I can't help but think that every time I look at the cherry blossom you tattooed onto my hand.*

*I think this cherry blossom which you made to look like a birthmark has special powers, Mr. Houshou. Every time we met, I felt like you were like one of those immortal hermits you read about in stories. You seemed like someone not of this world.*

*Since even my brother has given me grief because he thinks I faked an injury to get discharged, I'm keeping my left eye bandaged. My home now is a little barn where I sleep at night, but compared to the front lines, it's comfortable.*

*I think the war will be over soon. When it does, I'll come back to Tokyo as a student and throw myself into my studies. And I'd like to finish the painting I left with you, Mr. Houshou.*

*Looking forward to seeing you again,*
*Hiroaki Takami*

Thank goodness.

Enma gripped the letter, overjoyed that Takami was all right. His older brother was still treating him poorly, but he seemed to be alive and in good spirits.

Surely they'd meet again soon. No country that would send a child like that to run around on a battlefield could possibly win. Everything he'd seen since the Meiji Restoration told him that.

He looked over to the painting the boy had left with him and smiled. He'd lived a century, but this was the first time he'd felt a special bond like this.

At the time, Enma didn't notice it.

That someone precious to him was about to vanish from his side.

After he'd been in such a funk since Kuro's disappearance, Natsu was a little relieved to see Enma smiling again.

She was also happy for Enma having befriended that boy Takami. Even after his long, eternally young life, he'd made very few friends. Natsu understood very well that he couldn't make any aside from herself and Nobumasa.

True, he couldn't easily open up to others, possibly because he may have feared forming deep relationships with them. Even so, he was too lonely as things were, and she and Nobumasa didn't have much time left.

Natsu had actually once considered committing a murder-suicide with him. She couldn't bear the thought of leaving this sad creature all alone, and if he wouldn't kill himself, then she'd have to do it. Unfortunately, Natsu's nature was far too rational to ever allow her to commit the sin of taking another person's life.

That was why Enma needed a friend who could accept everything about him. Or else he needed the strength to go on living on his own.

She prayed that Enma's heart wouldn't be devoured by emptiness once Kuro, Nobumasa, and she were all gone.

She covered her face with both hands, feeling the deep wrinkles on them. Even at this age, she was still a woman. A hopeless longing would fill even her withered breast whenever she thought of Enma. She would go on hoping to the very end that he'd acknowledge her as a woman, but it wasn't always easy.

"You know…" she said to her junior colleague as she checked the medical chart.

"Yes?" Although she wasn't even fifty yet, the lady doctor was very talented. Her son was starting work as a doctor as well.

"I'm thinking of getting out of Tokyo."

Perhaps she'd been prepared for Natsu saying this. Dr. Kumegawa looked sad, but not surprised. "Where will you go?"

"I'll think about that. Since I'll only be able to practice a little longer and intend to die doing this job, I think I'll go to where I'm needed the most."

Would you approve of that, Father?

## —4—

He'd been careless.

He thought he had a bit more time before the country went to war. Thanks to that, he hadn't been able to get out of the country in time and had been stuck there for three years.

For half a century, he'd wandered all over the world and had seen a lot of things. As the flames of war began to rise all over, he couldn't afford to get careless, and so he'd left Macau and had ended up here in Nagasaki.

Still, the city had a foreign flavor which seemed to suit him, and the comforts it offered weren't bad. Yokohama, where he'd once lived, had a similar feel, and perhaps his body had acclimated itself to the stateless atmosphere.

Yasha was hiding out in a sanatorium in the suburbs, pretending to be a patient there. Since he'd never looked very healthy to begin with, nobody questioned his cover at all. The sanatorium was one to which he'd donated money. He didn't have a patron like Enma did, but he did have the wealth and brains to conceal himself in the background of society.

He'd done a lot of things which he'd be hated for, but what he had done had allowed him to live this long.

As he strolled quietly through the garden with its profusion of sunflowers, Yasha suddenly thought of the one other immortal he knew. He wondered what his brash junior colleague was up to. He had run into Natsu recently, but hadn't seen Enma in ages. Maybe he'd go look him up after the war was over.

He knew that Enma would most likely still hate him, but that didn't change his desire to see him again. Fifty years had passed since they'd last spoken, he realized. Perhaps, he thought, what I want is for him to save me.

Naturally, this would just be seen as trouble by his opposite. Hanging onto another person with long, sharp nails would just cause them pain, but who else did he have?

"Mr. Onitsuki."

A nun was walking up from the bottom of the hill. The way she walked in her habit was adorable, making her look a bit like a penguin. She wasn't young, but her gaze, so full of kindness, made her beautiful.

"Lovely weather today, isn't it?"

"It's hot. A bit too hot for my tastes, today."

Even though he very rarely perspired, there was a trickle of sweat curling around the back of his neck. He looked up at the blue summer sky spreading out overhead. Beneath it he could see the bell tower of Urakami Cathedral.

"Off to Mass? Thank you very much, as always." Yasha bowed deeply as he thanked the sanatorium staffer.

"Oh, no. It's a precious duty given to me by God."

She was possessed of a calm and devout nature, but she didn't sense the oni that dwelt within Yasha. Fortunately for him, she didn't seem to have any talent for demonic exorcism, which was why he could safely associate with her.

"Did you hear? Hiroshima apparently suffered some sort of terrible attack. It's horrible."

He'd heard about Hiroshima, but details were still sketchy about whether it had been a normal bombing or if it had been hit with some kind of new weapon. One ugly rumor going around was that the entire city had been destroyed in an instant.

"I hope this war ends soon."

She may have been a servant of God, but the prolonged war seemed to have exhausted her to her very core. It wasn't just from her work for the church. She also eagerly went around to the local hospitals to give encouragement to the patients.

Yasha had little interest in gods or buddhas, but even he was surprised by how effective the power of faith could be at times. Faith in some sort of god was one of the first things humans developed a belief in.

"It'll be over soon, since this country is going to lose," he said indifferently.

The nun seemed shocked by his candor. She nervously looked around to see if anyone had overheard him. "You're a bold man to say something like that," she said, "considering how much trouble you'd be in if somebody overheard you." Making certain there was nobody else around, the nun smiled wryly.

"Despite appearances, I live by making cunning calculations."

"And if you talk about yourself that way, I imagine you're a very childish man," the nun laughed.

A hundred and fifteen years old, and still immature. All Yasha could do was laugh with her.

"Oh, yes. I came to ask a favor of you today, Mr. Onitsuki. Could you take a look at these?"

He tilted his head as he regarded the rolled-up cylinder she handed to him. "What are they?"

"Watercolors painted by an art student I know. You'd normally use oil paints for a major subject, but he can't get any supplies now. But even watercolors can make a good painting in the hands of a skilled artist. What do you think? Would you hang any of them in the sanatorium?"

As he'd expect from the nun's endorsement, the paintings were all appealing. He especially liked the one of the smiling nun. Naturally, it was the lady standing in front of him now. "This one's nice. He captured your gentle expression very well, Sister."

The nun blushed and hurriedly shook her head. "Oh no, this is the one he gave to me. I think that one of the Nagasaki skyline is nice. It's such a pretty city."

Nagasaki spread out, sparkling in the sunlight. True, this one wasn't bad either, but it was the nun's portrait which most captivated Yasha.

Where did I…?

He had a feeling he'd seen a smile just like this a long time ago.

"I think it comforts him to know he's making the other patients feel better. He hasn't recovered yet from the wound he received in battle, but the boy has a real future in this." She spoke about him as proudly as if he were her own son.

"I see. I'll show them to the director as well. May I take these?"

"Yes, of course. I appreciate it." The nun bowed deeply. "Now then, I have to get back to the church. And you should go back to your room to rest. You'll get sunstroke if you stay out here too long."

He had to maintain his cover as an invalid. He said goodbye and turned back toward the sanatorium. He soon heard the nun talking to somebody else.

"Oh, hello there. Feeling better today?"

"Yes. It's such a nice day, so…"

Turning to look back, he saw the nun talking to a boy in the sunflower field at the bottom of the hill. A skinny kid that he'd never seen before, who had one eye covered with a bandage. With a straw hat on his head and an important-looking sketchbook held protectively under one arm, it could only be the art student with the bright future.

"May I sketch the Virgin Mary in the church, please?"

"Of course you may. Your paintings have such a gentleness to them, I'm sure the Holy Mother would be glad to have you sketch her. I was just asking if we could decorate the sanatorium with your paintings. By the way, you shouldn't leave that dirty dressing wrapped around your head for too long. Don't overdo things. Have you really had a doctor check that for you?"

The boy just smiled nervously as the nun fired off question after question, like a concerned mother. The sunflowers surrounding them both swayed in the breeze. It was a scene so tranquil that you could almost forget that there was a war on.

Giving one last look at the nun and the boy standing next to her as he headed into the sanatorium, Yasha felt a chill run down his spine.

He looked up into the sky.

An instant later, the world evaporated in a flash of white.

* * * * *

The news began to circulate that a brilliant white calamity had descended upon the cities of Hiroshima and Nagasaki in the sweltering days of August.

It had to have been a new weapon of the American military. Nowhere in the entire nation was safe now. They were like tiny flies buzzing in the palm of an enormous monster.

Naturally, Enma didn't take the news very well.

"I'm going to Nagasaki," he declared, and immediately began packing a rucksack with what he'd need for the trip. He may not be able to do anything even when he got there, but there was no way Enma could just stay where he was, doing nothing. After burdening Takami with the same fate as he, the boy was no longer a stranger. He was another him.

"Nagasaki? It'll take you days to get there the way things are now."

Natsu wasn't trying to keep Enma from going. She was just stating a fact. She doubted transport facilities would be operating at a time like this.

"I'm still going." Looking pale, Enma stood up. He looked as though he was about to collapse.

"All right. I'll pray that your friend is all right," Natsu said, her voice cracking a bit as she spoke.

Enma dashed out of the apartment without looking back. He didn't notice that Natsu's face was now wet with tears.

Travel proved more difficult than he'd imagined.

Catching a packed train, Enma set off for Nagasaki. When he missed his next connection, he started walking south.

By the time he'd gotten past Kyoto, he suddenly thought of Nobumasa Muta. Was he all right? A vision of all the people near to him vanishing one by one assaulted him, and his anxiety only grew.

A lot of news was flying about Hiroshima when he reached Okayama. It was full of refugees, and the stories he heard one by one froze his blood cold.

There'd been a blue-white flash that had filled the hot cloudless summer sky, the entire world turning blue-white in an instant. Red flames had leaped into the air, with black smoke covering everything… It got so that all he wanted to do was scream for them to stop telling him.

Enma then made a detour around the chaos of Hiroshima and entered his old home prefecture of Yamaguchi. It had taken him five days to get there. In that time, Japan surrendered, ending the war. Anger bubbled up inside of him when he heard the news. Idiots, he yelled, heedless of who heard him. Why hadn't they done it sooner?

He spotted a low-flying American plane along the way. It was a fighter, decorated with nose art of big, red lips.

His strength left him.

How could these people afford to do all this? It was absurd to have ever thought that they were going to win.

He bribed a fishing boat crew to get him to Kyushu. Finally, he started hearing things about Nagasaki, and none of it was good.

A week after leaving Tokyo, Enma finally arrived in Nagasaki.

He'd been warned against approaching the center of the blast. Word was that those who did had contracted some sort of infectious disease, and it was stymieing relief efforts.

Takami's home had been in the city proper. He walked from hospital to relief station on the city's outskirts, asking around, but there was no news. An immortality oni-gome was useless in the face of such a bomb. Takami may have vanished without any trace.

He wanted to go to Takami's home address according to the letter, but the city had been reduced to a wasteland, and there was no way to tell where anything had been. He saw the ruins of Urakami Cathedral in the distance.

Even God must have fled from this place…

He balled his hands into fists so tight they threatened to crush King Enma himself.

Finally, three days after arriving in Nagasaki, Enma got a clue.

"There's a monster there. It's so creepy, nobody will go near him. He shouldn't even be alive, but he goes on breathing, even without anyone giving him any help. They think it's a young man."

There could be no mistake. Asking where the monster was, Enma staggered out to find him.

The ruins of a sanatorium stood at the top of a low hill. The man who wouldn't die was in a partially destroyed shack standing next to them. The walls and roof of one section were only just barely standing, and it looked like it could collapse at any moment.

Something that looked human was lying on some straw. The only thing covering him was a large towel around his waist.

One arm and one leg were completely gone, while the remaining limbs were blackened stumps. Burns covered him from his chest to his belly, and fire had burned both eyes from their sockets. There was no way of telling now what he'd looked like. The slight rise and fall of his chest was the only sign that he was still alive.

Enma fell to his knees, unable to rise, as though he was having some sort of awful hallucination.

"Kid…" Kneeling across from him, he called to the boy. "It's me. Can you hear me?" There was hardly any skin left, so he couldn't even touch him.

"M…Mister… Hou…shou…" the lips moved slightly, the reply barely more than a breath.

"I'm sorry. It's all my fault. I… I just ended up making you suffer."

Enma didn't know if the immortality oni was doing all it could just to keep him alive or if he'd just not performed the technique properly. All he knew was that the wages of the sin he'd committed resided in the pathetic remains of the boy that lay before him.

"I did this to you out of selfishness, because I didn't want to be left alone."

He was ashamed of himself for not knowing better than to do this, even after a hundred years of life.

"I'm no immortal wizard, just a weak-hearted monster. I can't die easily and I can't get old, that's all. I just pretend to be clever. You shouldn't have any feelings for me at all."

Takami's lips formed into a hint of a smile. "Duh.. Don… Cr…"

Don't cry. That's what he was trying to say. Even in all of his suffering, all of his pain. In all of his years, Enma had never seen such a sad sight.

"Glad… you… here…"

How much mercy could one boy have? He wouldn't say anything against him.

Enma wanted to scream, to break down and sob. But there was something he needed to do first.

"I'm going to end your suffering now…"

Enma slowly drew out the boy's left hand from beneath the towel. The flesh was charred and the bone exposed, but the palm alone remained white, a cherry blossom floating upon it. There could be no more awful curse than this. And he had done it to him.

He drew a needle out of his bag. It was only used for extracting an oni.

"It's bad enough that I have to suffer this fate." He couldn't forgive his own stupidity. "And yet I thought I could take you along with me."

Enma walked out of the shed, then fell to his hands and knees and howled in anguish. Even as the sky grew dark, his wailing never ceased.

## —5—

Night gave way to day.

Spread-eagled on the ground, Enma watched the smoke rising into the air nearby.

Surely heaven awaited that child, beautiful in every way. All Enma could offer him was a humble cremation.

He couldn't move from the side of the burning corpse. His body and mind lay in useless tatters, and he was completely exhausted from the weight of a hundred years of life.

He heard footsteps on the ground, approaching him. Even so, he had no motivation to get up. The footsteps stopped and someone peered down into Enma's face, blocking his view of the blue sky.

"It's been a long time."

"You…"

The light was behind him and hair covered half of his face. Enma couldn't see it clearly at all, but he knew it was Yasha. He felt a sensation like goosebumps rising on him. His heart coldly stirred.

"You really haven't changed. I'm glad."

"What are you doing here?" Enma got up slowly, a dangerous rage seeming to hang in the air around him.

"Coincidence."

Enma didn't think so. It had all been arranged. The oni who wriggled in the darkness wanted to see these two humans burdened with immortality fight each other to the death. In the end, like it or not, they'd both been led here.

"I never expected something like that to fall out of the sky."

The field had been burnt to ash, with not even a weed to be found for 360 degrees all around.

"There used to be a white-walled sanatorium and a field of sunflowers here.

The view of the town was lovely." Yasha smiled, saying that Enma probably couldn't imagine it. "There are bodies everywhere in there. It happened instantly, without any warning. They probably never even knew what hit them," he remarked coldly.

Even in an air raid, you still had time to seek shelter. You could understand what was about to kill you. They hadn't even had that much of a chance?

"I found the boy lying over there. The poor guy had his arms and legs torn off and was burned from head to toe, but he still lingered on in agony."

No matter how horrific the weapon, if it didn't kill him instantly, an immortal would go on living. If one wanted to know why immortality and eternal youth were the greatest taboo of all, there was the answer. Takami had to live on in the worst possible way. All the boy could do was breathe, trapped in the wreckage of his body, unable to die.

"The child you'd tattooed the curse into was perfectly saved from death. Everyone was so disturbed by it that nobody would come near him, so I laid him to rest in the remaining shed here, even if it wasn't any of my business."

As the poisoned words hit him one by one, Enma's lips began to tremble. Yasha carried on with his malediction.

"Was he your stand-in for Natsu? Did you curse that dear child with the oni-gome of immortality and eternal youth? So that he could be mocked as an undying freak and linger on in torment?"

Yasha stared silently at Enma's lips as they trembled in rage. Enma didn't even notice the look of envy for all the rich emotions the other man saw in his eyes.

"You… You just stood there and watched him? You could have extracted the oni, couldn't you?"

Yasha nodded. "He was yours. Finishing him was something you had to do." Going for the coup de grace, he added, "Besides, if I kept him alive, I knew you'd come looking for him."

Enma froze. He felt the clear line he'd protected between the two Houshou practitioners vanish.

Almost in a trance, he grabbed Yasha by the collar. He drew his fist back to punch him, then stopped just short of his face.

"You're…"

Enma's eyes went wide with shock. The moment he grabbed Yasha's collar, some of the hair covering his face fell back. The left side of his forehead to below his eye was thick with burn scars.

Yasha hadn't escaped the blast unscathed, either.

"Do you see? I got it pretty bad, too."

Rolling his shirt up, he revealed everything from his back to his hips. Half of the yasha Baikou had tattooed onto his lower back had been burned away.

"It's been a while since it happened, but it just won't heal completely. I'm shocked, because this has never happened before."

So, it hadn't been because Enma was inexperienced at tattooing immortality. The thing that had fallen from the sky had been the worst curse of all.

Yasha combed his hair back and looked down upon the dead city. "It's amazing. Human beings are more frightening than any oni."

A tepid breeze swirled some ash into the air. The scene showed without any doubt that humans had surpassed the oni in terms of terror.

Looking at the now-silent Enma, Yasha brought his face close, as though to mock him. "I wonder if eating you would cure me."

Raising a face that seemed to have shed its soul, Enma looked at the devilish beauty. "I'll deal with you later," he replied quietly.

The fire was dying down now. All that was left of the cremated boy were his white bones. No matter how his rage boiled in his guts, he wanted to complete this funeral.

He carefully picked out the bones one by one and wrapped them in a towel.

"What are you going to do with the bones?"

"Cast them into the sea."

Countless bodies had been interred together in mass graves dug on the beach, but he didn't want Takami to end up in one of those.

He remembered Takami's wish. *Once the war's over and I'm free, there are all sorts of places I want to go see. I want to draw people from all different countries…*

Enma turned to Yasha. "You want to be killed by me, don't you? Come on, then." It was the only way now. Having reached this point, Enma could finally see that. Only Yasha's blood would slake the thirst of his raging heart.

"So, you're finally ready to do it."

Seeing Yasha smiling happily, Enma clucked his tongue in annoyance with the perverted freak.

Either he would kill or be killed. Either way would be fine with him.

They walked on in silence. The ocean wasn't that far away. The single bomb had blasted most obstructions away, and after a short walk they could see the horizon.

"You've probably been waiting a long time to avenge your sister, haven't you?"

Enma answered Yasha's question with an exhausted smile. "Avenge?" He shook his head slightly. "I'm in no position to start lecturing anybody about vengeance."

This guy killed my sister, he thought. But I used to be an assassin too. How could I ever talk about taking revenge? I'm going to kill this guy because he irritates me, that's all.

Whether it was for war or for vengeance, trying to justify murder just made him sick.

Coming to the remains of what might have once been a lighthouse, Enma halted.

They were fairly near the center of the blast, and the once-bustling port now lay in ruins. The seawall had fissures and cracks in it everywhere and was collapsing. He couldn't see a single ship anywhere; they'd all probably been wrecked and sunk beneath the water.

The waves sparkled, seeming to show the way to paradise. Enma opened up the towel-wrapped bundle. Holding the bones in one hand, he flung them with all his might. They quickly sank beneath the waves. The scattering of the remains now complete, Enma squatted and clasped his hands together in prayer.

He prayed for a long time, his hunched back trembling. Yasha stood still, watching from behind.

"Why did you make that child immortal?"

Enma finally rose. Dark flames flickered behind him. "Because I'm just another corrupt bearer of the Houshou name." He had no intention of making any excuses to Yasha. One of them wasn't going to be walking away from this. "Let's do it. A duel to the death between heretics. It's what you want, isn't it?"

Both of them carried oni inside of their bodies. No matter how much they may have wanted to die, they couldn't easily let themselves be killed. In the end, they had no choice but to fight each other for all they were worth.

"Except we have nothing to do it with. Maybe some steel framework will do."

They dragged some twisted metal out of the crumbling rubble, but it seemed hard to use.

"You know, it might still be there… Follow me."

Too tired to think, Enma simply followed quietly behind Yasha. They came to a half-wrecked building further down the port which looked like a shipyard or something. It might have once been a maintenance plant.

"Let's see, I think it was around here somewhere…"

The floor looked as though straw mats had been laid out on it, but they'd been burned to ashes. He easily brushed them and the other debris aside with his foot. Soon, a doorway appeared in the floor. Lifting up the stout iron hatch, he drew out a container from beneath the floor. Yasha took a key from his pocket and opened the lid on top. Its contents were individually wrapped in oiled paper, appearing to be paintings and swords.

"I use this place to store illegal exports. Since it was convenient to be able to ship things out quickly, I used it all the time. Woodblock art by Sharaku, Utamaro, and Hiroshige can fetch a high price. It'd be a waste if they just burned up in an air raid."

He said it without a hint of shame. What a traitor this man was. But then, oni didn't owe their allegiance to any nation, so Enma really couldn't blame Yasha.

"Here you go." Yasha handed him a sword.

"This is a *kiku-ichimonji*, isn't it?"

"You know your swords."

He could tell by its beauty that this really was the work of the old Imperial swordsmiths. He recalled a captain in the Shinsengumi he'd infiltrated so long ago had worn one proudly at his side.

"Are you sure about this? Despite appearances, I was born a samurai."

"Once, maybe. You can't compete when it comes to the number of people I've killed, even counting that child you just laid to rest."

I'll kill him, Enma thought, a dark murderous rage taking hold. It'll be easy if I just let the oni take control of my heart. Being human would only make it harder.

They both took hold of their swords and drew them from the scabbards. Casting them aside, they stepped back from each other.

He felt a strange excitement at holding a sword again after such a long time. The feeling of cutting an enemy in half seemed to reawaken within him. Was that the oni within him rejoicing, or the blood of the assassin growing excited? Doing this made all the years since the Meiji Restoration seem like a dream.

"It's been so long," Yasha said. "I feel as though I've always been waiting for this day."

"Yeah, I've been waiting for it, too. Waiting more than fifty years for the day when I could annihilate you."

An ecstatic smile came to Yasha's face. "How sweeter to hear than any lover's words."

Again and again, the glittering silver swords crossed. The profound shock that carried down to his palm and the high-pitched sound that only swords seemed to make filled his heart with excitement.

*There, you see?* the oni whispered to him. *Being an assassin is your true calling.* His eyes were probably bloodshot with madness. So many times before now, he'd risked his life, never quite managing to die. It had probably been the same for Yasha.

"You're the one constant I have left in my life," the senior apprentice laughed.

Stepping over the rubble which constricted them, they moved to a more open space which made it easier to maneuver. There was a hole in Enma's shoe, making it hard to move, but he couldn't go barefoot in this situation. Over his head was a blue sky and at his feet, nothing but sea and charred fields. And there he was, fighting a sword duel. But it was too late to be thinking about that.

Enma parried a thrust from Yasha's blade. He seemed to be mixing in Western fencing with his technique, and it was making it extremely difficult to fight him. Naturally, Yasha was fighting for all he was worth. He may have wanted to be killed, but the oni within him didn't want to die. It desired more lives to devour. Ultimately, his body could not resist the will of the oni.

His blow knocked back, Yasha shuffled back and immediately retook his fighting stance, moving like a flexing spring. He was stronger than he looked.

Quit being so stubborn!

Enma wiped away the sweat dripping from his chin.

As with Yasha, nobody could compete with the amount of carnage he'd witnessed in his life. Perhaps the essential nature of the immortality oni-gome wasn't so much as to make them extremely difficult to kill, but to override the will of the bearer to make them do whatever it took to survive.

Yasha said, "In the end, we're both being manipulated by the oni." He was right. Even now, they were watching them, no doubt delighting in making their puppets dance.

Enma felt like he would melt in the heat. They both struggled to breathe. Yasha hesitated a moment, and Enma's sword opened up a thin wound on his upper arm. As Yasha staggered back, Enma pressed the attack mercilessly.

"I have you now!"

As Enma raised his sword overhead to strike the killing blow, Yasha tossed some rubble at him. Barely dodging the blow, Yasha held his arm and ran to take refuge in the shadow of a crumbling warehouse.

I guess this won't be quick…

Yasha must have decided that he was at a disadvantage in a head-on sword fight. Knowing Yasha, he'd definitely use some underhanded trick to win. Where was he hiding? Enma couldn't see him anywhere. His eyes glittering, his senses focused completely on his surroundings, Enma lowered his sword into a ready stance and searched for Yasha. His opponent was wounded. He needed to finish him before he could heal.

He heard a pebble hit something behind him. A diversion. Yasha was probably trying to draw his attention away. Don't make any false moves. Next came a sound from the right. That was from something else he'd thrown.

Now you're just insulting me.

His hand was soaked with sweat beneath his glove. He wanted to fling it off, but it'd be dangerous to let go of the sword now. Sweat poured down his forehead and stung his eyes. Where was Yasha? What was he doing?

Enma walked on, coming towards the wreck of the warehouse. Parts of the building lay in ruins, while others still stood relatively intact. He heard some rubble shift and looked up. There was a catwalk overhead, damaged, but in no immediate danger of collapse. Nearby stood a crane which had somehow escaped destruction. It towered into the sky, casting a shadow that made it look like the skeleton of some petrified giant. A large load of half-carbonized lumber still hung from its boom.

Nervous excitement was turning to irritation now. Where would the attack come from? Enma stuck close to the teetering wall, creeping forward as he stalked his prey. He moved around a support, when some movement caught his eye. A brightly colored piece of paper had gotten caught on the remains of the wall and was flapping in the breeze.

A painting?

He drew closer. Part of it was burned away, and it was dirty and bloodstained, but there was a watercolor of a smiling nun. Without thinking, he picked it up. He'd never seen the woman before, but the way it was painted seemed so familiar to him… It seemed to radiate an air of gentleness that only one of Takami's works could have achieved.

What's this doing here?

He suddenly heard a noise coming from the crane. The lumber load had been released. A trap? But he was nowhere near it, so what threat could it possibly…

It was only then that he noticed the cable snapping up from the debris on the ground. One end was connected to the falling lumber, and the other…to the support he was standing next to.

By the time he realized what was happening, it was too late. In an instant, the support was yanked away and the remains of the catwalk smashed down upon Enma.

He grunted in pain as he was showered with broken wooden planks, brick, and several large fuel drums. One of them hit scant inches from him, breaking open and spilling its reeking contents out onto the ground.

Blood dribbled from his mouth. He may have been stunned, but the inside of his head was roaring. Had his ears been punctured? His head smashed? Even as he shrugged the rubble off of him, he couldn't move. Had his nerves been severed? He couldn't even tell if he felt pain or not.

His field of view was restricted, and all he could see was the harshly blue sky.

The immobile man felt a bit more weight on top of him.

"You're alive. I'm glad."

Putting his foot atop Enma's chest, Yasha looked down at him. As though he wanted to say killing him so easily would be boring.

"Looks painful," he muttered sarcastically, and then thrust his index finger covered with black powder toward Enma's half-open lips.

"Damn you…" He didn't need to ask to know it was the ashes of a human heart.

"Go on, lick it. It'll make the pain go away."

God, it pissed him off. Just how crazy was this guy? Enma spat at him.

When he thought about how he'd left Takami's painting there to trap him, his desire to kill flamed even higher. There was no way he would let him live now.

The painting, still clutched in his fingers, fluttered in the breeze.

"It's a nice painting, isn't it? The only one that survived. Ironic, isn't it, when you consider the woman in it left behind hardly any flesh when she died…"

The wind tore the scrap of paper from Enma's fingers. The figure seemed to smile as it fluttered into the air and disappeared out to sea.

"Now the sister got a burial at sea."

What the hell was he babbling about? Enma's head was pounding so hard he could barely make out what Yasha was muttering. His wounds were in the process of healing quickly, but they were too severe.

Yasha pointed the sword in his hand at Enma's chest, the tip aimed directly at his heart. "What's wrong? Is that it? How irresponsible of a man who takes property that someone else had previously reserved. Weren't you going to protect Natsu to the very end? Aren't you worried about what'll happen if you die and I live?"

Damn it…

By every means, he seemed to be begging Enma to kill him quickly. It was almost annoying. If Yasha had meant to do Natsu any harm, he'd have done it long ago. The fact that he hadn't meant that his dark obsession didn't extend that far. If he was obsessed with anything, Enma thought, it was being killed by me. In that case…

Yasha let out a short scream. With an anguished look, he looked down to see the sword stuck up into his thigh.

"That hurt…"

Enma had stabbed Yasha's thigh from below. Pulling the sword out, Enma kicked at the debris on top of him with his free leg. Yasha fell back.

"Natsu isn't some jewel for you to use as you please!"

Bracing himself with a piece of fallen steelwork, Enma struggled to his feet. His pain nerves seemed to have recovered, but the pain was still slow to come. All he could do for now was hide and then wait until he could move again.

His left leg hung limply at his side, his toes facing backwards. His spine still seemed to be in one piece, but his ribs were broken and poking through his flesh and lungs. The momentum of getting to his feet induced another gout of blood from his mouth.

One of his ears had been scraped off the side of his skull, and there was a roar in his head like a deluge. If he didn't get back into action before Yasha did, then…

Come on…

He ripped the glove off and pleaded with the oni within him. He had to get it to mend his broken body. He was a more assertive person than he looked, and he had no intention of losing this duel because of some cheap trick. But first he needed to get away and heal.

He spat in frustration.

Dragging his leg, he looked around for Yasha. What could he use as a distraction? He felt in his pockets, but all he could find were the matches he'd used to cremate Takami.

Matches.

Maybe he was luckier than he thought. Stumbling back towards the pile of rubble he'd crawled from, Enma struck a match and let it fall into the oil that had spread from the fallen fuel drum. It caught fire at once, sending up plumes of thick, black smoke.

He didn't think the fire would engulf Yasha, but as he'd hoped, the black smoke flowed towards him. It would be enough to conceal himself.

He hid in the shadow of the one remaining wall of the building. He would have preferred to get a little farther away, but his sense of pain seemed to be returning, and breathtaking agony now assaulted his entire body. He couldn't move. His heavily bloodstained clothes now felt even heavier.

No matter how many times he experienced it, he never got used to pain like this. He lay down, gritted his teeth, and endured. Enough, just finish me, already, he wanted to scream to an unseen god. All the determination he could muster was meaningless in the face of such agony.

He squeezed his palms shut to keep himself from clawing his fingernails off on the ground. Inflicting as much pain as it could, the oni happily healed his body. It jeered at him, daring him to hurt himself more.

He could relieve the pain if he drank some blood. But then he'd become even more like the oni, and that was the one thing he didn't want. Even if Yasha killed him here, he wanted to die as a human being.

Here he comes…

His ears seemed to be healed. He could hear footsteps approaching. It sounded like he was dragging one leg. Enma got up on one knee, readying himself to stand. He'd cross the summit of the pain now. Could he move his left leg yet? Even if he couldn't, his only choice was to fight.

"Found you!"

He saw Yasha standing a bit away from him, calling out in a mocking voice. His face was blackened with soot from the smoke.

Enma stood up. He still had no strength in his crushed left leg. Balanced on just his right leg, he took his stance, holding the sword in his right hand.

Yasha, holding his sword in both hands, broke his stance and rushed at him. His leg still seemed to hurt him, but he apparently intended to end this fight with one blow. Yasha's blade slashed at him. Enma barely dodged in time, then retreated back a step.

Sweat poured from their mangled bodies. The black smoking fire and late summer sun made it rise off the two immortal men like steam.

"I hate it when it's hot like this… It reminds me of that day."

Yasha looked up at the sky as he wiped the sweat from him. Perhaps a memory had crossed his mind, because fear twisted his mask-like face for just a split second.

"Let's. A man who has seen hell has nothing to fear."

Yasha drove his sword towards Enma with tremendous force. The sharp metallic clanging resounded into the clear sky. The famous sword, admired by all as a work of art, was just a shadow of its former self.

"C'mon, what's wrong with you? Weren't you going to kill me? I'm sick of living, now hurry up and kill me, my brother!" Yasha shouted.

It was as much a plea as it was a provocation. Quit crying while you laugh, Enma wanted to angrily shout back at his crazy antics. He hated him so much, had killed him over and over in his dreams more times than he could count. And yet…

He's me.

The man's pain and loneliness… With a start, Enma understood all of it.

Enma swung the sword over his head with both hands, then brought it down with a tooth-shattering blow. It shattered Yasha's sword as he attempted to block it, then sliced through his body from shoulder to waist.

Yasha's body arched backwards as blood erupted from it. With a silent scream, he fell back. Enma vomited blood and fell to his knees. The impact of swinging the sword with all of his might seemed to have broken a few more of his ribs. Surprisingly, the oni within his body seemed to be telling him to knock it the hell off.

The fallen Yasha unsteadily raised his body. Had his sword been in good condition, it probably would have killed him, but the edge had been dulled, and so it'd half slashed and half struck him. When he looked, Enma saw that his sword had broken as well.

"Heh-heh… My innards look like they're about to fall out."

Pressing the wound with both hands, Yasha began crawling away.

I'll go after him and finish him off, just as he wants. But even as Enma thought this, he couldn't move well. There was a wheezing sound coming from his chest, as if there was a draft blowing through it.

Yasha staggered into the crumbling lighthouse at the end of the pier. If he went in there, there would be no way out for him. He may as well have been telling Enma to come finish him off. The sun was radiant as it sank towards the sea.

Enma's footsetps echoed as he entered the cylindrical walls of the shattered building. Light streamed in from the top of the spiral staircase as if a section of the floor above had broken away.

"It's like a stairway to heaven… Come quick," said a voice from above.

"What are you talking about? The only place we're headed is to hell."

"You're probably right," Yasha laughed.

Enma saw a bit of blue sky when he looked up. With every step, the trembling he felt warned of the lighthouse's imminent collapse.

Barely anything was left of the domed roof. All he could see was the cloudless sky. Yasha sat leaning against the one remaining wall, looking completely spent, but raised his hand when he saw Enma climbing up.

"Don't move. That slash you gave me did its damage…" Yasha's shirt was stained crimson. The way his legs were sprawled out in front of him showed that he'd lost the last of his will to fight.

"I don't have a sword now, so you get to choose between me beating you to death or strangling you." Either way, Enma would have to be thorough and keep at it until his opponent was completely dead.

"Then strangle me with your own hands."

Enma nodded silently.

He wrapped both his hands around Yasha's slender neck, feeling the warmth of Yasha's body on his palms. It made Enma hesitate for a moment, but then he began to squeeze, harder and harder. He wondered how long it would take before this man was well and truly dead.

Sister…?

As Yasha's face twisted in pain, for a moment it overlapped with Sawa's. His sister's face had looked peaceful in death. Yasha had claimed that he could kill painlessly, but that had only been his own conceit. Dying wasn't easy or peaceful. It hadn't been for Chie and Takami.

How many people had he watched die? Did he really want to add one more corpse to that sad parade?

I… I can't kill him.

And with that realization, the demon that seemed to possess him finally fled. Enma relaxed his grip, looking down at Yasha.

"I quit," he said, and let go.

"You…what…?" Yasha gasped in protest.

Shut up. He stood up, not caring anymore. The lighthouse was shuddering even more violently now, down to its foundation. It'd probably collapse at any moment. He wanted a drink of water. He wanted a bath. He wanted to sleep on a soft futon. He wanted to do all the things you could only do by being alive.

As he stooped to climb down the stairs, he felt a sharp pain race through his back.

"You…son of a…!"

He'd been stabbed with the tip of the broken sword Yasha had been concealing.

"Loser…"

Staggering away from the cursing Yasha, Enma pulled the sword point from his back. He sank to the floor in pain. What the hell were they doing? It all seemed ridiculous now. When he thought how foolish men must seem to Natsu and Keiko, he wanted to laugh.

An awful cracking sound came from the building's walls, like a final warning.

"Let me tell you one thing," Enma said, grabbing Yasha's collar and jerking him closer. He glared at him, close enough to accidentally bite him. "Even we have a limited life span… I don't know how many centuries. The point is, we just live a lot longer than other people. So, just give it a rest already…brother."

Yasha opened his eyes. He smiled as he let out a long sigh. "If that's true, that changes my outlook on life…"

Baikou must not have ever told him. And if it hadn't been for Kuro, Enma wouldn't have known for certain.

"If you don't believe me, why don't you try seeing for yourself?"

The floor tilted wildly. With a raspy clatter, the lighthouse collapsed toward the sea, the air shaking with the roar of its destruction.

The two oni were flung into the air and fell with the rubble into the sea.

It seemed like he was going to sink, but then Enma somehow managed to get his body moving again. The water sucked the ruined lighthouse down with a gurgle. He couldn't see Yasha, but he had no time to worry about him. The additional injures he'd suffered wracked his body with pain. As he struggled towards the shore, Enma noticed a figure still being tossed on the waves.

Yasha must have been hit by a piece of concrete as he fell, because he was bleeding from the forehead. As if to prove the adage that beauty is only skin deep, the once-graceful face was now burnt and swollen. It was hard to make out, but Yasha was floating completely exhausted. Neither emerging from the water nor sinking, he remained in the sea.

There's the problem.

A large piece of iron rebar in the rubble had caught onto the cuff of Yasha's shirt. That was why he couldn't move.

Yasha wouldn't last much longer. With no time to hesitate, Enma changed direction and swam towards him with all of his might.

Yasha looked angry, wondering what Enma was doing. He probably thought he was going to die. Well, too bad, because I'm not letting you, Enma thought. He grabbed Yasha's shirt with all his strength to save him, nearly tearing it off. He wasn't going to let anything happen to him now.

I just told you, didn't I?

He was going to see for himself just how long he would live.

Keeping their faces just above water, he gasped for breath. Grabbing onto a piece of lumber floating by, he somehow managed to get them back to shore.

After that, washed up there like a piece of driftwood, he writhed in pain. He knew it was just the beginning as his blood and bone regenerated. Soon a tremendous pain would assault his body. Once that happened, he wouldn't even be able to think. Pain had now hijacked all of his senses. He writhed in an agony that would not allow the release of unconsciousness, as if it were punishment to teach him the folly of living his life off of the path given to other men.

In other words, the usual thing.

As the sea began to be colored by the sun in the west, Enma could finally move his body again. His injuries had mostly healed. The burning fire had finally gone out, and the breeze carried with it the smell of sea water and the barest hint of autumn.

Now that he thought of it, where was Yasha? He got up and looked around. There were drops of blood here and there that led towards the sea. It looked like he'd wasted no time making his exit from the scene.

The mad fool who'd tattooed immortality into himself wouldn't get his wish.

Sitting cross-legged and looking up into the sky, Enma smiled feebly.

**—6—**

Not really knowing where he was going or how he'd get there, Enma headed north. All he knew was that he was going home.

The few days he'd been there seemed like decades.

When he got back to Yamaguchi, he learned that the village he'd lived in once had been flooded by a dam. He was so exhausted at that point that he didn't even care.

His time as a Choushuu assassin seemed so long ago that it may as well have been a past life. It was too bad he hadn't been killed back then.

Sorry, Old Man…

In the end, he'd let Yasha live.

He thought back to the time when he'd tried to get Okazaki to kill him, and remembered something he'd never been able to admit to himself. All that he'd wanted then was to die at his friend's hands. Maybe that was how Yasha had felt, too.

It really was a nasty disease they had… It made them childish, selfish, and pathetic.

Riding a train packed with people, Enma finally made it to Kyoto.

Kyoto really hadn't changed much from the old days, having been spared the worst of the air raids. The sun was reflected in road mirages on the ground.

How much nicer it would be if everything he'd gone through had just been a dream. The meager, shimmering mirage on the pavement in front of him seemed to be full of empty dreams.

Enma headed for the Muta family villa. The purely Japanese estate with its tiled roof still maintained its beautiful appearance. Flowers were even in bloom, as if what he'd seen in Nagasaki had been a lie.

The entryway door opened before he could even knock.

"Keiko…"

Keiko stood there with tears in her eyes. Her normally doll-like features were now blurred with emotion.

"What's wrong? You must have known I was coming."

"I heard your heart screaming."

He was amazed she knew that much. Keiko's ability chose people. Enma had no idea that it displayed its maximum effect on him.

"Thank heaven you're all right…"

"Looks like I've caused you some worry."

His wounds had mostly healed, but the madness of the past few days had left him with a tattered appearance and a crazed look in his eyes like something out of a story.

"I have a change of clothes ready for you."

"I don't need it. More importantly, is Nobumasa still alive?" He barged in and headed towards Nobumasa's bedroom without waiting for a reply.

"Yes. He's resting now."

That was a relief. He didn't think he could deal with another death at that point.

Nobumasa was definitely alive. Lying on the bed was the same frail, wrinkled, spotted old man he'd seen before. But his face seemed to have regained some of its vigor.

Seeing Enma, he broke into a smile. Keiko leaned over the bed to help him sit up a bit.

"It's been a while. A shame you missed me last time." It may have been a little weaker now, but his voice hadn't changed. He sounded as arrogant as ever. "What happened? You look exhausted."

Enma's clothes were filthy and torn all over. His cheeks were drawn, and there were bags under his eyes. To Nobumasa, Enma seemed closer to death than he was.

"Well, this and that…"

"When you say 'this and that,' it usually means something fairly significant," Nobumasa said teasingly.

Enma didn't have the strength for a retort. He went for nasty sarcasm instead. "It looks like Kyoto hardly got hit in the air raids. I guess those rumors that the Americans didn't want to destroy historic buildings were true. In that case, I've got to laugh. So, they didn't care about people, but thought some old buildings were important. No wonder you spent the duration of the war here." Enma was immediately annoyed with himself for this angry outburst. What was he doing, being so sarcastic to a bed-ridden old man?

"That's absurd," Nobumasa snorted. "They have no interest in Japan's cultural heritage. They were probably just saving it for last. I love Kyoto, and I figured that, if I was going to die, I'd rather that I die here. Fortunately for me, Keiko's been working her pretty little fingers to the bone keeping the garden maintained so that I can have a nice view." He looked out the window at the garden colored with brilliantly blooming flowers as he said this.

"I see. I'm sorry for what I just said."

Nobumasa cocked a white eyebrow at Enma's unusual meekness. "What's with you? Since when do you ever apologize to me?"

Enma shamefully started at his feet. "Why do you go on living?"

Nobumasa smiled at the philosophical question. "Well, now that the war's over, there'll be a reconstruction. It'll be fun to start over from scratch, won't it? I'll profit off of it, I suppose, but the nation will come out of it better than ever. That's why I can't just roll over and die. I gotta stick around for another year or two, at least."

Enma chuckled. "So typical of you. I'm jealous. But…" He leaned over the bed and took Nobumasa's hand as he spoke. "Don't talk about how many years you have left. Don't die. Don't leave me."

Nobumasa probably couldn't believe what he was seeing. Here was Enma, clutching a withered old man's hand and his eyes filling with tears. "I have lived a long life, haven't I? But I never thought I'd live to see this."

"You can laugh at me if you must, but… Please don't die," Enma begged, shamelessly clinging to him.

"I don't know what happened to you, but don't worry about a thing. Think about yourself. I've made arrangements for you. No matter what happens to me, you'll be fine."

Enma shook his head at Nobumasa's persuasions. "You're wrong. I won't be fine."

Nobumasa smiled and said that he understood.

"A long time ago, I was a washout as an assassin," Enma said. He'd never told Nobumasa this, but the old man seemed to know already. "After I killed anyone, I'd be so scared and upset that I'd hide in bed, crying. I haven't changed a bit since then. All I do is tremble and run away… I can't take it anymore."

Enma's shoulders shook uncontrollably. He broke down crying like a baby in front of the man he least wanted to show weakness to.

"You were the one thing in my world that was different. You got stronger. No matter how heavy the burdens you carried, you'd see them through to the end. You always tried your best, and I admire you so much."

The old man reached out a large hand that seemed to just be skin clinging to bone and gently caressed Enma's cheek. Enma's lips looked drawn, like he was embarrassed by the unexpected kindness.

"I've asked Keiko to take care of you from now on."

Nobumasa looked up at Keiko, who stood off to the side. At his words, Enma hastily wiped his tears away. He'd completely forgotten that Keiko was there.

"I wasn't the only one. Natsu also asked this girl to look after you."

Keiko nodded. "She came here on her own about ten days ago."

Natsu had made it here in all this chaos, at her age? Enma was so surprised that he had to make sure. "Natsu did?"

"Dr. Natsu asked me over and over to look after her big brother if she should die. She told me that you're such a lonely man that she wanted someone to be with you," Keiko murmured as though criticizing the dumbfounded Enma. "You're lucky, Enma. But considering all that's happened, I didn't give Dr. Natsu an answer." She glared at him as if he were the enemy of all women.

He somehow understood what Keiko wasn't saying. For fifty years he'd hidden his true feelings and run away from Natsu's. Natsu had been seeking an answer from him.

"Do you have any idea what sort of feelings Dr. Natsu would have for you to make her bow her head to me?"

Enma shook his head like a spoiled child. "I don't want to know."

Keiko was a good girl. But she'd never be a replacement for Natsu. He didn't want to acknowledge that Natsu had asked anyone to be that.

Natsu and Nobumasa were making arrangements for their deaths, and he hated them for it.

"I have one request," Nobumasa said. "Would you extract the oni from my palm?"

Enma looked up in surprise.

"I want to share a drink with you."

His oni-gome had been a vow to give up all alcohol.

"I was able to get back on my feet, thanks to this. But, I don't think I need it anymore. I'd like to share a cup of sake with you. I don't think we'll get another chance." Nobumasa held out his withered right hand. The six-pointed star on it shone as brightly as ever.

"Fine..."

Enma wiped his face with his sleeve and prepared his needle.

"All right then, prepare some sake for us."

Keiko left the room.

"That girl's as patient as Natsu," Nobumasa laughed. "She'll say whatever's in her heart...eventually."

Enma didn't understand what he meant.

It was September now, but the heat hadn't let up at all.

Exhausted, Enma finally made it back to Tokyo. Its ruined streets wriggled with waves of people who seemed to draw excitement from somewhere.

Even as they took the blow of defeat, there was an odd liveliness in the city. It seemed as if everyone's souls were rejoicing with the realization it hadn't really been the end of the world.

"Everyone who lives in this era now is a person who has escaped death. You're not the only one now," Nobumasa had said. Enma recalled those words as he walked the path back home. "There's no way you didn't realize how Natsu felt about you," he'd gone on.

Of course he'd known. But he'd thought that thinking about Natsu as a woman would have been a blasphemy to Okazaki. He could never seriously love anyone in his condition. He didn't know if the both of them suppressing their feelings had been the right thing to do. They just hadn't been willing to cross that line. What would be the point in doing so now?

"Unlike you, Natsu's life is limited. Don't you think there's something you have to make clear before all you can do is cry over it?"

God, get a little alcohol in the guy after all these years and he became a sermonizer. Enma had completely forgotten what a weepy drunk the man was.

The western skies were reddening.

He saw the home where he lived with Natsu. As he had once also felt, so long ago, he was glad to have a home to return to. Enma opened the front door.

He knew something was wrong even before he called out that he was home. There was no sign of life in the room. Just the light of the setting sun streaming through the window. It didn't feel like someone had just stepped out. This was a vacant home.

There was an envelope on the low dining table. Enma opened it with trembling hands.

*Dear Mr. Enma. Or should that be Mr. Amane Ichinose?*

*This is the first proper letter I've ever written you. There were many over the years that I left unfinished, but they often came dangerously close to revealing thoughts best left unsaid, and our ordinary business ended up being conducted by telegraph or telephone.*

*I wonder what your feelings are as you read this letter. Was your friend all right? If you found unhappiness there, I imagine what I'm about to ask of you will only deepen your sorrow.*

*I think it's time that we went our separate ways.*

*I beg of you, don't take this too hard.*

*Back when I didn't accept that marriage proposal and determined that I'd spend my life with you, it was like the beginning of a very long baseball game. I knew from the start that I wasn't going to win.*

*In the beginning, I was your little sister. Then I became your big sister, your mother, and finally your grandmother. I really have spent an awfully long time taking care of you. And I really am tired now.*

*As much as you may have disliked it, I called myself your mother and grandmother. And I did it sincerely, praying that it might give a bit of hope and comfort to you.*

*It was foolish of me. All I did was back myself into a corner.*

*No matter how sincerely I wanted it, the two of us could never share a relationship simply as man and woman. That was my destiny; it was nobody's fault. Even so, I couldn't hold back the loneliness I felt. I knew that one day its weight would be too much for me to endure.*

*I'm over seventy years old now, and lately my legs and back have gotten weak. I may eventually fall into senility. I've decided to spare you seeing me that way by leaving now. Despite everything, I'm still a woman. Even if it's just a slight risk, I don't want you to see me reduced to such an embarrassing state. But I won't be able to prevent that if I become bedridden. Not to mention how I couldn't bear for you to see me as a senile old woman.*

*So please excuse me as I leave before that happens. I suppose I've always been jealous of Kuro. That's why I'm going to take his lead on this. He had a gallant pride which I must endeavor to emulate. At the very least, I can take pride in having lived my life as a doctor. I think Father would have approved.*

*I've asked Keiko to look after you from now on. She has a good head on her shoulders, and I know I won't have to worry leaving you in her hands.*

*And with a lifetime of memories in my heart, I'm going to spend the remainder of my days as well as I can. I was happy, and it was all because of you. I can't express my gratitude. While I will always be with you in your heart, I now withdraw this old body from your sight. I sincerely request that you not try to find me.*

*Natsu*

The paper fell from his fingertips.

No tears came. All he could do was slump against the wall, his mind reeling. His eyes stared blankly into space. The room, stained red by the sunset, had grown dark, but he didn't notice. He simply stood there silently.

Natsu must have left here and stopped off at Nobumasa's along the way. To name Keiko as her successor.

The deep darkness enveloped him, seeming to gently caress his cheek and calling to him to follow it. Oni scuttled towards him out of it. All he felt in his empty heart was pain. He stayed like that all night, his soul seemingly gone.

At last, night gave way to dawn, and as the room brightened, Enma noticed the painting above the cupboard for the first time. Natsu must have hung it up. It was

Takami's painting of him and Kuro.

The gentle painting seemed to address him with a message from the boy: Please be happy.

A thought suddenly occurred to him.

Why hadn't he gone looking for Kuro that time? Yes, Kuro had what pride an animal might have, but he was important to me, wasn't he, Enma thought. He would have wanted me to find him, to hold him, to watch over him as he fell asleep in my arms.

Enma stuffed the letter and the painting into his bag, then stood up.

What the hell do you mean you'll take Kuro's lead? Are you a cat? What the hell do you mean, "Don't try to find me?" You're family, dammit. When your family disappears, you move heaven and earth to find them, don't you? Don't be ridiculous. You think one letter is going to keep me from doing that?

Suddenly, he was pissed off.

He wouldn't feel right till he was holding that stuck-up overachieving woman in his arms and giving her a piece of his mind.

"Okazaki, forgive me."

At long last, he had a feeling he finally understood what that last samurai's request had meant.

Already packed for a long trip, Enma once again headed out towards Ueno station. He'd find her, no matter what. Natsu was a doctor. She'd go where she was needed the most. And he could think of two places which needed doctors more than any other at that moment. The two cities which had been overtaken by calamity: Hiroshima and Nagasaki. If Natsu had been determined not to see Enma again, then she wouldn't have gone to Nagasaki.

She probably went to Hiroshima then.

He'd find her, all right, and then he'd give her something to think about. He didn't know exactly what he'd say, but he would think of something once he was holding her in his arms.

I told you, Natsu...

If you ever disappeared, I'd search to the ends of the earth for you. I told you that back in Yokohama, fifty years ago. Don't you dare tell me you forgot that.

No matter how many years, how many centuries he'd live, in the end he'd always be human. Because being human wasn't such a big deal. He just had to take what life handed to him as it came, and eventually he'd die.

The city looked dazzling in the light of dawn.

"All I see now is the future before me," he sighed to himself, smiling as he squinted at the morning sun.

Now, Enma was going to give her his answer.

# About the Author

Fumi Nakamura was a mother of two in provincial Japan who wrote fiction as a hobby whenever her childrearing duties permitted. Submitting her works to various competitions, she found herself ending up a finalist more often than not. In 2010, *ENMA* shared the Golden Elephant Award Grand Prize with *A Caring Man* (also available in translation from Vertical). Its subsequent publication marked the unassuming housewife's debut as a pro novelist.